Praise for the novels of

BRENDA JACKSON

"Jackson's series starter proves once again that she rocks when it comes to crafting family drama with a healthy dose of humor and steamy, sweaty sex. Here's another winner....
Bring on the Granger brothers!"
—*RT Book Reviews* on *A Brother's Honor*, 4 1/2 stars, Top Pick

"Welcome to another memorable family tree created by the indomitable Brenda Jackson, a romantic at heart."
—*USA TODAY* on *A Brother's Honor*

"Readers can't deny that Jackson knows how to bring the heat, and more. Her characters are multidimensional, tantalizing and charming."
—*RT Book Reviews* on *Texas Wild*, 4 1/2 stars, Top Pick

"This deliciously sensual romance ramps up the emotional stakes and the action with a bit of deception and corporate espionage....
[S]exy and sizzling."
—*Library Journal* on *Intimate Seduction*

"Jackson does not disappoint...first-class page-turner."
—*RT Book Reviews* on *A Silken Thread*, 4 1/2 stars, Top Pick

"Jackson is a master at writing."
—*Publishers Weekly* on *Sensual Confessions*

BRENDA JACKSON

A MAN'S
Promise

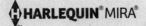

HARLEQUIN® MIRA®

Recycling programs
for this product may
not exist in your area.

ISBN-13: 978-0-7783-1625-1

A MAN'S PROMISE

Copyright © 2014 by Brenda Streater Jackson

For questions and comments about the quality of this book, please contact us at
CustomerService@Harlequin.com.

Printed in U.S.A.

To the love of my life, Gerald Jackson, Sr. My one and only.
Always and Forever.

To everyone who enjoyed reading Book 1 of the Granger Series,
A Brother's Honor, and couldn't wait for Caden Granger's story
to be told, this one is for you!

Provide things honest in the sight of all men.
—*Romans* 12:17

A MAN'S
Promise

Prologue

Fifteen years ago

She was going to die....

Sylvia Granger swallowed tightly as she stared into eyes that were as cold as glaciers. She lowered her gaze to the gun pointed at her. Her only chance was to talk her way out of this, at least to buy enough time before her husband, Sheppard, arrived at the boathouse for their meeting. He should be here any minute now. She began talking, pleading, practically begging.

"Please, don't do this. They are playing the two of us against each other. Why can't you see that?"

"Are they?"

"Yes."

The mocking chuckle made her skin crawl. "Haven't you figured things out by now, Sylvia? There is no one else. I only led you to believe there were others, just to see if you could be trusted. You failed the test."

Sylvia's mind went into a frenzy. *There's no one*

else? That can't be true. But after seeing the look of triumph flaring in the eyes staring at her, she knew it was true. "But—but how?"

"I don't owe you any explanation regarding the way I handle my business. You were smart, but not smart enough to betray me."

"But it wasn't that way at all." She spoke quickly as fear spread throughout her body, settling deep into her bones.

Another chuckle. "Yes, it was that way. You proved just how deceitful you are. Killing you will be a favor to everyone…especially your husband. He has no idea what you've been up to."

Sylvia slowly backed up as the gun was cocked. "Please. Don't. You won't get away with this," she said frantically. "Shep is on his way here. You can't leave without him knowing—"

The sound of laughter sent a chilling sensation all through her. "I can, and I will, get away with it. I have too many players in place to fail. The stage has been set. I'm the major star, and your services are no longer needed." The gun was lifted higher and, in an instant, a shot rang out.

Pain ripped through Sylvia's chest, and before she could blink, a second shot followed the first. She crumpled to the floor and took her last breath while gazing up into a pair of dark, evil eyes.

One

Present day

Shiloh Timmons's hands trembled as she set down the newspaper she'd just read. Emotions she'd been suppressing for the past four years were reemerging, and she refused to let them get the better of her. Caden Granger would never hurt her again; she would see to it.

Hearing someone clearing their throat, she glanced across the room and saw her brother standing in the doorway of her office. Growing up, Sedrick had been her hero, the big brother every girl needed and deserved. He'd been her protector. Even now, he was trying to protect her…especially since Caden had returned to town.

"It wasn't Caden, Shiloh," he said, referring to the newspaper article she'd just read.

"No, but it could have been. Did you read what that article said, Sedrick?"

He shrugged before coming into her office, closing

the door behind him. "Didn't have to. It's dominated the local news since the story broke a few days ago."

Shiloh drew in a deep breath. All last week she had been in California, in the heart of Napa Valley, making purchases for the grand-opening celebration of the wine shop she'd opened a few weeks ago. When she'd returned home last night it had been late, and since she wasn't a television watcher, she hadn't turned on the set. Instead, she had showered and gone to bed, knowing this would be a busy week at the Wine Cellar Boutique. She was gearing up for a party that would put her specialty shop on the map.

She'd been sitting at her desk, about to take her first sip of coffee, but nothing could have prepared her for what she saw in the morning paper. The headlines blared out at her in bold letters: Granger Narrowly Escapes Death.

Literally holding her breath, she read that Jace Granger, Caden's older brother, had been kidnapped from the parking garage at Granger Aeronautics. He had been just seconds from losing his life when the FBI had located him in the warehouse where he'd been held hostage. Arrests had been made, and the authorities were trying to determine whether there was a possible tie-in between the kidnapping and the reported ongoing trade-secrets investigation at Granger Aeronautics. Of course, the article took the opportunity to remind the readers that Jace's father, Sheppard Granger, was serving a thirty-year sentence for murdering his wife, Sylvia, fifteen years ago.

Shiloh stood and walked over to the window. If she were to tilt her head back and slant her gaze to the right, she could see the twenty-three-story building of Granger Aeronautics. Had it really been over a month since she had been there, attending the stockholders' meeting in her mother's absence? That day she had cast the deciding vote that allowed the three Granger brothers to retain control of their family corporation. Jace and Caden's younger brother, Dalton, had been friendly to her, but Caden had not spoken one word. And she could not forget the daggered looks he'd given her.

"You need to move on with your life, Shiloh. You tried telling Caden the truth about what happened and—" Sedrick began.

"And he didn't want to hear anything I had to say." Shiloh turned around, remembering that night a few weeks ago when she had gone to Sutton Hills, the Granger estates, to tell Caden that she'd recently discovered what her parents—specifically, her father—had done to ruin her life. Her mother was not blameless in the whole sordid business, either, because she'd known what her husband was capable of.

That was the same night Shiloh had moved out of her parents' home and taken a place in town after giving her mother a scalding earful. Her father would have gotten more of the same had he been alive to hear it. But he had died several months ago, probably thinking he had taken all his secrets to the grave. Nonetheless, there was one secret that hadn't quite made it. And it had been by pure accident that she had stumbled upon the truth.

She saw Sedrick's concerned expression. "I have moved on, Sedrick. Honest. However, I haven't forgiven Mom for the part she played in everything. But,

rest assured, Caden means nothing to me anymore."
The same way he had let her know that she no longer
meant anything to him. He'd even gone so far as to tell
her that he couldn't stand the sight of her. His words
had hurt, destroying her already broken and shattered
spirit. The words he had spoken that night had been
cruel, brutal and so undeserved. She doubted she would
ever forgive him for that.

"I hope one day you'll find it in your heart to forgive Mom, Shiloh. She needs you more than ever. She's
all alone now in that huge house. I wish you hadn't
moved out."

She felt Sedrick's words were unfair. "I don't see you
racing to move back home," she said curtly.

"Only because I need to be close to the hospital.
Surely you understand that."

Yes, she did understand. After medical school, Sedrick had moved back to Charlottesville, whereas she
had remained living in Boston after completing college.
She'd returned to Charlottesville only after her mother
had pleaded with her to come home seven months ago.
At the time, her father was dying of lung cancer. She
had been home only a few weeks before he'd passed on.

"You and I both know Mom was a bigger puppet
for Dad than we were," Sedrick said, interrupting her
thoughts. "Samuel Timmons expected everyone to obey
any orders he dished out. And we did."

"Not all the time," Shiloh countered. "When we got
older, we began thinking for ourselves," she said, recalling that time. It was after they had both moved away

to go to college that they were finally able to begin to really understand how things were at home.

"I regret the day Mom and Dad forbade us to have any contact with Jace, Caden and Dalton Granger. That was wrong. After their father was sent to prison, they probably needed their friends more than ever. Instead, they were ostracized," Sedrick said.

Shiloh regretted it, as well. One day, the two families had been close, and then the next, her parents had forbidden her and Sedrick to have anything to do with the Grangers. And all because her parents believed Sheppard Granger had killed his wife. They hadn't wanted their kids associating with the kids of an accused killer. She remembered Mr. Granger as a nice man and, for the life of her, she couldn't imagine him killing anyone. And she knew that Caden and his brothers were convinced of their father's innocence.

"Jace was my best friend growing up, and I lost him," Sedrick said, interrupting her thoughts. "Did I tell you that he didn't even recognize me that night he arrived at the hospital after his grandfather had that heart attack?"

Yes, Sedrick had mentioned it, and for him to bring it up again meant that he was bothered by it. Shiloh drew in a deep breath, remembering that Caden had been her best friend growing up. And in later years, after leaving for college, she had defied her father's orders by seeking out Caden, and they had become lovers.

"Well, since you're certain you've moved on, what about Wallace?"

She lifted a brow. "Who?"

"Wallace Aiken. Another heart specialist who transferred in from a hospital in Maryland. He's a good guy, and I like him. I introduced the two of you last month when you dropped by the hospital to see me. He's asked about you several times since. He told me last week that he would like to take you out."

Shiloh couldn't remember the man Sedrick was talking about, which meant he hadn't made a lasting impression on her. But then, very few men had, compared to Caden. But not anymore. "Fine. Fix us up."

Surprise showed on her brother's face. "You're serious?"

She chuckled. "Why not? We can start off by double-dating with you and Cassie."

Her brother and Cassie Mayfield, a respiratory therapist at the hospital, had begun dating a few years ago. As far as Shiloh was concerned, it was time for Sedrick to put a ring on Cassie's finger. Samuel Timmons hadn't liked Cassie, saying she was from the wrong side of the tracks. But he hadn't been able to tear the couple apart. One of his few failures.

"Great! I'll talk to Wallace and make all the arrangements," Sedrick said, smiling. "Is this weekend okay?"

She moved back to her desk to check her calendar. She sucked in a hiss between her teeth. She might have spoken too soon. "That's a week before grand-opening night, and I'm going to have a lot to do this entire week," she said, glancing over at her brother.

After seeing the *I figured you would come up with an excuse* look on his face, she quickly added, "But I will make time. It will probably be the last chance I have for some fun before getting really busy at work."

"Great. And by the way, I'm impressed with how this place is shaping up. I'm glad you're doing something you enjoy."

A smile touched Shiloh's lips. "Thanks, and I do enjoy this, Sedrick. I really do."

Two

Caden Granger frowned as he gazed across his desk at his younger brother. "You're kidding, right?"

Dalton released that crazy-ass chuckle that, at times, could grate on Caden's last nerve. "No, I'm not kidding. Just think of what could have happened to Jace if he hadn't had that tracking device on his phone."

Caden didn't want to think about it. When he and his two brothers had left Charlottesville for college years ago, each had vowed never to return. After college, they had moved to separate parts of the world, living their dreams. Caden was a well-known saxophonist touring in some of the most sought-after cities to sold-out crowds; Jace worked as an attorney for the government in California; and Dalton claimed he worked smarter and not harder by investing his money while living the life of a playboy/boy toy in Europe. In the end, Dalton was the one who'd become a billionaire. Go figure.

He, Jace and Dalton had returned to Charlottesville when their grandfather, Richard Granger, had had a fatal heart attack. It had been a couple of months ago that the three of them had made the deathbed promise to their grandfather to take over the family business, Granger Aeronautics. When they'd done so, they had no idea that in addition to inheriting a failing company, they would have to deal with employees intent on divulging trade secrets and someone they thought they could trust being a killer. The man had actually kidnapped Jace with the intention of ending his life. If it hadn't been for the tracker Dalton had convinced Jace to install on his phone, Caden didn't want to think of what might have happened.

"Fine. Put the damned tracker on my phone," Caden said, tossing a document he didn't feel like reading back into the in-box on his desk.

Dalton smiled. "I already have."

Caden's frown deepened. "You did so without my permission?"

"Yes."

Dalton eased up out of the chair as if he didn't have a care in the world, knowing full well that Caden really wanted to kick his ass. Caden might be two years older but, as far as Dalton was concerned, he was in way better shape than Caden. But he knew Caden wouldn't do any such thing. He and his brothers might give each other hell from time to time, but they always had each other's backs.

"So, Jace still hasn't said anything about what's going on with him and Wonder Woman?" Dalton observed.

Caden shrugged. Shana Bradford, whom Dalton

liked to refer to as *Wonder Woman,* was the person they had hired to help get the company back on a proper footing. She was a real fixer, which was lucky since it was her team that had figured out about the trade-secrets encroachments, as well as Vidal Duncan's duplicity.

"What's there to say, Dalton? It's been obvious from day one that he had a thing for her, although he claimed indifference. After this week's rescue, I'd say it's become pretty damned obvious."

Caden was referring to the fact that the FBI agents were barely in the door to stop Jace's head from being blown off before Shana had rushed in and thrown herself in his arms. "And I didn't see him rejecting that wallop of a kiss she laid on him," he added.

"Me, either," Dalton chimed in to say, glancing at his watch. He had an appointment that he planned to keep and didn't intend to be late.

At that moment, the buzzer on Caden's desk sounded. "Yes, Brandy?"

"There's a Sandra Timmons here to see you?"

Surprise shone on both Caden's and Dalton's faces. Sandra and Samuel Timmons had been neighbors and friends of their parents. When Sylvia Granger was murdered fifteen years ago, and their father wrongly convicted of committing the crime, the Timmonses and a lot of others had forbidden their children to continue to associate with the Granger kids. Caden had been fourteen, Jace sixteen, and Dalton twelve at the time.

"Send her in, Brandy," Caden said, standing, straightening his tie.

Dalton stood, as well. "I wonder what she wants."

"I have no idea."

"Then I wouldn't see her if I were you."

Caden glanced over at Dalton. "Why?"

"She's probably here to tell you to leave Shiloh alone. She'll probably make threats and get ugly about it. She could take up where old man Timmons left off—thinking we're nothing but scum."

Hearing Dalton bring up the name of the one woman Caden wanted more than anything to forget sent a flash of pain through his heart. "First of all, I'm not involved with Shiloh. She's the last woman I want to have anything to do with."

"There was a time the two of you were—"

"Best friends," he interrupted to say, refusing to fall victim to his younger brother's nosiness. For months Dalton had been trying to figure out what, if anything, was going on between Caden and Shiloh. Caden had confided in Jace and told him the full story, but he figured the less Dalton knew, the better.

The door opened, and Sandra Timmons was escorted in by Brandy. As always, she looked immaculate, not a hair out of place and her clothing of the finest quality from a top-notch designer. But there was a sadness in her eyes that Caden noted immediately. Was she still mourning the loss of her husband? From what Shiloh had once told him, her parents had an unorthodox marriage that was not based on love.

"I'm glad you could see me on such short notice, Caden," she said, giving Dalton a brief nod.

"You mean *no* notice, don't you, Ms. Timmons?" Dalton interjected.

Caden frowned over at Dalton. "I believe there's a meeting you're supposed to attend, Dalton?"

Dalton lifted a brow. "Is there?"

"Yes. I distinctly remember your telling me about it this morning."

Dalton looked at his watch. "Christ! I almost forgot." And then without saying another word, he rushed out of Caden's office, slamming the door behind him.

"I heard about what happened to Jace. That was simply dreadful. And just to think Vidal Duncan was behind it. I recall that he was once a close friend of your family."

Caden leaned back against his desk and shoved his hands into his pockets. "And, if I remember correctly, Mrs. Timmons, so were you."

Caden watched as the woman inhaled a deep breath. "Yes, and I'll be the first to admit I was wrong about a lot of things."

"Were you?"

"Yes. And I'm here to apologize to you personally. None of you boys were at fault for what your father did to your mother. I should have stood up to Samuel when he wouldn't let Sedrick and Shiloh have anything to do with you and your brothers."

"Yes, you should have." Caden decided not to add that, as far as he was concerned, his father hadn't done anything to his mother—much less murder her—but he figured it would be a waste of his time. Fifteen years ago, the Timmonses didn't mind letting everyone know they thought Sheppard Granger was guilty of murder.

"Is that why you came here today? To apologize?" If it was, her apology was fifteen years too late.

"Yes, to apologize for *everything* Samuel did. I tried apologizing to Shiloh, but she refuses to take my calls."

Caden raised a brow. "Take your calls? Isn't Shiloh living with you at Shady Pines?" he asked, surprised.

"No, she moved out the same night she went to see you at Sutton Hills. That was over three weeks ago."

Caden remembered that night all too well and he had no intention of discussing it with Sandra Timmons. "Mrs. Timmons, Jace will be out of the office for a few days, which means Dalton and I are pretty busy in his absence. If there's nothing else you'd like to discuss, then I must ask you to—"

"You don't know, do you?" she interrupted.

Caden drew in a frustrated breath. His patience with the woman was wearing thin. "Know what?"

She stared back at him, and he detected nervousness in her features. "That night, when Shiloh came to see you, didn't she tell you anything?" she asked softly.

"No. I didn't want to hear a word she had to say." He walked around his desk toward the door, intending to open it so she could leave. "Now if you will excuse me, I—"

"What do you mean you didn't want to hear anything she had to say?" the woman demanded in an angry tone, causing him to pause and look at her as if she'd lost her mind. A part of him was beginning to wonder if she had become unhinged. A lot of strange things had been happening since he and his brothers had returned to Charlottesville to take over the running of Granger Aeronautics, and this could be one more.

He turned around to face her. "I meant just what I said. I didn't want to hear anything Shiloh had to say that night."

"So, you have no idea where she was that weekend four years ago when the two of you planned to elope to Vegas and marry?"

Caden was surprised Shiloh had told anyone about their plans to elope four years ago. Plans *she* hadn't kept. "I already know where she was, Mrs. Timmons. I received photographs that were compliments of your husband, letting me know that he was still controlling Shiloh's life. The photographs showed her on the beach having a good time with one of Mr. Timmons's business associates. The same person he'd been trying to shove down her throat for a year or more. Your husband, Samuel Timmons, wanted me to know she'd finally caved in."

Sandra Timmons frowned. "And you believed that?"

Caden shrugged. "Seeing is believing."

The woman shook her head. "You saw what Samuel wanted you to see. Those photographs were altered with Photoshop. That was not Shiloh. She was nowhere near the beach that day."

Caden stared at the woman as her words sank in. "Then where was she?"

Sandra Timmons eased back down on the chair across from his desk, and Caden actually saw her trembling. And then he saw the tears. Whether they were genuine or not, they were there all the same. "I came here thinking that you knew. Certain that you did, and now to know that you have no idea…"

An uneasy feeling crept up Caden's spine. What did she mean that those photographs had been altered with Photoshop? That woman in the pictures had been Shiloh. Hadn't it? He narrowed his gaze at Mrs. Timmons as he crossed the room to her, and anger consumed every part of his body. "Where…was…she?"

The woman dabbed her eyes with a handkerchief, saying, "That same weekend, while you waited for her in Vegas, she was in a hospital in Boston, fighting for her life."

Stunned, Caden grasped the edge of his desk to keep his balance. "What the hell are you talking about?"

Sandra Timmons lowered her face to study her hands in her lap before lifting a tear-streaked face to Caden. "I don't know how, but Samuel found out what the two of you planned and flew to Boston to try to stop her. He said he was only going to talk some sense into her. They argued, and she asked him to leave. When he re-fused, she rushed from the house and darted into the path of an oncoming car."

Shocked beyond belief, Caden had to lean back against his desk for support. "Shiloh was hit by a car?"

"Yes. Things were pretty bad. She had to remain in the hospital for almost two months. The doctors man-aged to save her…but they couldn't save the baby."

The bottom of Caden's stomach dropped. "Baby?"

"Yes. She was pregnant with your child."

Three

Caden remembered very little after that. He recalled that the shock of Sandra Timmons's words had rendered him speechless, mindless and senseless. He'd been so stunned, so horrified by what he'd learned that he'd covered his face with his hands as an onslaught of emotions slammed into him. Shiloh had been pregnant? With their child? And when she had finally discovered the duplicity of her parents, she had come to him to tell him. And he had rejected her in a very cruel way.

He vaguely recalled hearing the sound of Mrs. Timmons walking softly toward his office door, whispering tearfully, "I'm truly sorry," before opening the door and leaving. He recalled clutching his stomach and remembered feeling suddenly sick as he agonized over and over about what Shiloh's mother had said.

He had believed the worst of her. If anyone should have recognized those pictures had been doctored, he should have. But he hadn't. Instead, he had accused her of the worst betrayal possible, calling her degrading names. Names she hadn't deserved.

And while he'd been indulging in his holier-than-thou attitude, she had been lying in some hospital room fighting for her life after losing their child.

Oh, God. The thought of her lying there in pain, hurting, brokenhearted, without him there to comfort her, filled him with anger. Intense rage. "Damn you, Samuel Timmons! Damn you!" he muttered under his breath with an alarming force because, at that moment, he knew how it felt to hate someone.

He thought he'd hated the man at fourteen, when he had ended his and Shiloh's friendship, but now he knew how real revulsion felt. At thirteen, she had been afraid to go against her tyrant father's orders; however, their friendship never really ended—it was just suspended. She would still smile at him whenever they passed in the halls at school, would silently slip birthday cards in his book bag and tape those *you're still my best bud* notes on his locker. And then there was the time on prom night when they managed to slip away from the watchful eyes of the chaperones to steal a kiss in the garden.

Then he finished high school and left for college. But he had thought about her often, wondering what she was doing and if she was still under her father's thumb. Had she broken free of him, now thinking for herself, living the full life she deserved?

He'd always thought about looking her up and he used to ask his grandfather about her during his visits home, but fear of what Samuel Timmons would do to her made him keep his distance.

He would never forget that night, six years ago, while onstage performing with his band, when he had looked out in the audience and had seen her. Shiloh was in her last year of college, and it was her birthday weekend. It had been years since he'd last seen her, but he had recognized her immediately. Gone was the kid he'd grown up with, the one who used to be his best pal, who would smile up at him through her braces. She had grown into a totally beautiful woman.

When the concert was over, he invited her backstage, and later they went to the after-party. When that party ended, he took her to a late-night restaurant for ice cream and cake to celebrate her twenty-third birthday. After that night, she would show up at his concerts whenever she could while working on her graduate degree at Northeastern University in Boston.

During his concerts he would search the audience, seeking her out, hoping to see her face. And then there was the night she had gone back to his hotel room with him after a concert and they'd made love. Wonderful, beautiful love, and he'd known that night that he loved her and that he had always loved her.

For two years, they'd kept their affair a secret from everyone and planned to elope to Vegas. She was supposed to meet him in Vegas that weekend, and once the ceremony was over they would fly to Paris for a brief honeymoon.

But she hadn't shown up that weekend. He had waited in that hotel room for three days; he had tried calling her. When he finally made a connection at one of her numbers, some man had answered her phone and said she was in the shower and couldn't be bothered.

He had just been about to leave, to fly to Boston to find out what the hell was going on, when he'd received a special delivery packet—a packet containing pictures that were still imprinted on his brain. He had taken one look at them and, combined with the conversation with the man who had answered her phone, he had immediately assumed the worst.

Caden moved away from his desk and walked to the window, a deep self-loathing within himself for the way he had treated Shiloh after that. He hadn't heard from her for more than three months after receiving those photographs, and now he knew why.

Believing the worst, he had deleted her number from his contact list and blocked any calls from her. Even when she'd shown up at one of his concerts eight months later, he'd asked Security to escort her out. He hadn't wanted her there.

She hadn't attended another concert…until that night last month in New York. He had looked into the audience and she was there, but still he had a hardened heart. And over three weeks ago, she had sought him out to tell him what had happened, and he hadn't wanted to hear anything she said. He closed his eyes when he remembered how he'd spoken to her, the mean, hateful things he'd said. How could he have been so wrong?

He had to apologize. He had to ask her to forgive him. But what if she didn't accept his apology? What if she didn't forgive him? Dread consumed him at those thoughts. He inhaled a deep breath, knowing he had to try. But first he had to find out where she was. Mrs. Timmons said she was no longer living at Shady Pines. Had she left Charlottesville? If she had, where had she gone? If she was still here, then where was she living? The last person he wanted to talk to again was her mother, but he would try her brother. Sedrick would know how to contact her. All he had to do was contact St. Francis Hospital and track him down.

Caden was about to move away from the window to use the phone on his desk when there was a knock at his door. Thinking it was Dalton returning, he said, "Come in, Dalton."

Instead of Dalton, his brother Jace walked in.

Taking one look at his younger brother, Jace said, "What is it, Caden? You look like shit."

Caden knew Jace's observation was probably true, because that was exactly how he felt right now. "What are you doing here, Jace?" he asked, instead of responding to his brother's inquiry. "We thought you wouldn't be back for a few more days. You didn't think Dalton and I could handle things till you got back? You aren't the only one who can run things around here." As soon as he'd said the words, Caden regretted doing so.

"Sorry," Caden said, moving to his desk, pulling out the chair to sit down. "Ignore me today. It hasn't been my best."

Jace stared at his brother for a moment. "Does it have anything to do with Sandra Timmons's visit? She was getting on the elevator when I got off. She seemed upset about something."

"And she should be. Damn, Jace—she and Samuel

Timmons did the unthinkable and, like a fool, I fell for it. How could I have been so damned gullible, so fucking stupid?"

Jace took the chair in front of Caden's desk. "I can't answer that until I know what you're talking about."

Caden drew in a deep breath and then told Jace the nature of Sandra Timmons's visit. He could tell from Jace's expression that he was just as appalled as Caden was, but he listened without interrupting.

Then Jace asked, "So what are you going to do? From what you've told me, you treated Shiloh pretty damned shabbily."

Yes, he had. And Caden wasn't proud of what he'd done. "First I intend to find out where she is. Then I'll go to her and apologize and then try like hell to convince her that I'm truly sorry for my actions."

"I'm playing devil's advocate for a minute," Jace said, staring at his brother. "What if she doesn't believe you and wants nothing to do with you?"

Caden tapped his finger on his desk a few times as he thought about what Jace was asking and had to face up to the fact that that was a real possibility. "I won't give up on her, Jace. No matter how long it takes, I will not give up. I will make it up to her. But first, I need to find out where she is. I need to go see her and talk with her. Then we'll go from there."

Four

Dalton Granger checked his watch before entering the private investigator's office. Great! He was on time for once in his life. He had toyed with the idea of hiring a private investigator for a couple of weeks, and now here he was.

He glanced around the sparsely furnished room and saw a woman sitting at a desk. She glanced up at him and smiled. He immediately thought she didn't look bad for her age, which he estimated to be late forties. And she didn't have a ring on her finger. While living in England, he was known as a man who preferred older women. In other words, he didn't mind being a cougar's cub. It had its benefits. A mature woman was usually independent, didn't have time for game playing and wouldn't create any baby-mama drama.

Since returning to the States, it seemed his tastes had changed, and now he was checking out women his own age or younger…just like the woman he'd met a couple of weeks ago at a local nightclub. The same woman who'd been so hot he still sizzled whenever he thought about her. This same woman had behaved as if he was a bother. She'd even had the nerve to refuse to give him her phone number. And when he told her he was interested in her and asked how he could reach her so the two of them could hook up, she'd had the audacity to tell him he'd have to find her first.

He'd been mad as hell. Dalton Granger didn't go looking for any woman. There were too many out there to suit his fancy, and usually it was the other way around. Women came looking for *him*.

So why was he here doing the very thing he swore he wouldn't do? Why was he willing to hire a private investigator to find the one woman who'd gotten away? The one who had snubbed him at the nightclub.

He could answer his own questions. Because she was a novelty. Different. Pretty damned refreshing. And, besides that, he had a feeling she would be hot in bed. Any woman who wore stilettos on legs like hers had to be. Damn. He would find this mystery woman and find out for himself just how hot she was. For her, he would make her an exception.

He walked toward the receptionist. "I'm Dalton Granger. I have an appointment with Mr. Harris."

"Yes, Mr. Granger. Mr. Harris is expecting you."

"Lead the way."

She stood and led him to a door and, without knocking, she entered. "Mr. Granger is here."

The man sitting behind the desk reading a sports magazine glanced up and stood, smiling. "Mr. Granger, thank you for coming in. I understand you want me to find someone for you."

Dalton nodded. "Yes, Mr. Harris, I do." The man had come recommended by Myron, the bartender/owner he'd met while frequenting McQueen's, a sports bar and grill not far from Granger Aeronautics. Myron swore that Emory Harris was one of the best in the business and that he specialized in missing persons. Usually it was deadbeat dads that Emory Harris tracked down, but Dalton figured if he was as good as Myron claimed, then he would give the man his business.

"Please have a seat, Mr. Granger," Harris said, gesturing to the chair in front of his desk.

"Thank you." Dalton heard the receptionist leave, closing the door behind her.

"Would you like something to drink? Thanks to Myron, I keep a pretty well-stocked bar."

"No, thanks. I'm fine. How did the two of you meet?"

Emory, who looked to be in his late forties, smiled. "Myron's wife and I went to college together and remained close friends." He paused and then said, "I understand you're looking for someone. A female. Is she your ex?"

Ex? Boy, was he way off, Dalton thought. "No, she's a woman I met one night at a club. She seemed to be in a hurry, and when I asked for her contact information, she rushed out and called over her shoulder that I should find her…and I intend to."

"She must be some woman if you're willing to go to the trouble."

For a second Dalton thought about what Harris had

just said. He'd already beaten himself up about what he was doing. It was so unlike him. But then all it took was for him to remember how she looked walking into that club—stilettos, legs and a shapely figure any man would appreciate. He had done more than appreciate it. He'd been lusting after her ever since. Shit, the woman was interfering with his sex life, making it hard for him to desire any other woman. He thought it would have passed by now, but so far, it hadn't. He needed to meet her, talk to her, have sex with her a few times to see why she had such an effect on him. And she definitely was having an effect. He got an erection every time he thought about her.

"Yes, I guess you can say she was some woman. So, you think you can find her?"

"I'm sure I can. I'll need the name of the club. She might be a regular there."

Dalton gave him the name of the club, which Harris jotted down.

"Did you see what kind of car she was driving?" he asked.

Dalton shook his head. "No. By the time I walked outside, she was driving away, and it was dark."

Harris nodded. "Describe her."

Dalton smiled, thinking. *Gorgeous legs. Firm breasts. Curvy ass.* But to Harris he said, "She was pretty. Sexy. Hot."

Harris stared at him for a minute and then asked, "What about her skin tone? Eye color? Hair color? Did you notice any of that?"

Dalton had to really think hard about it. "Brown skin. Brown eyes. Brown hair."

Harris nodded as he jotted the information down. "Notice anything else?"

"She was wearing Amarige."

Harris looked up. "Excuse me?"

"Her perfume was Amarige. Nice fragrance on a woman, and it smelled super nice on her."

Harris lifted a brow. "You're so familiar with fragrances that you can name one?"

Dalton shrugged. "Yes. I guess I can. I'm a bit of an expert."

Harris chuckled. "I would definitely say that you are." He leaned back in his chair. "I have a case I'll be wrapping up over the next week or so, and then I'm on it."

Dalton smiled. That was what he wanted to hear. He couldn't wait to see the woman again.

Five

Jace knocked on the closed door.

"Come in."

He entered the office, locking the door behind him, and his gaze immediately went to the woman sitting behind the desk. Shana Bradford. When he'd hired her almost three months ago, he had been attracted to her from the first. The sexual chemistry between them had been undeniable, and they both knew it. Being the professionals that they were, intent on keeping their relationship strictly business, they had tried ignoring the attraction…until it got the best of them.

They'd been having a secret affair. But now that was about to come to an end. She was pregnant with his child, and he intended to put a wedding ring on her finger.

Her smile was radiant and warmed not only the room but his heart. "Jace, what are you doing here? I left you in bed."

"I noticed. I thought we both decided to stay away

from the office for a few days, clear our heads, get our heart rates back in sync."

She leaned back in her chair. "You needed to do that more than I did. Did you talk to your dad?"

"Yes, Warden Smallwood let him take my call immediately."

"And?"

He drew in a slow breath, moving away from the door to stand in front of her desk. "And, unfortunately, he heard about the kidnapping attempt on the news. He was upset. He was glad I was okay and realized how close he could have come to losing me."

Shana nodded. "I know the feeling."

Jace didn't say anything for a second and then added, "And he's upset about Vidal. He couldn't believe it. The man had been a family friend for years. Now I'm sure he's wondering just how far back the man's treachery went and whether perhaps he could have been involved in my mother's death."

Shana sat up straight in her chair. "I hadn't thought of that."

"I have," Jace said. "So have Caden and Dalton. But I don't think he was."

Shana lifted a brow. "Why?"

"Vidal said a lot of things while holding that gun on me, convincing me I was about to take my last breath. He had no problems bragging about all his misdeeds— including siphoning funds for the company from right under my grandfather's nose. He seemed to take great pride in confessing all the things he'd done. If he had killed my mother, he would have bragged about it before killing me."

Shana thought about what he said. "You might have a point."

"I do," he said, coming around her desk, pulling her out of her chair and rubbing a hand over her stomach. "I had planned to tell my brothers about us and the baby today. However, Dalton left for an appointment someplace, and when I walked into Caden's office, he was dealing with a few issues."

Jace pulled her into his arms and smiled down at her. "But I can't wait to tell them, and we'll do so later today at Sutton Hills."

Caden tried to be patient as the phone rang several times. He released a sigh of relief when it was answered. "Dr. Timmons."

"Sedrick, this is Caden Granger."

There was a long pause and for a minute Caden thought the call might have been dropped. "Yes, Caden, what can I do for you?"

"I'm trying to locate Shiloh."

There was another long pause. "Are you?"

"Yes."

"Why?"

Caden wondered how much Sedrick knew about the situation and quickly figured he knew all of it since Shiloh and her brother were close. "I need to talk to her. Your mother came to see me today, and she told me everything."

There was a flow of muttered expletives from the

other end of the line that almost burned Caden's ears. "Mom had no right to do that. I'm surprised that you listened to what she had to say when you wouldn't listen to Shiloh when she came to see you." Sedrick's tone was sarcastic in the extreme.

Caden rubbed a hand down his face. "Yes. I believed things about her that I shouldn't have. I was wrong."

"Yes, you were. And you hurt her. Badly."

Hearing these accusations from Sedrick only reinforced how deeply Caden had wronged Shiloh and how much he needed to correct the mess he'd made. At this point, he couldn't place the blame entirely on Samuel Timmons and use the man as a scapegoat. He should have believed in Shiloh and trusted her. "I know, Sedrick, and I plan to make things right," Caden said solemnly.

"Not sure if you can. I just talked with her today. She's moved on with her life, Caden, and I think you need to just let things be and move on with yours."

It was on the tip of Caden's tongue to tell Sedrick that he really didn't give a royal damn what he thought. But now was not the time for that, especially when the man had information he needed. "I can't move on, nor can I let things be. If I ignore this situation, it means your father has won. And I refuse to let him continue to call the shots—even from the grave."

Something he'd said must have resonated with Sedrick because, after a few moments, he said, "I'll tell you where she is, but you have to promise me something."

"What is that?"

"That if she asks to be left alone, you do just that and leave her alone."

Caden knew he couldn't make such a promise. Even if Shiloh refused to forgive him for the things he'd done, he would not give up on her. He still loved Shiloh and hoped there was a chance that she still loved him.

"Caden?"

"I heard you, man, but I can't make you that promise, Sedrick. The only thing I can promise is to never hurt her again. And if you don't tell me where she is, I will eventually find her. It might take me longer, but I *will* find her."

Sedrick must have heard the determination in his voice. "Fine. I'll tell you where she is."

"Has she left Charlottesville?"

"No. She has a place in town and has opened a wine shop on Vines Boulevard. The Wine Cellar Boutique. She's there every day, except for when she's away on business. But fair warning—you're the last person she'll want to see."

"I'll just have to deal with that. Thanks." And then Caden quickly hung up the phone, grabbed his jacket and headed for the door.

Six

Shiloh Timmons glanced around her wine boutique, thinking that everything was coming together nicely. After that huge argument with her mother and the confrontation with Caden, she had thought about leaving Charlottesville and returning to Boston but, in the end, she was glad she had decided to remain in Charlottesville. It was where she wanted to be. Besides, she had already invested a ton of money to get the shop up to her standards. Also, she figured that by living in town she would rarely run into her mother. And as far as Caden was concerned, it would be just a matter of time before he left on another one of his tours.

She'd heard about the deathbed promise he and his brothers had made to their grandfather to take over the running of Granger Aeronautics. Of the three, she could see only Jace being the one to stick it out. Caden was a musician, for heaven's sake, and a very good one. He had a great following, and it was expected that his recent album would be nominated for another Grammy.

And as far as Dalton was concerned, she knew he considered Europe his home and he was probably champing at the bit to return.

"I just love this wine boutique, Ms. Timmons, and I appreciate you hiring me. I know I will enjoy working here."

Shiloh turned and smiled. The young woman she'd hired to work in the boutique was Tess, a junior at the University of Virginia. Tess was one of four students working for her. They were bright, energetic, dedicated and ready to learn the business. She understood how they felt since she had worked at a wine shop in Boston while attending college. She had learned a lot from the owner, Valerie Motley. Valerie had been more than an employer; she'd been a friend. And she still was. Valerie, whose family owned a winery in Italy on the island of Sicily, had taught her a lot about the business. Shiloh knew that if she could be half the businesswoman that Valerie was, then she would do well herself.

"Thanks, Tess. The next two weeks are going to be busy as we get ready for the grand opening. I'm going to need all hands on deck."

Excitement spread across Tess's face. "We know, and we can't wait. We're ready to do whatever you need. You do everything with class, Ms. Timmons. Just look at this place."

Shiloh glanced around again, and she couldn't help but be filled with pride. She had known this place would be perfect the moment the Realtor had shown it to her, and she couldn't think of any better way to use the money from the trust fund her grandparents had set up for her. She loved the location—right in the middle of Charlottesville's gorgeous historical district. The brick streets and sidewalks, the quaint shops, the old-fashioned light posts and the thousands of tourists ready to spend money were the perfect complements to her new business. The patrons could purchase a bottle of wine to take home, or they could sit and enjoy a glass of something special at one of the café tables in front of the shop. The huge overhanging oak trees helped provide shade in the summer and a blanket against the snow in the winter.

Once in a while, she would go outside and look up at the huge sign over the large storefront window. The Wine Cellar Boutique. She'd had the sign custom made to blend in with the shop's architecture, and just seeing it made her feel that at least she had accomplished one of the things she'd always wanted: to become an entrepreneur. One of her own choosing.

She knew her father had been disappointed that neither she nor Sedrick ever showed any interest in joining his million-dollar retail business. Samuel had ended up reaching out to his brother and nephews. He had brought them into the business. Her uncle Rodney was the complete opposite of his brother, and Shiloh often wondered how the two ever got along.

Shiloh looked out the large front window. It was late August and pretty soon it would be September. Forecasters were predicting a short fall and an early winter. Shiloh hoped they were wrong, especially since the winter being predicted would be colder than usual. She much preferred the fall, when the days were still somewhat warm and the nights were cool. What she loved the most was the changing of the leaves—the colors turned from a bright green to a rusty-red.

Inside the shop, the floors were covered with tile that had been imported from Italy, and she had installed shelves made of rich mahogany wood that held racks and racks of the best-tasting wine available anywhere. Most of the wine had been purchased directly from the vineyards. In addition to the wine, the boutique sold various kinds of cheeses, wineglasses and an assortment of breads that were delivered daily. And for those who preferred enjoying their wine inside, she had a separate seating area complete with Wi-Fi. It wasn't unusual for patrons to come and sit and sip for a while—some had already become regulars.

Most locals and tourists had been receptive to the new boutique, and business had been booming since day one. Originally, Shiloh thought she and Tess could handle things themselves, but within days she had had to hire Markel, Collette and Donnell.

Her office was located on the second floor, and the cellar below the shop was where all her stock was located. There was also a huge room adjacent to the shop itself that she could use for just about anything, and this week the decorator was busy transforming it into the reception area for her grand opening. Out back was the brick courtyard with a huge water fountain. She would be utilizing that area for the grand opening, as well.

The third floor of the building was a private floor where her living quarters were located. Right now, the two bedrooms, the one-and-a-half baths, the living room and the eat-in kitchen unit were all she needed. There was another huge room on that floor, and if she ever felt the need for more space, all she had to do was knock down a wall.

She glanced at her watch. She was expecting her accountant any minute. "Tess, I'm going down to the cellar to finish taking inventory. I'm expecting my accountant anytime now. Send him downstairs when he arrives."

"Okay, I sure will."

Caden walked into the Wine Cellar Boutique and glanced around. Nice. Classy. But then, he didn't expect anything owned by Shiloh to be any other way. The place was busy, but her employees were very efficient. Most appeared to be college age, and they were serving and greeting customers, referring to many by their first names. Instead of getting in line to buy something, he approached a young woman who was watering one of the huge plants.

"Excuse me, miss. I'm looking for Shiloh Timmons."

A huge smile touched the young woman's lips. "Welcome to the Wine Boutique, and I'm Tess. Ms. Timmons is expecting you."

Caden seriously doubted that. "All right."

"She asked me to send you downstairs to the cellar. The elevator is just over there to your right."

"Thanks." Caden turned toward the elevator, passing a huge display of wineglasses that were stacked in the shape of a pyramid that went all the way up to the ceiling. He stepped on the elevator and braced himself for what Shiloh would say when she saw him. Regardless of what Tess had said, he was not the person Shiloh was expecting.

The elevator ride took a few moments, and when he stepped out of it, he glanced around and immediately saw that the place was huge. The fresh smell of paint permeated the air. Hearing the sounds of shuffling papers, he moved in that direction. Rounding the corner, he saw her.

He paused and stared. Her back was to him and she was leaning over a huge crate, counting the contents. Dressed in a silky blue blouse, a black pencil skirt with a slit in the back and black high heels, she presented a picture that he couldn't help but appreciate. There was no doubt that Shiloh was a beautiful and desirable woman. Although their relationship had been built on more than just physical attraction, he would be the first to admit that the physical had been good. Damned good. But what he'd loved most about her was her bubbly and lovable spirit—something that shone through even when she had a tyrant for a father. But Samuel was dead, and Caden could blame only himself for being the one who'd now broken that spirit.

As he studied her further, he saw she had put her hair up. It swirled into an elegant chignon at the nape of her neck. She usually wore her hair up in the summer, when the July heat began getting to her. She had always preferred cold weather to hot, and he had always enjoyed keeping her warm during those cold nights when he'd visited her in Boston.

She straightened, and he watched as she flipped through the papers on her clipboard.

Figuring that now was as good a time as any to make his presence known, he said, "Hello, Shiloh."

Seven

Shiloh spun around, recognizing Caden's voice immediately. And he stood there in her cellar as if he had every right to be there. The shock of seeing him was replaced with anger, and she raised her chin and narrowed her gaze while trying to ignore how good he looked in his business suit. When he performed he wore casual attire—a nice shirt with either jeans or slacks. Seeing him standing there looking as if he had stepped off the pages of a *GQ* magazine almost took her breath away. *Almost...but not quite.*

And why did he look more handsome than ever? His neatly trimmed beard might have something to do with it. Did he have to look so sexy standing there and staring at her with those gorgeous light brown eyes of his? And his nutmeg-colored features appeared creamy smooth against the whiteness of his dress shirt.

"What are you doing here, Caden?" Her tone was sharp, and she meant for it to be.

"I came to see you."

Her eyebrows shot up. He had to be joking. "Why would you do that when you told me just last month that you couldn't stand the sight of me?"

"I was wrong, and I came to apologize, Shiloh. I said a lot of things that night that I had no business saying. I know the truth now, and I should have listened to what you had been trying to tell me."

She wondered who'd told him anything, but it truly didn't matter. "Yes, you should have listened to what I had to say, but you didn't. Not only that, you showed me how much faith and trust you had in me, Caden. A whole lot less than I had in you."

"What was I supposed to think, Shiloh?"

It infuriated her that he would have to ask. "That nothing short of death could have kept me from marrying you that weekend. But you didn't think about that. You thought I would lie around on the beach with another man. So much for what you thought of my character."

"But there were pictures, and when I tried calling, a man answered the phone. Of course, I now know all of it was arranged by your father."

"And that made you believe the worst about me?"

He didn't say anything for a minute and then said, "I was wrong. I'm apologizing. Like I said, I thought—"

"I know what you thought. I get it. Now, will you please leave?"

He shook his head at that request. "And I know about the baby. Our baby," he said instead. "I wish I could have been there with you," he said softly.

A pain sliced through her heart. Caden was forcing

her to remember a period in her life that had been so painful. She didn't want to recall that she had wanted him there. The pain of broken bones had been bad enough, but then to be told she had lost their child had been an agony no one should go through. Even now, an ache still remained inside of her. And she often wondered if her child had survived whether it would have been a boy or a girl. It would not have mattered to her. She would have been a better parent to that child than her parents had ever been to her.

And she had cried every night for Caden to come, refusing to believe her father when he'd said he'd contacted Caden. Her father had told her that Caden didn't want her and that he couldn't have cared less about her pregnancy.

"What about you, Shiloh? It's been four years. If you had so much faith in me, why didn't you contact me and tell me about the baby?"

His words made something inside her snap. "I *did* try to contact you. For months, while I lay in that hospital bed, broken up and in pain, I didn't believe any of the things my father was telling me about you. He even showed me newspapers that listed where you had gone on tour and the women the tabloids claimed you were sleeping with. I didn't want to believe it. I refused to believe it."

She paused a moment. Later, when she'd been released from the hospital, she *had* discovered that he'd been sleeping around with those women. "And when I could travel, I found out where you were. I wanted to know why you had betrayed me and why you hadn't come to me when I needed you. I believed there had to be a reason, and I needed you to tell me that reason. But when I attended your concert, you had Security escort me out. Again, you didn't want to hear what I had to say."

Caden cursed himself, shamed by the memory. Yes, after he had received those photographs and had believed the worst, he had begun having affairs, hoping she would hear about them. He had wanted to hurt her the way she'd hurt him. Seeing her in the audience at one of his concerts had been a huge distraction and he'd acted like a fool. He'd had no idea she had come to tell him about the baby.

He looked over at her and saw her lips trembling, saw the anger in her eyes in a way he'd never seen before. He had wronged her in so many ways. Yet, she had come to pay her last respects to his grandfather by attending the memorial service. And she could have been spiteful during the board meeting, voting against him and his brothers to prevent them from retaining control of Granger Aeronautics.

When she had discovered the truth of what her parents had done, she had sought him out again, and he had said words to her that no man should ever say to the woman he loved.

Looking at her now, he knew those same words applied to himself. She couldn't stand the sight of him.

Caden knew he had to plead his case and hoped she would give him another chance. He took a step toward her and felt agony all the way to his feet when she took a step back, away from him. "You have every right to despise me, Shiloh," he said in a soft tone. "And I deserve all the hatred you might be feeling toward me right now. I let you down. I did the one thing I'd always promised not to do, and that was to let your father come between us again. And you're right. You believed in me more than I believed in you."

He paused a moment and then said, "There has been a lot of hurt and anger on both sides. I suggest we pick up the pieces and move on. Together. And I think—"

"Right now, I don't care what you think, Caden," she said, interrupting him. "I hurt too much to care. The only thing I want you to do is leave me alone. I want to move on…without you."

He stared at her for a moment, not believing she could really feel that way, and he knew now was not the time to push. But he definitely needed her to understand something. "I love you, Shiloh. I know you doubt that right now, and I understand. But if there's one thing you should know about me, it's that I'm a survivor. I survived the death of my mother and the injustice done to my father. Right now, the only thing that threatens my survival is you, because I need you…and I always have. And I intend with every breath in my body to make you believe in me again. I will regain your trust."

He paused to get himself together. At that moment, he was filled with all kinds of emotion, and at the top of the list was the fear that he might have lost her for good. What he'd just told her was true. He was a survivor, but only because he'd always known she was there and always would be.

"I'm making you a promise, Shiloh—a man's promise to the woman he loves. I promise that I will do what it takes to win you back. I promise to regain your love and trust."

Shiloh shook her head sadly as tears filled her eyes. "I'm not sure that's possible, Caden. So much has happened, so many hurtful things have been said. Things I'm not sure I can forgive you for saying. Like I told you, I just want to move on. If you love me as much as you claim you do, you'd let me do that."

Caden drew in a deep breath. "And because I love you as much as I do, I *can't* do that."

She stared at him for a moment and then, without saying another word, she turned and quickly headed toward the elevator.

Shiloh barely made it to her office, closing the door behind her. Leaning against it, she tried to stop the tears that flowed from her eyes but could not. How could a man say he loved her but trust her so little? He had taken one look at those pictures and accepted them at face value, assuming she had betrayed him. Knowing that was something she couldn't get beyond.

Her cell phone began ringing and she recognized the ringtone immediately. It belonged to Sedrick.

Wiping the tears from her eyes, she tried to speak in a normal voice. "Hello, Sedrick."

"Did Caden Granger contact you?"

She frowned. "You knew he would try?"

There was a pause on the other end before Sedrick answered. "Yes, he called me here at the hospital and asked me how to find you."

"And you told him?" she accused.

"He would have hunted you down eventually. He was desperate to talk to you. I would have called sooner to warn you but I had an emergency with one of my patients."

"Who told him what had happened? How did he find out?"

"Mom. He said she came to see him. She assumed he already knew. Figured you told him that night."

"I would have had he wanted to listen to me," she said angrily. Pain settled around her heart every time she thought of that night. "Why would Mom go see him anyway?"

"I guess she was reaching out to him to help patch up things between the two of you. Shiloh, she regrets what she did, and one day, you're going to have to meet with her and talk about it. Hear her out. Like I said, you and I both know the old man had her under his thumb."

There was a moment of silence, and then Sedrick asked, "Well, did he contact you?"

"He came here to tell me how sorry he was for what he did and said."

"And did you and Caden kiss and make up?"

Was she hearing hope in her brother's voice? "Is that what *you* want?"

"It's not what I want, Shiloh. It's what you want. Whatever will make you happy."

She thought about her brother's question. She'd always thought being with Caden would make her happy. It seemed she had loved him forever. She had never imagined the day would come when the thought of him would fill her heart with so much pain. And, for some reason, she was having a problem getting beyond it. Those two years when they'd become lovers had been the best she'd ever had. But now all she felt was heartache and anger.

She was doing the very thing she'd said she would never do, and that was cry over Caden Granger. But she refused to do so again. "What will make me happy is what I plan to do, and that is to move on. I can't imagine having Caden back in my life. Too much has happened. Too much has been said. I need to get beyond that, Sedrick. For years, my life had been wrapped around Caden's, even those years when Father forbade me to have contact with him."

She paused a moment and then said, "Caden told me he loves me."

"Do you believe him?"

"No. What man can love a woman and treat her the way he treated me?"

"He thought you had betrayed him, Shiloh."

She was irritated by his words. "Why are you defending him?"

"I don't think I'm doing that. I just want you to make sure you know what you're doing because, personally, I don't see Caden giving up on you. I heard it in his voice today."

She couldn't help but remember the promise he'd made to her. A man's promise. If his promise was meant to give her hope, it had missed the mark because, at that moment, all she felt was regret. "It doesn't matter what he does. I intend to live my life without Caden in it."

"Shiloh, I know how much Caden means to you.

To be fair to my colleague Wallace, I don't think you should get involved with him until you're sure that you are over Caden."

"I am over him, Sedrick. Caden coming here today means nothing to me. I don't know how much plainer I can be."

Sedrick didn't say anything for a minute and then asked, "So everything is still on for this weekend?"

She drew in a deep breath. "Yes, everything is still on."

Caden got into his car and had buckled the seat belt when his cell phone went off. The ringtone meant it was Dalton. "Yes, Dalton?"

"What are you doing in historic downtown?"

Caden cursed under his breath, recalling the tracker his brother had placed on his phone. "None of your damned business. What do you want?"

"A little grouchy, are we?"

Deciding now was not the time for Dalton to get on his last nerve, he said, "Unless there's a reason for this call, I suggest you call me back later."

"Oh, there is a reason for it. Big brother asked me to call and inform you of the meeting at Sutton Hills. Don't ask me what it's about, because I don't know. I think his Wonder Woman is going to be there. And he included Hannah." Hannah had been the family's house-keeper for years and had grown to become more than that. She was like a part of the Granger family, and he and his brothers simply adored her.

Caden eased into traffic. "What time's the meeting?"

"As soon as you can get here. Jace and Wonder Woman are on their way. Tonight's Ladies' Night at McQueen's, so I'm missing out on checking out several hot babes. This damned meeting better be good."

Caden rolled his eyes. "I'm on my way."

After he clicked off the phone, he couldn't help wondering about the meeting Jace had called away from the office. Was something going on that made Jace feel they couldn't have a secure conversation at Granger Aeronautics? Had Shana and her team uncovered another diabolical plot against the company? But then, Dalton had said Hannah would be attending the meeting, so maybe the meeting had nothing to do with the business after all. He would know soon enough. Jeez, he longed for the days when all he had to worry about was his concert-tour schedule.

Deciding he didn't want to dwell on work problems for the moment, he turned his mind to his own major problem. Shiloh. Regaining her trust wouldn't be easy, but he was determined to do it.

His goal was to put her back in his life, where she belonged.

Eight

"Welcome to Sutton Hills, Shana."

Shana smiled over at Jace. "This place is beautiful."

Jace told her Sutton Hills, the Grangers' estate, encompassed over two hundred acres near the foothills of the Blue Ridge Mountains and consisted of the most beautiful land anywhere.

As they drove on the long winding road canopied by large oak trees, he pointed out several places of interest. "That's the equestrian center to your right. Those horses are my father's pride and joy. And my grandfather felt the same way."

She looked over at him. "There are so many horses in the pastures."

Jace chuckled. "Yes. Sutton Hills is considered a horse ranch because of the beautiful Thoroughbreds we have here. A number of them are entered into the major races each year."

Shana knew that managing the stables alone was

a huge undertaking. "Who handles the horses while you're running Granger Aeronautics?"

"We have a ranch foreman who takes care of that end of things for us. Patrick has been with Sutton Hills for over forty years now, since before I was born. He'll be retiring next year, and his son Clyde has already been groomed to take his place."

Shana nodded. She had heard about Sutton Hills. Had even read about it during her research. She'd known it was large, but hadn't imagined it was this immense.

"Sutton Hills is divided into four major areas," Jace continued. "My grandparents lived in the main house, which is probably a mile or so from the equestrian center, and it sits on fifty acres of land. It's two stories and backs up against Mammoth Lake."

"That's where you're staying now? In your grandfather's home?"

"Yes. If you look through those trees, you'll be able to see the roof of my parents' home. After Mom died and Dad went to prison, Granddad closed up the place and brought us to live with him. None of us has been back in that house ever since."

Shana could understand why they wouldn't want to return. Through the trees, she saw an outline of the structure's rooftop. It was huge.

"And over there," he said, slowing down. "At the mouth of the lake is the boathouse." Quietly, he added, "That's the place where my mother was found murdered fifteen years ago. She had two gunshot wounds in her chest."

Shana did not say a word. She knew Jace had more to say.

He paused a moment, then said, "Dad found her. He went into the boathouse, and one of the first things he saw when he walked in was his gun lying in the middle of the floor. I wish to hell that he hadn't picked it up—it turned out to be the murder weapon. Then he went toward the back of the boathouse, and that's when he found Mom, lying on the floor in a pool of blood. He called 911. Within hours, he was arrested for her murder. Since only his fingerprints were found on the gun, he ended up being charged with her murder."

Shana decided not to ask if anyone had been to the boathouse since that tragic day. In all likelihood they had not. Jace told her he'd been sixteen when his mother was killed, Caden fourteen, and Dalton had been about to celebrate his twelfth birthday.

Changing the subject and the somber mood, Jace said, "You're going to like Hannah, and she's going to like you."

Shana smiled. "What makes you so sure of that?"

"Because I like you. Better yet, I love you."

A warm feeling always stole over Shana whenever he told her that. "How do you think everyone will react once they know about us and the baby?"

Jace chuckled. "My brothers have suspected something for a while, although I've never owned up to it. But after that little scene with you during my rescue, there is no doubt in their minds that we are more than business associates."

Shana grinned sheepishly. "I couldn't help myself.

I was so scared that we wouldn't find you, and then, when we did, nothing else mattered to me. Certainly not our secret affair."

"I felt the same way. At that point, I didn't give a damn who knew about us. And as far as the baby news goes, I think once the shock wears off, my brothers will love the idea of being uncles. Hannah will be beside herself. She's been hinting at me to settle down, remarry and make babies for years. I told you that she didn't like Eve."

"Yes, you told me." Shana didn't say anything, but she was tempted to say that after meeting his ex-wife, she could see why Hannah hadn't liked her.

"Here we are." Jace pulled into the circular driveway of the largest house Shana had ever seen. The lawn was immaculate, and the architectural structure of the house was breathtaking.

"Jace, it's beautiful."

"Thanks. It was built and designed by my great-grandfather. I see Dalton's and Caden's cars over there. That means they are here already," he said, bringing his car to a stop behind Dalton's two-seater sports car.

After killing the ignition, Jace glanced over at her and smiled. "Ready for us to go tell everyone our good news?"

Shana couldn't help smiling back over at him. "Yes, I'm ready."

"Your email in-box full again, Mr. Granger?"

Sheppard Granger glanced over at Ambrose Cheney,

one of the prison guards, and smiled. "Yes, it looks that way. How are your sons doing?"

The two of them exchanged pleasantries for a few minutes before Ambrose moved on. Shep knew that, as prisons went, he'd been pretty damned lucky. When he'd entered the prison system fifteen years ago, he'd been assigned to Glenworth. He had refused to get an attitude about being wrongly convicted or about being sent to Glenworth. Instead, he'd decided to make the best of the situation he was in. While there he had met fellow inmates with the same mind-set…like Luther Thomas, who'd been wrongly convicted of rape. Together, he and Luther had begun programs in prison such as Toastmasters, Leaders of Tomorrow and the GED program. Their efforts had been successful and were recognized by the media and even the governor. And together, he and Luther had helped to turn around the lives of several inmates like Lamar "Striker" Jennings, Quasar Patterson and Stonewall Courson.

Luther was eventually acquitted and was now a minister in Hampton, Virginia. Five years ago, after serving ten years of his sentence and being termed a model employee and a born leader, the governor had approved Sheppard's transfer to Delvers, a prison that housed low-risk offenders. He worked closely with the warden as a trustee, initiating various projects to ensure that the less-serious offenders didn't become serious offenders in the future.

He was proud that, so far, all the men whose lives he had helped turn around at both Glenworth and Delvers had stayed on the straight and narrow. They came to

visit from time to time now that they were on the outside, and he was proud that they were making positive
impacts on their communities. And what he liked more
than anything was that, from time to time, when they
couldn't visit, they would send Sheppard an email to let
him know where they were and how they were doing.
Some had gone back to school, many even to college,
and others were business owners—successful men in
their communities.

He opened an email from Andrew Logan. Andrew
had been in trouble since the age of ten, when stealing
had been his favorite pastime. He had been in and out
of youth detention as a way of life. Now Andrew had a
college degree and worked on the right side of the law
as a police detective in Alexandria.

Like most of the other emails he'd opened so far,
Andrew's reported that he had heard the reports on the
radio and television about Jace. Although they'd never
met Jace, they knew Jace was his son. They had all written because they knew Sheppard would be upset and
feeling useless since he couldn't do anything to help
his son while he was in prison. They all said how glad
they were that Jace had been rescued before anything
bad had gone down during the kidnapping.

Shep drew in a deep breath, thinking that no one
was gladder about that than he was. If anything had
happened to Jace or any of his three sons, Shep didn't
know what he would do. Thank heavens, the FBI had
gotten there in time, and he appreciated Dalton for putting that tracker on Jace's phone.

At the end of the email, Shep tried not to get emotional when he read what Andrew had written:

Mr. Granger, a lot of the guys whose lives you touched at both Glenworth and Delvers got together this past weekend at my place. We went to a ball game then came back here for chips and beer. Matthew Fontane was here, and since he was the last one released from Delvers, he brought us up to date on everyone and assured us you were doing well...at least as well as can be expected under the circumstances. We all know you've been given a raw deal, being an innocent man in prison and all. And I hope this doesn't sound selfish, but we all agreed that we thank God that you were at Glenworth and Delvers for us. We all know that if it hadn't been for you making us see the light, the majority of us would still be serving time. Now, you of all people know I'm not a religious man...as much as Reverend Luther Thomas wishes otherwise...but we believe there was a reason you were sent to prison. Because someone knew you were needed for the six guys who'd lost their way. So, although you may have lost time with your three sons while being locked up, we all want you to know that you've gained six others. And one day, when you're finally found innocent and released from prison, we're going to make sure all nine of your sons get together and give you the biggest homecoming party ever.

Shep leaned back in his chair and closed his eyes for a second. He'd done what any other human would have done for those guys. They'd been young, foolish and like Andrew had said…lost. But he'd looked beyond their tough and rough exteriors and had seen guys who'd been denied love and affection, attention and a chance to succeed. Some even had the attitude that the world owed them something. He would be the first to admit it hadn't been easy getting through to some of them, and Andrew and Matthew had been two of the hardest.

He opened his eyes and chuckled. But then, Courson and Striker had been real badasses, too. In the end, he'd gotten through to them and was proud they were back on the outside as productive citizens.

Shep went through several more emails before coming to one with a sender name he didn't recognize. He started to delete it, but something about the subject line—Suggest You Read This—aroused his curiosity, so he clicked on it.

Granger. You don't know me, but I know you. If I were you, I would make sure your sons don't get it into their heads to prove your innocence. Something tragic could happen.

Breath was snatched from Shep's lungs, and for a moment he found it difficult to breathe. Once he got his breathing under control, he looked at the sender's email address and frowned. Again. He didn't recognize the name and figured it had been sent from a public computer.

When he saw Ambrose making his rounds across the room, Shep called out to him. He'd grown close to Ambrose, who, in his middle forties, was a hard worker, a dedicated and fair prison guard, and a family man with a wife and two sons who were the same age Caden and Dalton had been when Sheppard had gone off to prison.

"Yes, Mr. Granger? You need something?"

Shep nodded. "I need to get in touch with my attorney right away."

Ambrose lifted a brow. "Is something wrong?"

"Yes." Shep slid his chair out of the way and motioned for Ambrose to take a look at the email that he still had up on the computer screen.

He watched as Ambrose's eyes sharpened to a steel-blue. "Holy Toledo! I'll contact your attorney right away."

Nine

"Hannah, I'd like you to meet Shana Bradford."

The first thing Shana thought was that the older woman was beautiful, although it was obvious that she didn't flaunt it. According to Jace, Hannah was in her early seventies, yet her skin was smooth with very few wrinkles. Her hair was pulled back in a knot, but Shana knew when she wore it down and around her shoulders it would frame her face dramatically. Another thing Shana noticed was that her eyes were sharp, intuitive and perceptive. They had to be if she'd raised these three Granger boys. She bet they had been a handful.

"It's nice meeting you, Ms. Bradford."

Shana smiled. "Same here, and please call me Shana. Is it okay for me to call you Hannah?"

Hannah beamed. "It certainly is. I just found out about the meeting a couple of hours ago, but that still gave me time to prepare refreshments. Oatmeal cookies and my special fruit punch."

"You shouldn't have gone to any trouble," Shana said.

"Yeah, Hannah, you shouldn't have," Dalton said, chewing on his fourth cookie.

Jace rolled his eyes. "And he's still stuffing his mouth as he speaks." He then looked over at Caden, who was standing at the window looking out. He seemed preoccupied with something. He had greeted them when they'd first arrived, but he now had eased back into his own little world. Jace had noticed that same behavior earlier today, as well. Caden had quickly left the office without telling anyone where he'd gone. Jace figured he'd gone looking for Shiloh. If he'd found her, how had it gone?

"I hope this meeting is important, Jace. I have a hot date." Okay, so he was lying through his teeth, Dalton thought, since he really didn't have a hot date. But he planned to hit that club just in case his mystery lady showed up again tonight. That was a long shot, but when you were desperate, what else could you do?

"No problem. We can get started since we're all here," Jace said, breaking into Dalton's thoughts. "If we can get you away from the cookie platter and the punch bowl. And, Caden?"

Caden glanced up upon hearing his name. "Yes?"

"We're ready for the meeting to start."

"Oh, all right." He then strolled over to sit on the sofa beside Hannah.

Jace glanced over at Dalton, who merely shrugged and sent a silent message. *Don't know what's going on with Caden, so don't ask me.*

"Jace, has something bad happened?" Hannah asked in a soft, concerned voice, gently rubbing her hands together. Caden reached out and took them in his.

"No, Hannah, nothing bad has happened," Jace said in a reassuring tone. "In fact, I called this meeting to share some good news for a change."

He smiled up at Shana, who was standing beside him. "As you know, Shana was hired to fix the problems at Granger Aeronautics. Well, she's done a lot more than that. She's fixed things with me, too—namely, my heart. I've fallen in love with her, and Shana and I are getting married."

"Married?"

"Married?"

"Married?"

All three—Hannah, Dalton and Caden—echoed one another at once.

Jace chuckled at the three shocked faces. He and Shana had evidently hidden the depth of their relationship pretty well. "Yes, married. But that's not all."

"Damn, what else is there?" Dalton asked, walking over to the liquor cabinet. He needed a drink. When had things gotten this serious between them? He'd figured they were probably sleeping together, although around the office they were decorously discreet. But marriage? Who in his right mind still did that these days?

"We're expecting a baby in the spring."

"Holy shit!" Dalton swung around so quickly that he dropped the whiskey decanter from his hand. He had to act fast to keep it from crashing to the floor.

Hannah let out a huge, joyous cheer, and Caden just sat there, staring at his brother, a surprised smile on his face.

* * *

"It's a little late to ask, but do you have a problem using condoms?" Dalton asked Jace, when he was able to pull him aside for a little private conversation. Shana and Hannah were across the room sitting on the sofa while Hannah showed her pictures of Jace as a child that were in one of the family albums. Caden had excused himself to step outside to take a phone call from his agent.

Jace lifted a brow. "Why would you think that?"

Dalton rolled his eyes. "Wonder Woman *is* pregnant. There are ways to prevent such things, and the use of a condom is one of them. Don't you know it's like an American Express card? You should never leave home without one."

Jace fought hard to keep from grinning because he knew Dalton was so damned serious. There was no need to explain their birth-control methods to his baby brother. The fact was that he and Shana had decided not to use condoms since she was on the pill. However, she'd gotten pregnant at some point during the two weeks she'd been on antibiotics for flulike symptoms, which had rendered the pill less effective.

"It was an accident, Dalton. It happens sometimes."

"But it shouldn't. Not to a Granger. We don't get women pregnant. We enjoy them and move on to the next."

"That's your way, not mine."

"Haven't you learned anything after being married to Evil Eve? Getting married is bad enough, and now a baby. Jeez. I offered to give you pointers when I first detected you were hot for Wonder Woman, but you claimed you had your shit together."

"I did, and I do. I fell in love, Dalton. The thought of doing something like that might seem foreign to you, but to some people, it's a natural way of life."

"But you haven't known her long enough. People have hidden secrets and hidden agendas. I figured you were rusty, out of touch with how to handle your business. I should have—"

"Done nothing." Jace reached out and placed a hand on his brother's shoulder, leaning in to stare into his eyes, and in a serious tone, he said, "I love her. She loves me. We're getting married. We're having a baby. We're both happy about it. Simply ecstatic. And just think, you're going to be an uncle. Uncle Dalton."

Dalton didn't say anything for a minute, and Jace watched the way his brother's eyes lit up when Dalton finally pushed all the bullshit from his mind about condoms and his dislike of marriage. A slow smile touched Dalton's lips. "Uncle Dalton…" he said, as if testing the sound of it.

"The one and only," Jace said. *Thank God.* He didn't know what he'd do if he had another brother like Dalton.

"Private party?" Caden asked, walking over to join them.

"I'm going to be an uncle, man," Dalton said, sticking his chest out and grinning from ear to ear.

Caden rolled his eyes. "You aren't the only one."

Dalton frowned as if just realizing that fact. "But I'm going to be the favorite." And with that said, he walked off.

Caden shook his head. "You sure he's really our brother?"

Jace chuckled. "You wonder about that at times, too?"

"Yeah, but there is the undisputed fact that he looks more like the old man than either one of us," Caden pointed out.

"True," Jace agreed, glancing over at Shana. He could tell that Hannah liked her already, and he felt good about that because she had disliked his ex-wife, Eve, on sight.

"And speaking of our father, have you told him?"

"Not yet. We'll talk with the fathers by the end of the week—both hers and mine. Shana's dad is an ex-cop, so wish me luck. I haven't met him yet."

"Fathers can get kind of crazy when you get their daughters pregnant."

"Thanks for the warning." Jace paused a moment and then asked, "How did things go today with Shiloh?"

Caden lifted a brow. "How did you know about that?"

"I didn't really. Just figured you would find her or die trying."

Caden looked down at the carpeted floor, remembering his meeting with Shiloh. He looked back at his brother. "She's not as forgiving as I'd hoped, which means I'm going to have to work hard to regain her trust and love."

"And you will."

"You sound so sure of that."

Jace smiled. "I am. You're a Granger, and our motto is to never give up."

* * *

Shep waited in one of the private rooms off the prison library. It was a huge room without windows, and he knew meetings were often held in here to determine the fate of inmates, to decide whether they were ready to become productive citizens on the outside.

He drew in a deep breath. Ambrose had told him a few moments ago that his attorney would be arriving any minute and had brought him here to wait. A few years ago, the warden had given permission for Shep to be alone for any meetings with his attorney. That privilege wasn't given to all prisoners, just those considered trustworthy. Truth be told, since Shep had found favor with both the warden and the governor, a lot of rights and privileges had been extended to him, and he appreciated each and every one of them.

There was a knock on the door, and Shep stood when Ambrose walked in followed by Shep's attorney. "I understand you need to speak with me, Mr. Granger."

Shep glanced over at his attorney and smiled. "Glad you could come on such short notice, Carson." Ambrose left, closing the door behind him.

"For you, anytime."

Shep truly believed that, which was why he covered the distance separating them, and without saying another word, he reached out and pulled her into his arms. "But I need this first."

And then he lowered his head and kissed her.

The kiss was leisurely and long, and as he'd said, he'd needed it. Shep took her mouth with a hunger he always felt when kissing her. He had met Carson Boyett about five years ago when the family of Craig Long, one of the young men he was mentoring, had hired her to represent their son. She had come out to Delvers a few times to visit with Craig, and their paths had crossed since he'd been Craig's mentor.

The attraction had been immediate, although he'd fought it. She was sharp, intelligent and beautiful, and he was an inmate with nothing to offer her. But she hadn't cared once they had been honest about their feelings. His father, Richard Granger, had merely raised a brow when he'd told him he was getting rid of his present attorney and replacing him with Carson. After all, as far as Shep was concerned, the man whom Vidal Duncan had recommended had done a piss-poor job while defending him during the trial.

Now Shep wondered how much of everything was merely a well-thought-out plan to make sure he was the one to serve time for Sylvia's murder. He couldn't help but have his suspicions, especially after what had been discovered about Vidal. It hurt him deeply that a man his family had trusted—whom he had trusted—could have been so evil. The thought of what the man had done to Jace literally soured his stomach just thinking about it and, at the same time, it brought fear to his bones at the thought that things weren't over yet. Not if he believed that email he'd just received.

Recalling that email and the reason he'd sent for Carson made him break off the kiss. He then drew in a deep breath and licked his lips. "Thanks—like I said, I needed that."

She smiled and licked her lips, as well. "And like I said, for you, anytime."

And he knew she meant it. Carson was ten years younger than Shep and a divorcée who had ended her marriage to an abusive husband and fought hard to become her own woman by putting herself through college and law school. She wasn't afraid of hard work, fighting for what she believed in or standing up for those she loved. He felt honored to be in that number.

Although they had been involved now for close to four years, she seemed okay with dating a man locked up behind prison walls with fifteen more years to go before he would be freed. She often mentioned the chance of a parole, but because of the way his sentence had been handed down, he had to make at least eighteen of the thirty years before any idea of parole could be entertained.

Shep also knew Ambrose always allowed them more private time than strictly permitted, thus giving them the opportunity to engage in conjugal visits if they so desired. But as tempted as he'd been to do so, Shep hadn't taken advantage of that. Carson deserved more than a quickie based on lust. He intended to make sure she got what she deserved, even if it meant that they both had to wait another three years to get it. She'd always told him she would wait because she loved him. And he knew with every bone in his body that he loved her.

He hadn't told his sons about her and figured one day he would get around to doing so. He and Carson had talked about it and both decided to keep the relationship between them quiet until they decided the time was right to share it. His life was pretty much an open book, and he preferred having Carson as the one part of his life he could keep private. She was everything he could possibly want, and he knew she was everything in a woman he'd never truly had.

Even when he thought he'd loved Sylvia, it hadn't felt like this. And he had stopped loving his wife a year or two after Dalton was born—when he'd found out about her first affair. By the time she'd died there had been many others. But he had remained with her for the sake of his sons.

"When Ambrose called, he sounded serious," Carson said, breaking into his thoughts. "What is it, Sheppard?"

Her comment once again reminded him of why he had summoned her. He took her hand in his and led her over to the table where the two of them could sit down. "This came in through my email account," he said, pulling out the paper he'd printed and handing it to her.

She scanned it quickly and then glanced up at him. "I can have it checked out, but I'm sure you know, chances are the IP address is probably from a public computer, one found in the library or someplace of that nature."

He nodded. "I know."

"And I assume you're going to take this person's threat seriously?"

"What else can I do, Carson?"

She didn't say anything for a moment before reaching over and placing her hand over his. "You can let your sons know what's going on, Shep. Let them know about this threat so they can be mindful and watchful. They are adults, and you can't protect them forever."

Shep drew in a sharp breath. "I know, but right now, they are all I have. A part of me almost died inside when I heard what happened to Jace."

"And you still think Vidal Duncan might have had something to do with your wife's murder?"

"Hell, the thought crossed my mind when I first heard about it. He'd had an affair with my son's wife, so why shouldn't I believe he was having an affair with mine? But after talking to Jace about everything Vidal said while he held Jace at gunpoint, I'm not so sure. Jace is convinced the two incidents aren't connected, and if that's true, then the person who killed Sylvia is still out there."

"That's why I want to push for a new investigation and—"

"No, Carson. I can't risk it if it means I could lose my sons."

Carson didn't say anything. "So what do you want me to do, Shep?"

"Hire someone to watch my sons."

"Without them knowing?"

"Yes. That means the person has to be good. My sons are sharp, and I don't want them to suspect anything."

"Are you sure that's what you want?"

"Yes, and I want you to arrange everything for me. Will you do that?"

A smile touched her lips and she leaned over and placed a light kiss on his. "Like I always say, Sheppard Granger. For you, anything."

Ten

The next morning, Caden came down for breakfast to find Dalton helping himself to a generous amount of bacon and eggs. He glanced to where Jace was sitting and, speaking loudly enough for Dalton to hear, said, "I thought he didn't live here anymore?"

Jace chuckled. "I thought so, too. However, he seems to find his way back whenever he feels entitled to a free meal."

"Why should you guys gain all the weight?" Dalton asked. "Besides, I know how to take it off easily."

Caden figured it had to be some way that was sexual. "So what time did everyone finally go to bed last night?" he asked, grabbing a glass of juice and a bowl of fruit. When he'd retired about ten, Jace, Shana, Dalton and Hannah were still up talking.

"I left around midnight," Dalton said, sitting down beside Jace and across the table from Caden. "I thought about spending the night when Hannah mentioned she would be preparing a huge meal for breakfast this morning, but then I heard you playing that damned saxophone and figured the best thing to do was haul ass if I wanted to get any sleep."

Caden took a sip of his orange juice and ignored Dalton's comment. He hadn't been able to sleep, and whenever that happened, he would take out his sax and play it for a while. Hannah and Jace never complained, and as far as he was concerned, Dalton didn't count since he'd moved into his own place last month.

"So, Jace, have you and Shana set a date yet for your wedding?" Caden asked his brother.

Jace smiled. "I'm leaving all that up to her, but I don't think she wants a huge wedding with the white gown, bridesmaids and a ton of guests and stuff."

"Hell, I hope not," Dalton said, chewing on a piece of bacon. "The moment she walks down the aisle, everyone is going to know she's knocked up. Shit, a pregnant bride is almost as bad as a pregnant nun."

Caden looked over at Jace. "Just ignore him."

Jace smiled. "I do. All the time."

"I hate being talked about," Dalton said.

"Then keep your damned mouth closed," Caden suggested.

Dalton had opened his mouth to say something when Hannah stuck her head in the door and said, "Don't forget your lunch on the way out, Dalton."

"Thanks, Hannah. I won't." Dalton smiled when he saw his two brothers glaring at him. "What?"

"You asked Hannah to fix your lunch?" Jace asked, barely holding back his anger.

"No, she volunteered, and I didn't want to hurt her feelings by saying she didn't have to."

"Yeah, I bet," Caden said, sipping his juice. He looked at his watch. "I think I'll head into the office."

"What's the rush?" Dalton asked, looking at his own watch.

"I have a meeting this morning with Shelton Fields. I want to see what his products and design department is all about."

"When you find out, let me know," Dalton said, chuckling.

"And what's on your agenda today?" Jace asked Dalton. He knew his brother got bored easily and he wanted to make sure that didn't happen. A bored Dalton somehow became a womanizing Dalton, and that was the last thing they needed.

Dalton shrugged. "I have a meeting with the guys in the security department. They want to make sure I'm familiar with all the new security gadgets on the market."

"Heaven help us all," Caden muttered, rising to his feet.

Dalton smiled. "I heard that."

"Good." He stared at Dalton. "And don't put another damned gadget on my phone or anyplace else without my permission."

Dalton waved off his words. "Whatever." As Caden was leaving, Dalton called out, "And you never did say why you were in the historical district yesterday."

"And I don't intend to." Caden threw the comment over his shoulder as he walked out of the dining room.

* * *

Carson hung up the phone and sighed. It had taken some time, but everything Sheppard had asked for had been arranged. She had called on her good friend Roland Summers of the Summers Security Firm and told him what she needed. He thought he had just the right people she was looking for to do what needed to be done. He had access to men who were trained body-guards, and several of them had served time with Shep and were now respectable, discreet and above reproach. And she made sure Roland understood they had to be ultra-discreet and remain at a safe distance.

She understood Sheppard's desire to keep his sons safe, but she felt they should be made aware of what was going on. Carson had an uneasy feeling about this, but it was Sheppard's decision.

She was about to pull a file from the in-box on her desk when her phone rang. Answering the call, she said, "Okay, Brett, what have you got for me?" Brett Holden was the guy she used on occasion as a private investigator.

"Just as you suspected. The email was sent to Sheppard Granger at Delvers from a computer belonging to the Wesconnett library."

"Thanks for checking."

"No problem. If you need me to do anything else, let me know."

"Will do." Carson clicked off the phone and said to herself, "Okay, Sheppard, your sons are being guarded. Now what?"

She opened the desk drawer and pulled out a copy

of the email Sheppard had given her that day. The person responsible for his wife's death was still out there and was crazy enough to try to kill again...even after fifteen years.

Sitting at her desk, Shiloh stared at the huge, beautiful bouquet of flowers delivered to her that morning. She had been totally surprised when Tess had walked into her office carrying them. The card attached had simply said, "Remember my promise."

She pushed away from her desk, walked to the window and looked out. Caden was not playing fair. He'd sent her a dozen roses. All white. Her favorite. He'd known that and was using it to break her down, and she didn't want that.

Shiloh glanced back at her desk and wished the bouquet wasn't so beautiful and that what he'd written on that card hadn't made her remember his promise. A man's promise to the woman he claimed to love. When Tess had placed the flowers on her desk and she'd read the card, she had been tempted to tell Tess to keep them because she didn't want them. But then she figured there was no reason she should not enjoy a dozen beautiful white roses. The bouquet wouldn't change a thing.

Just like it didn't matter that she was still plagued with memories of how Caden had looked the day he'd paid her a visit here at the boutique. Why did he still have to look so ruggedly handsome in a smooth sort of way? It didn't make sense. How could a man look both rugged and smooth? She wasn't sure, but Caden managed it. And then there was that sexiness he exuded so well. Her heart rate increased whenever she thought about it.

Feeling frustrated, she welcomed the ring of her cell phone, a ring she recognized right away. It was Valerie. Moving away from the window, she went to her desk to answer the phone. "How did you know I needed my mind refreshed?"

She heard her friend laugh. "Not sure. Do you?"

"Desperately. Caden sent me flowers. White roses."

"Oh, a man after my own heart. He doesn't plan on giving up without a fight, does he?"

Shiloh nibbled on her bottom lip as she studied her flowers. "I guess not." Valerie had met Caden and she was the one to encourage Shiloh to go to that concert during the time she was in college. Valerie had been able to see through Samuel right from the start.

"I want to get over him, Val," she said in a soft voice.

"I'm hearing the words, but I'm not convinced."

"You should be. I have a date this weekend."

Valerie laughed. "Any reason you don't sound excited about it?"

"Probably because it's a blind date. Actually, that's not quite correct. Apparently, I've met the guy. At least that's what Sedrick claims. He's a doctor at the hospital where Sedrick works, and Sedrick swears he introduced us. I don't remember."

"Hmm, that's not good if he wasn't worth remembering."

She wasn't going to tell Valerie she thought the same thing. Instead, she said, "Sedrick says he's a nice guy, and I'm taking his word for it. Sedrick can be overprotective, and he wouldn't hook me up with just anyone."

"Then you should have nothing to worry about. Where are you going, and what are you wearing?"

She told Valerie it would be a double date with her brother and his girlfriend, Cassie, and her and Wallace. Sedrick was selecting the place, and once he told her, she would know what outfit to wear. They spent another ten minutes more talking about how plans were shaping up for the grand opening. Valerie and her husband were arriving from Boston a couple of days early to help out with last-minute details.

After Shiloh ended her phone call with Valerie, she leaned back in her chair and stared at her flowers, remembering the first time Caden had given her white roses. There had been three of them…on her sixteenth birthday. Her father had spies at the high school, namely the principal, Mr. Waverly, and one of the teachers, Mrs. Joyner, who reported back to him on her behavior. Caden had sent the flowers to her best friend at the time, Cindy Brooks, to give to her. You would have thought Cindy had handed her a million dollars that day.

Bringing her thoughts back to the present, she checked the clock on the wall. In a few hours, she had an appointment with Nannette Gaither, the woman coordinating Charlottesville's annual Live-It-Up Ball to benefit cancer research. Shiloh was on the committee that met every two weeks, but since the event was next month, they were getting together more regularly.

She and Nannette had attended high school together, and instead of moving away for college, Nannette had remained in Charlottesville and attended college here. She was engaged to marry Vance Clayburn, a wealthy businessman who'd moved to town a few years ago. Shiloh had never met the man, but it was rumored that he was old enough to be Nannette's father.

Deciding she had been held up in her office long enough, Shiloh stood and was headed toward the door to go check on things below when the phone on her desk rang. Tess was transferring a call that had come in through the boutique.

She went back to her desk and picked up the phone. "Yes, Tess?"

"A Mr. Caden Granger is on the line and wants to speak with you."

Shiloh drew in a deep breath. She should take the call and at least thank him for the flowers, but then she thought better of it. The last thing she wanted to do was encourage Caden. If he thought he was breaking down her defenses, he would continue with this, and she preferred that he didn't.

"Tell Mr. Granger that I'm busy, Tess."

"Okay, I'll tell him."

Tess hung up on her end, and Shiloh hung up on hers. If Caden thought he would get close to her with a bouquet of flowers, he was sadly mistaken.

Caden held the phone in his hand a full minute before hanging it up. Shiloh had told her employee to tell him she was busy. That was fine. He wouldn't push for now, but he damn well wouldn't give up. He knew all about the grand opening of her boutique next weekend, and he intended to attend.

He glanced toward the door when he heard the knock. "Come in," he called out and then wished he hadn't when Dalton walked in. "What do you want, Dalton?"

Dalton smiled as he plopped down on the chair across from his desk. "Still in a bad mood, I see."

"What do you want, Dalton? Some of us have work to do."

"So do I," Dalton countered. "I just came from that meeting with those Security guys, and you wouldn't believe some of the technical shit they have now. Trying it out, I felt like a regular James Bond. And just so you know, you don't have to tell me why you were in the historical district yesterday."

"I don't?" Caden asked, staring hard at his brother.

"No, you don't. I was able to backtrack all the places you went yesterday with the tracker I put on your phone." A huge smile spread across Dalton's lips. "Why didn't you tell me Shiloh owns a wine shop?"

"Does she?"

"I'm sure you know that she does. So tell me, what's the real deal with you and Shiloh? And don't tell me there isn't one. All it will do is keep me digging."

Caden leaned back in his chair and built a steeple with his fingers while staring at his brother. "Has it ever occurred to you that it's not any of your business?"

Dalton continued to smile. "Yes, that did occur to me, but I dismissed it as a crazy idea."

"And why would you do that?"

"Because you're the middle child, and I promised Dad I would keep an eye out for you, so everything you do *is* my business, Caden."

"Bullshit. But two can play your silly little game. Where were you yesterday? On the way out, I asked Brandy to let you know I was leaving the office, and she mentioned you hadn't returned from your appointment with a private investigator. Why were you meeting with a P.I.?"

Caden watched the expression on his brother's face, and it was apparent he didn't like being the one in the hot seat. In fact, Caden noticed that Dalton actually seemed to be squirming.

"You wouldn't believe me if I told you."

No doubt it will be damned interesting, Caden thought, keeping an eye on Dalton. "Try me."

Dalton was silent for a minute, then he said, "I hired a private investigator to find a woman for me. I met her in a nightclub, and she left without telling me who she was and how to contact her."

"And you hired a P.I. to find her?"

"Yes."

Caden couldn't help but chuckle. "You're right. I don't believe you."

Eleven

Shana grinned over at Jace. They were on their way to her father's home, and he'd gotten quiet all of a sudden. "If I didn't know any better, I would think you were nervous, Jace."

He took his eyes off the road when he brought the car to a stop at a traffic light. "I am. It's not every day I meet the father of a woman and tell him I got his daughter pregnant and ask for her hand in marriage in the same meeting."

Shana smiled. "Take it easy. Dad's a swell guy. Besides, he's wanted grandkids for the longest time…as well as a son-in-law. Now he'll get both. But you better be glad my sister, Jules, is out of town and won't be here. She would give you a hard time just for the hell of it."

She paused a moment and then said, "Your family seems to have taken the news well. Except maybe for Dalton. It was obvious he was kind of put out about it."

"You should know Dalton by now. Dalton is Dalton," Jace said as the car moved forward again. "The thought of my having unprotected sex was beyond his comprehension."

"You didn't tell him what happened?"

Jace shook his head. "No. It's none of his business. Let him think whatever he wants, which is Dalton's way."

"Caden seemed preoccupied with something last night. Is everything all right with his band?"

"Yes, everything is fine with the band. It's an issue concerning Shiloh Timmons."

Shana's brow bunched. "Timmons? Where do I know that name from?"

"Probably from seeing it in the listings of all our shareholders. Samuel Timmons was her father, but he died several months ago. All his shares in the company went to Sandra Timmons, her mother. In our board meeting a few months ago, when Titus Freeman tried to take over Granger Aeronautics, Shiloh saved the day by casting her mother's votes our way."

"That was pretty darned nice of her."

"Yes, it was. Without those votes going our way, we would have been prevented from running the company the way my grandfather wanted us to." He paused a moment and then said, "If Samuel Timmons had been alive, he would have voted with Freeman and, to this day, I don't understand what happened."

She looked over at him. "What happened about what?"

"My parents' relationship with the Timmonses. They used to be close friends, and we all did things together… which is why their son, Sedrick, and I were close while growing up, and why Shiloh and Caden were close. But after my mother was killed, they, like everyone else, were convinced my father was guilty. They even testified at Dad's trial about overhearing one of my parents' arguments when Dad threatened to kill Mom."

Jace paused a moment and then said, "Caden, Dalton and I overheard a similar argument. The night before Mom died. But we knew he was upset with her and that it was an idle threat."

"Even when she was murdered the next day?"

"Yes. We were confused about a lot of things, but I think, deep down, none of us really thought Dad was capable of killing Mom."

"Not even in the heat of passion like the prosecutors claimed?"

"Not even then. We knew Dad. As far as I'm concerned, the Timmonses should have known him equally well, and that he'd made an idle threat. It seemed as if for some reason Samuel Timmons wanted everyone to think Dad was capable of killing Mom."

He paused again and then said, "And then after Dad was sentenced, the Timmonses and some of the other neighbors—the country-club gang—treated my brothers and me like we had the bubonic plague. They refused to let any of their kids associate with us."

"That's awful."

"Yes, it was," Jace said. "I lost my best friend, and Caden lost his."

"So what's the problem now?"

Jace took a few moments to tell her what Caden had told him. Retelling it made Jace realize just what a genuine ass Samuel Timmons had been. "Caden realizes he made a mistake and is determined to get her back."

"I hope that he does."

"Me, too." They were silent again, and then when they came to another traffic light, Jace glanced back over at Shana and said, "Prepare me for your dad. What am I to expect?"

She smiled. "Ben Bradford is an ex-cop who raised his two daughters after the wife he loved with all his heart passed away of pancreatic cancer. Mom knew she was dying, so she prepared us somewhat. She made Jules and me promise to be good girls, and we tried to keep that promise. Dad made it easy by being such a terrific father. He worked during the day while we were in school and made sure he was home at night. At one time he was promoted to detective, but when he saw it was interfering with his time at home, he gave it up and went back to being a street cop. He said money wasn't everything. It was more important for him to spend quality time with us."

Jace nodded. "And he never remarried?"

"No. And he never brought a woman home for us to meet, although Jules and I know he was sexually active."

"How could you and your sister know something like that?"

"Because we found condoms in his dresser drawer once. That's where he kept extra money for special things like our hair appointments and school trips and stuff like that. As we got older we knew what the condoms were for. I guess he didn't think when he tossed the packet into that particular drawer. He'd forgotten we went into it from time to time."

"And now he's dating Mona, the blind woman."

"Yes. They'd only known each other a short while, and now he says he's in love with her."

"True love. There was a time I didn't believe in it."

"Yes," she said, grinning. "I recall you once saying that."

"Things have changed, and I hope you don't find it hard to believe that two people can fall in love quickly, Shana. We've known each other a short while, and I know for certain that I'm in love with you."

"And I'm in love with you," she said, smiling over at him. "But…"

"But what?"

"I guess I'm overprotective of Dad, yet at the same time I want to see him happy. He deserves it."

"Then let him be happy."

Jace pulled the car into Shana's father's driveway and killed the ignition. He glanced over at her. "He is expecting us, right?"

Shana smiled. "Yes, he's expecting us, and please relax, Jace. My father is nothing like Samuel Timmons."

Jace let out a deep breath before smiling over at her. "Hell, I hope not."

"Yes, Sedrick?" Shiloh asked, connecting to the incoming call on her phone.

"Everything is all set for Saturday night. I've made dinner plans at the Matador."

"All right." The Matador was a very nice restaurant in town.

"Wallace wants to come pick you up. Do you have a problem with that?"

Because he'd asked, she figured he thought that she would. "No, I don't have a problem with it. I'm looking forward to seeing him again."

"Great! And like I said, Shiloh, he's a nice guy. He'll be there to pick you up at seven."

"Fine. I'll be ready."

She hung up the phone thinking that she sounded more excited than she actually felt. Each time she went into her office and saw those darned white roses on her desk she thought about Caden.

Then why did you keep the darned things? You could have trashed them, her mind mocked. No matter how she felt about Caden, there was no way she could have done such a thing for spite. She was more mature than that. *In that case, why did you have Tess tell Caden you were busy when he called? You could have at least thanked him for the flowers.*

She knew the answer to that one. The last thing she needed was to hear his voice. That deep, rich, sexy sound always did things to her. She recalled teasing him about his voice changing when they were kids. He took all of her jesting in stride. But then, Caden had always been the most easygoing person she knew. At least he was until he got angry, and then he was the one who'd become spiteful, not only sleeping with other women but also refusing to have anything to do with her. And then for him to say all those awful things to her that night and...

She drew in a deep breath when she felt tears fill her eyes. Why couldn't she just let go of the pain? Wiping the tears from her eyes, she decided to take a shower and get into bed early. More than anything, she needed a good night's sleep.

Twelve

Ben Bradford offered Jace his hand as he looked directly into his eyes. "So you're Jace Granger." The older man then smiled. "I'm so glad my daughter has finally brought you over for a visit. Come on in. I've prepared dinner, so I hope you're hungry."

"Yes, sir, I am," Jace said as he and Shana followed her father through the foyer into a spacious living room. He glanced around at all the framed photographs lining the walls. He walked over to look more closely at Shana in various stages of her growth. One photo was of her on a bicycle with her sister on a tricycle. Another on her graduation day from high school. Then another showed her graduating from college.

"She was a cute little something," Ben said, chuckling. "Both my daughters were. I'm proud of my girls."

Jace turned toward the man. "And you have every right to be." Benjamin Bradford was just as he'd pictured him to be. Tall, ruggedly built and in good shape for a man his age, which he would put in his middle fifties, like his own father.

"Thanks, Dad. What's for dinner?" Shana asked, turning to head for the kitchen.

Ben chuckled. "Only my child can thank you for a compliment and then beg for food in the same sentence."

"I wasn't begging, just asking out of curiosity. It smells good, whatever it is," Shana said as she walked into the kitchen.

Ben and Jace followed. Ben glanced over at Jace. "So, Jace, I read about that kidnapping attempt in the paper. Glad you came out without a scratch, young man."

"And I have your daughter to thank for that."

"Hmm, better not let Dalton hear you say that," Shana said, sitting down at the kitchen table.

Jace chuckled. "Yeah, I have to give my brother credit as well, but he would not have known I was missing had it not been for Shana and her team."

Ben was very astute in reading people, and he'd been reading the body language between these two from the moment they had entered his home. His daughter, his finicky daughter where men were concerned, was in love. There was a glow on her face that he'd never seen before. Ever. And he hadn't missed the looks these two had been giving each other.

He wasn't surprised Shana hadn't brought Jace around before now. His daughter had to be sure of things, and for her to bring him now meant her mind was made up.

She had finally met a guy she felt was worthy of her affection.

Ben figured these two hadn't known each other too long. But then, he of all people knew you could fall in love in an instant. He'd done so twice in his life and figured when it came to his girls, things for them wouldn't be much different. He'd noticed how Jace was looking at Shana, and he knew those feelings went beyond the physical.

There was no doubt in his mind there was a strong physical attraction between the two of them. He'd seen Jace's sports car parked in Shana's driveway more than once when he'd come to visit. Seeing she had company, he had kept going, knowing she would bring him around eventually if he was a keeper. These two were in love, and he wondered whether they'd figured it out yet.

"You can join Shana at the table, Jace. As you can see, it's already set."

"Yes, sir. Thank you."

Jace had manners, and Ben appreciated that. He'd done his homework on Jace Granger and liked what he'd discovered so far. Shana had mentioned the deathbed promise he'd made to his grandfather, and Ben couldn't help but think highly of him for fulfilling it.

"I grilled steaks, made a salad, baked bread, steamed veggies and made a banana pudding."

"Everything sounds delicious."

"And it will be. Didn't I tell you my dad was fantastic?" Shana said, grinning.

Ben couldn't help smiling. It was good to see all the starchiness gone from his daughter. She appeared relaxed, carefree, and it was obvious she had let her hair down a bit—literally, since it flowed past her shoulders. She looked content. Happy.

Over dinner, they discussed a number of things—the economy, upcoming elections, world affairs and such. Then Ben took Jace out back to show him his garden that he'd started with Mona's help. For some reason, he ended up telling Jace about Mona and what a wonderful woman she was.

"I intend to marry her one day," Ben said. "I just need to bring her around to my way of thinking about our future."

Jace nodded and then looked Ben in the eyes and said, "And I intend to marry your daughter. I hope to get your permission and blessing."

"You got it," Ben replied so quickly it made Jace blink. The older man chuckled. "Was that too fast for you?"

Jace shook his head, grinning. "No, sir. It was just perfect."

Ben smiled. "I give my permission and blessing, but Shana has to have a say in this." He then looked to where Shana was sitting on the patio, stretched on his lounger with her eReader. "Shana?"

She looked up. "Yes, Dad?"

"This young man says he intends to marry you."

A smile spread across her lips. "That's good, because *I* intend to marry *him.*"

A joyous flutter moved in Ben's stomach. "Glad to hear it, since I gave him my blessing and permission."

"Thanks," Shana replied. She then stood, put her

eReader down and came to join them, standing beside Jace and taking his hand in hers. "Did he tell you the rest of it?"

Ben lifted a brow. "There's more?"

Shana nodded. "There is." She tilted her head back to meet her father's gaze directly. "Benjamin Bradford, come next spring, you'll get that grandbaby you've always wanted."

Ben stared at his daughter for a minute to make sure she was saying what he thought she was saying. Seconds passed, and he could tell from the look in her eyes that they were on the same wavelength. Happiness flowed through him, tears misted in his eyes and he pulled his oldest daughter into his arms. "You sure know how to spring one on the old man."

He glanced over at Jace. "A son-in-law and a grandchild. The two of you have definitely made my day."

"Carson?"

"Yes, Sheppard?"

"The warden said you called. I was in a Toastmaster's meeting. We had three new members join."

"That's wonderful. I just wanted you to know that I've taken care of that matter you requested."

Shep drew in a deep breath. "Thanks. I was hoping I'd be able to sleep better tonight, but I'm not sure now, especially after Jace's phone call earlier."

"Jace called?"

"Yes. He wants to come see me tomorrow. Said it was important and he didn't want to tell me over the phone."

"I wonder what it's about."

"I have no idea. But I guess I'll find out tomorrow."

Miles away, in a very private location, a group of individuals had assembled. It had been years since some of their paths had crossed, and most had preferred it that way.

"What is the purpose of this meeting?" someone asked in an annoyed tone. "Everything is going the way we had planned, and we all agreed years ago not to ever—"

"The meeting tonight was necessary."

"Why?"

"Because Sylvia Granger's murder case might be reopened." That statement got everyone's attention, and an immediate hush silenced the room.

"But I thought we took care of that matter involving the private investigator Richard Granger hired a few years back," someone finally added.

"We did. However, Sylvia's sons have stepped into top positions at Granger Aeronautics and, from what I'm hearing, they intend to prove their father is innocent of their mother's murder. And all of us know that can't happen. We have too much at stake."

There was a brief pause and then, "Do I have everyone's permission to proceed in whatever way I see fit?"

All heads in the room nodded consent.

Thirteen

"Now who's the one getting nervous?" Jace asked, smiling over at Shana. They had left Charlottesville early that morning for the drive to Delvers, where they would tell his father about their impending marriage and the baby.

The baby.

It was hard to believe that it was only a couple of months ago that he and his brothers had been summoned home because of his grandfather's heart attack. An attack Richard Granger never recovered from. But before he died, he'd had them make promises they intended to keep…although at times the three of them wondered what the hell they'd gotten themselves into. Especially since they'd all been living separate lives all over the country and the world. At least Jace knew his life before returning home was nothing compared to what it was now, thanks to Shana.

"I can't help it. I've heard so much about him and—"

"You're positive you want to meet him?" Jace asked,

interrupting and raising his eyebrows. "Most people actually believe he killed my mom—and that is nothing to be excited about."

"But you and your brothers don't believe that, and that is good enough for me."

It was a statement more than a question. "No, we don't, and I intend to find out who is actually responsible. But every time I talk to Dad about reopening the case to prove his innocence, he freezes up on me. He thinks Mom was into something that went deeper than that affair with Michael Greene."

Shana lifted a brow.

"I have no idea what he was referring to, and he won't say," Jace continued. "Do you know what I think?"

"No. What do you think?"

"That Dad is against reopening the case because he believes that if we do, it might place us in some kind of danger."

"He told you that?"

"No, but it's what he's not telling me that has me thinking that way."

Shana frowned. "What could your mom have been involved in that was so sinister that it could lead to her death?"

"I don't have a clue, but I'm determined to find out."

"Have you talked to your brothers about it?"

"No. I haven't even told them what I discovered about Mom's affair. I'll have to tell them eventually, although Dad doesn't want me to."

Shana didn't say anything for a minute, and then

she asked, "Do you think he'll be happy you're getting married and that we're having a baby?"

When the car came to a traffic light, he reached out and took her hand in his, a wide smile spread across his lips. "Just like your father, Sheppard Granger is going to be ecstatic."

Tess was on break and Shiloh was assisting customers with their wine purchases when she suddenly felt heat envelop her body. She glanced up and looked across the room. When had Caden Granger come in?

She tried ignoring him as he browsed around her shop but it was difficult to do so. And just like the other day, he was dressed in a business suit that seemed tailored just for his body. At least she wasn't the only one checking him out. She saw several other women finding it hard to keep their eyes off him.

Forcing her gaze away, she focused on the woman who had quickly become one of her regular customers, Mrs. Owens. Her husband owned several computer stores throughout Virginia and Maryland. It seemed the Owenses were always entertaining. "Another party, Mrs. Owens?"

The woman, who looked to be in her mid-sixties, beamed a smile at her. "Yes, another party."

Shiloh could tell from the woman's tone that she wasn't put out by the prospect of hosting yet another party. In fact, she seemed excited. Shiloh recalled that her mother had been that sort of person. One who had enjoyed hosting all of Samuel Timmons's parties, and there had been plenty. Owning a slew of retail stores had paid off for her father, and he was constantly traveling to increase his business.

"I remember when your parents used to give parties. Your mom was the perfect hostess. She was so good at it."

That wasn't the only thing she was good at, Shiloh thought, wondering how many other of her husband's secrets her mother was hiding. "Yes, she was."

"And I understand you're helping with this year's ball for cancer research. That's wonderful. We need more young people to get involved." The woman looked at her watch and then said, "Well, I'll be going. I have a few more stops to make."

"Have a good day, Mrs. Owens, and I hope you'll attend my grand opening next weekend."

"Harold and I both will be here. I love this place, and you have the best of everything."

"Thank you."

By now, Caden was standing in line at the cash desk, and there were two customers ahead of him. Shiloh hoped Tess's break would end so she could deal with Caden, but it didn't happen. Moments later, he was standing in front of her. He placed a bottle of Riesling on the counter. "Will this be all?" Shiloh asked.

"Not unless you're willing to forgive me for all my wrongdoings, Shiloh."

Shiloh didn't say anything, because at the moment she couldn't. There was so much regret lining his features that she couldn't stand it. Caden had always been her weakness, to the point that she had risked her father's wrath for him. He'd had no right to hurt her the way he had.

She wished there was another customer behind him so she could hurry him on, but there was no one. In fact, most of her customers had either left or were drinking their wine in the outside café, where Donnell was making sure they had everything they could want. In other words, this little scene was in Caden's favor. But it wouldn't be for long.

"I'm short on forgiveness today. I'm all out. Anything else?" she asked briskly, clearly letting him know she wasn't in the mood.

"Yes, there is something else. Would you go out with me Saturday night?"

She stared at him. When would he give up? He really thought they could move on after everything that had happened. It was time for her to let him know she *had* moved on, but in a different direction. "Sorry, I have a date Saturday night."

He didn't have to say anything. His expression said it all. If she had intended to hurt him, she'd done a perfect job. Now he would know how it had felt when she'd learned he had slept with those women while thinking the worst of her. But, no, he would never know how it had felt for her. Despite that, she had been there for him and his brothers when they could have lost their family business.

"Anybody I know?"

"Excuse me?"

"Is your date anyone I know?" he asked. She could

hear the anger in his voice, although his tone remained level.

"I doubt it. But then, I don't know everyone you know. If there won't be anything else, I have some work to attend to in my office," she said as she saw Tess returning from her break.

"No, there won't be anything else. For now."

Good, she thought, ringing up his order and placing the bottle of wine inside the store's signature wine bag. He handed her his charge card, and although she tried to be careful, their fingers still touched, and a zing of electricity passed through her.

Shiloh quickly processed his card and, instead of handing it directly back to him, she wrapped his receipt around it and placed it on the counter beside his wine bag. She plastered a smile on her face. "Thank you for your purchase, Mr. Granger. Do have a nice day."

Sheppard stood at the window in the prison library and watched as Jace got out of his car. Shep hadn't slept much last night, wondering why his son had called this meeting and why he was being so evasive about it.

He lifted an eyebrow when Jace went to the passenger side of that little sports car of his and opened the door…for a woman. And Shep had to say she was a beautiful woman. As he watched the couple, he could tell something was going on between them. It was in the way Jace automatically took her hand in his as together they strolled toward the entrance.

He then watched as another car pulled up to park beside Jace's car, and he noted a man sitting inside who made no move to get out. Shep wondered whether it was one of the guys he had hired to protect his sons.

He felt a presence come to stand beside him. "Looks like your visitors have arrived," Ambrose said.

"Yes, it sure looks that way."

"It will take them a minute to get through security, and then I'll bring them on up to the same private room you used before."

Shep nodded. "Thanks, Ambrose."

Shep turned away from the window and drew in a deep breath, thinking about his sons. The last woman Jace had brought home for them to meet had turned out to be a disaster. And from what Jace had told him, she had betrayed him in the worst way. So for him to be involved with another woman meant he'd moved on and had left Eve behind. Shep certainly hoped so.

He also knew that although Caden pretended otherwise, something had happened between him and Shiloh. Whatever was going on, Shep hoped they got things together. He'd always liked Shiloh and he didn't blame her for the fact that her parents had forced her to end her friendship with his sons. He hoped his sons didn't blame her, either.

His thoughts shifted to Dalton. Sheppard had no idea what woman Dalton was into, and maybe it was best he didn't know. His baby boy had started noticing girls early and, unfortunately, girls had started noticing him, too.

Moments later, Ambrose knocked on the door before entering. "Your visitors are here, Mr. Granger."

Jace walked in with the beautiful woman by his side.

A huge smile covered his son's face. "Dad, it's so good seeing you again," he said, giving him a huge bear hug while Ambrose basically looked the other way rather than reminding them of the rule against physical contact.

"I'll be outside the door if I'm needed," Ambrose said. Shep knew the man would probably wander off, giving him the privacy he felt Sheppard deserved.

"Good seeing you, too, Jace," Shep said, looking his son up and down. He looked good. He looked happy.

"Thanks. And I want you to meet someone. This is the woman we hired to turn Granger Aeronautics around. A woman I can thank, along with Dalton, of course, for saving my life. But most importantly, Dad, she's the woman I intend to marry next month. Shana Bradford."

Shana, who had been hanging back so Jace and his father could have their private moment, walked over to Shep and offered her hand. "It's nice to meet you, Mr. Granger."

Instead of taking her hand, Shep pulled her into his arms for a hug. "Welcome to the family, Shana. And thanks for your part in saving my son's life."

"We have something else to tell you, Dad."

Shep released Shana and glanced over at Jace. "You do? What?"

A huge smile covered Jace's features when he said, "You'll become a grandfather in the spring."

It took a second for Jace's words to sink in, and when they did, another huge smile touched Shep's face. Emotions he'd never felt before took over. All the emptiness he'd felt when he'd lost his father was being replaced at the thought that he was gaining a grandchild.

"A grandchild?" His first. He felt overwhelmed. So damned happy.

"Yes, Dad," Jace said, grinning and wrapping his arms around Shana's waist. "A grandchild. Another Granger."

Fourteen

There was a knock on Caden's office door. "Come in."

Dalton walked in, smiling. "It's all set."

Caden leaned back in his chair. "What is?"

"Our celebration for Jace and Shana. We're taking them out to dinner Saturday night."

Caden lifted a brow. "We are?"

"Yes. Don't you remember? I mentioned it this morning, and you said for me to go ahead and plan it."

No, Caden didn't remember. But then, his mind hadn't been working right since Sandra Timmons's visit and the bombshell she had dropped. And then there was that incident earlier today when he had dropped by the wine shop. Shiloh had let him know in no uncertain terms that she had not forgiven him. She even told him she had a date for Saturday night. Those words had been like a knife in his heart.

"Caden?"

He drew in a deep breath and met Dalton's gaze. "To be quite honest with you, I don't remember discussing anything about it with you. But it doesn't matter. Sorry. What do you have planned?"

Dalton looked at him strangely for a second before saying, "Dinner Saturday night at the Matador. The four of us. Reservations have been made for six-thirty."

"Fine. I'll be there."

He expected Dalton to leave, but when he continued to sit there and stare at him, Caden asked, "Is there something else?"

"Yes, there is."

"What?"

"I know I can be a pain in the ass sometimes, and—"

"Sometimes?"

"Okay, probably the majority of the time, but I care about you, man. You're going through something, but you won't tell me shit. I might not have any answers, but I can listen. Besides, I leveled with you about what was going on with me."

Caden rolled his eyes. "You really want me to believe you hired a P.I. to find a woman?"

"It's true. I know that is *so* not me, but people do strange things at times. And, like I told you, she was hot." Dalton didn't say anything for a moment, and then he asked, "So what's going on with you and Shiloh? I know it has something to do with her, Caden. You can't be holding a grudge against her because her old man kept her from being friends with us all those years ago. Samuel Timmons was crazy—we all knew that."

"Is that what you think? That I'm holding a grudge against her?"

"What else could it be when the two of you hadn't been in contact with each other for years?"

Caden leaned forward in his chair. "That's where you're wrong, Dalton. Samuel Timmons tried keeping us apart, and he succeeded for a while. But Shiloh and I finally hooked up years later when she was in her last year of college, and the band and I were beginning the concert tours."

Seeing the look of surprise in Dalton's eyes, Caden said, "I might as well start from the beginning."

Caden began talking, telling Dalton everything, including his and Shiloh's plans to marry in Vegas, the photographs he'd received and how he had treated Shiloh afterward, believing the worst about her.

He told Dalton about the night Shiloh had come to Sutton Hills and the mean things he'd said to her. He then told him what Sandra Timmons had wanted when she'd shown up to see him that day—the bombshell she had dropped, and how Caden had been trying to make things right with Shiloh ever since. He even told Dalton about going to see her today and her unforgiving attitude…and her date with someone else this weekend.

To Caden's surprise, Dalton listened without saying a single word, not one. Caden couldn't even fathom what his brother was thinking since Dalton's expression was unreadable. When he finished and Dalton still didn't say anything, Caden asked, "So you don't have anything to say?"

Dalton held his gaze. "Oh, I have a lot to say, but first I have a question."

"And what is your question?"

"Where were you and Jace when Richard Granger was giving out his endless lectures about unprotected sex and the use of condoms? Because it seems that somehow along the way, the two of you must have missed that class."

Caden stared at his brother, thinking his question couldn't be a serious one, but when he saw that it was, he answered. "First of all, Jace and I did get those lectures, trust me. However, neither of us was as sexually active as you were in high school, and Granddad knew it."

Dalton lifted a brow. "He knew it?"

"He couldn't help but know it when you used to brag about your conquests over the breakfast table."

"But I spoke in codes so only you and Jace could know what I was saying, and I whispered most of the time. And if I remember correctly, Granddad was ignoring us and reading his newspaper."

"And listening to your every word while doing so."

"No kidding?" Dalton asked, smiling as if such a thing was good news.

"Jace and I wondered if you knew. In fact, we thought you were embellishing a lot of the stuff you told us about because you figured the old man was listening."

Dalton rolled his eyes. "I didn't have to embellish anything. I was giving you guys the facts."

"And you still wonder why you got more lectures than we did? Let's move on from that. I want to hear what you really have to say," Caden said.

"Okay, here goes. I think you made a real mess of

things but that it can be fixed. The reason I say that is because evidently Shiloh still cares about you."

"I don't know how you figure that. I told you what happened when I dropped by her wine shop earlier today."

"Yes, and she's still in pain from the hurt you caused her. And the reason I say she still cares for you is because you're sitting there and I'm sitting here."

Caden was confused, and it showed on his face. "I don't get your point."

Dalton rolled his eyes. "The only reason we were able to hold on to this company amid a hostile-takeover attempt was because Shiloh saved the day by voting her mother's shares in our favor. That was after you did all those mean things to her—like having her ejected from one of your concerts and sleeping around for spite. And even with all that, according to you, she recently attended another one of your concerts, and when she found out the truth about what her father had done, she came to Sutton Hills to tell you."

Dalton paused a minute and said, "Shiloh has every right to be angry with you, Caden. But I don't think she has totally fallen out of love with you. She only thinks she has, and understandably so."

Caden stared at his brother. For someone who had never been in love, Dalton was talking as if he were an expert on the subject matter. As if Dalton could read his mind, he said, "You don't have to know a lot about love to figure out your problem, Caden. You just have to know a lot about women. And they are my specialty."

"If what you've said is to be believed, how am I supposed to get back into her good graces? How can I make her realize she still loves me as much as I love her?"

Dalton smiled. "It's rather simple. Come up with a plan to get her to fall in love with you all over again. If I were you, I would do everything to prove that the two of you belong together, that you still love her and that she still loves you. But most important, remind her that you're worthy of her love."

Fifteen

For Shiloh, the time had flown by this past week, and Saturday was here before she knew it. She had been so busy getting things organized for her grand opening that she hadn't noticed the passing of the days. She'd also found time to meet with Nannette about the charity ball and had agreed to handle the entertainment aspect of the event. That shouldn't be hard. Nannette had even given her a list of local talent she could choose from.

One good thing was that Caden hadn't dropped by, and she wondered whether telling him she had a date had finally made him realize things were over between them. She doubted that she would forget the look on his face when she'd told him. She had tried not to let it bother her, but she found herself turning the moment over in her mind anyway. And to make matters worse, she had been tempted more than once to call Sedrick and cancel tonight's double date. But each time, she had talked herself out of it, refusing to let Caden's visits and those flowers weaken her resolve. Her relationship with Caden had ended, so there was no reason she should feel guilty about going out with another man. He hadn't thought of her when he'd slept with those other women. Regardless of the fact that he had unwittingly been played by her father, he should have trusted her more.

She had just finished fixing her hair when the buzzer sounded. Wallace was a few minutes early. "Who is it?" she asked, after hitting the intercom.

"Wallace."

"Take the elevator up to the third floor and then come to the first door." She took a deep breath, thinking, *Okay, this is it.* This was her initial step in moving on, something she should have done years ago. After hearing his knock, she opened the door and had to stare up at the man standing there. He was tall. Almost as tall as Caden. Now, why had she made that comparison?

He was handsome. Any woman would agree with that assessment. He had a nice smile and looked good in his brown slacks and mint-green dress shirt. And, according to Sedrick, he was a nice guy. So why wasn't she feeling a little excitement? Why wasn't there an increase in her pulse? An extra beat from her heart? "Wallace, please come in while I get my purse."

"Thanks," he said, stepping over the threshold and closing the door behind him while glancing around. "Nice place."

"Thank you."

"I'm looking forward to tonight," he said, smiling over at her.

She again thought he had a nice smile. But then, so

did Caden. Growing annoyed with herself, she said, "I'll be back in a minute."

She quickly rounded the corner and grabbed her purse off the breakfast counter. Why was her mind constantly going back into the past? Some things you couldn't change. And the history between her and Caden was one of them. Her goal was to move forward and not look back. She believed if she gave him the chance, Wallace could be the man to help her take those steps.

When she returned, he was standing in the spot where she'd left him. "I'm ready." And she inwardly told herself that she was ready not just for dinner but to get on with her life.

He nodded, smiling. "I'm ready, as well. Ready to start getting to know you better."

She returned his smile. "I'd like that."

"Sheppard, that's wonderful news. Congratulations."

"Thanks. After I saw Jace and Shana walk in together and how into each other they seemed, I figured there was a reason he was bringing her here to meet me," Sheppard said, shifting the phone to his other ear. "His announcement that they were getting married didn't come as a shock. But for them to tell me about the baby... Wow! It was incredible."

He paused a moment and then said, "And then I got to thinking, Carson. The baby will have a grandfather in prison. A grandfather he or she won't be able to spend any time with except during visits. I don't want my grandchild seeing me here, unable to understand that

I'm not a criminal. And do you know that by the time I'm released from jail, he or she might be the same age Jace was when I went in?"

Carson didn't say anything. Sheppard Granger rarely held a pity party, so as far as she was concerned, he deserved this one. The one thing she admired about him more than anything was his integrity and his fierce desire to protect those he loved.

"You'll be up for parole in a couple of years, Sheppard." She paused and then added, "And if you would let me arrange for your case to be reevaluated, I'm sure—"

"No. You saw that email. You read it. I can't lose my sons, and if you get too involved, I could lose you, too. That would destroy me, Carson. Just let things be. Please."

She heard the plea in his voice and decided to do as he'd asked and let things be. And she would. For now.

"Welcome to the Matador," the maître d' greeted Dalton.

"Thanks," Dalton said. "We have reservations for a party of four. The Grangers."

"Certainly, Mr. Granger. Your table is ready. Right this way."

Dalton had been looking forward to tonight. Although he'd initially been shocked by Jace's marriage announcement and hearing about the baby had almost made him lose his cool, he was okay now, and the more he was around Jace and Shana, the more he saw how right they were for each other. And tonight he and

Caden planned to officially welcome her to the family, Granger style.

They had invited Hannah to join them because she was considered part of the family, but she had made plans to visit her daughter, who was in New York on business. They intended to take in a Broadway show.

Jace and Shana had decided to marry in a private ceremony with only close family and friends next month at Sutton Hills. All the arrangements were being made, and Hannah was so excited that she had volunteered to cater the entire affair. It would be her gift to the bridal couple.

They were seated and menus given to them when Dalton inquired, "So how did the fathers handle the news?"

Jace and Shana told Dalton and Caden how they had shared the news with Ben and Sheppard and how joyously both men had reacted. After visiting Sheppard, the couple had gone straight to a jewelry store, where Jace had purchased Shana an engagement ring. Dalton would admit it was a mighty nice-looking rock, but then, he hadn't expected anything less from his older brother.

"I understand you have a sister, Shana. You could have invited her to join us," Dalton said.

Shana smiled. "She would have liked that, but she works out of town on occasion and won't be back for a few weeks or so."

Dalton was just about to ask Shana what kind of work her sister did when the arrival of a group across the room caught his attention. *Damn.* Eventually Caden

would see them, he thought, so he might as well mention it. "It seems this is a popular place tonight," he said
to everyone seated at the table. "Shiloh Timmons and
her brother, Sedrick, just walked in…with their dates."

Caden's head snapped up, and he gazed across the
room at the same time a sharp pain ripped through his
heart. Shiloh had told him she had a date tonight, but
he hadn't wanted to believe her. And seeing her with
another man froze him solid.

Shiloh must have felt his gaze on her, because at that
moment, she glanced in their direction. From the sudden look that appeared on her face, it was obvious that
she was as surprised to see him as he was to see her.

"Caden?"

Jace said his name. He heard the concern in his
brother's voice. Without breaking eye contact with Shiloh, he said, "I can deal with it."

But even as he said the words, deep down he truly
knew that he couldn't.

The moment Shiloh was seated, she felt a blast of
cold air come her way. Glancing across the room, her
gaze caught Caden's. For a moment she went still because she read everything in his expression and the
icy-cold eyes staring at her. Telling him she intended
to move on without him and that she had a date tonight
was one thing, but actually seeing her with someone
else was another. And, at that moment, she felt both
his anger and his pain. The intensity of both almost
closed her throat.

"Shiloh? Are you all right?" Wallace asked, getting the attention of the others seated at their table.

She met Sedrick's gaze, and she saw concern in her brother's eyes. She could see the wheels turning in his head, wondering what was wrong with her. Obviously, he hadn't seen the Grangers yet, and she had no intention of pointing them out.

Shiloh knew she had to pull herself together and do so quickly. Forcing a smile at Wallace, she said, "Yes, I'm fine. I was trying to remember if I unplugged my curling iron. I don't like leaving it plugged in."

Okay, what she'd said sounded lame, and she wasn't surprised when Sedrick looked at her strangely. And bless Cassie's heart, she tried coming to her rescue by saying, "You never want to leave them plugged into an outlet if you can avoid it. Small fires are known to happen."

Cassie had gone a little overboard with that statement, and from the expression on both Wallace's and Sedrick's faces, they probably knew it.

Wallace leaned close to her and said, "If you like, I'd be glad to take you back home to make sure you did unplug it."

It was a kind offer, and it would be so easy to tell him, yes, she wanted him to take her back home, because deep down she didn't know how she could enjoy her meal knowing Caden was in the same building and sitting at a table where he could see her every move. But she knew leaving was the coward's way out, and Sedrick would be upset when he discovered the real reason. He had warned her not to get involved with Wallace if she wasn't ready to move on. She had assured him she was.

"Thanks for the offer, but now that I think about it, I'm pretty sure I unplugged it. No big deal."

"You sure? A few minutes ago, you had an expression on your face as if you were really bothered."

"No, I'm fine now." She drew in a deep breath, wishing that were true.

"Caden, how are you managing to balance your work at Granger and your music?" Shana asked.

Caden smiled, understanding her ploy. The sight of Shiloh with a date had rendered him speechless, and he'd had little to say during most of the meal, leaving Dalton to keep things lively for the engaged couple. Every so often, he would glance across the room at Shiloh. She had refused to look at him again after that initial eye contact. Although she smiled occasionally at her dinner date, he could tell she was nervous. Only someone who had once been as close to Shiloh as he had could detect her nerves from across the room. She kept her hands so busy while she talked that she barely had time to eat and she kept brushing her hair back from her face.

Knowing Shana was waiting on his response, he said, "Luckily, this time of year is our downtime. The guys like being home for the fall since it leads into the holidays, and they enjoy the time they get to spend with their families."

"No females in the band? I recall there was one on your last album."

There had been, he thought. Rita Crews. She had been his bass guitarist, and she'd been a damned good one. She'd also been his lover at one time. Although she'd accepted his sex-only rule in the beginning, after a few months she hadn't wanted to play by the rules. He'd told her the same thing he told all the others—he didn't intend to get involved in a serious relationship. They would be lovers and nothing more. Rita's possessiveness had become obsessive, and he made the decision to let her go from the band after several altercations with fans when her jealousy got the best of her.

"We did have a female bass player once, but she moved on." He didn't add that she didn't have a choice and hadn't been happy about doing so.

"I'm glad everything worked out in your favor with your tour schedule."

He was glad, too. He was also glad Shana hadn't inquired about what he intended to do in January, when it was time for him and the guys to begin touring again. He felt committed to his band but, at the same time, he was committed to Granger Aeronautics. A promise was a promise, and he and his brothers had given their grandfather their word on his deathbed. They all intended to keep that promise.

Luckily for Caden, Dalton steered the conversation to another topic by asking Jace and Shana where they would live after getting married. It was then that Caden realized what Jace's marriage would mean to him personally. If Jace and Shana decided to make their home at Sutton Hills, that meant he would need to find somewhere else to stay. Moving to his parents' home was out of the question, and moving into the boathouse was unthinkable.

"We haven't decided where we'll live yet," Jace responded.

Caden wondered what there was to think about. As the oldest, Jace would inherit their grandfather's house…until their father was released from prison, and then it would be up to Sheppard as to what he wanted to do with it.

The waiter returned to suggest dessert, and everyone declined. The food had been delicious, although how the food had tasted was the last thing on Caden's mind. They sat there a few minutes longer, talking over coffee, and then it was time to leave, which meant they would have to walk by Shiloh's table.

Dalton saw his dilemma and said, "I can always ask the manager to let us sneak out the back door if you'd rather not encounter Shiloh."

"Go to hell, Dalton."

His baby brother only gave him a wide grin as he stood. "Well, since you're being a meanie, I think I'll mosey over and say hello to the Timmonses."

Before Caden could stop him, Dalton walked toward the table where Shiloh was sitting. Damn him.

Sixteen

"Well, if it isn't Shiloh and Sedrick Timmons. Fancy running into you here," Dalton began.

Sedrick was talking, and the table went quiet when Dalton Granger approached, his presence causing a momentary lull in their conversation. Shiloh had been hoping that the Granger party would ignore them on their way out. It seemed that would not be the case.

Not only had Dalton stopped by their table, but the others in his group did so, too. She forced herself not to look at Caden as Sedrick introduced everyone.

When Jace introduced Shana as his fiancée and indicated they would be getting married in a few weeks, congratulations were offered to the engaged couple. While growing up, Shiloh had always liked Jace, mainly because he'd been older and so sure of himself. Whereas Dalton, the youngest of the three, had mostly been the pain that only younger brothers could be.

"Wait a minute," she heard Wallace exclaim, grinning all over after being introduced to Caden. "You're

Caden Granger? *The* Caden Granger—the Grammy Award–winning saxophone player? The Caden Granger who doesn't put out a CD that I don't run out and buy?"

Before Caden could say anything, Dalton spoke up and said, "Yes, he's *that* Caden Granger. For a minute there, I thought you were going to ask if he was the same Caden Granger who was once engaged to marry Shiloh, because, yes, he's that one, as well."

"Oh," Wallace said. His surprised expression indicated he definitely hadn't known that piece of information.

He looked at Shiloh, who quickly added, "That was a *long* time ago."

She then sent Dalton a frosty look, but he only smiled at her. He'd done that on purpose, and she didn't appreciate it. A quick glance at Caden and his annoyed expression indicated he hadn't appreciated his brother's statement, either. At least she was grateful for that.

"Well, we'd better get going," Jace said quickly, trying to smooth things over. "It was very nice meeting you. I hope you enjoy your meal." He then all but shoved Dalton toward the exit.

Caden hung back somewhat, and Shiloh held her breath, wondering what he would say. As far as she was concerned, Dalton had said enough. Too damned much.

He glanced her way, but instead he looked past her to Wallace and said, "Thanks for supporting my music. I appreciate it." Then to the rest of the table he said, "Please, enjoy the rest of your evening."

Shiloh watched as Caden left the dining room.

"He seems like a nice guy," said Wallace.

Shiloh swung her gaze back to Wallace. "Who?"

"Caden Granger. I'm glad I got to meet him. I should have asked for his autograph."

She nodded and then drew in a deep breath, avoiding her brother's gaze that she knew was not missing a thing. "Yes," she said to Wallace. "You should have gotten his autograph."

Dalton, to Caden's surprise, was waiting for him beside his car in the parking lot. And he had the nerve to be smiling. "Jace told me I was crazy to wait for you, because you would probably kick my ass," Dalton said. "But I assured him you wouldn't since I helped you out."

Caden narrowed his gaze at his brother. "You think you helped me out?"

"Sure. Now Dr. Aiken has been given fair warning that there used to be something between you and Shiloh. So he won't be surprised when you get her back."

Caden drew in a deep breath. "Dr. Aiken is not my concern in terms of getting Shiloh back."

"So you do intend to get her back?"

"Yes."

"At least you're admitting to that. And I hope you don't plan to be a Mr. Nice Guy about it. I studied Wallace Aiken at dinner. He likes her, and I take it that Sedrick is pushing the relationship. If I were you, I—"

"Damn it, Dalton, you aren't me. You handle your business your way, and I'll handle my business my way. Now, move out of my way before I do kick your ass."

Without another word to his brother, Caden got into his car, slamming the door behind him, and drove off.

He wished he could say something for Dalton to mull over but knew that would never happen. His brother would never fully understand the emotions he was feeling until he fell in love, and Caden didn't see that happening anytime soon, if ever. Dalton thought he should be worried that Wallace Aiken was his competition. However, as far as Caden was concerned, Aiken wasn't even in the picture. It was all about Shiloh and making sure she understood a few things. If she thought all the history they shared could be tossed aside, she was wrong, and he intended to prove it to her.

He knew Jace would be spending the night at Shana's place, especially now that they were engaged and expecting a baby. And with Hannah being away for the weekend, it meant he had Sutton Hills to himself. Whoop-dee-doo.

He headed for home, knowing that he definitely wouldn't do things Dalton's way, but he fully intended to get the woman he loved back—the Caden Granger way.

"Oh, Ben. You're going to be a grandfather. That's wonderful. I'm so happy for you."

Benjamin Bradford couldn't help but smile as he glanced across the candlelit table at someone he thought was a very beautiful woman. He and Mona Underwood had met months ago in the produce section of the neighborhood grocery store. He had been a cop on the streets of Boston and had worked for a while as a detective, so he could read people pretty well.

She had been getting around the store with minimal use of her cane, but he immediately knew she was blind.

But that hadn't stopped him from admiring her beauty or striking up a conversation with her.

Now several months later, they'd had a number of dates, and she'd met both of his daughters, Shana and Jules—short for Juliet. They liked her, although they wanted him to take things at a reasonable pace. They were protective of him since he hadn't been involved in a serious relationship since their mother Sharon's death of pancreatic cancer thirteen years ago. At the time the girls had been in their early teens and they'd needed their dad.

Ben liked everything about Mona. She had a quiet manner and appreciated life, although one would think life had given her a bad rap. A car accident had rendered her legally blind. Then her husband had left her, married someone else and had given his young bride the child he had denied Mona for years.

Yet Mona never felt sorry for herself. Instead, she became independent and self-sufficient. She didn't see her blindness as a handicap. Instead, she saw it as a challenge—a way of life for now, since her doctors felt there was a possibility her sight could return.

However, it mattered not at all to Ben whether Mona ever regained her sight because, in his heart, he'd already fallen in love with her and intended to make her a part of his life. For always. He'd told her as much, and she was trying to get used to him and his bold assumption that their lives would always be entwined. He was okay with that, because he didn't intend to go anywhere. He had plenty of time on his hands and couldn't see using it any other way than spending it with her whenever he could.

"Thanks, Mona. I'm excited about it. I must admit my girls had me worried for a while. It's okay to build a career and work hard at it, but at the end of the day, it's always nice to have someone to come home to."

She nodded slowly, hoping he was hinting at their situation.

Mona was a political-science professor at the University of Virginia and Ben smiled at the thought. He'd always done his duty by voting, but until he had met Mona, he had never discussed politics with anyone. She was well versed in the issues at all levels of government and she had a wealth of knowledge. He loved her intellectual mind and, as far as he was concerned, Mona was still a beauty at fifty-three. He was nine years older at sixty-two and he thought the age difference was perfect.

He reached across the table and captured her hand in his. "So, did you enjoy dinner tonight?"

"Yes. I enjoyed it very much."

He watched as her features lit up. With her creamy brown skin, expressive dark brown eyes, full glossy lips and cute perky nose, all framed by a mass of short curls that cascaded around her face, he thought she was simply beautiful, totally desirable. The latter was what he'd been fighting now for a few months. Her desirability.

"I prepared dinner for Shana and Jace the other night and plan to do so again when Jules returns home. Will you come?" he asked.

She smiled. "It sounds like a family gathering."

"It will be. I want to get to know my future son-in-law better. He's captured my daughter's heart, that's for sure. And from the time I spent with him the other night, I can tell he's what she needs. He's solid, strong, a man of distinction."

"All the qualities you possess."

He chuckled, appreciating her compliment. "Thank you. So, getting back to my invitation to dinner. Will you come to dinner?"

"And you're sure that your girls won't mind?"

He smiled. "Positive. They like you." And besides that, he thought further, he'd made it clear to his daughters that they had their lives and he had his. They knew he'd loved Sharon, but now it was time for him to enjoy his life with the woman he wanted.

"If you're sure…"

His hand tightened on hers. "Positive. I'll give you sufficient notice in terms of the date. I'm just waiting for Jules to come back to town. You never know with her and those cases she works," he said of his daughter, who owned a private-investigation firm.

"Where is she now?" Mona asked.

"Last we talked, she was skipping through Montana." He paused a moment, then said, "There is another matter I'd like to talk to you about."

She lifted an arched brow. "Oh? What?"

"A trip. How would you like to go with me to New York to see a Broadway play? We can stay a few days and enjoy ourselves and the city."

She didn't say anything as he watched her features, knowing what he was asking of her. Taking her away from Charlottesville meant removing her from her comfort zone. He knew she had very particular ways to deal with her blindness. Her clothes were coded for easy identification, and she used what she called her "magic wand" to get around so as not to bump into anything. And whenever they went out, he would arrange her plated food so that she knew where everything was. If she were to accept the offer, it would mean her total dependency on him for the entire time they were gone.

"New York?" she asked softly.

"Yes, New York. I figured we could stay for a few days." He was letting her know this trip wouldn't be a day trip like the time he'd taken her to the beach or driven her into D.C. He was talking about them staying overnight. Together.

He watched her features, saw the indecisiveness and knew she was thinking of all the reasons she shouldn't go. He gently tightened his hand on hers. "Trust me to take care of you, Mona. Trust me to never hurt you."

He watched her beautiful, strong, dark brown eyes fill with tears as she asked, "Are you sure you want to do this?"

"Positive," he replied quickly. He reached up and wiped a tear that tracked down her cheek. "It will be okay, baby. You'll see. Just trust me," he whispered.

She nodded slowly and then said, "I do trust you. Okay, I will go to New York with you."

Ben let out the breath he'd been holding, doubting that Mona had any idea about just how happy she had made him at that moment.

Seventeen

Shiloh glanced around the room at the attendees who were there for the grand opening of her wine boutique. The place was packed, but she had been prepared. She and her staff had worked tirelessly for the past weeks finalizing last-minute details in preparation for tonight.

Valerie had arrived a week ago, and she'd been a godsend, helping out wherever she was needed. And then, two days ago, Valerie's husband, Jack, had arrived, surprising Shiloh with additional wines from Valerie's family's vineyard in Italy. The wine had been a gift from Valerie's grandparents.

Shiloh smiled when she saw Jack sneak his wife a kiss and thought more than once that the couple had such a touching relationship, the kind she'd always wanted for herself and Caden.

Caden.

Why had her mind conjured him right then? It had been a week ago tonight since she had seen him and his family at the Matador. Luckily, Wallace hadn't seemed bothered by Dalton's revelation that she and Caden once shared a serious relationship. On the drive back to her place, he hadn't even brought it up. In fact, she'd been somewhat annoyed with how he'd carried on and on about what a big fan of Caden's music he was. He'd even had the gall to suggest that if she ran into Caden again, she might get his autograph for him—if she didn't mind. Sedrick had said Wallace was a nice guy, but as far as she was concerned, he was being way too nice.

When he'd walked her to her door, Wallace hadn't asked for another date; however, he had indicated he would attend her grand opening tonight. And when he'd placed a chaste kiss on her lips, she hadn't felt a thing. Not even the tiniest spike in her pulse. He had called once this week when he'd been on break at the hospital, and because she'd been busy, the conversation had been short. He hadn't called again, and she hated to admit it, but she hadn't thought of him since.

Until tonight.

And only because Valerie had mentioned she was dying to meet Wallace. But Shiloh knew her friend. Although Valerie claimed she was being neutral when it came to her love life, Shiloh knew Valerie had a soft spot in her heart for Caden. It had everything to do with the time Caden had been on his European tour and had dropped by the Rizollis' vineyard and had ended up spending a couple of nights. Valerie's family loved him and had made Caden an honorary son.

"Nice turnout, and it's still early yet."

Shiloh turned at the sound of Sedrick's voice. Once the Grangers had shown up at their table at the Matador, it hadn't taken her brother long to figure out why she'd been acting so strange when they'd first arrived. Although Wallace hadn't said anything about Dalton's comment, Sedrick had said plenty in private to her and none of it nice. He thought Dalton's comment had been out of line and had been made intentionally to make Wallace feel uncomfortable. Shiloh didn't doubt that was true, but she had explained to Sedrick that she had more to do with her time than try to figure out Dalton Granger's motives.

She smiled up at her brother. "Hopefully, that's a good sign. I'm glad Uncle Rodney was able to make it." Her uncle, her father's younger brother, ran the Timmons retail empire on the West Coast.

"I am, too. It's always good seeing him. I spent the last thirty minutes talking to him. I wasn't aware that he'd been ill."

Neither had Shiloh. The last time she'd seen him was at their father's funeral. He had looked pretty fit then. "What's wrong?"

"Skin cancer, which doesn't surprise me since we know how he loves to hang out in the sun on that yacht of his."

"But he's okay now?"

"He said he was. He underwent surgery followed by radiation, and his doctors told him everything went well."

Shiloh nodded as she took a sip of her wine. She and Sedrick owed a lot to their uncle Rodney. Their paternal grandparents had set up trust funds for all of their grandchildren, and when Shiloh and Sedrick hadn't shown any signs of wanting to take part in the family business, and had chosen other careers, Samuel had tried to take away the trust fund in protest. But Uncle Rodney wouldn't let him. He defied his brother and stood behind her and Sedrick, saying that they had a right to do whatever they wanted with their lives without having their trust funds held over their heads as blackmail.

For years, the brothers stopped speaking and Rodney Timmons expanded the family business in California. But the death of one of Uncle Rodney's sons a few years ago brought about a reconciliation between the brothers. And, according to her mother, Uncle Rodney had flown in several times to visit Samuel when he'd become ill.

Shiloh glanced around the room. "Where's Wallace?" She hadn't asked about Cassie, because Shiloh knew she would be arriving later.

"An emergency came up at the hospital, and he had to cancel his appearance here tonight. Do you really care?"

She knew Sedrick was still upset about the incident at dinner last week. He'd felt that she could have done more. Just what he figured she could have done, she wasn't sure. She had spoken up and quickly explained that her relationship with Caden had ended a long time ago.

"You might not believe this, but I like Wallace. He's a nice guy."

"But nice guys finish last, right? Or sometimes not at all."

She wondered why her brother was in such a funky mood and figured he must have had a tough day at work. "You could have warned me that Mom was coming."

Sedrick froze while taking a sip of wine and gazed up at her over the glass. "Mom's here?"

From his reaction, it was evident he was unaware that their mother was attending. "Yes. She's outside in the courtyard talking to the Greenes."

He frowned. "The Greenes are here?"

He sounded surprised.

"Do you really think they would miss an opportunity to campaign for their son? And I expect him to show up at some point tonight."

Michael and Yolanda Greene had been close friends of their parents, and their oldest son, Ivan, was running for mayor. Shiloh never got to know Ivan growing up since he was a good thirteen years older than she was. But she had known his sisters, Kerrie and Deidra. The one thing she remembered more than anything was that Kerrie and Sedrick used to have a thing for each other back in the day. In fact, they had dated through most of their senior year of high school. She'd almost forgotten about that.

"Do you keep up with Kerrie Greene?"

Her question surprised Sedrick, and from the look on his face, she knew immediately that he kept up with Kerrie. Why? If she recalled, Kerrie had dumped him the first year she'd left to attend a university in Florida.

"Why would you ask me that?"

And why don't you just give me a simple yes or no? Shiloh thought. Instead, she shrugged. "Just curious. I remembered the two of you used to be hot and heavy at one time."

"Like you and Caden?"

Why was he trying to switch things on her? "If I recall, Caden and I were never hot and heavy in high school. Dad made sure of that." She took a sip of her wine and asked, "So where does Kerrie live now?"

"Texas."

"I wonder how you know that."

Sedrick gave her an annoying look. "Because I've asked her parents about her from time to time."

Shiloh wondered if that was all he had done and was about to ask as much when that feeling, a sudden increase of her pulse, alerted her to the fact that Caden was in the building. She was about to glance around when Sedrick leaned close to her and said, "Maybe I should be asking if you're keeping up with Caden Granger, because he definitely seems to be keeping up with you."

Caden grabbed a glass of wine from the tray of a passing waitress and took a sip as he glanced around. It didn't take but a second for him to spot Shiloh across the room, where she stood talking to her brother. She glanced over and caught his gaze. He could tell by her expression she wasn't exactly happy to see him. Oh, well.

He took another sip of his wine, thinking she looked absolutely stunning in a formfitting dress that looked as if it had been specially made for her body. She was definitely the most beautiful woman present. And, as usual, that sensuous undercurrent neither of them could deny was at full throttle, messing with his senses, emitting an electrical charge that he could feel all the way across the room. She was still holding his gaze, and he knew she had to feel the same thing whether she wanted to or not.

Caden believed that the special link they'd always shared would be what would reunite them. And that was what Dalton couldn't understand. The connection he and Shiloh shared was more than physical. It was as emotional as it could get and had always been that way. Samuel Timmons hadn't understood it, either. Caden knew he had hurt her, and now *only* he could erase the pain he'd caused. It would take time, so he needed to be patient with her. It would also take persistence on his part, because he intended for Shiloh to see he wasn't going anywhere. The bottom line was that he loved her. Always had and always would.

"Excuse me?"

He gazed at a woman who'd stepped in front of him, blocking his line of vision to Shiloh. "Yes?"

"You may not remember me, but we went to high school together. I'm Nannette Gaither, and this is my fiancé, Vance Clayburn."

Caden recognized Nannette. It had been years, but he immediately recalled that after the trial, the Gaithers, who were from old money and were one of the wealthiest families in Charlottesville, had forbidden their children from associating with him and his brothers. However, before the trial, just like the Timmonses, the Gaithers had been good friends of his parents.

He glanced at the man by Nannette's side. Had she just introduced him as her fiancé? The man looked old enough to be her father. "I do remember you, Nannette," he said, offering her his hand. "And it's nice meeting you, Vance." He offered the man his hand, as well.

The man flashed a perfect, white-toothed smile, and it suddenly hit Caden that he'd seen the man before. When? Where? Had he once been an associate of his father? His grandfather?

"Your face looks familiar, Vance. Have we met before?"

The smile slid from Vance's face. "Don't see how that's possible. I just moved to Charlottesville a few years ago."

"Vance owns several huge industrial firms around the country," Nannette said, tooting her fiancé's horn and beaming with pride. "Charlottesville was lucky when he chose our town as a location for one of his factories. That was two years ago and it has boosted our local economy tremendously."

Caden nodded as he took a sip of his wine, thinking that was all very nice; however, he was sure that his and Vance Clayburn's paths had crossed before at some point. And it had to have been years ago. If it wasn't here in Charlottesville, then where?

"I just love your music and know you have an extensive following, Caden," Nannette enthused. "I'm going to suggest to Shiloh that she ask you to be our entertainment headliner for the fundraiser this year."

"Shiloh?"

"Yes. Shiloh's working with me and she is in charge

of entertainment. The city's annual ball will raise a lot of money for cancer research. It would be simply wonderful if you would perform for us."

"When is this?"

"During the holidays. I know it's probably short notice, but I hope you will consider it."

Caden smiled. "I will consider it. But, of course, I'll have to check my schedule."

Nannette's face lit up. "That's wonderful. I'll have Shiloh get in touch with you."

"Yes, you do that."

The couple walked off, and Caden glanced over to where Shiloh had been standing moments ago. But she was gone. He figured he would mingle for a little while, and if he didn't run into her, he would simply go and find her.

Shiloh saw Caden out of the corner of her eye. He was surrounded by a group of women asking him to autograph the napkins they'd grabbed off a drinks tray. Smiling, he obliged them, and before he could get away, even more women approached him.

"Young Granger certainly has his hands full. The women are buzzing around him as if they're bees and he's the honey," Harold Owens said, chuckling and grabbing Shiloh's attention.

Helen Owens nodded. "Can't blame them too much. He's a handsome man. Gets his looks from his father, and everyone knows how handsome Sheppard was. Besides, I'm sure Caden Granger's celebrity status doesn't hurt when it comes to the ladies." Helen paused a moment and added, "I always knew those boys would make something of themselves even if their father was a cold-blooded murderer."

Shiloh thought about what Mrs. Owens had said about Caden's father. It seemed she was one of those people who still thought Sheppard Granger had killed his wife fifteen years ago.

"I wish you wouldn't do that, Helen," Mr. Owens said with a frown, breaking into Shiloh's thoughts.

His wife raised an eyebrow. "Do what?"

"Call Sheppard Granger a murderer."

"And why not? A jury found him guilty."

"Yes, but I never believed he did it. He wasn't that sort of guy. I played golf with Richard and Sheppard numerous times. He was one of the most honest and kindhearted men I knew."

"Who happened to discover his wife was having an affair. That's why he killed her."

"I disagree." Mr. Owens looked at Shiloh. "You knew the Grangers. In fact, I recall you and your brother being their playmates when you were younger. Do you believe Sheppard Granger could kill his wife so heartlessly?"

Shiloh drew in a deep breath. This was the first time anyone had asked her what she thought about Caden's father's guilt or innocence. Growing up, her opinion had been somewhat colored by what her parents had claimed, which had all been negative. But as she recalled, everyone assumed it was Sheppard Granger who was involved in an affair, although the prosecution had never been able to produce the name of the other woman implicated. They claimed he killed his wife because she refused to give him a divorce. This was the first time she'd heard anything about Sylvia Granger being the one involved in an affair.

She looked at the Owenses, who were waiting for her response. "I've never given any thought to Mr. Granger's guilt or innocence. If you recall, I was young, in my early teens, when the trial was going on. But I do recall Jace, Caden and Dalton believing their father was innocent. And, up until now, I'd always assumed that *Mr.* Granger was the one involved in an affair and not the other way around."

Was it her imagination or had the Owenses suddenly gone unusually quiet? Harold Owens seemed to study a speck on his tie, and Helen said nothing as she stared into her glass of wine.

She found their actions very odd and was about to restate her question when she felt heat at her back. She knew Caden was less than a few feet away. Was that the reason the Owenses were acting strange? Shiloh thought there was more to it than that, because they were looking over her shoulder and appeared surprised to see Caden approaching.

"Good evening, Shiloh. Mr. and Mrs. Owens."

Caden's deep, husky voice caressed her skin when he came to stand beside her. He then reached out his hand to the Owenses. "Good seeing you again. It's been years."

A smile spread across Helen's lips. "Why, Caden Granger. You've grown into a very handsome man, and I've heard nothing but wonderful things about you and that saxophone of yours." She paused a moment and then added, "And it seems you still get all the girls."

Caden chuckled. "I think you have me mixed up with my brother Dalton."

"And how are your brothers?" Harold asked as if he genuinely wanted to know. "We heard about that kidnapping incident with Jace a few weeks ago. That was awful, and to think the mastermind was someone you thought could be trusted."

"But isn't that how it usually is?" Shiloh asked, not looking at Caden. "The people you trust the most are the ones who will cause you the most pain." Not waiting for anyone's reply, she said, "If all of you will excuse me, I need to mingle with my guests."

She walked off and could actually feel Caden's stare in the center of her back.

Eighteen

"Is there a reason he's still here?" Sedrick asked his sister.

Shiloh didn't have to glance around to know whom her brother was referring to. Although the party had wound down and most of the people had left, Caden was among the handful that remained.

She lifted her chin. "I don't know. Why don't you ask him?"

Her brother frowned. "I think I will."

Cassie shot an arm out to detain Sedrick. "Really, Sedrick, is that necessary? Maybe you need to let Shiloh handle her own business."

He removed Cassie's hand from his arm. "And maybe you need to attend to your own business."

Shiloh saw the hurt flash in Cassie's eyes before she walked off. She spoke up and said, "Cassie's right. Caden is my business, Sedrick, and I'll handle him. And did you have to be so rude to Cassie just now? What in the world is wrong with you? You haven't been yourself since you arrived here tonight. I think you owe Cassie an apology."

He frowned. "Just like you claim Caden is your business, Cassie is mine. You handle yours, and I'll handle mine." He then walked off.

Shiloh drew in a deep breath. What in the world was wrong with Sedrick? He'd arrived in a surly mood, and it had gotten worse after he'd spent some time with the Greenes.

Tonight, Shiloh hadn't been able to help but notice that all the influential families who had ostracized Caden and his brothers years ago had been falling all over themselves tonight, smiling, shaking his hand and asking for his autograph.

Except for the Greenes.

It seemed they had deliberately avoided him. Why? Even when Ivan had arrived, he'd appeared to be put out to see Caden here. The man who wanted to be mayor had made his rounds, shaking hands with almost everyone present, except for Caden. Shiloh wondered whether Caden had noticed the Greenes' avoidance of him tonight. Knowing Caden the way she did, Shiloh knew that if he had noticed, he probably didn't care.

"Time for us to call it a night," Valerie said, coming up behind her and interrupting her thoughts.

Whenever Valerie came into town alone she stayed with Shiloh, but whenever Jack came with her, Valerie preferred staying at the Fairgate, a hotel known for its romantic setting. The hotel was built so each and every room had a beautiful view of the mountains. On top of that, each hotel room was really a large suite with a fireplace and huge garden tub.

"Thanks for staying as long as you did," she said, giving Valerie a hug. "I couldn't have done this without you."

"Hmm, it seems that some of us plan to stay even longer."

Shiloh knew she was referring to Caden. Obviously, Sedrick hadn't been the only one to notice.

"Yes, I saw you over there mingling with the enemy," Shiloh said, looking pointedly at her friend.

Valerie chuckled. "Caden might be your enemy, but he isn't mine. I admit I was a little put out with him about the way he'd been treating you. But that was before you told me what your father had done. I still don't agree with the things Caden might have done and said, but now I understand why he did them. That was pretty low of your father. To think a father would go to that extreme to keep a man away from his daughter only makes me wonder why."

"I know why," Shiloh said, putting down her wineglass and glancing across the room to where Caden was talking to Jack. "Dad disliked the Grangers. For some reason, my parents, especially my father, seemed to take Sylvia Granger's murder personally. Not only did they want Sheppard Granger to pay for that sin, but they wanted his sons to pay for it, as well."

"That's a lot of hatred, Shiloh. Have you ever wondered why?"

When Shiloh didn't say anything, Valerie pressed on. "Samuel Timmons is dead, yet you're still letting him win. He always wanted you and Caden apart, and he's getting just what he wanted." Changing the subject, she said, "Good night, Shiloh. Jack and I fly out early in the morning. I'll call you sometime tomorrow to let you know we made it back home safely."

Shiloh watched as Valerie crossed the room to where Jack and Caden stood. She slid her arm into Jack's, leaning up to kiss Caden on the cheek before pulling Jack toward the exit.

It was then that Caden glanced over at her. She had deliberately avoided him all night, and the one time he had approached her when she'd been chatting with the Owenses, she had walked off. Later, Nannette had approached her, putting her on the spot by insisting that she consider Caden for this year's entertainment at the ball. Shiloh agreed he would be a huge draw, but the thought of working with him on any project was too much for her to think about.

She glanced around and realized that everyone had left—everyone except her, Caden and the catering staff. When had Sedrick and Cassie left? She was surprised her brother hadn't hung around long enough to make sure Caden wasn't the last one to leave. Her brother's behavior tonight was now more confusing than ever.

She drew in a steady breath when Caden began walking toward her. She wished he didn't look so darned good. His appearance had definitely been appreciated by some and resented by a few. Her thoughts shifted again to the Greenes, but not for long as Caden came to a stop in front of her.

"You had a nice turnout, Shiloh."

She tilted her head back to look up at him. "Why did you come here tonight, Caden?"

He held her stare, shoving his hands into his pockets. "And why wouldn't I come?"

"You know the answer to that and, frankly, I don't want to go over it again."

A smile touched his lips. "Good because, frankly, I don't want you to go over it again, either. I know how you feel."

She shook her head. "No, you don't. If you did, you wouldn't be here."

He took a step closer. "Because I do know how you feel. That's why I am here."

She frowned, thinking what he said didn't make sense. "Everyone has left. The party is over, so you can leave now."

"Before I go, there's something I'd like to ask you about."

"What?"

"Not here." The caterers were breaking things down, and they were in the way. She had a feeling that whatever he wanted to ask her he wanted to ask in private. A part of her knew she should tell him that he didn't have a right to ask her anything, but another part of her was curious about what he wanted to know. Besides, there was something she needed to ask him, as well. Something Valerie now had her pondering.

"Fine. We can talk privately out in the courtyard."

Caden followed Shiloh as she opened the French doors. He ducked under the top of the door and walked out onto a brick courtyard. He'd noticed people coming and going into this space during most of the evening but hadn't ventured out himself.

It was the first week in September, and already the night air was growing cool. Caden figured that in a couple of weeks, most people would be wearing their winter clothes. He watched as Shiloh led him toward one of the patio sofas, covered in cushions. She slipped off her shoes and then sat down, curling her bare feet beneath her.

"Now, what is your question? Because I have one of my own," she said, looking over at him.

He was so taken by how she appeared at that moment, sitting there with the reflections from the lanterns making her look even more beautiful. He almost forgot she was talking. But he did catch the tail end of what she'd said. "You have a question for me, as well?"

"Yes. Please go ahead, and then I'll ask mine," she said, leaning back in the seat.

He took a chair across from her. "First, I'd like to state that I have a reason for asking you this, so please don't get all bent out of shape."

Her gaze bored into him. "I won't make any promises. What is it that you want to know?"

He paused a moment and then asked, "Is there or has there ever been something going on between you and Ivan Greene?"

Shiloh stared at Caden, certain she had misunderstood his question. But when it was obvious she had not, anger ignited her entire body. She immediately sat up, and her feet hit the brick floor with a thump. "You have a lot of nerve asking me something like that. The answer is no, but if I had been involved with him, it would be none of your business."

"I had a reason for asking you that."

Shiloh thought he had better have a damned good reason. "And what would that be?"

Caden leaned back in his chair. "Tonight, for whatever reason, I felt deep animosity coming from not only Ivan but also his parents. And I can think of no other reason for it other than perhaps he has feelings for you and he sees me as a threat."

"Rest assured, Ivan Greene is not interested in me. Besides, he's almost fourteen years older than I am."

"To some women, age doesn't mean anything. It definitely doesn't seem to matter to Nannette Gaither."

"Well, it does to me. And as far as the Greenes' animosity toward you, I have no answers. If I recall, Michael Greene worked for your father's company at one time, didn't he?"

"Yes, and Dad fired him. I never knew the reason why, but it happened a few months before my mother's death."

"Do you think he's holding a grudge from that time?"

Caden shrugged. "I don't know why he would. After leaving Granger, he started his own business and became highly successful. I think he would consider his departure from Granger Aeronautics a good move and not the opposite."

Caden didn't say anything for a moment and then added, "Maybe I imagined things tonight."

"No, you didn't," Shiloh said. "I picked up on their

coolness to you myself and wondered the reason for it. With Ivan running for mayor, you would think he would be friendly to as many people as he could. I don't know why the Greenes snubbed you tonight, but it has nothing to do with me. I barely know Ivan Greene…although if you remember, Sedrick and Ivan's sister Kerrie dated seriously back in high school."

Caden nodded. "Yes, I do recall that." Since returning to Charlottesville, he was beginning to remember a lot from his childhood. Some good, and some bad. "Now, what is your question?" he asked.

Shiloh met his gaze. "Do you have any idea why my parents started hating yours? Dad went to a lot of trouble to keep us apart and, before now, I never wondered what motivated him. I just accepted it as his way. Now I want to know why."

Nineteen

Caden held Shiloh's eyes. Her question was one he'd been pondering himself lately. All he had to do was remember that packet he'd received in his hotel room in Vegas, and how carefully Samuel Timmons had manipulated things in his favor, using distorted photographs to plant doubt in Caden's mind over Shiloh's love and loyalty. Only hatred could drive a person to that extreme.

"I honestly don't know, Shiloh. I've been thinking about my father's trial a lot. Things were fine, and then one day Granddad picked us up from school and broke the news that our mother was dead and Dad had been charged with killing her."

He paused a moment and then said, "And that's when the ugliness began. I remember wanting to talk to you then. I called your house, as usual, and your dad answered the phone. Instead of the kindness he'd always displayed to me, he showed me another side. A bitter, hateful and vicious side. He told me never to call his house again, and he also said he would not have his children associating with the kids of a murderer. It was as if he'd already decided my dad was guilty."

She nodded. "And things got worse from there," she said. "After giving us orders never to be friends with you and your brothers again, he began drinking heavily. I thought it was guilt because of the way he had begun treating you, but I don't think that was the case. Drinking just made him even more hateful toward your family. Because of his threats, Sedrick and I did what he told us to do, although I would go out of my way, whenever I could, to let you know I would always be there for you."

Caden remembered that. The smiles. The notes. The cards.

"Years later, my father used my convalescence to keep us apart, to play his hand, knowing if he played it right, you would believe it. And you did."

"Yes," Caden admitted ashamedly. "I did."

Hearing him admit to that brought back memories of all the pain she'd endured. Both the physical pain of the accident and the emotional pain of his rejection when he'd believed the worst about her.

She quickly stood. "You've asked your question and I've asked mine, but it seems we still don't have answers."

He stood, as well. "No, we don't. Honestly, I don't give a damn about the way the Greenes feel about me. Their behavior tonight has only made me curious. And in terms of your father's hatred of my family, I think the only person who could shed some light on everything is your mother. Maybe you should ask her."

Shiloh inwardly shuddered at the thought. "I'd rather not."

Caden studied her for a moment, looking beyond the resentment in her features to the happy-go-lucky woman she'd always been. "You're going to have to learn how to forgive, Shiloh," he said softly.

She lifted her chin. "Why? You think that will give you a way back into my life?"

Caden took a step toward her, closing the distance between them. "Something you simply refuse to acknowledge, Shiloh, is that I am already back in your life. In fact, I never truly left. Even when you wanted to hate me, you couldn't. There has always been a you and a me, even when there wasn't supposed to be. I've made you a promise that I intend to keep. One day, you'll believe how sorry I am for all I did and accept that we all make mistakes. I love you and only you. Those other women were just a physical way to purge my pain. You are the only woman I can and will ever love."

Shiloh broke eye contact with Caden. The intensity of the gaze boring into her nearly took her breath away. His words had been so profound that it stirred things within her that she hadn't wanted to feel. But still…

"I need time, Caden."

"No. You need *me*. Just like I need you. Too much time has been wasted already."

And with that said, he reached out and pulled her into his arms.

* * *

Shiloh knew she should push him away. She wasn't ready for this, but when his mouth began feasting on hers, the only thing she could do, the only thing she wanted to do, was enjoy it. The kiss was as natural as snow falling on the mountains in late December and as natural as a hungry man eating for the first time in months.

Caden had a way of kissing that always filled her with feverish intensity, and it was happening now. Her senses were awakening, and her entire body was responding. She could feel the solid hardness of him pressed against her. She could smell his manly aroma filtering through her nostrils. And more than anything, she was loving the pure taste of him.

Why was it always this way with him and with no one else? Why was her body, her mind, her entire being so tuned in to him? His kisses were hot, possessive and intoxicating to the point that she felt weak in the knees.

Then just as suddenly as he had begun kissing her, he stopped. Slowly, he unwrapped his arms from around her and whispered against her damp lips, "I love you, Shiloh. No matter what, always believe that. I'm not going to rush you, but I want you to be sure of me. To be sure of us."

And then he headed for the wrought-iron gate that led out toward the parking area on the street. Before opening the gate, he turned and said, "You look simply radiant tonight, Shiloh, and you have a nice shop that I know will do well. I'm very proud of you."

Then he was gone. She moved toward the gate to

watch him walk down the brick walkway to the street. The lights that lined the streets shone on him and his muscular form. He walked like a man sure of himself. A man who'd had tough times in his life but who was determined to survive, and he had.

That kiss had been everything she remembered a Caden Granger kiss could be. Four years hadn't changed the impact he had on her. Again, he had brought up that promise tonight. She of all people knew that Caden didn't make promises lightly, but she wasn't sure she was ready to let him back into her life.

Breathing in the cool night air, she felt a chill go through her body, and she wrapped her arms around her sleeveless dress, feeling the change in the weather. She watched Caden cross the street to his car, and she was about to turn around to go back inside when she noticed a car pulling out behind a parked car.

Suddenly the car accelerated and picked up speed. Her breath caught when she saw that the car was headed straight toward Caden. It brought back terrible memories of the night she'd been hit.

She screamed Caden's name, and he snapped his head around and looked back. The car's headlights must have blinded him, because instead of getting out of the way, he stood there as if frozen in place.

Then she watched as someone appeared out of nowhere and pushed Caden out of the way, forcing both men to the ground to roll out of the car's path. The speeding car had come within inches of hitting them both, and the driver had kept on going.

Shiloh began running toward Caden as fast as she

could, ignoring the fact that the length of her dress made movement difficult. She almost lost a shoe, but she didn't care. When she reached the two men sprawled on the ground, the huge hulk of a man who had pushed Caden out of the way was pulling himself up off the ground and hauling Caden up with him. Both were breathing hard as if they'd run a marathon.

"Are the two of you all right?" she asked in a frantic tone when she reached them. The big guy moved aside as she took a good look at Caden. His jacket was ripped, dirt was smeared on his pants, and he was flexing his fingers. He must have fallen on his hand.

She moved toward Caden, and his gaze met hers. She reached for him, and he drew her into his arms. Her body was shaking, trembling, and he tightened his arms around her. She buried her face in his chest, trying to stop her body from quaking.

Breathing deeply a few times to pull herself together, she finally lifted her head and gazed up at him. "You could have been killed," she said in a quivering voice. "I can't believe what that driver did. He must have been drunk. I—"

Shiloh never finished, because Caden lowered his mouth and kissed her. At that moment she wasn't sure who needed it most. When she'd seen that speeding car headed toward him, she had stopped breathing. She suddenly realized how close she'd come to losing him. Had that car hit him, there was no way he would have survived the impact. That realization had her shaking to the core, returning his kiss with all the fiery desire of her own.

The clearing of a throat had them breaking apart to glance at the man whom they'd forgotten all about. The man who had saved Caden's life by moving quickly and pushing him out the path of the speeding car.

"I take it you're okay," the man said, smiling and brushing dirt from his jeans. Like Caden's, his jacket was ripped, and Shiloh noticed the scrape on the side of his face. He was huge, taller than Caden, and she figured he stood at least six-six. He looked to be in his early thirties and, judging from his physique, she would say that he was definitely into bodybuilding. He was all muscle.

"Yes, I'm fine, thanks to you," Caden answered. "I never saw that car coming. The man must have had too many drinks and plowed down on the accelerator by mistake."

The man nodded. "Yes, he must have. My name is Striker, by the way," he said, offering Caden his hand. "But people call me Lucky Strike."

Caden chuckled. "Well, Lucky Strike, you definitely brought me luck tonight. Where did you come from? When I was crossing to my car, I swear I didn't see another soul out tonight."

"I was taking a walk," the man said easily. "Right over there," he said, pointing to the sidewalk shaded by large trees. "I had stopped to make a call on my cell phone, and that's when I saw that car speeding toward you. I knew I had to move quickly."

"And you did, thank God. Like I said, you saved my life."

Just like your dad saved mine, Lamar "Striker" Jennings thought, gazing at Caden. Yes, this was definitely Shep's son. He looked just like him. Striker recalled seeing Caden a few times when he had come to visit his dad in prison a few years ago. That was before Shep was transferred to Delvers. He doubted Caden remembered him, and that was a good thing. Otherwise, his cover would have been blown.

"I think you guys had a rough time of it tonight. Would you like coffee or wine or something to eat? I definitely have a lot of everything," Shiloh said, breaking into Striker's thoughts. "And you have a bruise on the side of your face, Striker. Please, let me take a look at it."

"Thanks for the offer, but I need to move on," Striker said quickly. He was ready to blend back into the darkness from where he'd come. And he needed to report this incident to Roland. Unlike what Granger and the woman thought, that car had intentionally tried to plow Granger down. "I still need to make that phone call, but thanks anyway. Have a good night." He looked at Caden. "And you, my man, stay safe." And then he was gone.

Neither Shiloh nor Caden said anything for a minute as they stood there staring at each other. And then Caden reached out and pulled her into his arms, holding her tight before brushing a kiss across her lips. "Does that offer for coffee, wine or food still stand?"

Shiloh nodded and, taking his hand, led him back across the street.

Dalton entered his condo, placed his jacket across the back of a chair and headed for the refrigerator for a beer. He had gone back to that nightclub again thinking he would run into his mystery lady but no such luck. He shouldn't get impatient, but he was.

The private investigator he'd hired had explained that he would need to wrap up another case before starting on Dalton's request, and Dalton had assured the man that that was fine. But what Dalton hadn't counted on was his nightly dreams of the mystery woman. Damn, even her scent was embedded deep in his head. The woman was messing with his love life—he hadn't been attracted to another woman since meeting her.

He was about to take another swallow of beer when his cell phone rang. He recognized the ringtone. It was Lady Victoria Bowman calling him from England. Because of the time difference, her day was just getting started while his was winding down.

He smiled, thinking of the relationship he and Victoria shared. They were friends with benefits and had been for a few years. She was twenty years older than he was, but she'd kept up with him in the bedroom. Hell, sometimes it was him keeping up with her. It hadn't mattered to him that for years he'd been considered Victoria's boy toy. He had enjoyed her company, and she had enjoyed his…both in and out of the bedroom.

"Victoria, how are you?" he asked, walking out of the kitchen to take a seat on the living-room sofa, stretching his legs out in front of him. It had been weeks since he'd spoken to her.

"I'm fine. I have some news to share with you."

"And what news is that?"

"I've decided to marry Sir Isaac."

Dalton didn't say anything for a minute. The last time they'd talked, she'd said Sir Isaac had proposed. He was happy for Victoria. Her first husband had done a job on her, and she deserved better. Dalton believed Sir Isaac would do right by her. And he knew the reason she was calling was because she wanted to do right by him. That meant she was letting Dalton know their stint as occasional lovers was over.

"I'm happy for you, Victoria. I think Sir Isaac is just the man you need." The man was older, and he was extremely wealthy. The latter meant he would be able to keep Victoria in the lavish lifestyle she was used to.

"I'm going to miss you, Dalton."

"I'm going to miss you, too. We had some good times, and I will always consider you a special friend," Dalton said.

"I told Sir Isaac about you, although I didn't have to. He's heard about our affairs."

Dalton chuckled. "I'm sure he has."

"He has made one stipulation."

Dalton nodded. "Let me guess. He doesn't want me messing around with his wife."

"Do you blame him?"

"No. You should have told him I don't do wives. When we started our affair, you were free from that asshole you'd been married to, so, technically, you were not anyone's wife at the time."

"I told him, but people talk. If we're seen together they'll speculate. They'll start nasty rumors."

"To hell with them all—but I understand. Sir Isaac does not want our paths to cross."

"Yes, that's what he wants."

"And you should give your future husband what he wants. He will be good to you, and you should be good to him. I want only the best for you, Victoria."

"I know, and that's what makes this so hard. But I believe one day a special lady will come into your life and—"

"If you say you think I'll fall in love, then I will hang up on you, here and now. I enjoy women. I sleep with them. I don't marry them."

"Some woman is going to make you sing a different song, Dalton."

"Not in this universe."

Wanting to change the subject, he brought her up to date on everything that had happened since their last conversation over a month ago, including the attempted kidnapping and murder of Jace. They talked for a half hour longer while she gave him all the English gossip. He didn't miss Europe as much as he'd thought he would and he enjoyed being here with his brothers, although they let him know when he was getting to be a pain.

He smiled. They complained and they cussed, but they loved him as he loved them.

"Dalton?"

"Yes, Victoria?"

"Have you told your brothers everything? About the work you did for your government while living over here?"

"No. That's something they never need to know about. Finding out I was a billionaire was bad enough. Finding out about my involvement with the United Security Network would blow their minds. Besides, I was only in it for a couple of years, and it's a time I honestly prefer to forget."

"Sorry I brought it up."

"No problem. You were the only person I could talk to about the USN, but now it is over."

"Dalton, I'm going to have to go now. I'm meeting Isaac this morning and we are off to attend a polo match. Just so you know, the wedding will take place in November." She paused a moment and then said, "It will be a private affair."

He chuckled. "In other words, don't expect an invitation, right?"

She laughed. "Right. It would be rather awkward."

"Yes, I guess it would be. I want you to be happy, Victoria."

"And I will be. You've been a good friend, Dalton. You were always there when I needed one. I'll never forget you."

"Nor I you."

"Goodbye, Dalton."

"Goodbye, Victoria."

He clicked off the phone knowing that the one woman he could always depend on would no longer be a part of his life.

Twenty

Shiloh led Caden back into the courtyard, and that was when he noticed the side elevator hidden behind a huge security gate. He'd learned that her home was located right above her business, and this elevator would have been convenient for moving things up and down.

"It won't take long for the coffee to brew, and while we're waiting, I want to take a look at your hand," Shiloh said when the elevator door closed behind them. It stopped on the third floor.

He followed her off the elevator and they stepped into a spacious hall with two doors. She moved toward the first door, unlocked it and went inside.

"You have another tenant on this floor?" he asked, nodding toward the other door.

"No, it's an extra room that I can use for expansion if I choose. Right now, I use it for extra storage."

He nodded, then glanced around her home. He breathed in and thought it smelled nice.

He immediately felt that the place suited her. The

living room was huge, and the balcony overlooked the courtyard below. Her walls were painted a canary-yellow that made the entire place appear bright and cheerful—just like the Shiloh he remembered.

She had a large eat-in kitchen, and he watched as she moved to turn the coffee on, then she disappeared through a hallway.

Shiloh had always loved flowers, so it didn't surprise him that the fabric on her sofa was a floral print. And he noticed the roses he'd sent her almost two weeks ago were sitting in the middle of her coffee table. He was surprised they'd lasted this long. And even more surprised that she'd kept them.

"Okay, have a seat so I can take a look at your hand," she said, coming back into the room carrying a first-aid kit.

He removed his jacket before sitting down on the sofa. She sat beside him and took his hand in hers. And that was when he looked at his hand for the first time—a couple of fingers were bruised, but he didn't think anything was broken.

She used a swab to apply disinfectant to the abrasions, and it stung like hell, but he wasn't about to tell her that. Just the thought of her holding his hand and tending to it meant everything to him. Her touch was gentle, and she was taking her time with what she was doing.

She was also quiet, so he followed suit and figured when it was time to talk, they would. Her hands were trembling somewhat, which meant she was probably still shaken by what she had just witnessed. When she'd screamed out his name and he had looked up to see that car bearing down on him, he'd been like a deer caught in the headlights.

He was convinced that if that man had not knocked him out of the way—risking his own life while doing so—he would probably be dead. Too bad there hadn't been enough time to get the car's license-plate number.

He looked around as Shiloh continued to administer first aid to his fingers. He imagined she spent a lot of her time here, reading, cooking and knitting. At least she used to knit, and he wondered if she still did. He certainly had received a lot of knitted items from her over the years, even when they weren't supposed to have any contact. A knitted cap or mittens would always find their way into his school backpack.

He glanced down when he felt something moist on his hand and realized they were tears. She was crying. "Shiloh?"

She started to get up, and he reached out and stopped her, tugging her back down and gently pulling her into his arms. "Don't cry, Shiloh. Everything is okay."

She pulled back and shook her head as her tears continued to fall. "No, everything is not okay. When I think about what could have happened to you tonight, I—"

"But it didn't," he said softly, trying to calm her.

"But it could have," she countered in a voice filled with emotion. She pushed back and looked up at him. "I saw that car coming toward you, Caden. That guy was drunk and shouldn't be behind the wheel of any car. You were lucky. He's not safe and should not be on the road tonight. We should call the police."

"And tell them what? I have no idea of the make or model of the car, much less what color it was. Do you?"

She frowned thoughtfully. "No."

He gently pulled her back into his arms. "It was a close call, but thanks to Striker, I'm fine. And I'm sorry that I didn't get his full name or his contact information. He disappeared just as quickly as he appeared."

When Shiloh didn't say anything, he pulled back and studied her features. She had stopped crying, but he could tell she was still filled with emotions. "Talk to me, Shiloh. Tell me what you're thinking, what you're feeling. Tell me."

She met his gaze, and her eyes filled with tears again. "I thought you were going to die. And at that moment, nothing mattered. Not the pain I've been feeling or the anger and bitterness that had consumed me. Seeing you come close to dying made my heart stop, Caden. I knew then that if you died, I might as well die myself."

Caden didn't say anything as he stared at her and saw the earnestness in her gaze. Her words touched him, and he reached up and wiped a tear from her eye. Then he lifted her off the sofa into his lap and wrapped his arms around her. She laid her face against his chest.

He rocked her into his arms, holding her gently yet tightly, not sure if he would ever let her go. He was filled with profound emotions and leaned in close to her ear. "Had I died tonight, Shiloh," he whispered huskily, "I would have died loving you."

Caden's words caused Shiloh's heart to catch in her throat. She leaned up and looked at him. It wasn't just the words he'd spoken, but the look in his eyes, as well.

He loved her. She could see it in the depths of his brown eyes. He had said it plenty of times in the past few weeks. She'd heard him, but this was the first time she'd actually listened.

She reached up and cupped his chin with her hand. Tears shimmered in her eyes. "But you would have died not knowing that I loved you," she whispered in a broken voice.

And she knew she did love him and had never stopped loving him. The pain and hurt had overshadowed her feelings, but they had not destroyed her love for him. The two of them had been through so much together over the years. He was a part of her and, deep down, she knew she was a part of him. She had to believe in what he'd been trying to get her to see all along. Yes, they should move on. But they should move on together, in the same direction, with the same goal and cause. Why did it take him nearly dying for her to see that?

"Shiloh—" Caden pulled her to him and held her. After the way he'd been treating her over the past few years, he hadn't been sure he would ever hear her words of love ever again. Now that he had, he knew he would never do anything to make her stop saying them.

He continued to hold her, his senses absorbing the feel of her in his arms, the scent of her skin and the gentle sound of her breathing. He pulled back, needing to look at her. Their gazes locked. Heat thrummed through them. He felt it and knew she felt it, as well.

And when the heat became more intense to the point that it was unbearable, he groaned deep in his throat. Leaning in, he captured her mouth with his, and a wild surge of desire shot through him. He deepened the kiss, feeding off her lips with a hunger that he felt in the pit of his groin. He wanted her. He needed her. But most important, he loved her.

Caden slowly stood with her in his arms and then slid her body down his until her feet touched the floor. It was obvious that he was sexually aroused, but if she wasn't ready to be intimate with him just yet, he understood.

That thought was thrown to the wind when she leaned up on tiptoes and whispered, "Make love to me, Caden."

Twenty-One

Shiloh held Caden's gaze as he placed her on the bed. He quickly glanced around the room, noting that, just like the other rooms in her house, it was *her*. "Nice bedroom."

"Thanks."

He stood back and glanced down at his clothes. His shirt was torn at the sleeve, and he felt dirty from rolling on the ground. He glanced back at her lying on her white bedspread. "May I shower first?"

She smiled and eased off the bed. "How about if we shower together?"

Thoughts of how that could turn out sent heat to Caden's groin. They had showered together numerous times before and had always enjoyed doing so. "I think that's a great idea," he said in a deep, raspy voice.

Already she had begun removing her clothes, shimmying out of her dress, and as he watched her, he knew no other woman could arouse him to this degree. He loved every inch of her shapely body—the perky and firm breasts, small waist, shapely hips and thighs and long, gorgeous legs.

When she stood before him completely naked, he reached out his hand to her. "I think you better lead the way before I take you here and now."

She laughed, and it was a throaty sound that only added to his torment. "Okay, but first, we need to take off these things," she said, running her hands over his shoulders before tugging on his shirt, popping off buttons and then ripping it off him. "It was torn anyway. Beyond repair," she said as a way of explaining her actions.

He smiled. "Doesn't matter. I didn't plan to ever wear it again."

"Then I took care of it for you," she said, reaching lower to remove his belt.

He stood there and let her have her way because he intended to have his later. But when she eased down his zipper, wiggled her hand inside the opening of his briefs and got ahold of his shaft, he began thinking maybe this wasn't such a good idea. Not if he wanted to keep his sanity. He fit perfectly in her hands, and she knew it as much as he did.

"Still in good shape, I see," she said, easing up on tiptoe to whisper the words against his mouth while her hand continued to stroke him.

"The shower. Remember," he said through clenched teeth, forcing back a moan.

"I remember." She released him and slowly pulled back and smiled. "The bathroom is down the hall to your right. Go ahead and get things started. I'll grab some towels and join you in a minute."

Caden had the shower going full blast, but no matter how hard the water beat down on him, it couldn't wash away the memory of seeing that speeding car heading straight toward him. It was a freaking nightmare, especially coming so close to Jace's incident. It was something he wouldn't forget for a long time.

For a second, he'd seen his life ending right before his eyes and had been unable to move. He had been frozen in shock at what was happening. Evidently, the Man Upstairs didn't think it was time for him to go yet and had kept him here for a reason.

Caden had been so deep in his thoughts that he couldn't recall the moment Shiloh opened the shower door to join him. All he knew was that she was there. Touching him. Rubbing her hands across his wet shoulders and then taking the soap from his hands.

She turned him around to face her as water splashed down on both of them. She began lathering his chest, moving lower to lather the curls of hair covering his groin before bending and easing down his legs. The soap smelled of a combination of strawberries and coconut. Then she reached up and adjusted the showerhead to rinse him off, making him feel squeaky clean.

"Now let me return the favor," he whispered close to her mouth.

Using the same soap, he worked up a lather in his hands and washed her all over, covering her breasts, moving down her flat stomach and lower still to her narrow hips and shapely backside, clutching her butt cheeks in his hands, then releasing them to skim his hands up and down the apex of her thighs. "I love touching you here," he whispered hotly.

"Is that all you can do? Touch?"

He grinned, knowing action was a lot better than words. He rinsed her off, watching how the water washed away the soap. Then he reached out to her, pulling her slippery wet body close to his, wrapping his arms around her. He could no longer hold back from wanting her but knew he didn't want to take her in the shower. Not this time.

Opening the shower door, he pulled her out with him and grabbed the huge bath towels she had placed on the vanity. He began drying her off, loving how the towel felt rubbing against her soft skin.

And then he dried himself while watching her watch him. Seeing her standing there naked with desire in her eyes, waiting for him, was a total turn-on. He was stimulated beyond reason. His gaze traveled from her eyes to her lips as they moved wordlessly. But he made out what she was saying nonetheless. *I love you.*

"Oh, baby, I love you, too," he said, tossing the towel aside and sweeping her into his arms and carrying her back into the bedroom. He placed her on the bed and joined her there.

Caden wanted to make love to her tonight at a level he'd never reached before. They had been separated too long, and he intended to bond with her in the most primitive way known to man. He didn't want to just take her to the edge; he wanted her to go over it with him.

Sitting back on his heels, he gazed down at her, loving every inch of the body he saw. Wanting to taste it, he leaned forward and glided his tongue over her body, loving the flavor of her skin. He started at her neck, moved lower to her breasts, nibbling and then sucking hard on her nipples. He had missed their taste, their feel. He couldn't get enough, laving his tongue over them again and again.

He heard her moan and loved the sound. She was overcome with passion, and so was he.

He reached his hand down and parted her thighs, and while his mouth was busy with her breasts, his fingers eased inside her womanly core. She immediately clenched his intruding fingers with her inner muscles and moaned his name.

And then his mouth left her breasts to travel past her stomach to join his fingers below. He grabbed her hips, lifted them to his mouth and buried his head between her legs. The instant his tongue slid inside her inner warmth, he felt her shudder. And then with the ease and peace of mind he felt when playing his sax, he used his mouth to play Shiloh just as he would his instrument, curling his lower lip the same way, plowing into her as her voice raised several pitches. Then he used his tongue to help her reach a higher octave. Never had he tasted anything as sweet and erotic as Shiloh.

The sound of her moans was music to his ears, blending in with the melody he was creating in his head. She whispered for him to stop, saying she couldn't take any more. And then, seconds later, in that same murmuring voice, she would demand that he not stop, saying she loved how he was making her feel. He wanted to show her just how much he'd missed her, just how much he'd missed this.

He had no problem prolonging her pleasure, mixing it with torture of the most delectable kind while being infused with her heat. He thought about one particular song he had created just for her but had never performed. At this moment, he knew that he was performing it now in its most erotic form, transmitting his thoughts and the essence of his music to her. Even during his darkest hours, his music had been all he'd ever wanted, all he had thought he needed. Until Shiloh. That was why the thought of her betraying him had been so difficult to take.

Caden lifted his mouth and pulled back to ease his body beside hers. She looked over at him. "Why did you stop?" she asked, dragging in a deep breath through her nostrils.

He leaned up over her. "Baby, it's just getting started. But first I need to take care of protection," he said, sliding off the bed.

Shiloh eased on her side and watched Caden. She had seen him prepare himself for their lovemaking many times, and each one was always an intimate thrill for her. The way he would encase his erect penis in latex was enough to make her womanly juices overflow.

Like they are beginning to do now.

He was standing there, naked, displaying the most gorgeous body any man could own while ripping open the condom package. His erection was huge and he was ready, knowing what was coming and what it would be like to get there.

He reached down and the sound of her breath catching made him look up at her smile. "You want to try it?"

She blinked. Had he just really asked her that? "I wouldn't know how."

He chuckled. "Yes, you would. You've watched me enough." He walked back over to the bed. "Go ahead," he said, handing the condom to her. "Try it."

She paused a minute before taking the condom from his hand. Sitting up on the edge of the bed, she reached out and took him in her hand. She had stroked him many times, had even taken him in her mouth, but never had she prepared him for their lovemaking, and the thought of doing so sent sensuous shudders through her body.

He felt hard, thick and engorged in her hand, and she slowly sheathed his penis in the condom. She smiled at her handiwork. "I did it!" she said, pleased with herself.

"Yes, you did, and now for what's next."

He eased back on the bed and pulled her into his arms and kissed her. When she moaned, he used that opportunity to deepen the kiss, using the tip of his tongue to lap her up, with hunger engulfing him.

He pulled back, breaking the kiss to ease over her spread legs. He looked down at her. "Ready for this?"

She drew in a deep breath. "Yes."

"Just know there's no going back for either of us, Shiloh. Ever. I don't ever intend to lose you again."

She reached up and stroked the side of his jaw with

the palm of her hand. "And I don't ever intend to lose you again, either," she whispered.

He tilted his head sideways to kiss her hand before gazing back down at her. And then he eased into her, penetrating deep, feeling the way her muscles clenched him tight. He forged on until he couldn't go anymore. Until he'd reached the hilt.

She wrapped her legs around his waist and back. "Just in case you change your mind about this," she said, smiling, "I've got you just where I want you."

"Not changing my mind." And then he began moving, thrusting slow at first, then picking up the pace, thrusting hard and fast.

"Caden!"

He heard her moan his name as she approached her ecstasy. She dug her nails into his back, his shoulder, his arm. Her passion was a powerful aphrodisiac and he kept going, pumping into her in a rhythm that was like a symphony to his ears, whipping her to a feverish pitch.

His gaze held hers and he knew the exact moment a climax ripped through her. She screamed his name louder, shattering into a million pieces under him, and he felt each and every one. And the magnitude of her orgasm was what triggered his own, making him throw his head back, the cords in his neck ready to pop. Only making love to her could have this effect on him, send him flying over the top in the most primal fashion.

He growled out her name and his orgasm seemed to last forever, tearing through them, taking no prisoners and leaving pleasure in its wake.

Moments later they were both weak, too limp and too drained to do anything but cuddle in each other's arms and drift off to sleep.

Twenty-Two

Refusing to wake up from the best sleep he'd had in weeks, Dalton shot out an arm from underneath the covers to turn off his alarm, only to find out it wasn't his alarm going off but his phone ringing.

"What the fuck?" he grumbled, opening his eyes and easing up in bed to snatch his cell phone off the nightstand. It was Caden. "Why are you calling me so damned early on a Sunday morning?"

"It's almost noon."

Dalton's frown deepened. "That's beside the point. I like sleeping late on the weekends. Getting up and going into that damned office every morning, five days a week at eight a.m. ain't no joke."

"Stop whining. You never make it in at eight."

Dalton rolled his eyes. "What do you want?"

"I need a favor."

"This time of morning, it better be good."

"I need you to go to Sutton Hills and bring me a few items."

Dalton shifted up in bed as his eyes widened. "Sutton Hills? You didn't spend the night there last night?"

"No."

"Then where *did* you spend the night?"

"You ask too many damned questions. Just do what I ask."

"Hmm," Dalton said, smiling. "Sounds like someone made a booty call last night. I'll be damned. I didn't think you had it in you, with you so hung up on Shiloh Timmons and all. So, who is she? That big-breasted redhead who's been coming on to you at McQueen's?"

"Shut up, Dalton."

Dalton threw his head back and laughed. "Okay, tell me what you need."

"A shirt and a pair of pants, preferably jeans. Undergarments. Also, another jacket would be nice."

"What happened to the clothes you had on?"

"Don't ask."

"Damn, did she tear them off you? Sounds like you got a little nympho on your hands. Ask her if she's into a ménage à trois."

"She's not."

"Let her speak for herself."

"She doesn't have to."

"Okay, then don't share," Dalton said, grinning.

"I never do, and I didn't know that you did, either."

Dalton laughed. "You'd be surprised what all you don't know about me."

"No, I wouldn't be. I'll be waiting for you. Now, goodbye."

"Hey, wait! You didn't say where you are."

"I'm at the Wine Cellar Boutique. Enter through the courtyard gate on the side and use the intercom by the elevator to let us know you're here."

Dalton's eyebrows came together in a frown as he threw back the covers to ease out of bed. "The Wine Cellar Boutique? Isn't that place owned by Shiloh Timmons?"

"Yes. I'll see you when you get here." Caden then clicked off the phone.

Shiloh curled up against Caden after he ended his call and placed the phone back on her nightstand. "So, Dalton thinks I'm a nymphomaniac, does he?"

Caden chuckled as he pulled her even closer in his arms while covering their naked bodies with the sheets. "Well, you did tear my clothes off."

She smiled and then playfully bit his arm. "They weren't fit to be worn again anyway." She didn't say anything for a minute and then chuckled. "Ménage à trois? Dalton?"

"I wouldn't be surprised. Who knows what kind of kinky stuff he might have been involved in while living in England? He enjoys being a ladies' man. Always has."

Caden leaned down and placed what was to be a quick kiss on Shiloh's lips but he lingered a minute, then two. When he pulled back, he smiled down at her. When he saw the worried look in her eyes, he asked, "What's wrong?"

She shrugged. "I never was one of Dalton's favorite people."

Caden didn't say anything for a minute. He wished

he hadn't called Dalton but he'd had no choice since Jace and Shana had spent the weekend at Jace's cabin in the mountains. "Dalton took being ostracized worse than Jace and I did. He was younger and didn't understand. He was hurt by it and grew resentful. But, believe me, he's lectured me for holding it against you."

"You never did," she stated.

"But Dalton didn't know that, so he thought I did. I never told him about us. In fact, I never told Jace, either. I only confided in them about it recently."

She didn't have to ask why he'd never told his brothers about their wedding plans. It had been their decision not to tell *anyone*. They figured everyone would find out after their elopement.

"You know, that's what I don't understand, Shiloh."

"What?"

"How did your father find out about our plans?"

"Dad found out because Mom told him. I was so happy about it I just had to tell someone, so I told Mom. Since my parents were having marital problems during that time, I assumed Mom had become fed up with my father's ways and had turned into someone I could trust. I thought she and I were beginning to share a close relationship. That was the one time I had confided in her. Boy, was I wrong to do that."

"She admitted to telling him?"

"Mom didn't have to. There was no way he could have found out without her telling him."

Caden didn't say anything for a moment and then asked, "And did she admit to knowing about the distorted pictures that were sent to me?"

"Yes. I did confront her about it and she admitted to knowing about it…although she claimed Dad forced her to keep the truth from me. She could have told me the truth after Dad died. But she didn't."

"How did you find out?"

She let out a deep breath. "I accidentally came across a safe-deposit key belonging to Dad. He'd glued it behind a painting in his office. One day, the painting looked crooked, and I reached behind it to straighten it and found the key. It took a while to find out what bank it was from and, when I did, I went there and found a packet with the pictures in his safe-deposit box."

Shiloh was silent for a minute and then she said, "It took me a moment to figure out what they meant since the woman in the picture wasn't me. Inside the packet was a copy of the note, containing instructions. The note said the pictures were to be sent to you at the Wayfarer Hotel in Vegas. When I saw the specified delivery date, I was horrified. I put two and two together and went home to confront Mom. She admitted to things happening just the way I'd pieced them together. I went directly to Sutton Hills to see you that night."

And Caden knew the story from there. He had rejected anything she'd had to say. Damn, he wished he'd listened. Things would have ended up so much differently if he had.

She reached out and touched his arm, and he looked at her. "It doesn't matter now, Caden. We both know the truth. Samuel is dead, and no one can hurt us again. We won't allow it."

He reached out and caressed her cheek with the back

of his hand. "No, we won't. We were played against each other for the last time."

He leaned closer and kissed her, sliding his tongue into her mouth and then sipping her like the fine wine she sold. Then he deepened the kiss, and when he heard her moan, he intensified it even more by sucking hard on her tongue.

Moments later, he pulled back and reached for another condom. In seconds, he had put it on. He intended to make love to Shiloh right now, before Dalton arrived with the extra clothes and a list of questions.

He would deal with Dalton later. Right now, he wanted to make love again to the woman who had his heart.

Sheppard glanced up when he walked out of the prison chapel. Ambrose was waiting for him, and he could tell by the look on the guard's face there was need for concern. He walked over to the man.

"What is it, Ambrose?"

"Your attorney is here."

Shep frowned. He wondered why Carson would make an unexpected trip to see him. Usually, Sundays were her days to wind down and relax. "Where is she?"

"Waiting in the library meeting room. I'll take you there."

Shep followed, and dread ached through him with every step. Ambrose was walking quickly through the halls and chambers, moving from one building to the next. He recalled that the last time the guard had escorted him with such urgency had been when Sheppard was summoned to meet with the warden to learn that his father had passed away.

When they reached the meeting room, Shep took a deep breath before opening the door and walking in. Carson had her back to him as she stared out the window at the courtyard below. "Carson?"

She turned quickly, and the look on her face was just as worrisome as Ambrose's had been. "What is it? What's wrong?"

She inhaled deeply. "I wanted to come tell you myself. To assure you that everything is fine now, but—"

"But what?" he asked, crossing the room to stand in front of her.

She inhaled deeply again. "Roland called. The bodyguard protecting Caden reported that an attempt was made on Caden's life last night."

Shep felt weak in the knees and he grabbed the back of a nearby chair for support. "How?"

"When he was leaving a social function in downtown Charlottesville, a car tried to run him over."

"What?"

"Fortunately, Striker was able to save him."

Shep's brow flew up. "Striker?"

"Yes. You know your boys, Sheppard," she said as a small smile touched her lips. "When they got wind that your sons were in danger, they convinced Roland they were the ones who needed to protect them. Striker was able to push Caden out of the way in time."

"How are they? Striker and Caden?"

"Sore, but okay. I talked to Striker myself this morning. He was still on duty. He said that after the incident, instead of going home, Caden spent the night with the woman who owned the place he was leaving."

"Do we know her name?"

"Shiloh Timmons."

Sheppard didn't say anything as a smile curved his lips. He really shouldn't be surprised. He'd suspected even when they were younger there was a special bond between those two. He'd figured something was going on because, when they were younger, he would hear too much protestation in Caden's voice whenever Shiloh's name was brought up. Evidently, they were now trying to work out whatever problems were between them.

"And you're sure both Striker and Caden are okay?"

"They are both fine and, according to Striker, neither Caden nor the woman suspects foul play. They assumed the driver had too much to drink and was acting irresponsibly."

"But Striker thinks otherwise?"

"Yes. He believes the attempt was intentional, but he doesn't have enough to go to the police, mainly because of how quickly things went down. The car sped away before he could get a make, model or tag number."

Sheppard didn't say anything for a minute and then asked, "What about Jace and Dalton?"

"Guards are on them. Quasar is protecting Jace, and Stonewall is on Dalton."

"Quasar? Stonewall? For heaven's sake, Carson, I don't want those two to get themselves into any trouble."

"And they won't. Roland has them under control. They know not to take anything into their own hands."

Sheppard nodded. Yes, Roland, who'd once been

an inmate himself, could handle Striker, Quasar and Stonewall.

"You might want to think about letting your sons know what's going on, Sheppard, so they won't be caught unaware."

He drew in a deep breath as Carson's words consumed him. "I never wanted them to live having to look over their shoulders, Carson."

"Then hire someone to find out the truth and bring the person responsible to justice."

Sheppard walked to the window, looked out and then turned around to her. "Dad did that himself. Then the private investigator he hired had a questionable accident just days after contacting Dad saying he might have found a breakthrough in the case."

Carson raised a brow. "Questionable? But I thought he was killed in an accident while drinking."

"That's the report that was put out, but I know Marshall Imerson didn't drink."

"But what about those reports of financial problems with his company and proof that he was into something illegal that was about to be exposed? That would be enough to make any sober man begin drinking, Sheppard."

"I never believed any of it. And all those rumors surfaced after Marshall was killed. I think it was done deliberately so no one would question why he was drinking that night. People who knew Marshall wouldn't believe it, so someone came up with a reason."

"Who?"

"The same person who doesn't want anyone reopening my case and who will do just about anything to make sure they don't."

Carson shuddered. "I don't like any of this, Sheppard. That's why I think your sons need to know what's going on. You should think seriously about telling them before they find out on their own."

He nodded. His sons were astute and he really needed to consider Carson's advice.

Twenty-Three

Dalton opened the side gate at the wine boutique and entered the courtyard. He rarely came into this section of town, but the drive had been a breeze with not too much traffic. It was Sunday and was turning out to be a rather nice day, unlike last weekend, when it had rained most of the time. Today the weather was sunny, although there was a little chill in the air.

It had been hard getting in and out of Sutton Hills and gathering up the clothing Caden had asked for without arousing Hannah's curiosity. Of course, she had finally asked him outright.

No one could lie worth a damn when it came to Hannah, so he'd given her a straight answer, telling her that some woman had torn Caden's clothes off, and he needed something to put on. Hannah had stared at him for a minute, then she'd shaken her head and walked away. So much for honesty. He had a feeling she hadn't believed a word he'd said.

Closing the gate behind him, he glanced around the

courtyard, admiring the setup, especially the water fountain in the center and the park-style benches. He wasn't a person who liked a lot of plants, but the ones here outdoors added an air of peacefulness to the surroundings. If you chose to live close to your place of business, then this would be the way to go. Although, for the life of him, he couldn't imagine living close to Granger Aeronautics, no matter how nice it was. He needed his breathing space.

He walked toward the elevator and pushed the intercom button. "Yes?" a feminine voice asked.

"It's Dalton."

He heard a click, and the security gate to the elevator was unlocked. He stepped inside, and the only button lit on the panel box was for the third floor. On the ride up, he couldn't help wondering how his brother had managed to patch things up with Shiloh so quickly. He wasn't sure what technique Caden had used, and he really didn't care. He was just glad he wouldn't be moping around the office anymore looking as if he'd lost his best friend.

The elevator opened up to a huge hallway with two doors. He stepped off the elevator, deciding to try the first. It opened on his second knock. "How are you, Dalton?" Shiloh asked, moving aside to let him in.

"Just fine, even though it *is* a little early," he said, stepping over the threshold and closing the door behind him. He glanced around. "Nice place."

"Thanks."

"Where's Caden?"

"In the shower. You have the items he asked for?"

"Yes," he said, handing her the bag.

"Thanks."

He must have been looking at her strangely, because she smiled and asked, "What's wrong? Haven't you seen a nymphomaniac before?"

Her question caught him by surprise, and this became one of those rare moments when he was lost for words. But he recovered, although not as quickly as he would have liked. He couldn't help but grin and say, "I take it Caden told you what I said."

"He didn't have to. He had you on speakerphone."

Shit! Dalton swiftly tried to recall all he'd said. And what he remembered wasn't all that pretty. "I can explain."

"Don't bother. I cooked breakfast, so help yourself. Caden and I will join you in a minute."

"Okay. Thanks." Rolling up his sleeves, Dalton walked toward the kitchen.

Ten minutes later Caden and Shiloh walked in to find Dalton sitting at the kitchen table with his plate filled to capacity.

"I hope you left some for us," Caden said, frowning at his brother.

Dalton looked up and smiled. "Sure I did. If anyone needs plenty of nourishment, it's you two. And this food is good by the way, Shiloh," he said, biting into a honey-glazed biscuit. "You can invite me to breakfast anytime."

Shiloh chuckled as she sat down with a plate of fruit. "I'll remember that."

Dalton looked at her fruit. "That's all you're eating?"

"Yes." She then glanced over at Caden, his plate just

as filled as Dalton's. "I think you need to tell Dalton the real reason you needed the clothes. Otherwise, he'll continue to think I'm some oversexed superwoman."

Dalton grinned. "And you're not?"

"No."

"I'm disappointed," Dalton said, smiling.

"Mind your own business, Dalton," Caden said, leaning across the table to place a kiss on Shiloh's lips.

Amazing, Dalton thought, how two people could be so at odds with each other one minute and tearing off each other's clothes and locking lips the next. Whatever they were using, he needed some of it. "So, what's the story you're telling about your clothes?"

"Not what your dirty mind is assuming. I came close to getting hit by a car last night."

That got Dalton's attention. He put his fork down. "You almost got hit by a car?"

"Yes, I was leaving here last night after the opening and I crossed the street to go to my car. Some drunk came along speeding, driving straight at me."

The expression on Caden's face as he recalled the details of last night suddenly made Dalton believe every word he said.

"So you had to jump out of the way?" Dalton asked, all playfulness gone from his eyes.

"Not exactly. I froze. Luckily, within seconds, I was shoved out of the way."

"By whom?" Dalton asked, switching his gaze from Caden to Shiloh.

"No, it wasn't me," she said, reading his thoughts.

"I told you I'm not a superwoman. Oversexed or otherwise."

His eyes moved back to Caden. "Who was it, then?"

"A passerby. Some guy named Striker. And, man, he was fast. He had to be to get us both out of the car's path. He pushed me down, and then the two of us rolled out of the way, tearing our shirts and jackets."

"And the driver of the vehicle?"

"Kept going. Everything happened so fast we didn't have a chance to get the make of the car or the license-plate number."

"Damn. But you're okay?"

"I'm okay." He then smiled over at Shiloh. "Thanks to Striker and Shiloh. She saw the car coming and screamed out to me. That's what alerted me of the danger. That car would have plowed me down and kept going. And if she hadn't screamed, Striker would not have known I was in trouble and taken action the way he did."

She shook her head. "You're giving me too much credit, Caden."

"No, I'm not. I know for a fact if it hadn't been for you and Striker, I would probably be dead."

Hearing his brother say that sent chills through Dalton's body. Shit, he didn't need to lose another family member. Their grandfather's death months ago was still raw. "This Striker guy? Do you have his contact information? I'd like to personally thank him. Hell, if anything were to happen to you, I'd have to deal with Jace on my own," he said, a semblance of his lightheartedness returning.

Caden took a sip of his coffee and then said, "No, he left just as quickly as he appeared."

At that moment, Caden's cell phone rang, and recognizing Jace's ringtone, he said, "Yes, Jace?"

Caden didn't say anything for a moment, but he did glance over at Dalton, then frowned as he said, "Oh, he did, did he? I'll be at Sutton Hills later today, around five. I'll explain things then." He clicked off the phone.

He then stared hard at Dalton for a moment before saying, "You actually told Hannah that the reason you needed to bring me more clothes was because some woman had torn them off me last night?"

Dalton smiled. "You know I can't lie to Hannah. What was I supposed to say?"

"Nothing."

"Yeah, right. You know Hannah like I do."

Yes, Caden thought, he knew Hannah. "Well, lucky for you, Hannah didn't believe a word you said."

"No," Dalton said, grinning. "It was lucky for *you*."

Twenty-Four

"Welcome back, Jules."

"Thanks, Dad," she said, giving her father a huge hug.

Ben was proud of his daughters and knew his deceased wife would be proud of them, too. And now Shana would be making him a father-in-law and a grandfather, and he was beside himself with happiness.

"So what's been happening since I've been gone?" Jules asked, plopping down on the sofa.

"Like you don't know." And when she gave him an innocent look, he said, "And please don't pretend like you don't, because you do. There's no doubt in my mind you know what's going on with your sister. You probably knew before she did."

Jules couldn't help but smile. There was no need to inform her father she'd been with Shana when she'd purchased the pregnancy-test kit. "Now, Dad, you give me way too much credit."

Ben snorted and sat in the chair across from Jules. "So what do you think of Jace Granger?"

Jules shrugged. "I haven't met him yet."

Ben raised an eyebrow, surprised. "You haven't?"

"No. I knew about him, but our paths had never crossed. Shana was in denial about her true feelings for him, and then I finally got her to admit otherwise. Right after that, Shana found out she was pregnant. When I left town on that case, she hadn't even told him."

Jules paused a minute and then said, "I heard about Jace Granger's kidnapping. I called Shana and got the details firsthand. She also told me that she and Jace had resolved their issues—she'd told him about the baby, and they were getting married."

Ben nodded thoughtfully. "She's happy."

"And I'm happy for her. I was beginning to think Jonathan had ruined her for any other man. She had trust issues."

"And you think Jace Granger can be trusted?"

Jules wondered why her father was quizzing her. He was a good judge of character, so if he had doubts about something…

"Dad, you met Jace Granger. Is there a reason you're asking me these questions about him?"

Ben held her gaze for a minute and then said, "I like him, but I know you. There's no way you haven't had him investigated, the same way you checked out Mona."

Jules didn't say anything. Her father was right. He knew her. "He's clean, a regular nice guy. I haven't met him, so I'm going on what I've learned. However, there is the issue of his father being charged for his mother's murder. I understand Jace doesn't believe his father is guilty."

"Well, someone had to have killed her."

Jules nodded, knowing her father was thinking like an ex-cop, and so was she. If Sheppard Granger hadn't killed his wife, then who had?

"Sheppard Granger has already served fifteen years with another fifteen years to go. If he's really innocent, then he's had a raw deal."

Wanting to change the subject, Jules asked her father about Mona and saw how his face lit up when he began talking. He truly loved the woman, just like Shana had said. Seeing her father fall in love wasn't as bad as she'd thought it would be. It just needed some getting used to.

Something her father said caught her attention. She raised her eyebrows. "New York? You're taking Mona to New York?"

"Yes, to see a Broadway play. Do you want to come?"

Jules knew he only asked because he knew she would not go. "Thanks, Dad, but no, I don't want to go." She leaned over and smiled before saying, "You can let go of your breath now."

A couple of hours later, Jules entered her condo thinking there was no place like home. Since January, she hadn't spent more than fifty days here. The others had been spent traveling while handling cases. Now that she was back, she intended to get in her bed and sleep for the next two weeks. She chuckled, wishing that were possible. But like always at the end of a case, there was a lot of paperwork to do.

But once all that was done, she would enjoy some time off for a while with no interruptions. One of the advantages of using a fictitious name for her P.I. agency was not having to worry about anyone tracking her down, making a nuisance of themselves. To everyone in the business, she was known as J. B. Sweet, using her initials and her mother's maiden name. She got a kick out of answering her phone saying, "The Sweet agency."

Another advantage to using a fictitious name was that clients didn't know whether she was male or female until they met her face-to-face or spoke with her on the phone. It also helped when she had clients who assumed she was a man and were surprised to find out differently once they'd met her. The looks on their faces were always priceless.

Deciding to touch base with her sister before she got too comfortable, she pulled her cell phone out of her back pocket to call Shana. According to her father, Shana had gone to the mountains with Jace this weekend but had called a couple of hours ago to let him know she had returned. More than likely, she and Jace would spend the rest of the day…and the night together.

Her sister answered on the first ring. "Jules, tell me you're back."

She heard the excitement in Shana's voice. "Okay, I'm back."

"Seriously?"

Jules laughed. "Yes, seriously." She moseyed to the kitchen, grabbed an apple from the refrigerator and bit into it. "So what's going on with you other than being knocked up?"

"Hey, behave yourself. I can't wait for you to meet Jace."

"Oh, you finally want to introduce me to your man? The same man you claimed for months you weren't interested in?"

"And you know why I was reluctant in the beginning."

Yes, Jules knew why. But she believed this time would be different for her sister. Although she hadn't met Jace Granger, she had a feeling he would be a positive influence in Shana's life. "So what are you doing later today? I might stop by after my nap."

"We're going to Jace's family estate for dinner with his brothers, but I intend to be back here by eight. Why don't you drop by and meet Jace then?"

"I think I will, if I don't oversleep. My bed is calling my name big-time. If I don't make it tonight, let's do dinner tomorrow at Lenny's around five."

"That would be nice. You get your rest. You're tired. I can hear it in your voice."

"I will. Talk to you later."

Leaving her kitchen, Jules went into the living room and checked the incoming messages on her landline. Dale Henslowe had called a number of times while she'd been away, and she wished he hadn't. She had told him the last time he called that she had no time for players or wannabe players. To be honest, she didn't have time for nonplayers, either. A man was the last thing she needed in her life. They all had a tendency to complicate things. Her work was her life, and that was enough.

Now that Shana was making her an aunt, she would

be satisfied with that. *Aunt Jules.* She liked the sound of that and smiled as she headed to her bathroom for a shower.

Caden brought his car to a stop in the circular drive of his grandfather's home at Sutton Hills and glanced over at Shiloh. He could tell she was nervous about being here. He wanted to make her feel comfortable before they went in to meet Jace and Shana, who were waiting for them. Dalton would be joining them as soon as he took care of an errand—right in time for the dinner Hannah was preparing.

"Remember that tree over there?" he asked her, pointing to a huge oak at the side of the house.

She smiled. "Yes, I remember."

When they were kids, the two of them would sit up in the tree and talk for hours. He had tried talking his grandfather into building a tree house in it, but his grandmother had been dead against it after Dalton had fallen out of the tree and broken his arm.

Shiloh looked past the tree to where the roof of his parents' home could be seen in the distance. "You and your brothers still haven't gone back there?"

He followed her gaze. "No. Neither have we gone to the boathouse. For a while, I thought Granddad would tear it down, but he didn't."

"You think your father will when he's released from prison?"

Caden thought about her question for a minute. "I honestly don't know. When Dad is released, he will have a lot on his hands just getting acclimated back into society. A lot has changed, although he's managing to keep up with changing technology. My dad is a very intelligent man."

Shiloh heard the admiration in his voice and recalled it had always been there whenever Caden talked about his dad. Even when they had been kids. On the other hand, she and her own father had never been close. Samuel Timmons had pretty much alienated both of his kids. She knew that Sedrick and their father had made some kind of peace. However, during the time she had moved back home when he had become ill, he had ignored her. He had acted as if she didn't exist. And she knew why. She had gotten pregnant by Caden, and he had told her that he would never forgive her for doing that. Not that she had cared how he felt at the time.

"Can I ask you something?" Caden asked, breaking into her thoughts.

She looked over at him. "Yes."

"What is your fondest memory of Sutton Hills?"

She knew the answer without thinking about it. "Spending time here with you." And she really meant that because, in her mind, Sutton Hills and Caden went together like wine and cheese. Whenever she had come here, it was to play with him.

He smiled. "Good. Now you're back. To spend time with me again."

She didn't say anything as she thought about what Caden had just said. Although the two of them had admitted to still loving each other, they both knew they had work to do in order to fully heal their relationship. And they were willing to take the time to do that, while at the same time trying to find answers to things that were still confusing to them.

"Ready?" he asked her, opening his car door.

"As ready as I'll ever be. I figure Dalton likes me a little better now since he kept telling me how good breakfast was, but now I have to win Jace over."

He touched her arm. "You don't have to win anyone over. I love you, and that's all that matters. My family knows you and has known you for years, Shiloh. They know we've always had a close friendship even as kids growing up. And they also know why our friendship ended. They don't blame you for any of it, like I never blamed you."

And then he leaned over and placed a kiss on her lips. "Come on. Everyone is waiting."

Moments later as they walked up toward the front door, he took her hand in his, leaned close and whispered, "You're going to like Shana. She's just what Jace needs."

Shiloh smiled while thinking that Caden was what she needed, as well.

Caden was right, Shiloh thought a short while later. Shana was a nice person and just what Jace needed. She had to say that everyone treated her like an old friend. Hannah was Hannah and made her feel immediately welcome, saying that she had known Shiloh was coming and she had prepared a batch of her favorite brownies in her honor. The older woman still remembered her favorite dessert.

Jace gave her a hug, and if he was surprised to see

her and Caden together, he didn't show it. He told her he was glad to see her again. No one mentioned running into her last weekend at the restaurant, and she was glad. She still had the issue of Wallace to resolve and didn't look forward to it because of Sedrick. He would be upset about it and understandably so, since he'd asked her more than once if she was truly ready to move on in her life. At the time, she had thought she was, but now she knew differently.

Dalton joined them a few minutes later and was his playful self again, but things turned serious when Caden began telling Jace about what had happened the previous evening.

Just as Dalton had, Jace clung to his brother's every word, and the emotions that appeared on his face told Shiloh everything. The three brothers may have gone their separate ways after leaving here for college, and only hooked up occasionally, but the love she saw between them was real. The three of them agreed it was imperative to find Striker to thank him for his act of heroism.

"And you didn't see the car while crossing the street?" Shana asked, pouring gravy on her mashed potatoes. They were all seated at the dinner table enjoying the delicious meal Hannah had prepared.

"No. The car was parked, and when I was crossing the street, he suddenly pulled out. I would not have seen it if Shiloh hadn't screamed."

Shana asked him a few more questions, and then Dalton suggested they change the subject to discuss something he'd noticed at the office.

"And what have you noticed?" Jace asked with concern in his voice. Things had been running pretty smoothly ever since that kidnapping attempt, but Shana's presence in the office sent a message that the company was still trying to find ways to reinvent itself.

"Brandy."

Jace rolled his eyes. Brandy Booker was one of the administrative assistants. She was attractive, young, single and flirty, and Dalton had had the hots for her from day one, which was why Jace had refused his request that Brandy be his personal administrative assistant. "What about Brandy? You've been noticing her from day one. What else is new?"

"I think she's a spy."

Now, that got everyone's attention. "What makes you think that?" Shana asked, on full alert.

"I noticed things."

Jace rolled his eyes. "Could you be more specific?"

Dalton didn't say anything for a moment and then said, "She deliberately hangs back after I leave."

"Since you leave early almost every day," Caden pointed out, "how would you know?"

"I forgot something last week and had to come back to the office. She was still there, claiming to be working late on some special project."

"And she probably was, Dalton. You know we have a number of employees working on special assignments. I still don't understand your concern," Caden said.

"She was in my office."

Jace frowned. "Your office? Don't you lock your office every day?"

Dalton answered Jace. "I thought I did, but when I asked her how she got in, she said it was unlocked and that she needed a file."

"Did she say what file she needed?" Shana asked.

"Yes, the one about the Evander Project. I told her I didn't have it and that Caden did."

Caden frowned. "I don't have it."

Dalton smiled. "I figured if she really needed the file like she claimed she did, then she would ask you for it. Since you didn't mention anything about this, I knew she'd been lying. So I set her up."

"Set her up? How?" Jace asked.

Dalton smiled. "I had Security install a camera in my office."

"And?" Jace asked.

"And she was recorded entering my office again a few evenings later…with a key."

"Where would she get a key?" Caden asked.

"Not sure, but it opened the door. And she was looking on my desk and trying to go through my drawers, but they were locked. She also spent some time looking behind the pictures on my wall, like she figured there was a safe or something behind them. And she used a mini-camera to take pictures."

"Of what?" Shana asked.

"The framed pictures on my wall. She took several shots of one particular picture."

"Which picture was that?

"The one showing fireworks for a Fourth of July celebration."

Jace frowned. "Why would that picture interest her more than the others?"

"I don't have a clue," Dalton said, taking another sip of coffee.

Jace stared hard at his brother. "And why is this the first time I'm hearing about any of this?" he asked, and it was apparent he was trying to keep his anger under control.

"All this was revealed to me Friday afternoon," Dalton said calmly. "If you recall, you and Shana left the office early to get a jump start on your weekend trip to the mountains. And of course, it was one of those very rare moments when Caden had left early, as well."

"Did you ask Brandy about it?"

"No. It was late evening when Security brought me the footage, and she had left for the day."

"Isn't she still involved with Shelton Fields?" Caden asked. Fields had been second-in-command under Cal Arrington, who'd been indicted for sharing trade secrets with a rival company.

"No. That little affair ended right after Jace's kidnapping," Dalton said. "I figured Shelton was so afraid Jace was going to terminate him because of his involvement with Brandy that he dropped her like a hot potato. If you noticed, Shelton doesn't come within five feet of her anymore."

"I noticed," Jace said.

"So have I," Shana added.

"Well, I haven't," Caden said, frowning.

"Probably because your mind has been rather occupied lately," Dalton said, grinning over at his brother. He then said to Jace, "So, what do you think we should do?"

Jace put it back on him. "What do *you* think we should do?" He'd placed Dalton in charge of security to keep him out of trouble. Now it seemed as if trouble was going to knock on Dalton's door regardless.

"I suggest we, along with Security, confront her about it when she returns to the office."

Both Jace and Caden nodded, agreeing with Dalton's suggestion.

"And if it's okay," Shana said, "I'll have Bruce check out her computer to make sure she hasn't sent any Granger Aeronautics files to anyone outside the company." Bruce Townsend was a computer whiz who worked on occasion for Shana.

"You think she might be divulging trade secrets like Arrington was doing?" Jace asked.

"Not sure, but I'd love to look at that video you've got, Dalton," Shana said.

"No problem. I'll order you a copy from Security. And I checked the calendar on Friday. Brandy has vacation scheduled for the first two days of next week and won't be back in the office until Wednesday."

"Then we'll meet with her on Wednesday. First thing," Jace said.

A few hours later, on the drive back to Shiloh's place, Caden asked if they had bored her to tears when they had been discussing business, and Brandy in particular.

She shook her head. "No, I find it all very interesting, and it seems as if you and your brothers have adapted."

"Adapted?"

"Yes, none of you entered the corporate world after college, but you were forced into it recently. Yet, you seem to be adjusting and taking care of business. It's as if the three of you are naturals."

Caden didn't say anything for a minute and then said, "I admit it can grow on you, but I still love my music."

"I know, but I think this could become your love as well if you were to allow it. Same for Dalton, who gets bored easily. He seems to enjoy that security work."

Caden chuckled. "You noticed, huh?"

"Yes. I think he's found his niche. He seems to be good at it and very comfortable with it."

"I think you're right."

"And since you brought up your music..." Shiloh said. "I'm sure you're well aware that Nannette Gaither wants me to book you for the entertainment at this year's charity ball."

"Yes, she did mention it."

"Well, will you do it?"

"Hmm, it depends."

She lifted a brow. "On what? Your schedule?"

"No, on how nice you are to me."

Shiloh laughed. "Sounds like blackmail."

He chuckled. "Baby, a man's got to do what a man's got to do."

Hours later, Jace and Shana were finishing up the last of the brownies Hannah had sent home with them. They had been too full after dinner to eat any, but a round of lovemaking had fueled their appetite.

The one thing he'd noticed since they'd gotten to her place was that she was quiet. The only time she had let loose was during their lovemaking, but now she was quiet again. He glanced across the table at her. He'd gotten to know her and knew when her mind was busy at work, and this was one of those times.

"What's going on in that brain of yours, Shana?" he asked, taking a sip of apple juice. Usually they would enjoy a glass of wine together, but with her pregnancy, she was now drinking only apple juice.

She glanced over at him. "What makes you think anything is going on?"

"I can tell. Are you worried about the wedding plans? Your sister? Your dad? What Dalton told us about Brandy? What?"

She smiled over at him. "Actually, none of the above. The wedding plans are in place, and now that Jules is back home, they can be finalized. And because she's back home, I'm not as worried about her as I usually am. Dad is fine, and as far as what Dalton told us about Brandy, it seems he handled it, and there's nothing more that can be done until she comes back on Wednesday and you question her about it."

Shana paused a moment and then said, "More than likely, she will deny things, but Dalton has that tape. I can't wait to hear what she has to say."

Jace nodded. "Well, if none of those things is on your mind, then what is?"

She held his gaze for a moment. "Not sure you want to hear it, and I might be wrong, but I have a nagging feeling that won't go away."

"About what?"

"Caden's accident."

Jace lifted a brow. "What about it?"

"It's something no one mentioned," she said, still holding his gaze.

"What?"

She paused, as if choosing her words carefully. "There is a distinct possibility that what happened last night wasn't an accident."

Jace returned her stare and felt his forehead contract into worried lines. After a moment, he shook his head. "No, it was an accident. You heard what both Caden and Shiloh said."

"Yes, I heard what they assumed. If you noticed, I asked them specific questions about it, and I'm convinced their answers were based on what they thought they saw."

"But you're thinking otherwise?"

"Not sure. What's bothering me is that, according to them, the car was parked, yet the ignition didn't start until Caden was about to cross the street. That's when the car started and pulled out of that parking spot."

Jace nodded. "Yes, and it could have been a coincidence that the driver was leaving at the same time."

"From where? If I recall, there aren't any nightclubs in the area, so why would an intoxicated person be parked there? Unless he had attended the grand opening of Shiloh's wine store. Otherwise, again, why would an intoxicated person be parked in that neighborhood?"

Before he could answer, she said, "And I would assume he became intoxicated *before* parking. Parallel parking is pretty damned tricky on that street even for a sober driver, not to mention a drunk one."

Shana could tell by the worried lines etched in Jace's forehead that she had him thinking. She hadn't wanted to voice her suspicions, but he had asked.

He drew in a deep breath. "Okay, let's explore your theory for a minute."

"Wait, Jace. I'm not saying what I'm thinking actually happened, but when you have a father who's a retired cop and homicide detective, and a sister who used to be a cop but is now a private investigator—and you add in the line of work I do—you never take things at face value. I have to see other possibilities in everything."

He reached across the table to take her hand in his. "And I understand that. But if there's any chance that you're right, who would want to hurt my brother? Of the three of us, Caden is the most laid-back and outgoing."

Shana shrugged. "Again, it just might be my mind working overtime. But if you don't mind, I'd like to run it by Jules. She texted me a short while ago. She's up from her nap and wants to come over and meet you."

A smile touched Jace's lips. "And I'm looking forward to meeting her."

Twenty-Five

After making love, Shiloh had dozed off awhile, only to wake up a short while later to discover it had grown dark outside and Caden was standing at the window looking out. He was naked, and from behind, the man looked like a real live Adonis, 100 percent pure man. He'd always been in great physical shape and, as a woman, she couldn't help appreciating that fact.

"Any reason you left me alone over here?"

At the sound of her voice, he turned around and crossed the room to rejoin her in bed. "I woke up because I thought I heard a noise down below in your courtyard."

She chuckled as she cozied closer into his arms. "Probably a stray cat. Even with the gate closed, they get in from time to time looking for food, which is why I don't put my trash out at night."

Caden tightened his arms around her. She hadn't said anything about him leaving; nor had she invited him to spend the night. Tomorrow was a workday for both of them. But there was something he wanted to know, and now was as good a time as any to ask.

"So, what do you plan to do about Dr. Aiken?" he asked, looking down at her.

She lifted a brow and chuckled. "Why do you want to know? Feeling territorial?"

"Yes." He was being totally honest. He hadn't liked seeing her that night at the restaurant with another man, and when they had returned from dinner at Sutton Hills tonight, he hadn't missed noticing Dr. Aiken had called and left a message, although she hadn't played it back yet.

She didn't say anything for a minute and then she said, "That's a good question, and in a way I feel bad about it."

"About what?"

"Going out with him in the first place. That was our first date although, according to Sedrick, he's been interested in me for a while. I thought it would be a nice way to get back into dating as a way to move on. Sedrick warned me not to go out with Wallace if I really wasn't over you. Then. I really thought I was."

"Now that we're back together…?"

She sighed. "I'll talk to him. He's a nice guy."

Caden shrugged. "That may be the case. But I'm nicer."

Shiloh pulled back to look up at him and grinned. "Are you really?"

"Need me to prove it again?" He really didn't care what her answer would be because he intended to make love to her anyway. He would not be spending the night, but he intended to make her miss him, yearn for him and only him when he wasn't here. They had agreed to take things slowly, but he also intended to be thorough where she was concerned. He wanted to be the only man she ever thought about, when she was awake or when she was asleep.

"You're taking too long to answer," he said, pushing back the bedcovers to reveal her nakedness.

"I'm thinking."

"What's there to think about?" he asked, lowering his hands between her legs. "But if you believe there is, then maybe I haven't been convincing enough."

He parted her thighs and then slid his fingers inside her heat. Her breath caught, and he heard it. He liked the sound of it. When he heard her moan he knew he'd hit the spot he'd been looking for.

"You, Caden Granger, are a naughty man," she said breathlessly, barely getting the words out.

"And you, Shiloh Timmons, are a very sensuous woman." And that was no lie. Like he'd told her, he might have had sex with other women, but he'd made love to only one. Her. And only her.

Leaning toward her, he dipped his head and used the tip of his tongue to trace a path along her collarbone, liking the sounds she made in response. He also liked the taste of her skin; he liked her scent. He liked every damned thing about her.

"You don't intend to be good, do you?" she asked in a husky whisper.

He leaned up and smiled at her. "On the contrary,

sweetheart. I intend to be good. So good you'll barely be able to stand it."

With that said, he leaned down and kissed her, but he didn't just kiss her. He ravished her mouth with a greed he couldn't control. He slid his tongue all over her mouth, stroking it along her gums and then taking hold of her tongue and sucking on it in a way that even had him moaning. And all the while his fingers were still busy stroking her, making her wet just the way he liked her.

He released her mouth, his entire body reeling from the frenzy of the kiss. Damn, it had been mindlessly hot, satisfying, and it had nearly drained him in one sense but had invigorated him in another. He eased his hand from between her legs and while she watched he slid each finger into his mouth, licking and sucking on it in a way that let her know how much he enjoyed tasting the dewy essence of her.

"Caden…"

The sound of his name off her lips triggered his erection, and it began to throb mercilessly. His body was coiled tight with a need that only she could appease. Reaching under her pillow, he retrieved the condom packet he'd put there earlier, ripped it open and quickly put it on. He needed to be inside of her yesterday and wished like hell he could stay until tomorrow.

In other words, he needed her now.

Lord have mercy, but he intended to make love to her until neither of them had strength left for anything. They must have shared the same thoughts, because they reached for each other at the same time. And when he eased his body in place over hers, she wrapped her legs completely around him as if she never intended to let him go.

He thrust inside of her and felt the full length of him slide straight to the hilt. Her inner muscles clenched him, and he stared down at her, feeling each and every pull they made on him. He bared his teeth in a sensuous growl and felt his iron-hard erection fully embedded inside of her.

And then he began moving fast, thrusting in and out of her, working every part of his body. She raised her hips, meeting him stroke for stroke. He could feel heat spread through his loins and hers. It fueled the intensity of their lovemaking and drove him to increase the tempo and the rhythm.

When his body arched in a bow, she was there with him. When he came down on a final thrust before his world shattered in one orgasmic explosion, she was also caught in the blast. The intensity of the climax had him tightening his hands on her hips and had her tightening the legs wrapped around his back.

"Caden!"

"Shiloh!"

Simultaneously they called out to each other as their worlds continued to erupt in pleasure so keen and sharp it left them gasping for breath. And as he slumped to his side and pulled her down with him, fighting for breath, the only thing he could think of was that he'd been given another chance with this woman. His woman. And he made another promise—that he would never let her down again. No matter what, their lives were entwined. She was his. He was hers, and she would never have reason to doubt it again.

"I'm glad I finally get to meet you, Jace," Jules said, smiling over at the man her sister had fallen in love with. "And sorry to show up so late. I had to grab a few winks. Otherwise, I would be a danger to myself and others on the road."

"I'm just glad we're finally meeting," Jace said. "I've heard a lot about you."

He and Shana were sitting on the sofa in her living room, and Jules sat across from them in a wingback chair. Jace could see a resemblance between her and Shana. They both had Ben's nose, but that was where the similarities stopped. Jules had more of her father's features than Shana did. Shana had told him that she resembled her mother more. But in his opinion, both were beautiful women. Jules was an inch or two shorter than Shana, and he couldn't imagine her as a cop taking down guys larger than she was. According to Shana, Jules was an expert at self-defense and marksmanship.

"Glad you got some rest," Shana said to her sister. "I worry about you."

Jules looked over at Jace and winked. "Typical big sister, although she's only older by a few months."

"Twenty months," Shana spoke up and said. "That's more than a few."

"Okay, I stand corrected. Jace, let it go on record that Shana is twenty months older than I am."

Jace smiled. The camaraderie Shana and Jules were

sharing was similar to that of his brothers, and he enjoyed listening to them.

"So how are the wedding plans coming along?" Jules asked.

Shana reached out and took Jace's hand in hers, tightening her fingers around his. "As you know, it will be a small wedding with just family and close friends. We plan to keep it under fifty people."

"That *is* small," Jules said. "Anything I can do to help move the process along?"

"Why?" Shana asked, grinning. "You want me married before I start showing?"

Jules threw her head back and laughed. "Doesn't bother me if it doesn't bother you. You're the one who's always been a stickler when it came to rules and what people thought. The opposite of me…unless it affected Dad negatively or something like that."

Jace could see Jules was something of a rebel. Dancing to the beat of her own drum and no one else's. But it was clear she cared about how her actions might affect her father, and he admired that.

"So I understand you used to be a police officer and are now a private investigator. That sounds interesting," Jace said. Although he was enjoying the conversation he was having with Jules and Shana, he couldn't push from his mind what Shana had said earlier. She had suggested another possibility concerning Caden's near-fatal accident.

"Jace?"

He glanced over at Shana. "Yes, sweetheart?"

"I was just telling Jules how delicious the dinner was. Hannah did a great job."

He wrapped his arms around Shana's shoulders to bring her closer to his side. "She always does. We should have invited you, Jules. You could have met my brothers and Hannah. We consider her family, as well."

Jules set her coffee cup aside. "Thanks, but I couldn't have made it. I was a walking zombie after I got back. I stopped by Dad's on the way from the airport. He fed me, and then I went home and slept like a baby. But I am definitely looking forward to meeting your brothers, and Hannah, too."

"And speaking of Jace's brothers," Shana said, straightening up in her seat as a serious expression appeared on her face, "there was an incident involving one of them last night, and I would like your opinion about it."

"Sure."

Shana told Jules everything that Caden and Shiloh had told them. Jace watched Jules's expression as she hung on Shana's every word. He could see her mind working, absorbing and dissecting every single detail.

When Shana finished, Jules had a couple of questions, which were some of the same questions Shana had asked Caden. Had Caden noticed the car's engine running when he'd first walked onto the street? Had the car appeared to be coming straight at him, or had it zigzagged erratically on the road?

Shana provided Jules with the same answers Caden had given her. No, he hadn't noticed the car running, and he couldn't say the car was zigzagging, because he wasn't sure. All he recalled was turning to find the car coming straight at him.

Jules didn't say anything for a minute, and then she said to Jace, "Caden is a great sax player, by the way. I enjoy his music." Then she paused a moment and asked, "Do you know if he has any enemies? Crazy fans? Jealous ex-lovers?"

Jace shrugged. "I'm the last person you should ask. Are you thinking the same way as Shana? That there's a chance it wasn't an accident?"

Jules leaned forward in her seat. "Not necessarily. I think your kidnapping has my sister suspicious of anything, maybe even a bit paranoid in a sense," she said, ignoring the frown Shana shot at her. "But then, you never know. I'll have some free time on my hands since I'm not taking on another case until after the holidays. If Caden wants to talk with me about it, I'd be happy to offer my opinion. I can check out a few things."

Jace nodded. "I'll run it by him, although he's convinced it was a drunk driver behind the wheel last night."

"And that might be the case, but I have a couple of questions I'd like to ask him while the incident is still fresh in his mind."

Jace nodded. "Okay, then, I'll arrange it."

Twenty-Six

Caden glanced up when he heard the knock on his office door. "Come in."

Dalton walked in smiling. Caden glanced at his watch and wondered what the hell was going on. It was a Monday morning, and it wasn't nine o'clock yet. Dalton was in the office at a reasonable time for once, and he was smiling. He must have gotten laid pretty damned good last night.

"What's going on with you, Dalton? What's the smile for?"

"No reason. It's just good to be alive."

Bullshit. As far as Caden was concerned, every day was a good day to be alive, so there had to be another reason behind Dalton's megawatt smile. "You have a date last night?"

"No."

"No date?"

Dalton chuckled. "No, no date. After I left Sutton Hills

I went home and watched a game on TV and then went to bed. My team didn't even win."

Caden chuckled. "So I heard. I figured you'd be wearing a sad face all day, so, again, I'm asking, what's up with the smile?"

Dalton slid into the chair across from Caden's desk. "If you must know, I got a call from that investigator I hired. He's found her."

Caden heard the excitement in Dalton's voice. "You were really serious about hiring a P.I. to find a woman for you?"

"Told you I was, and it's not just any woman. She is *the* woman. Can't wait to see her face when I show up and she realizes I've found her. That will teach her to throw out a challenge to me."

There was another knock on Caden's door. "Come in."

Jace walked in but, unlike Dalton, he wasn't smiling. In fact, he appeared disturbed about something.

"And what's your problem this morning?" Dalton asked his brother, grinning. "Shana cut you off already?"

Jace shook his head. "No. Shana got a call from Marcel Eaton."

Caden raised a brow. "That FBI guy?"

"Yes. He gave her some disturbing news."

"What?" Dalton asked, feeling worry vibes coming from his oldest brother.

"Brandy Booker was found dead in an apartment in D.C. It appears she committed suicide."

"Shit," Dalton and Caden exclaimed at the same time.

* * *

Shana hung up the phone and leaned back in her chair, thinking her conversation with Marcel just now had been rather interesting. Although the D.C. authorities had ruled Brandy Booker's death a suicide by overdose, her mother wasn't buying that story…mainly because of the suicide note that was left.

In the note, Brandy told her parents she'd been depressed lately and didn't want to live anymore and that was the reason she was taking her life. She asked her mother and father to forgive her. She also told them to tell her sister she loved her.

The only problem with this account was that Brandy Booker didn't have a sister. She'd been an only child. Her mother was convinced her daughter had left that intentionally misleading statement as a clue that she was being forced to end her life. If that was true, then by whom?

This wasn't, strictly speaking, an FBI issue. The reason Marcel had contacted her at all was because, at the time of her death, Brandy's Granger Aeronautics ID badge was found in her purse along with her other belongings. Since the FBI had recently worked a case involving Granger, the FBI was notified about Brandy. So far, there was nothing to connect the two cases.

Shana stood and walked over to the window. It was a beautiful September day, and her view of the mountains was excellent. Unlike that morning, when fog had blanketed the city, there wasn't a trace of fog anywhere. And the sun was peeking out over the mountains.

She drew in a deep breath. She hoped she wasn't becoming paranoid like Jules had said, even though she had been teasing at the time. But Shana was beginning to wonder, especially with the recent events surrounding Granger Aeronautics. The kidnapping of Jace had been bad enough, but then Caden's accident Saturday night, which she wasn't completely sure was an accident…and now Brandy's suicide this weekend. And Brandy's death had come right before they planned to question her about why she had been snooping around in Dalton's office.

She turned at the knock on her office door. "Come in."

She wasn't surprised when Jace and his brothers walked in. She could tell from the looks on Caden's and Dalton's faces that they were as shocked as she and Jace were about Brandy.

"I need a drink," Dalton said, heading for the coffeepot in her office. She figured he'd prefer something a lot stronger, but he would make do with coffee for now. It was still early.

"All of us will need a drink before this is all over. I just hung up with Marcel, and there's more."

Dalton turned and looked at her. "*Christ*. And here I thought that today would be one of those rare days where everything went my way."

Ignoring Dalton, Jace crossed the room to Shana. He could see the troubled look in her features. "What else did you learn?"

"Brandy's mother doesn't think it was suicide. She's trying to convince the D.C. authorities that her daughter had no reason to take her life. She believes Brandy was murdered and forced to write that note."

Caden frowned. "What makes her think that?"

"The suicide note itself. In it, Brandy apologizes to her parents for ending her life, and then she asked them to tell her sister she loved her."

"Brandy doesn't have a sister."

Everyone in the room turned and looked at Dalton with raised brows. He shrugged. "In one of our conversations, Brandy mentioned she was an only child. That was the same day she'd also said both her parents used to work here."

"Her parents used to work here?" Shana asked, quickly walking over to her computer. "Jace, did you know that?"

"No. That's news to me," Jace said, still staring at his brother.

"And I don't recall that information coming up in my investigation of everyone here at Granger," Shana said, sliding into her chair and rebooting her computer.

Jace came and leaned on the edge of Shana's desk. "And just what else did Brandy tell you?" he asked Dalton.

Dalton shrugged for a second time while pouring his coffee. The thought of Brandy's death bothered him. "Not a whole lot. Her mother left here to embark on a career in nursing. Her father left the company shortly after his divorce from her mom and moved to Texas. I believe she said that was eight or nine years ago."

"This listing shows five Bookers who have worked for Granger Aeronautics since the company was founded," Shana spoke up to say. "There was a Rosalyn Booker who left the company nine years ago, and her husband, Neil, left the year after she did. But according to this, he didn't leave voluntarily. He was fired."

"Why?" Caden asked, taking the chair across from Shana's desk.

"It doesn't say. We'll have to pull old employment records to find out. The reason I didn't link the three is because Brandy checked 'no' on her employment application where it asks if any relatives work or have ever worked for the company."

Jace raised a brow. "I wonder why she did that."

"Probably because her father was fired, and she was afraid the connection would jeopardize her chances of being hired," Caden surmised.

"Yet she took a chance and told Dalton," Jace said, staring at his brother.

Dalton took a sip of his coffee. "I guess I'm the kind of man women feel they can confide in."

"When? During pillow-talk time?" Caden inquired.

Dalton frowned. "Let me go on record as saying that although Brandy was a hot number, she and I never slept together. She and I were never involved." He then looked over at Jace. "Are you going to call everyone together and tell them? Brandy was well liked in this department."

"Yes. But first I'll tell Shelton Fields, because they'd been involved in an affair. I've called a meeting for ten o'clock to tell the staff."

"Do you think she'd been depressed about the breakup?" Caden asked. "What if Brandy had assumed there was more to the affair than Shelton intended? He sure didn't have any problems dropping her when the going got rough."

"I don't recall Brandy being depressed at all," Dalton said. "After her breakup with Shelton, she had moved on to her next conquest."

Jace lifted a brow. "How would you know?"

"She mentioned she was seeing someone. Some older guy, but she didn't give any details. Whoever he was, she was falling for him fast. She didn't give good old Shelton another thought." Dalton lowered his head. "I guess we'll never know why she was snooping around my office."

"Bruce was here earlier," Shana said, referring to the computer expert she hired on occasion. "He took Brandy's hard drive and will call me if he finds anything. I mentioned to Marcel that Brandy was to be questioned when she returned on Wednesday. He was interested in that piece of information but said if the authorities rule her death as suicide, there's no reason for the FBI to get involved unless we discover something."

"But what about her mother's accusations? It does seems funny she would write about a sister on her suicide note when she didn't have one," Caden said, frowning.

"Yes, it does," Shana agreed.

Dalton glanced at his watch. "I hate to run, but I have an appointment."

Jace raised a brow. "This early? With whom?"

"That private investigator I hired," he said, heading out the door.

Shana gave Jace a questioning look. He shook his head and said, "Don't ask."

Twenty-Seven

A jubilant Dalton entered Emory Harris's office all but whistling. The man's secretary looked up and smiled.

"I believe Mr. Harris is expecting me," Dalton said.

"Yes, he is," she said, standing. "Right this way, Mr. Granger."

Moments later, Emory Harris was rising to his feet when Dalton entered his office. "Mr. Granger, like I told you on the phone this morning, I found the woman you were looking for," he said, gesturing for Dalton to take the chair in front of his desk.

"I began work on your case on Friday."

Dalton nodded. "And you were able to find her this quickly. I'm impressed."

The man chuckled. "You shouldn't be. In fact, I feel bad about taking your money. This was the easiest case I've had in a long time."

Dalton lifted a brow. "Really? What made this one so easy?"

"Two reasons. The first is surveillance footage. I

went to that club and got the owner to let me see the surveillance tape for that night. At first, he gave me some
crap about privacy laws, so I had a friend of mine who
works at police headquarters request a copy for me.
Imagine my surprise when I watched the footage and
immediately recognized the woman you're looking for."

Dalton wasn't sure he liked the sound of that. Just
what kind of work could this woman be in that she was
easily recognized by Harris?

"And how were you able to identify her so easily?"

Harris smiled. "And that's reason number two. I always make it my business to know a colleague."

"Excuse me?"

"Your girl is a P.I. like me and a damned good one."

Dalton blinked. *A private investigator?* He recalled
the night he'd first met her she'd told him she was looking for a man. He'd thought he knew what she meant.
Now it seemed he'd been wrong about that.

"Yeah, like I said, Sweet Pea is a damned good investigator."

"Sweet Pea?"

"It's a nickname she was given by other local P.I.s.
Her agency is the J. B. Sweet agency, so we call her
Sweet Pea…although I'm probably eighty percent cer-
tain J. B. Sweet isn't her real name."

Dalton frowned. "Why would she make up a name
for her agency?"

"She's a woman. Most people prefer to have a man
handle their investigative work. By using initials, she
makes sure, initially anyway, you don't know whether
she's male or female. Once face-to-face contact is made,

she has the opportunity to convince the client she's the right person for the job."

Harris took a sip of his coffee then added, "And then a lot of private investigators use fictitious names for privacy as well as protection. The last thing you want is for someone—like a deadbeat dad you've had arrested—to show up on your doorstep or in a dark alley. Nothing wrong with playing it safe."

But did she have to look so damned sexy? Dalton wondered. He drew in a deep breath. Shit, he didn't care what the woman did for a living. He had to see if he still found her as desirable as he had that night. Dalton had a strong feeling that he would.

Minutes later, he was walking out of Harris's office with the address of the private investigator known as Sweet Pea safely tucked in his pocket.

"Come in."

Jace walked into Caden's office and went straight for the chair in front of his brother's desk and sat down. He was certain his face still had an ashen look. Telling the staff about Brandy's death had been hard on him. Brandy had been well liked and had gotten to know a lot of people during her three years with the company. No one should get to an emotional state that would make her choose death over life.

"Well, that's over," he said. "A lot of people are in shock, and understandably so. Of course, some approached me afterward expecting me to divulge details."

Caden nodded. "What about Shelton? How did he take the news?"

"Worse than I expected. And according to Shelton, Brandy dropped *him,* not the other way around. He said she even threatened him with a sexual-harassment charge if he spoke to her or came near her again, which was why he'd been keeping his distance. Now, that's strange," Jace said, shaking his head.

He didn't say anything for a minute and then he said, "The reason I came here is to talk about you, Caden."

Caden looked surprised. "Me?"

"Yes. It's about the other night, when that car almost hit you."

Caden rubbed a hand down his face. "I've been trying to forget about it."

"I can appreciate that and I do understand. But we need to talk about a possibility we haven't discussed."

A bemused expression showed on Caden's face. "And what possibility is that?"

Jace leaned back in his chair and then said, "That it was no accident, and that someone tried to kill you."

Twenty-Eight

Caden stared at his brother. "Is that supposed to be a joke?"

Jace shook his head. "I wouldn't joke about something as serious as that, Caden."

"Then why would you think something like that?" he asked, his face filled with indignation. "Why would anyone want to kill me? How did you come up with such a crazy idea?"

Jace absently tapped his fingers on the arm of his chair. "Trust me. I want to think it's crazy as well, but…"

"But what?"

"But," Jace said, standing, "like Shana suggested, we have to consider all possibilities."

"Shana?"

"Yes. We talked about it last night, and she's concerned it might not have been an accident."

Caden released a breath that was part frustration and part disbelief. "Why? Your fiancée is concerned someone wants to harm me just because someone tried to kill you? Damn it, Jace, that's not fair."

Jace frowned. He leaned forward and braced his hands on Caden's desk to stare him down. "And it's not fair that you assume her thought processes are based on emotions. I admit that when she first brought it up, I thought the same way you did. However, we might be jumping to conclusions about it being an accident. We need to consider all the facts," he stated, the tone of his voice edged with deadly calm.

"What facts? I told you what happened, and Shiloh saw the entire thing. Don't you think she would have said something if she thought it was intentional?"

"Not necessarily," Jace said, returning to his chair. "All Shiloh noticed was a car heading straight for you. She even said as much."

Caden rubbed a hand down his face in frustration as he cursed under his breath. "Look, Jace, I want to put what happened Saturday night behind me. I sure as hell am not going to start looking over my shoulder just because Shana thinks someone is out to get me."

"All she's saying is that *might* be a possibility, Caden. Just think of all we don't know. Who was the driver? What was the make and model of the car? Why was anyone drunk and parked on that street when there aren't any bars or nightclubs in the area?" Jace asked.

"Hell, I don't know."

"I don't, either, but I think we should find out. It might be nothing, and I'm hoping that's true. But I want to be sure. I admit I hadn't thought of any foul play until she brought it up. But you know Shana. She's good at what she does because her brain never stops working. She even ran it by her sister last night."

"Her sister?"

"Yes. Jules is an ex-cop who owns a P.I. firm, and I understand she's good. She agrees that we shouldn't rule out the possibility of foul play."

Caden walked over to the window and glanced out, but his fury clouded everything. His body was tense, and he felt frustrated. The weekend with Shiloh had been wonderful, more than he could ever have wished for. They had resolved their differences and were back together, where they belonged.

Although he hadn't planned it, he'd ended up spending last night at her place anyway, which meant getting up early to go back to Sutton Hills to dress for work. He looked forward to seeing her again tonight, and like he had told Jace, the last thing he wanted was to feel he had a reason to start looking over his shoulder. He resented this unexpected theory of Shana's. He didn't need it; nor did he want it.

He turned back to Jace. "And how are we supposed to rule out the possibility it really wasn't an accident? Like I told you, I can't even tell you what kind of car it was, and Shiloh can't, either."

"What about that guy who saved your life? Think he might remember?"

Caden shrugged. "Not sure. He was there one minute and gone the next. I don't know how to contact him."

Jace didn't say anything for a long minute. "Would you be willing to at least talk to Jules, Caden? Answer a few questions she might have, and then let her rule out the possibility of—"

"I'd rather not," he said, coming back to his desk and sitting down. "I don't want my life turned upside down on the possibility of a far-fetched idea."

"Will you do it for me? I made a promise…we all did, that we would watch each other's backs. If anything were to happen to you and I felt I could have prevented it, I wouldn't be able to live with myself. If you think the whole idea is far-fetched, then let Jules prove you right."

Caden didn't say anything as he picked up a pen and rolled it back and forth between the palms of his hands. He thought about how he'd felt when he'd learned Jace had been kidnapped. All he could think about was that he had let his brother down by not watching out for him. Not protecting each other like they'd promised their father and grandfather they would. He knew exactly how Jace would feel if anything were to happen to him. He'd been down that road already and didn't wish it on either of his brothers.

"Okay, I'll talk to Shana's sister. I'll answer her questions. And when she discovers I'm right, you owe me a damned case of Scotch."

Relief ran through Jace. "And I'll be glad to buy it for you," he said, standing up. "I'll make arrangements for Jules to meet with you this week. The sooner, the better. And she'll probably want to talk to Shiloh."

Caden tossed his pen on the desk. "Fine. I'll let Shiloh know."

* * *

Jules sealed the envelope containing documents that finalized the paperwork on her last case, thinking this was the story of her life. One case after another. At least her sister had found true love. She couldn't help but smile, feeling pretty happy about it. After all, she would be an aunt in nine months or less. Definitely less.

She tossed her pen on her desk, leaned back in her chair and gazed out the window. For some reason, she was feeling edgy, hot—and her feminine urges were kicking in. Damn, when was the last time she'd been fucked? She frowned, thinking that sounded rather vulgar and needed to be rephrased. Okay, then, when was the last time she'd had sex?

Thinking of it as making love was totally out of the question. Who did that these days…except for Jace and Shana and a few more happily married people out there—people like her dad. She rolled her eyes. Christ! Who wanted to think of the possibility of her parent getting some when she wasn't?

Standing, she went over to the coffeepot and poured herself a cup. It was after lunch already and she'd skipped it, as well as breakfast. That meant she'd have to eat something nourishing at dinner. She needed to feed her body.

She needed to take care of something else with her body, too, and it was beginning to speak loud and clear, demanding that its needs be fulfilled. She thought about her life again and decided she needed something to shake her up. Her personal life had become boring, and she didn't see any improvement ahead. She had no man, and her battery-operated toy was getting damned worn-out.

She went back to her desk, thinking that she might be getting back into another case—as a favor to her soon-to-be brother-in-law. Hopefully, Shana was wrong about what she thought had happened Saturday night. That would be quick to prove, and her involvement would be over. Then what? She wouldn't take any cases that would require traveling until after the holidays. That meant she had the rest of this month, then October, November and December to continue to be bored.

She took a sip of her coffee, thinking that the only real excitement she'd had recently had been last month with the man she'd run into at the club. He'd been a cutie. Hot with a capital *H*. Fine with a capital *F*...in italics and bold. He had crossed her mind a number of times since that night, and she would even admit he had crept into her dreams a time or two.

Yes, he was handsome, and damn it, he'd known it. He could have had his pick of any woman at the club that night. But she had given him the brush-off. Served his ass right for thinking he was all that and a bag of chips...even if he had been.

She wasn't crazy. The man had wanted sex that night. She had seen it in his eyes, had read it on his lips, even without speaking the words. Hell, he had *horny* written all over him...just the way she had it scribbled all over her right now.

Jules took another sip of her coffee. Manning, who worked as her administrative assistant, had left already for a doctor's appointment. With little to do, she had told him not to worry about coming back today since she would be leaving early herself.

The phone on her desk rang, and she saw who it was. Smiling, she answered. "Hello, Dad."

"Would you like to explain why Caden Granger was sneaking out of your place this morning before seven o'clock?"

Shiloh glanced up from the stack of papers on her desk to see Sedrick standing in the doorway of her office.

She studied her brother and noticed two things. He was wearing his white medical coat, which meant he was probably on his lunch hour, and second, he was frowning. She released a deep sigh. Her weekend had been too beautiful for her to let Sedrick or anyone else try to blemish it.

Shiloh leaned back in her chair. "What were you doing around here that time of morning?"

"The road was closed on Fifth and MacConnie, and I figured I'd make better time detouring through downtown. Imagine my surprise when I was sitting at the traffic light and saw Caden sneaking out of your place."

"Caden was not sneaking out. I invited him to stay the night."

Sedrick's frown deepened. "That's a switch from Saturday night. If I recall, you were acting as if you couldn't stand the sight of him."

"Yes, I guess it was a switch, since he spent Saturday night with me, as well."

Her brother just stared at her. She could feel his anger

and couldn't understand the reason for it. "Would you like to explain how that happened?" he asked.

"I will, but not because I feel that I have to, Sedrick. I'm an adult, and I make my own decisions about my life."

He came into the office, closing the door behind him. "True, and I think I've always treated you as an adult, Shiloh…except for those times you showed up at my place crying your eyes out like a child because of how shabbily Caden had treated you."

"That was when he thought I had wronged him."

"Doesn't matter what he thought. I still comforted you as a big brother would his kid sister."

Shiloh didn't say anything. She remembered those times. There had been only two—the night Caden had had her thrown out of his concert and last month, when she had gone to Sutton Hills to see him and he had refused to listen to her.

"So how did he get to you? How did he get you to change your mind about moving on in your life without him?"

Shiloh walked over to the window and stared out. It was a beautiful day, but nothing could be as beautiful as the weekend she had shared with Caden. A weekend that could have ended in tragedy.

She turned back to Sedrick to find him staring at her. "To be honest, Sedrick, it wasn't anything Caden did. It was something that almost happened."

She saw the look of confusion on his face. "And what almost happened?"

Shiloh swallowed deeply, remembering. "Caden came close to being killed Saturday night."

Sedrick went stock-still, looking as thunderstruck as she'd felt that night. "What do you mean, he came close to being killed Saturday night? When I left your party, he was still here, and he seemed pretty damned fine to me."

She went back to her chair to sit down. "It was after you left. After everyone left and he was leaving. A drunk driver lost control of his car and almost ran him down."

"Is this what he told you?"

"No, that is what I saw with my own eyes, Sedrick. If a Good Samaritan hadn't knocked him out of the way, he would have been killed." Her voice was breaking, and there was no help for it. Talking about it made her remember every little detail.

"What Good Samaritan?"

"We don't know really. Some guy was walking by and saw what was about to happen. However, instead of going into a panic and screaming like I did, he went into action and pushed Caden out of danger."

Sedrick didn't say anything for a moment, but Shiloh could tell what she was saying was now sinking in. "The guy who saved him… Is he all right? What about Caden?"

She nodded. "They're both fine. Bruised up but fine."

"Did anyone call the police? Did the car stop? If not, did anyone get a tag number?"

"No to all three. Things happened so quickly, and

there was no need to call the police when we had no information to give them."

Sedrick didn't say anything for a minute, and then he came and plopped down on the chair across from Shiloh's desk. "I don't like the sound of this," he said angrily. "You're upset about what happened, and I can understand that. But there's something else you might want to consider about what happened."

Shiloh lifted a brow. "What?"

"That the entire damned thing was staged."

She stared at her brother, and his expression clearly said he honestly considered that a likelihood. "That's not possible."

"And why not? If he wanted to play on your sympathy, then what better way to do it? It definitely got him a night in your bed."

Shiloh leaned over her desk, releasing an angry breath. "It was not staged, Sedrick. I saw the entire thing. There was no way for that driver to know when Caden would be leaving my party. It happened just like I told you, whether you choose to believe it or not. Caden could have lost his life Saturday night."

"Well, forgive me if I have trouble believing it. It worked in his favor too damned well to suit me."

Shiloh stared at her brother, not understanding this hostile attitude he had toward Caden. It hadn't been there two weeks ago. She could clearly recall him telling her all he wanted was her happiness, and at one time he'd acted as if he'd wanted her and Caden to get back together. What had happened? She then recalled something she had noticed at her party Saturday night.

"Are the Greenes the reason you've suddenly developed this dislike for Caden?"

"What are you talking about?"

"I saw you hanging with them at the party. And it was pretty obvious they were acting rather badly toward Caden. He noticed it, as well."

Sedrick's gaze hardened. "Trust me, they couldn't care less what he noticed."

She again heard the venom in his voice. "Why? Why do they dislike Caden so much? And why has their dislike now spread to you?"

"I don't know what you're talking about," Sedrick said, standing. "I have to get back to work." Then, without saying anything else, he walked out of her office.

Twenty-Nine

Dalton parked his car across from the tall building where the J. B. Sweet Investigative Agency was located. It was in a newly developed area of Charlottesville located near other businesses such as clothing stores, restaurants and various types of home-design stores. The landscaping was nice, and the building's modern architecture featured steel and glass.

Entering the building, he went to the receptionist's desk. "May I help you?" she asked.

He returned the woman's smile. "Yes, I'm looking for the J. B. Sweet Investigative Agency."

"It's on the tenth floor. The elevators are to your right."

"Thanks."

Dalton's heart rate kicked up a beat and his pulse increased as he walked toward the elevator. What the hell was wrong with him? She was just another woman he wanted in his bed. No biggie.

He stepped on the elevator, wondering who in hell

he was trying to fool. This *was* a big deal. He'd spent his money and his time; he had passed many sleepless nights and had suffered through countless dreams about her. What other woman had put him through that kind of shit?

As the elevator door swooshed shut behind him, he pressed the button for the tenth floor while thinking about what had driven him to this point. He knew the answer without having to think about it. From the moment she had walked into the nightclub that night, he had wanted her. Pure and simple. And she'd been determined to make everything complicated.

An amazing body, gorgeous legs and a beautiful face. There had been something that had drawn him to her besides being sexy as hell. His libido had been out of control ever since. He hadn't known why his attraction to her was so strong—she was like a magnet and he a piece of metal. Even now he didn't know. But one thing he did know was that he wanted her and he intended to have her. Neither his mind nor his body would be at peace until he did.

He stepped off the elevator and walked down a wide corridor until he came to a door with the name of her business on it in big, bold letters. Opening the door, he entered, stepping into a nice lobby area.

He heard her voice, the same sexy sound he remembered from that night, and the scent of Amarige floated on the air. There was no doubt in his mind that his mystery woman was seated a few yards away. She was talking to someone on the phone in what was probably her office. The door was open, but he wouldn't disrupt her phone call. He would wait until she ended the call before letting her know he was there.

He sat down on one of the comfortable-looking chairs.

"Mr. Granger, there's a Ms. Timmons here to see you."

Caden lifted his face from the stack of papers he was reading and rubbed the bridge of his nose, wondering what the hell Shiloh's mother wanted. Sandra Timmons had seen him at Shiloh's party Saturday night and hadn't even acknowledged his presence. He was beginning to think that, with the exception of Shiloh, her family had mental issues.

He drew in a deep breath. "Okay, Teresa. Please send her in."

Standing, he slid into his jacket and adjusted his tie. The office had been pretty quiet ever since everyone had been told of Brandy's death. Most had heard the details, and news had spread quickly. Shelton had left the office early, which was probably a good thing. When Caden had passed him in the hall earlier, he'd looked as if he'd still been in a state of shock. Jace had personally made a call to Brandy's family, conveying the company's condolences and letting them know that Brandy's personal belongings at the office would be delivered to them this week. Jace had said that her mother had seemed grateful for the call.

Caden raised a surprised eyebrow when his office door opened and the person who walked in was not Sandra Timmons but Shiloh. An overwhelming feeling of love and warmth flowed through him, and he walked from behind his desk to meet her.

"This is a pleasant surprise," he said. And as soon as Teresa left, closing the door behind her, he pulled Shiloh into his arms and kissed her.

He heard her purse drop to the floor when she let go of it to wrap her arms around his neck. She tasted like heaven and was a sensual delight in his arms. He had been thinking of her a lot today, and now she was here.

He finally broke off the kiss, and he watched as she gasped and breathed the word *wow*.

"Ditto," he whispered, not ready to let her go yet. So he stood there and held her, loving the feel of her in his arms. "I don't know what brought you here, but whatever the reason, I'm grateful," he said.

She leaned back and smiled up at him. "I was in my office, standing at the window looking out at this building, which can be seen in the distance, and wondered which one of the offices was yours. So I grabbed my jacket and purse and decided to find out."

He forced his gaze away from what he considered a too-sexy mouth to look into her eyes. "I want to officially welcome you to my office and to let you know you're welcome to visit anytime."

Her lips widened into a smile, and the impact touched him. Not in one particular spot but all over. "Come here. Let me show you the view from my window," he said, taking her hand and leading her over to the window.

He heard her sharp intake of breath when she stood beside him at the window. "The mountains are beautiful from here. How do you get any work done?"

He chuckled, tightening her hand in his. "This view isn't my number one challenge in getting anything done around here," he said. "That is," he said, gesturing to the saxophone case in the corner of the room. "I bring it into the office with me on occasion. You wouldn't believe the number of times during the day I've been tempted to take it out and play it."

"And you haven't?"

"So far, no."

"You can play it for me one night."

"I intend to." As far as he was concerned, he owed her a whole damned concert and intended to perform just for her one of these days.

He led her over to the love seat in his office and sat down with her beside him. "I was going to call you later to see if you wanted to do dinner. There's something I need to discuss with you."

"I'd love to do dinner, and there is something I want to talk to you about as well…which is another reason I'm paying you a visit."

Hearing the nervousness in her voice, he asked, "What is it?"

She nervously nibbled on her bottom lip before saying, "It's Sedrick. He came to see me today. It appears he was in the area this morning and saw you leave my place."

He nodded and tightened his hand on hers. "And that bothers you?"

"No," she said, shaking her head. "I'm an adult and can do as I please. But what bothers me is the way he's handling the whole idea of our getting back together.

Just weeks ago, he claimed he wanted me to be happy, even if that meant working things out with you."

"And now?"

"Now he has a horrible attitude, and I don't know where it came from…although I have an idea."

"The Greenes?"

Her eyes widened. "Yes. How did you know?"

"A mere guess since I saw him hanging with them at the party Saturday night. I wasn't aware he was that close to the family."

"He's not. At least he hadn't been since he and Kerrie broke up ages ago."

"He sure seems to be back in tight with them now."

"Seems that way, doesn't it?" she said, shaking her head. "I told him what happened to you on Saturday night, and do you know what he said?"

"No. What did he say?"

"That he didn't think it was an accident at all."

Caden stiffened, wondering if perhaps Sedrick's opinion was the same as Jace's and Shana's. "What does he think it was?"

"Staged."

"Staged?" Caden said, nearly choking on the word. Not believing what he was hearing.

"Yes. Can you believe something so crazy?"

Caden smiled. "Just as crazy as what Jace and Shana think happened."

A quizzical look appeared in her eyes. "What do they think?"

He stood. "Come on. We can grab dinner at Smiley's and talk about it."

* * *

"How would you like to come over for dinner?" Ben Bradford asked his daughter. "I'm putting pork chops on the grill and—"

"I'll be there," Jules said, interrupting quickly. She couldn't help the smile that touched her lips. It would be just like Ben Bradford to continue to look out for his daughters, even when he really didn't have to. And she didn't need to know what would be served along with the pork chops. Her father was an excellent cook, and she was hungry enough to eat a whole tray of pork chops.

"Okay, can I expect you around four o'clock, then?"

"More like three, Dad. There's not much left to do here, and I gave Manning the rest of the afternoon off. He had a doctor's appointment."

"Okay, I'll see you around three. Then you can help me with the other stuff."

She shook her head, grinning. She knew the routine with Ben Bradford. He would start off giving her what he considered an easy chore, like making the salad or slicing the veggies to be steamed. And when she didn't do it just the way he liked, he would eventually send her out of the kitchen, suggesting she watch television until things were ready.

"Okay, Dad. See you at three."

Jules hung up the phone and slid her chair back to stand up and stretch. She licked her lips. Already she could taste her father's pork chops. He would have marinated them overnight, and there was no doubt in her mind they would be mouthwateringly tender.

Suddenly, she sensed another presence and glanced toward her door, thinking Manning had returned, although she'd told him not to. She drew in a sharp breath and stared wide-eyed for about two seconds, not sure she could believe what she was seeing. Standing in the doorway of her office was *him*. The man she had met that night at the club while she'd been working a case.

The man who had invaded her inner peace ever since.

And he was staring at her the same way he had that night. Looking at her with an intensity that she could actually feel. She drew in a shallow breath, wanting to break eye contact with him, but she couldn't. So, instead, she stiffened in automatic defense, while fighting for control of her senses and her body's reaction to him.

What was he doing here? She was trying to find her voice to ask him that very thing when he spoke. Flashing a roguish grin, he said, "I found you."

Thirty

Dalton never had a problem being attracted to most women. For him, it was a natural phenomenon. As natural to him as breathing. And he would admit he'd been attracted to some more than others. There were those who could make him hard on contact. But he would have to say that he was standing across the room from a woman who could do that and more. Never had he felt the need to brand a female. Claim her. Declare any and all rights to everything she had…especially that lush body in jeans and a tank top.

And her scent was pumping through his nostrils, making him want to walk across the room, strip her naked, lay her on that desk and…

"So you found me. Big deal."

Her words interrupted his thoughts. Just as well. He needed to get a grip. Get his mind and body back under control. She was standing there with her hands on her hips, staring him down while he was doing the same, wishing she would move from behind that desk so he could see more of her.

He crossed his arms over his chest, not caring that doing so made it damned obvious he had an erection. Solid as a rock, hard as nails, straining against the zipper of his pants. "It *is* a big deal. So what do I get in return for my effort?"

Lordy, who is this man? Jules asked herself. Not only did he look good all over, but he was arrogant as sin. Arrogance was not a trait she admired in a man, but she was finding it quite stimulating coming from him. "Who are you?"

He smiled, and the area between her legs began to sizzle with heated lust. "I'm not telling you who I am until you tell me who you are."

She frowned, not liking his response, but decided to answer anyway. "J. B. Sweet."

He chuckled. "That's your professional name. What's your real name?"

If he thought she would divulge that information, then he was crazy. She kept her real name confidential for a reason. "That's the only name you'll get."

He nodded. "Okay. Then the only name of mine you get is Dick."

The lashes shadowing her cheeks flew up. "Dick?"

"Yes." A trace of humor lit his eyes as if he knew where her thoughts had gone. "Short for Richard."

Yeah. Right. If he thought she believed that, then he had another think coming. "So, Mr. Dick, I think—"

"Just Dick."

She was convinced there was nothing "just Dick"

about him. He looked better than she remembered. That night it had been dark, but now she was seeing him in the brightness of day, and what she was seeing was making it hard for her to keep a firm grip on reality. "The office is technically closed for business until the beginning of the year. I would suggest that you try us again in January," she said.

He dropped his arms and stepped into the room. He looked powerful but not in a threatening way. More in a "lock up your feminine body parts" way, because he looked like the type to capture, claim and conquer… all in one tantalizing sweep. And why did the thought of him doing all three send erotic shivers up her spine?

"What if what I want can't wait until January?"

"Then I'm afraid there's nothing we can do."

He chuckled, and the sound was smooth and enticing, too appealing for her peace of mind. Of all the days he could have shown up, why today, when she'd already confirmed her body was suffering from sexual neglect? And him standing in her office was making the neglect that much more noticeable.

"There's plenty 'we' can do," he said, intruding into her thoughts. "Starting tonight. I've found you. Now it's your turn to find me. But I'll make it easy for you. I'll be at the place it all began. That same nightclub. At seven. I'll be there waiting." And then he turned and walked out.

It took Jules a minute to regain her composure, dropping into her chair when she heard the door close behind him. Was he crazy? She never actually thought he would find her. How had he managed it? She'd been so shocked at seeing him that she hadn't bothered to ask.

And did he actually think she would show up tonight? Seriously? What sane woman would do something like that? Meet a man she didn't really know for no telling what?

Jules took a deep breath. But the "what" was part of the puzzle she did know. There was no doubt in her mind what that man wanted. It was the reason he had found her and the reason he obviously thought he was entitled to have her.

She pushed back the chair from her desk to cross her legs when she felt that deep throb in her center. Sexual drama was the last thing she needed—she had to think logically. The man apparently had a strong sexual appetite. He had stood there the entire time with a hard-on and done nothing to hide it. It was obvious he wanted her to know he wanted her. Okay, so she knew. What now?

What now is that he wants you to meet him tonight at seven, a little voice in her head said. *And it won't be to chitchat. He would probably suggest the two of us go somewhere and get it on, tear each other's clothes off, scorch the sheets, enjoy orgasm after mind-blowing orgasm.*

She forced all those erotic thoughts to the back of her mind, thinking, *Who needs that?*

You do, that same voice taunted. Wasn't it just hours ago she'd complained of boredom? Well, with him, she wouldn't be bored, and there was no doubt in her mind he could provide the excitement she longed for. But should she risk it?

She could handle herself, so she wasn't worried about that, but what bothered her was his cockiness—he behaved as if he had her all figured out. And not just her, but women in general. He acted as if they were all easy pickings, just for his enjoyment. All he had to do was crook his little finger…or in her case, issue an edict as to where to meet him. As if the call was his to make.

Well, he would know who was in charge when she didn't show.

Shiloh glanced over her menu at Caden. "Everything looks delicious. Thanks for bringing me here."

"You're welcome. Have you decided what you're going to have?"

"Yes," she said quickly. "The Capricorn Chicken sounds good."

"It is. I had it the last time I was here."

She nodded. "You come here often?"

He shook his head. "I've only been here once with Jace and Dalton. We try to eat out every once in a while to give Hannah a break. She'd cook every day if we let her. We try telling her we're adults and can fend for ourselves, but you know Hannah."

Shiloh smiled. "Yes, I do know Hannah." Since she had been Caden's playmate, the older woman had been a part of her life almost as much as she'd been part of Caden's. "I like her. Always have."

Caden smiled. "And she likes you. Always has, too. She told me Sunday that she'd always known something was going on between us, even though we tried keeping it a secret."

Shiloh's eyes sparkled. "Really? How did she know?"

"She claims from the way my eyes would light up whenever your name was mentioned. Except for recent years, when I seemed so angry. She couldn't understand why."

She could hear the deep regret in his voice and reached across the table to take his hand in hers. "We said we would put that behind us, remember?"

He nodded and took a sip of his wine. "So what do you have planned for the weekend?"

She shrugged. "Work. The boutique is open half days on Saturday, and then I have some restocking to do."

"I can help you."

She wondered how much work she could get done with him around. "We'll see. Have you decided if you'll be our entertainment for this year's Live-It-Up Ball? Nannette called again today asking if you had made a decision."

A smile ruffled Caden's lips. "Yes, I'll be able to do it, and my band will back me as well that night. I confirmed with them yesterday."

Shiloh couldn't stop the grin that spread across her face. "That's wonderful, Caden. Thanks."

"For you, anything. Besides, it's for a good cause."

The waiter came and took their dinner order. After he left, Shiloh glanced over at Caden. "So what do you want to discuss? You said something about Jace and Shana having another theory about Saturday night."

Caden drew in a deep breath, not wanting to talk

about it now but knowing he had to, especially since Shana's sister wanted to talk to both of them at some point this week.

"You'll probably think this is as far-fetched as I do, but Jace and Shana don't want us to rule out the possibility that what happened Saturday night might have been an intentional act."

Shiloh almost choked on the sip of wine she'd just taken. "What?" she said, not believing what she'd just heard. "Are you serious?"

"As a heart attack. Jace mentioned it today. In fact, he's so serious about it that he wants me to talk to a private investigator about it. Give her the facts and let her dig into a few things."

"Wow," Shiloh said, shaking her head. "Why would anyone want to harm you?"

"As far as I know, there isn't one good reason. I don't have any enemies that I know of. There are people I know who still avoid my brothers and me because of Dad, but that's about it."

She nodded. "You're mainly talking about the Greenes, right?"

"Yes."

"Is that why you think they're acting strangely toward you?" Shiloh asked.

"What other reason could there be? I mentioned it to Jace, but he hadn't run into them and said not to give a damn about it, so I'm not."

She took another sip of her wine. "So, are you going to talk to this private investigator?"

"Yes. It's Shana's sister, so hopefully it won't be so

bad. And she wants to talk to you, too. To get your account of what happened that night."

"Sure, but I barely remember anything except that speeding car coming straight at you. I basically blocked out everything else, except for that guy knocking you out of the way."

Caden nodded. "I wonder if he recalls anything before knocking me out of the way."

"Not sure. But how can you find him to ask? He didn't leave any contact information."

"But today, my brother proved that a good private investigator can find just about anyone," Caden said, shaking his head. He then told Shiloh about the private investigator Dalton had hired to find a particular woman.

"I can't imagine Dalton doing something like that," Shiloh said when he'd finished.

"Neither can I, sweetheart. Neither can I."

"You're awfully quiet, Jules."

Jules glanced up at her father. "Am I?"

"Yes. You ate all your food, which meant you were hungry, but you were quiet as a mouse. You didn't interrogate me at all today."

She couldn't help but grin. "Do I really do stuff like that?"

"All the time. You would have made a good detective had you stayed on the force long enough."

She didn't say anything for a minute. Leaving the force to branch out on her own had been risky. But she believed in her ability to figure things out. And then there were her gut feelings about things, which also benefited her.

So why couldn't those same gut feelings come into play with the man who wanted to call himself Dick? The two of them were playing a game by not coming clean with their names. It added a sense of mystery, intrigue and suspense into the mix. At least she was no longer bored. She glanced at the clock on the wall. It was almost five o'clock.

"Have someplace to go?"

She shifted her gaze to her father. "Why do you ask that?"

A smile touched his lips. "You've been clock watching since you got here."

Have I? She shrugged. "I was invited to be somewhere at seven, but I'm not going."

"Oh. Okay."

She watched her father take a swallow of lemonade. That was what she liked most about her dad. She might interrogate him like he'd said, but he never interrogated her. If she told him something, he listened. If she asked for advice, he gave it. But he never pried into her affairs…not that she had any to pry into.

She leaned back in her chair. "So, are you ready for your trip to New York this weekend?" she asked, deciding to change the subject.

The smile that spread across his lips told her everything. "Yes, and I think Mona is, too. The tickets to the Broadway show we're seeing came in the mail last week, so yes, we're ready."

She then asked him the question she'd wanted to ask him since meeting Mona. "Dad?"

"Yes, sweetheart?"

"Do you think Mona will ever see again?"

He shrugged as he stood to begin cleaning off the table. "Not sure. But it doesn't matter."

"You sure?"

He glanced at Jules and sat back down. "I love her, Jules, and not having her eyesight means nothing to me. I will be her eyes if that's what I need to do."

Jules drew in a deep breath, deciding to broach something else with her father that she would admit bothered her when she knew it shouldn't. He was happy with Mona, and it was happiness he deserved to have. But…

"Spill it out, Juliet. There's something else that's bothering you about my involvement with Mona."

Yes, there is. "She's nice, and I like her."

"But? And I know there's a but. We wouldn't be having this conversation if there weren't."

He was right. "She's not Mom."

A small smile touched the corners of his lips. "No, she's not. Your mom was my life for years, and I knew I loved her the first time I saw her. We had good years together, and she gave me you and Shana. Our life was going great. We had plans for how we would live the rest of our life together. First we would get you girls through school, then college, and quickly marry you off to any man crazy enough to take the two of you off our hands," he said, grinning. "And then she and I would retire here, to the city where we met all those years ago, and live our life the way we wanted, doing whatever we pleased…with grandkids and two nice sons-in-law visiting with our daughters every once in a while."

At that moment, she saw the pain that came into his eyes. "No one will ever know how I felt that day when the doctor told us about her cancer and that she had less than a year to live. It was a death sentence, not just for her but for me, as well. I could not imagine going through life without her. But it was your mother who made me see that I didn't have a choice. I had two beautiful daughters who needed me. I promised her I would always be there for our girls. She died believing that and believing in me."

His voice had broken, and he was quiet for a moment as he leaned back in his chair. "She also told me that she didn't want me to go through the rest of my life alone and had the nerve to suggest that one day I should marry again. She said I had a lot of love to share, and that one day I would meet a woman who needed the kind of love that only Ben Bradford could give. I didn't want to believe it or accept what she was saying. I *didn't* accept what she said. I went through the years believing that my job and raising my girls were enough. Then my girls suddenly had lives of their own and, although at times I was lonely, I couldn't allow myself to open up a heart that still belonged to your mom. Until the day I saw Mona."

He drew in a deep breath. "I saw her that day, and it was then that I remembered your mother's words…that one day I would meet a woman who needed the kind of love she believed I could share. Mona is that woman. I will always love your mother, but Mona has carved out a special place in my heart, as well."

Jules didn't say anything for a moment as she fought back tears. She reached out and took her father's hand in hers. "Now I understand, Dad. And I am truly happy for you. You were the best dad ever for Shana and me, and we want you to be happy."

He nodded slowly. "Thank you. Hearing you say that means a lot. As far as Mona ever being able to see again, the doctors haven't given up on her, but they aren't making any promises, either. We take one day at a time and can only hope and pray."

He then stood. "And you better get going if you want to make your seven-o'clock appointment."

She blinked. "I never said I was going to try to make it."

Ben chuckled. "No, you didn't. But you're acting anxious about it, though at the same time, you're undecided. Not sure whether you want to keep it or not. And if it involves a man, I have all the faith in the world you can handle it. Maybe too well for your own good."

"Dad!"

"Well, it's true."

"You don't know this guy." *And neither do I,* she thought to herself.

"I don't have to know him. I know my daughter," Ben said, grinning. "And I can hope that one day you'll get to meet a nice guy, settle down and give me grandkids like Shana is."

Jules laughed. "Release the pressure, will you, Dad? First of all, I don't have a steady boyfriend, I seldom have time to date, and my tolerance level is low when it comes to the B.S. a lot of the guys put out. They don't make many Ben Bradfords anymore."

He chuckled. "The man for you is out there somewhere. And you'll know it when you meet him, although knowing you, you'll probably fight against it like hell."

She smiled as she stood. "You're probably right. I'll help you with those dishes."

"All I'm going to do is load them in the dishwasher, Jules. I think I can manage that without you, but thanks for the offer. What you need to do is decide what you're going to do about that seven-o'clock appointment."

Thirty-One

"Thanks for dinner, Caden," Shiloh said, looking up at him. "Sure you don't want to come in and stay awhile?"

"You're too much temptation," he said, leaning down and placing a kiss on her temple. "And I have a stack of documents I need to read for a departmental meeting early in the morning."

"You don't have to explain. I understand. Your work is important."

But nothing was more important in his life than she was, and he proceeded to tell her so. Afterward, he tightened his arms around her and held her for a while before leaning back to look down at her face again. A beautiful face that he would never tire of seeing.

"With Cal Arrington indicted for trade-secrets violations, we can turn our concentration to reclaiming the company's position in aerospace technology. I'm working to make sure that happens."

After they'd made love on Saturday night, he had

told her about the deathbed promise he and his brothers had made to their grandfather.

He leaned down and kissed her, needing the taste of her tongue mingling with his, mating hungrily, greedily. And when he deepened the kiss, she moaned, and the sound electrified everything within him. He loved her so damned much, and he intended to spend the rest of his life proving it. "Go away with me this weekend."

She lifted a brow. "To where?"

"It's a surprise."

She chuckled. "Then how will I know how to pack?"

"Don't. I'll buy everything you need when we get there."

She shook her head. "Caden, be serious."

"Sweetheart, I *am* serious. Just be ready when I pick you up Saturday morning around seven. Will you?"

She looked up at him. "I'll have to give Tess and the others notice that I'll be away, but I know they'll be able to handle things at the shop in my absence. They've done it before when I left on wine-buying trips, so it shouldn't be a problem."

"So, will you go away with me?" he asked, seeing the curiosity in her eyes. She had questions he wouldn't answer yet. And then, above all else, he saw trust in her gaze, and it touched him deeply. After all he had put her through, she could still trust him.

"Yes, I'll go away for the weekend with you."

Jules's cell phone rang the moment she walked into her house. Recognizing her sister's ringtone, she said, "Yes, Shana?"

"Jace's brother and Shiloh have agreed to talk to you about Saturday night."

She made her way into the kitchen to put the leftovers her father had sent her home with in the refrigerator. "Okay. I can do it on Wednesday. Tomorrow is already booked pretty solid, starting with a dental appointment at nine and ending with a day of beauty at the spa. I intend to get the works."

"Sounds like it. How did your day go today?"

"Not too badly," she said, going into the living room, where she kicked off her shoes and dropped down on her sofa. "I had to finalize documents like I usually do at the end of a case. And I had dinner with Dad."

"He told me. He called to see if Jace and I were free, but we'd already made plans to meet with a wedding planner and decided to grab something while we were out."

"Wedding planner? You're hiring a wedding planner when you're only inviting fifty people?"

"I would hire a wedding planner for ten people. Neither Jace nor I want the headache. If it were up to us, we would fly to Vegas and get it over with."

"And Dad would die at being cheated out of the opportunity to give you away," Jules said and laughed.

"Don't you know it," Shana replied, sharing her sister's amusement.

Jules's humor faded when she glanced over at the clock. It was a little after six. She gritted her teeth. Why was she letting sexual tension get the best of her?

"You okay?"

Good grief, had she made a sound? "Not really."

"What's wrong, Jules?"

She heard the concern in Shana's voice and drew in a deep breath. "He found me."

"Who found you?"

"That man I told you about weeks ago."

"The one you met at that nightclub when you were working undercover?" Shana asked. "How did he find you?"

"Not sure. But he did. Imagine my shock when I looked up and he was standing in the doorway of my office today."

"Your office? How did he get past Manning?"

"Manning left early today for a doctor's appointment and didn't lock the door. So the man came in."

"What did he say?"

"Stood there gloating that he'd found me. Then suggested I meet him tonight at that same club at seven."

"I take it that you're not planning to do that."

"No. Just who does he think he is?"

Shana chuckled. "The man evidently went to a lot of trouble to find you. And if I remember correctly, at the time when you told me about him, you said if he were to find you it meant he was truly interested."

Jules nibbled on her lower lip. She had said that, hadn't she? He was truly interested…but in one thing. Her body. "Well, I've changed my mind."

"Why?"

"I just have."

"Bull. You would not have changed your mind unless you had a reason, and I think I know what it is. I have a feeling you know he's a man you can't handle."

Jules frowned. "What do you mean?"

"Come on, Jules. You like being in control, and I have a feeling this guy is probably aggressive, arrogant and overconfident. Sounds a lot like you, kiddo."

Jules's frown deepened. "I don't like him."

"Why? Because you finally met a man who sounds like your equal? I have a feeling you find him intriguing but won't admit it."

"Okay, I find him intriguing. Big deal."

"But not intriguing enough to meet him at seven?"

Shana's words infuriated her. "Look, Shana. I need to get laid, in a bad way. But I'll be damned if I'll give this guy the honor. He's so damned conceited that he had the nerve to tell me his name was Dick."

Shana burst out laughing.

"Glad I could bring humor to your day again," Jules said curtly.

"Sorry. But I bet he assumes your name is J. B. Sweet."

"What of it?"

"Then the both of you are playing an interesting game that can backfire."

Jules rolled her eyes. "He knows that's not my real name, which is why he told me his was Dick."

She quieted for a couple of seconds before asking, "And you honestly think I should meet him tonight, Shana?"

"All kidding aside, I think you should do what feels right for you. Evidently, this guy bothers you on a lot of levels, so if I were you, I would go with my gut feelings. And if those feelings are telling you not to go, then don't. Look, I have to run. Jace is taking me to a movie tonight."

"Enjoy yourself."

"Thanks. No matter what decision you make about that guy, I'm sure it will be the right one. Goodbye."

"'Bye." Jules clicked off the phone. It was twenty past six. She frowned as she recalled parts of her conversation with Shana. Then she stood and began stripping off her clothes as she headed toward her bedroom. She would take a shower, get dressed and go meet *Dick.* Shana was wrong about her not being able to handle him. And when she finished *handling him,* he was going to wish he hadn't found her.

Dalton glanced at his watch. It was seven o'clock on the dot, and J. B. Sweet wasn't here. He tried to make light of it and figured she was running late like women had a tendency to do at times. Surely she wouldn't stand him up.

But what if she did?

He refused to consider that possibility. He was a man who knew women, and it was obvious there was sexual chemistry between them. Strong. Sizzling. Hot. And at her office today, he had recognized that look he'd seen in her eyes. She wanted him just as much as he wanted her.

He glanced at his watch again before looking at the door. He had chosen this particular table so he could see her when she came in, and so she could see him. Now it was a waiting game. And if she didn't show up…

Hell, he refused to consider that possibility. Instead,

he glanced around. The place wasn't packed, but there were a lot of single women there. Most were openly checking him out. But he wasn't interested. The only woman who interested him was the one he'd hired a private investigator to find. The look on her face when she'd seen him had been priceless.

He could recall the defiant look in her eyes when he'd told her to meet him here at seven. She hadn't liked it. Would her anger overrule her desire for him?

Dalton was about to check his watch again when he heard the door to the nightclub open. He glanced toward the entrance and almost fell out of his chair. Holy shit! It was her and what in the world was she wearing?

If he thought the last outfit was a heart-stopper, an erection-maker, then this one should be outlawed from public display. It reminded him of one of those skimpy dance outfits Beyoncé wore while performing. One that could tantalize the senses and invigorate your testosterone way beyond a normal level.

The short dress was made of skin-tone lace that left it hard to tell what was fabric and what was skin. It hugged her curves, cuddled her hips and embraced her small waist in a way that had every man in the club's jaw dropping and eyes bulging. Was she even wearing underwear?

And the high-heeled leather boots that went past her knees made her look like a sexy cowgirl, ready to ride. And he was more than willing to let her. The only thing missing was a hat. And she didn't need it. He preferred nothing covering up the mass of hair flowing over her shoulders.

After his eyes traveled the length of her once more, they retraced their way back up to her face. She angled her chin and stared at him. He tried to read her mood through the haze of desire clouding his senses and found doing so difficult.

And when she began walking toward his table, a jolt of sexual hunger shook him to the bone with every step she took. She was holding his gaze, and he couldn't look away even if he wanted to.

When she took the chair across from him, he let out a whoosh of air. If it was her goal to get attention, she had succeeded. All eyes were on her…and him. He swallowed and found his voice. "We're stirring up too much interest. I suggest we leave and go somewhere that will afford us more privacy."

She shook her head. "I only came here to give you some advice."

He frowned, not liking the sound of that. Advice wasn't what he wanted. "What kind of advice?"

She leaned closer over the table, and he got a whiff of her aroma. Damn, she smelled good. Her perfume was doing a number on him. His attention latched on to her lips, and his gut twisted. He couldn't wait to taste them.

"Forget you found me," she whispered.

"Afraid I can't do that" was his quick comeback.

"*Dick,* you don't have a choice."

A smile touched the corners of his lips, although he found none of what she was saying amusing. "So you want to play hard to get, is that it?"

She lifted her chin a notch. "I don't want to play at

all. At least not with you. You're conceited, arrogant and overconfident."

"Why? Because I went after something I want?"

Her gaze narrowed. "No, because you're egotistical enough to assume you will get it. And that's where you're wrong."

"You're certain about that?"

"Positive."

Blood pounded at his temples, and it was taking all his control to keep his rising anger at bay. "And you came all the way over here to tell me that?"

"Yes. I wanted to make sure you heard it from my own lips. Figured it would be worth the trip. I hope that we now understand each other."

She eased out of her chair and turned to leave, but he grabbed her arm, probably with a little more force than he'd intended. He could feel the way her muscles tensed under his touch. But at the moment he didn't care. No woman acted as if he were yesterday's garbage. Just who the hell did she think she was? "I *won't* come looking for you again."

She cracked a smile. "Trust me. I don't want it any other way." Then she strutted out of the club.

Thirty-Two

Dalton arrived at Granger the next morning in a foul mood and figured the best thing to do was keep his shitty attitude to himself and stay in his office. The less contact he had with anyone today, the better.

He would have booked off today if he hadn't had a ton of paperwork to review from Security. They had a new device they planned to install on all the computer hardware this weekend. Since Jace had made him top man of that department, his approval was needed on just about anything they did.

But he canceled the two other meetings he had scheduled that day, deciding to leave at lunch and not come back. He needed time to get his senses reprogrammed. Get his act together and forget about J. B. Sweet, or whatever her name was.

He went to the window and stared out. What in the hell was wrong with him? When had he let a woman, any woman, get to him this way? He was Dalton Richard Granger. He had his pick of women, always had.

Never had he been obsessed with one. And her parting words before strutting her curvy ass out of the club had left him cold and angry.

Dalton rubbed his hand down his face, admitting that last night his pride had taken a damned hit. Even the woman that he'd eventually left the club with last night and had fucked senseless hadn't done a thing for him. In his mind, she hadn't been *her*.

He heard the knock on his door and glanced around. "Come in."

His brother Jace came in smiling, but he took one look at Dalton and the smile faded. "I take it things didn't go like you wanted yesterday."

Dalton narrowed his gaze. "And how do you know about yesterday?"

Jace shrugged. "I'm only going by what you told us. You said the P.I. you hired had found the woman you've been looking for. Did he find the wrong woman?"

Dalton chuckled derisively. "No, he found the right one, but we don't mesh."

"So, in other words, she didn't put up with your bullshit."

Dalton immediately took offense. "What the hell are you talking about?"

"I'm talking about your holier-than-thou attitude with women at times. Like you're the Prince of Peace and Pleasure. A prize worthy to be claimed. A—"

"Who the hell are you to judge my way with women? How I deal with them is my business, not yours. When I need your advice, I'll ask for it. But then, maybe not.

Shit, you don't even have the sense to wear a damned condom when you fuck somebody."

Jace's anger flared. "You've said enough, Dalton."

"I haven't even fucking started."

They both turned when they heard the door slam. "What the hell is wrong with you two?" Caden asked, coming to stand in the middle of the room. "I could hear you out in the hall. Luckily, the woman who took Brandy's place wasn't at her desk. What's going on?"

Dalton drew in a deep breath. "Big brother is trying to get into my damned business again."

Jace frowned. "Is that what you think I was doing?"

"Weren't you? Trying to tell me how to handle my affairs. Have I ever tried telling either of you how to handle yours?"

"Yes," both brothers said simultaneously.

Dalton's frown deepened. "The two of you can go to hell." And he went back to stand at the window, dismissing both.

Caden glanced over at Jace. "What the hell is wrong with him?" he asked in a low tone.

"Evidently, things didn't go well with that woman he hired the private investigator to find."

"Oh." Caden shook his head. "Knowing him, he probably handled it wrong."

"That's what I tried telling him, but you know at times you can't tell him a damned thing."

Caden nodded. "He's taking it pretty hard."

"Obviously."

Dalton turned around, shoving his hands into his pockets. The expression on his face was fiercer than ever. "Is there a reason the two of you are still here? I have work to do."

"With your present attitude, you might want to work from home today," Jace suggested sternly. "There is a matter that Caden and I need to discuss with you, but we can do so at another time. When you're in a far better mood."

And then Jace and Caden left the office.

"The Wine Cellar Boutique. This is Shiloh."

"Good morning, Shiloh. This is Wallace. I wasn't sure you got my last message, and I didn't want you to think I'd forgotten about you."

Like I've forgotten about you? she thought to herself, feeling bad she hadn't called him back. "Yes, I got it, and sorry I haven't gotten back with you, but I've been busy." *Making up time with the man I love,* she bit back from saying.

"No problem. I was wondering if we can do lunch today. This is one of my rare days away from the hospital."

She considered turning down his invitation and just telling him that she was back in an exclusive relationship with Caden, but she thought telling him over the phone wasn't the way to do things. "Yes, I would love to have lunch with you. There's something I need to talk with you about anyway."

"There is?"

"Yes."

"Okay. How about lunch at Ricky's? I can pick you up at—"

"I prefer meeting you there," she interrupted. "Will noon be okay?"

"Noon is fine. I'll see you then."

She clicked off the phone. Moments later, she was about to go downstairs to check to see how things were going when her office phone rang again. "The Wine Cellar Boutique."

There was no response, but Shiloh could hear breathing on the other end. "Hello?"

When once again there was no response, Shiloh hung up, thinking it was probably someone who'd dialed the wrong number.

"So, what did you decide to do last night with that guy?"

Jules had expected her sister's call and was surprised Shana hadn't contacted her sooner. Luckily, she had left her dentist's office, finished her annual eye exam and come home to grab a quick lunch before heading out to spend the rest of the day at the spa.

"I figured you'd be waking me up early this morning," she said, placing her sister on speakerphone while she sat down at the kitchen table with the leftovers her father had sent her home with.

"I would have, but I had a doctor's appointment myself this morning. Jace went with me, and we could see the baby's heart beating on the ultrasound."

"Oh, Shana, that is wonderful. The doctor said everything's okay?"

"Yes. According to him, I'm doing fine. Jace and I are so happy we can't stand it. We can't wait until the wedding at the end of this month. We only have a few weeks to go. Of course, you will be my bridesmaid and Jace's brothers will be his best men."

"Sounds great. I hope I haven't eaten one pork chop too many and will look decent in the dress you want me to wear."

"You're going to look great. Now, back to my earlier question, did you or did you not meet up with that guy last night?"

Jules let out a deep breath. In a way, she was trying not to remember last night. "Yes, I met up with him. But I did it with a purpose in mind."

"What purpose?"

"To set his arrogant ass back a couple of notches."

"Jules, please tell me you didn't."

"Okay, I won't tell you."

Shana didn't say anything for a minute. "You'll never find anyone if you keep running them off."

"First of all, he wasn't a keeper. All he wanted out of me was one thing. Hell, I hadn't sat down before he was suggesting that we leave and go somewhere. Probably a hotel."

Jules took a sip of her lemonade. "But I told him to forget he found me. In other words, I let him know I wasn't interested. You should have seen the look on his face. You would think he'd never been turned down by a woman."

"He looked that hot?"

"I admit, even hotter. But I refuse to put up with bullshit, and he was full of it last night. I hope when they made him they not only broke the mold but threw it away."

"Wow. I guess he didn't make an impression on you."

"No, not a positive one. In a way I wish he had, though. Going without sex is killing me."

"Hmm, too much information. Got to go now. And by the way, Caden said he and Shiloh can meet with you tomorrow evening. We can do it here, at my place, around five."

"That's a good time, and your place is a good central location. I'll see you then."

Jules clicked off the call and finished off the rest of her meal while trying not to think about Dick, or whatever his real name was. But if she was completely honest with herself, even when she'd come home and stripped out of the hot little outfit she'd worn just for him to see what he wouldn't be getting, her mind had been filled with thoughts of him. Despite his attitude, she had still given him his dues in the looks department.

At least she didn't have to worry about him showing up at her office again. She knew about men, especially the conceited types. They didn't appreciate it when a woman burst their egotistical bubble by letting them know what they really thought. It was sad when women convinced them they owned a golden dick or something.

Well, she thought, getting up from the table to put her plate in the sink and discard her trash, *at least I don't have to worry about ever seeing him again. Good riddance.*

* * *

"I take it Dalton took your advice and went home," Caden said, coming into Jace's office.

Jace leaned back in his chair. "Hell, I hope so. He was in a damned bad way this morning. I don't know what that woman said or did to him, but he was fit to be tied."

Caden nodded. "You know Dalton. Sometimes he acts as if women, like everything else he comes in contact with, are an entitlement."

"I thought he was getting better with that."

"He is, but he still has room for improvement. I guess you can say he's a work in progress." Caden didn't say anything for a short while and then added, "But I wouldn't trade him for the world."

Jace chuckled. "Me neither." He then sat up in his chair and studied his brother. "I take it things are going well with you and Shiloh."

Caden smiled, thinking how well things were going. "Yes. I know there are a lot of questions still out there regarding whether what happened on Saturday night was intentional or an accident. But you know what I think about it?"

"No. What?"

"I almost lost my life that night, but I consider it a blessing because I *really* did get my life back, Jace. Shiloh has been and always will be my life, and I got her back."

Jace didn't say anything for a moment as he thought about what Caden had said, the implications he had made. "I am happy for you."

"Thanks. But Sedrick doesn't think what happened Saturday night was either an accident or an attempt on my life."

Jace raised a dark eyebrow. "Then what does he think?"

"He told Shiloh he believes the whole thing was staged by me to play on her sympathy to get her back."

"You're kidding."

"I kid you not."

Jace shook his head. "I'm surprised Sedrick would say something like that."

"I'm not. He's been acting wishy-washy lately. He was all caring, concerned and sympathetic at the hospital when Granddad died, but that night at Shiloh's open house, he hung with the Greenes, and they all shot me dirty looks like I was a piece of shit on the floor."

Jace frowned. "The Greenes?"

"Yes, you probably remember them from years back. Michael and Yolanda Greene."

Caden missed the flare of resentment that flashed in Jace's eyes when he said, "I remember them."

"Michael Greene used to work here, years ago."

"I remember that, as well," Jace replied, trying to keep his voice neutral.

"Ivan Greene, present mayoral candidate, is their son, and they have two daughters, Kerrie and Deidra."

Jace didn't say anything for a minute. "I recall Sedrick and Kerrie dating back in the day."

"Yes, I'd forgotten about that. Shiloh reminded me."

"Going back to what you said earlier about the

Greenes and Sedrick shooting you dirty looks," Jace prompted.

"Yeah, man. It was strange. I've never done anything to them, but you would think they resented me for some reason. If looks could kill, I would have been dead that night."

Jace built a steeple with his fingers as he thought about what Caden had said. "You're right. That *is* strange."

"But, of course, I didn't give a damn."

"I'm sure you didn't. And by the way, everything is set for tomorrow evening at Shana's place. You and Shiloh are invited to dinner, and Jules will be there, too. We'll all enjoy a nice meal, and then afterward, Jules will ask you and Shiloh some questions about Saturday night."

"Okay, that will work. What about Dalton? Have you mentioned that other possibility about Saturday night to him yet?"

"No. I went into his office to do so this morning, and you know how that turned out. His balls have taken a kicking, so I'll let him get over it before telling him anything. He needs to come to terms with the fact that he doesn't take rejection well."

"I agree. And just so you know, I'm taking Shiloh away this weekend."

"Where are you going?"

Caden then shared with his brother his plans for the weekend.

A smile spread across Jace's face. "She's definitely going to be surprised."

Caden nodded as he returned his brother's smile. "I'm counting on it."

"Bruce, what do you have for me?" Shana asked, relaxing in her office chair. The man she considered a technological genius had taken Brandy's hard drive to have a look at it after Dalton had reported a video showing Brandy searching around in his office and taking pictures. Now Brandy was dead from an apparent suicide, although her mother was still crying foul play. Shana would admit it seemed pretty coincidental to her.

"I went through the hard drive twice and couldn't find a thing. No suspicious inside emails or documents, nor were there any questionable outside emails. If she was forwarding information to anyone, it wasn't on this particular computer. I can't even see that she visited any other websites while at work."

Shana found that odd. Most people at some point in time, whether at work or not, would surf the Net. Brandy was a smart dresser, and it was hard to believe she never was tempted to go check out a few online sales during company time.

"If I didn't know any better, I'd think her hard drive had been given a complete wipe somehow."

Shana thought about what he had said. "Is that possible?"

"Yes, but that would take real calculation on someone's part. No one would know unless they suspected someone was onto them. A complete wipe is done when the original hard drive goes to its original state. The process was ruled illegal back in the nineties, when some company in Arizona was wiping hard drives clean so they couldn't be used as evidence in court cases involving child pornography. When the prosecution got ready to present their cases, all their digital evidence had disappeared."

Shana recalled reading about something like that in college. "Is there any way you can tell if the hard drive you took off her computer has been wiped clean?"

"Yes, it's doable, although it will take quite some time. There's only one company that I know of in Japan that can do it. I'll check into it."

"Thanks, Bruce."

Shana thought about all Bruce had said, and then she placed a call to Marcel. "Marcel, this is Shana. Have you heard anything else on the Brandy Booker suicide?"

"No, other than that the parents are on opposite sides of the fence with this one. While her mother doesn't believe it was suicide, I understand her father does. It seems he heard from Brandy on Friday night, and she sounded depressed and said things weren't going for her the way she hoped. She told her father that she needed to get away for a while, which is why she took that trip to D.C. Her friend from high school who owns the house was out of the country. She'd always told Brandy she was welcome to visit anytime and had left instructions about where to find the key."

"No security cameras in the complex?"

"No. A lot of the tenants are politicians who want to enjoy their privacy."

Or who want to engage in activities they wouldn't want captured on film, Shana thought. "So the D.C. authorities are still ruling the death a suicide?"

"Yes, since everything seems to lead that way."

"And they aren't taking what she said in the suicide note into account?"

"No. Her best friend, the one who owns the condo, says Brandy was referring to her in the note. She claims that over the years, because of their close friendship, she and Brandy had begun to think of each other as sisters. And since that's where Brandy supposedly chose to end her life, everyone figures Brandy is apologizing for that."

"Is Brandy's mother buying that reasoning?"

"Not really. But there's nothing else for anyone to go on. Did Bruce find anything on her computer?"

"No." She then told Marcel about Bruce checking to see if perhaps the hard drive had been deliberately wiped.

"Good luck with that. Even if he determines that's the case, it will be hard to prove, and trying to find out what was erased will be close to impossible."

A smile touched Shana's lips. "You know Bruce. He thrives on challenges, and I have a feeling he's going to have fun with this one."

Thirty-Three

Dalton sighed heavily as he tossed the papers he'd been reading onto his coffee table and leaned back against his sofa. Damn, he needed to get away for a while. This was probably the longest he'd stayed in one place for years. He missed England and would fly there this weekend if his arrival wouldn't cause speculation and get the rumor mill rolling.

Victoria's wedding announcement had been in last week's paper. If he were to return to England now, some would assume he was back to reclaim his place in her life. He wouldn't give them the satisfaction of such drama. Victoria deserved better.

He stood, stretched and walked barefoot into the kitchen for a beer. He was glad Jace had suggested he get out of the office. His mood and attitude had been crap. Now he had reclaimed his senses. Sort of. He was still pissed about yesterday but refused to let any woman bring him down. There were too many out there to get fucked up by just one.

In fact, he intended to go out later and have one hell of a good time with a woman he'd met just that day. After leaving the office, he had stopped by McQueen's for brunch and had met her then. She'd been leaving when he had been arriving. He had convinced her to hang around for a few more minutes, which hadn't been hard to do. Nor had it been hard to get her to go out with him tonight.

He had popped the top off his beer and was about to take a swig when his cell phone rang. The ringtone indicated it was Jace. He clicked on. "I don't need you checking up on me, Jace."

"I wasn't. Just calling to say Brandy's funeral plans have been finalized. The services will be held Friday morning. I thought you and I could make plans to attend."

"What about Caden?"

"He's taking Shiloh away for the weekend, and they're flying out Friday morning. So, will you go?"

"Yes, I'll go. Brandy was okay. I still can't imagine her taking her own life. Did Shana's computer guy find anything?"

Jace told Dalton what Bruce had reported. "Even if he discovers the hard drive was wiped clean, will he be able to tell what was removed?" Dalton asked.

"Probably not. But at least we'll know someone is trying to cover up something."

"I think that's obvious with the video showing her snooping around in my office. I would love to know what she was looking for."

"So would I. And by the way, we're having dinner at

Shana's this evening. She wanted to make sure I issued you an invitation. I've already told Caden and Shiloh, and they will be there. And Shana's sister, Jules, will be dining with us, as well. This will give you a chance to meet her."

"Thank Shana for the invite, but I've already made plans for the evening. I happen to have a date with a woman I met when I dropped by McQueen's after leaving the office today. I'll have to meet Shana's sister some other time," Dalton said, taking a swallow of beer.

"Okay, I'll tell Shana. And enjoy your date."

"Trust me. I intend to."

Jules glanced at the two couples as she sipped her wine. Dinner had been great, and since she knew her sister was no more of an ace in the kitchen than she was, she figured Shana had had the meal catered. Everything had been delicious, and Shana was the perfect hostess. Jace was forever by her side, helping whenever needed. They would make a good team, and Jules was happy for them.

Then there was Jace's brother Caden and the woman he was undoubtedly in love with, Shiloh Timmons. The love was obvious from the way he would look at her and touch her when there really was no need to do so, as if he needed to verify she was there in the flesh. Just like he was doing right now.

Jules wondered what Caden and Shiloh's story was and had a feeling there was one. That was one of the pitfalls of being a P.I. It was easy to get investigator inquisitiveness. She was sure her curiosity about them would be answered during her inquiry. Jace had mentioned his other brother—the youngest, whose name was Dalton—had a date tonight and couldn't make it.

"I know all of you have work tomorrow, so I'll begin asking my questions now, if you don't mind," Jules said, when it was apparent everyone was getting too relaxed. That was one of the downsides of a good dinner. You had a tendency to become content and sleepy, and she needed Caden and Shiloh very much alert when she began asking questions.

"All right," Caden said, taking Shiloh's hand and moving closer to where Jules sat in a wingback chair. Caden sank down on the sofa, and Shiloh eased onto on the floor by his feet to lean back against his legs. He leaned forward slightly to place his hands on her shoulders. Jace and Shana sat on the love seat, and Jace wrapped his arm around Shana's shoulders. Both couples, Jules noted, had gotten rather comfortable and cozy.

"I will need the two of you to remember everything about Saturday night, even something you might not think is important," she said, addressing Caden and Shiloh.

"Okay, ask away," Caden said. "But just so you know, Shiloh and I talked about it on the way over here, and we still feel that what happened Saturday night was nothing more than an accident."

Jules stood to pull a mini-recorder from the back pocket of her jeans. Before turning it on, she asked their permission to record the conversation, and they agreed.

"Tell me exactly what happened that night, Caden, leading up to your near-fatal accident."

Out of the corner of her eye, she saw Jace flinch. It was easy to see that the thought of nearly losing his brother still bothered him deeply.

In a clear voice, Caden told her that he'd left Shiloh's grand-opening celebration and had walked out through the courtyard to go to his car. He explained what had happened after that, detailing how he'd heard Shiloh scream his name just in time to turn and see a vehicle speeding toward him. It seemed the car was mere inches from hitting him when he was knocked to the ground and out of the car's path. He'd had the breath zapped from him and was thankful for the man who happened to be walking by that night.

Jules then heard Shiloh's version, which pretty much lined up with what Caden had said. "When did you realize Caden was in trouble?"

Shiloh's eyebrows drew together, and Jules could tell she was thinking really hard. "I didn't notice anything at first, mainly because I was mad."

Jules arched a brow. "Mad?"

"Yes, at Caden. We'd had a disagreement. I watched him cross the street. I saw the driver of the car when he turned on his lights and pulled from the curb. But I figured he would stop because Caden had the right of way when crossing the street."

Shiloh paused a moment, remembering. "It was only when I noticed that the sound of the engine had grown loud and the car had picked up speed that I knew the driver was probably drunk. He had to be not to see

Caden. I recall glancing at the car, and in that quick second, I saw Caden and knew that if the car didn't stop, it would hit him."

"Can you recall whether the driver was male or female?"

"I think male, but I'm not sure. All I remember is that my throat froze and I was afraid I wouldn't be able to warn Caden to look out," Shiloh said.

Jules watched as Caden took her hand in his and held it tight. These two Grangers were men who didn't mind touching the women they loved. She'd never considered herself a romantic person by any means but would admit that seeing such affection warmed her.

"What about you, Caden? Do you recall seeing the driver?" she asked.

He shook his head. "No. The bright headlights coming toward me were blinding, and that's all I saw. I literally froze in my tracks, like a deer caught in the headlights. If it hadn't been for that Striker guy pushing me out of the way, I know I wouldn't be here now."

"And this guy, who identified himself as Striker, happened to be walking by?"

"Yes, and I'm glad that he was. Talk about perfect timing."

"Do you know how to contact him if I need to ask him a few questions?"

"Unfortunately, no. He left before I could get his contact information," Caden replied.

"And do you know his full name?"

"No, he just said Striker. He said his friends call him

Lucky Strike but, for me, he was more than simple luck. I'm convinced he was a godsend."

Jules didn't say anything for a minute and then said to Shiloh and Caden, "The two of you are so convinced it was an accident and not intentional. Why?"

Shiloh shrugged her shoulders and leaned forward somewhat. "I just assumed it was an accident. I guess the reason I don't think it was intentional is because I don't know of anyone who'd want to deliberately hurt Caden." She glanced up at Caden, and a smile touched her lips when she added, "He's such a lovable guy."

Caden released a husky chuckle. "I think I'm a lovable guy, as well." Amusement faded from his face when he said, "Although at Shiloh's party that night, I got a few hateful stares."

Jules lifted a brow. "Really? From whom?"

"Mainly the Greenes."

"Who are the Greenes?" Jules asked, watching how Shiloh leaned back against Caden's legs again.

"Michael, Yolanda and their son, Ivan. They also have two daughters, Kerrie and Deidra, who live in another state somewhere," Caden replied, as his hands left Shiloh's shoulders to spread down her arms.

Jules watched as Shiloh lifted her hand to Caden and he took it, placed a kiss in the palm of it and smiled down at her. She thought what had just transpired between the two was incredibly romantic. "Ivan Greene? The one who's running for mayor?" Jules asked, while thinking that her sister and Shiloh were two lucky women.

"Yes, one and the same," Caden replied. "His father,

Michael Greene, used to work for Granger years ago in the information-systems department. Not sure why he left. I was in my early teens but remember them because one of their daughters—Kerrie, I believe—was a classmate of Jace's. I seem to recall that she came to school one day saying that her dad didn't work for our company anymore and that it was all my dad's fault."

Jules glanced over at Jace and saw how his expression had hardened. There was something about the Greenes that bothered her future brother-in-law, and she intended to find out what. "I assume this was before your father went to prison?" she asked, addressing both of the brothers.

It was Jace who answered. "Yes, that's right. Less than a year before."

She was glad it was Jace who'd responded. She had a feeling he knew more about what had happened with the Greenes than Caden did. "Is that why the Greenes were giving Caden hateful stares, Jace?" Jules asked, meeting his gaze directly. "Fifteen years is a long time for a family to hold a grudge because someone lost his job. Could there be another reason?"

Jace hesitated a moment and then said, "No."

Jules had a feeling there *was* something else, but she wouldn't push. But on the other hand, she'd been asked to see if an attempt had been made on Caden's life, and that was what she was trying to do. And to be successful, she needed everyone to be totally honest with her.

"What time did the Greenes leave the party?"

Shiloh's face went blank for a minute. "I don't know.

I never saw them leave, but then, I didn't notice a number of other people leave, either."

Jules returned her attention to Caden. "Was it one or all of the Greenes who were showing some level of animosity toward you?"

"It was all three of them, which was strange. I hardly know those people, so I don't know what their problems are with me specifically, or with the Grangers as a whole."

Jules switched her glance to Jace and decided to call him out. "But you do."

She and Jace held each other's gazes for a minute before she said, "The only way I can be effective in determining whether Saturday night was an accident is for me to know everything, Jace. And I mean *everything*."

Jace drew in a deep breath and broke eye contact with her to glance over at Caden. "One night, while we were working late, Shana and I discovered a secret compartment inside the sofa in Dad's office."

"A secret compartment inside the sofa? In Dad's office?" Caden asked, to make sure he'd heard correctly.

"Yes."

Jules wondered if she was the only one wondering why Jace and Shana were in Sheppard Granger's office one night while working late, and how they'd managed to find a secret compartment in his sofa.

"And what was in the secret compartment?" Jules asked.

"Photographs that Yolanda Greene sent to my dad."

"Photographs?" Caden asked. "Why would she send him photographs?"

Jace paused a moment and said to Caden, "The photographs were proof that her husband was having an affair with our mother."

Thirty-Four

It was obvious that Jace's revelation had shocked Caden to the point that he couldn't speak for a moment. He simply sat there and stared at his brother. When he finally spoke, he said, "That's bullshit."

"I wish it were, Caden, but that's the reason Michael Greene was terminated from Granger. I don't know when Yolanda Greene found out about the affair, but she hired a private investigator who proved her suspicions…if the pictures are anything to go by."

Caden didn't say anything for a minute, as if allowing what Jace had said to sink in. "You told Dad about finding the file?"

"Yes, and I asked him why he let the prosecution make it appear as if *he* was the one having an affair. All those hotel receipts they attributed to Dad with the initials S.G. had been Mom's receipts, not Dad's."

"What did he say? Why didn't he provide that information during his trial?" Caden asked in a frustrated tone.

"He knew they couldn't pin anything on him, because

he didn't *have* an affair," Jace said. "But he reasoned that had they found out about Mom, the prosecution would have gone after another motive—saying he killed Mom for being unfaithful."

"I can hardly believe this."

"Another reason he didn't say anything about Mom's affair was to protect her reputation in the media. She was our mother, and he didn't want us to have to contend with that."

Jules sat listening to the exchange between the brothers. From their conversation, it sounded very much as if Sheppard Granger was an honorable man. She could see her own father doing something similar to protect his daughters, just the way Sheppard had protected his sons.

"What about Yolanda Greene?" Caden asked. "She had a reason to kill Mom. Why didn't Dad's attorney come up with a defense strategy and put reasonable doubt in the jurors' minds by suggesting that Mrs. Greene could have done it out of jealousy?"

"Because the Greenes had proof they were on a cruise when Mom was murdered."

"How convenient," Caden said curtly.

"They took the cruise together as a way to repair their marriage. According to Dad's attorney, their story checked out, and he confirmed their alibi."

While Jules sat quietly and listened attentively, her mind was racing. When Shana had first mentioned she had been hired by Granger Aeronautics, she had checked the company out and learned about Sheppard Granger serving time for his wife's murder. The case had looked pretty cut-and-dried, especially since his fingerprints had been on the murder weapon.

It was alleged he was having an affair, although the prosecution was never able to discover the name of the mystery woman, nor did Sheppard ever reveal anything. He also claimed the hotel receipts in question were his own.

From what she was hearing, the receipts and the affair were all Sheppard's wife's doing. And he had taken the rap just so his sons' image of their mother wouldn't be tarnished.

"When you found out about Mom, why didn't you tell me, Jace? Didn't you think I had a right to know?" Caden was now upset *and* angry.

"Yes, I knew both you and Dalton had a right to know, but Dad forbade me to tell you. Although I said I understood his feelings, I told him I couldn't promise."

Caden nodded. "Dad didn't want us to know the truth about Mom." He shook his head. "Can you imagine how Dalton is going to react if he ever finds out? He was closer to Mom than the two of us and he thought she walked on water."

"I know, but he has to be told. I'd rather he hear it from us than anyone else," Jace said.

"You think there are others who know about this, apart from the Greenes?" Caden asked.

"I'm not sure."

"I believe there are," Shiloh said, adding to the discussion. "Saturday night at my party, shortly after you arrived, I was talking to Harold and Helen Owens, an older couple who're known around town for their lavish parties."

Caden nodded. "I remember them and I recall you were talking to them when I first approached you."

"Well, when they saw you they began talking, and one of the things they said was that your mom had been involved in an affair. I spoke up and told them I'd never heard that before, repeating what everyone had believed back then—it had been your father who was the adulterer. Mr. and Mrs. Owens both looked at me and then quickly changed the subject."

"Well, if Helen Owens knew something, then there are others who know, too. One thing I recall about her is that she liked to gossip," Jace said.

Jules knew it was time to intervene. It was getting late, and she needed to make sense of why the Greenes disliked the Grangers. That information would help her determine whether it was connected to what had happened to Caden on Saturday night.

"But it doesn't make sense for the Greenes to hold any animosity toward you and your brothers, Jace. From what you said, I would think Mr. Greene would feel some sort of shame and not anger. And if Mrs. Greene should be angry with anyone, it should be toward her husband and your mother."

Jules drew in a deep breath before saying, "And Ivan Greene's attitude is baffling. Even if he knew about his father's affair with your mother, surely he realized you and your brothers were young. You were just in your teens and had no control over the actions of your mother or your father."

"Honestly," Caden said, "I don't know what to think about all this, but I can say I was not imagining things on Saturday. Shiloh picked up on it, as well."

Jules glanced at Shiloh. "Has there ever been anything going on between you and Ivan? If so, could he be jealous?"

Shiloh shook her head. "Caden asked me the same thing on Saturday night, and the answer is no. I've never been involved with Ivan . He's come into the wine boutique to make a few purchases, but he's barely said two words to me."

"What about with you, Caden?" Jules asked. "Has there been any jealousy toward you from other music professionals or band members? What about the women you dated in the past? Do any of them have a beef with you?"

Caden shook his head. "There has never been any jealousy. I get along with my band members and fellow musicians. As far as women are concerned," he said, glancing down at Shiloh, "I've only loved one woman. However, while we were apart, I did have lovers but I always made sure they understood up front it was for sex and nothing more."

"And none of them had a problem with that?" Jules asked, watching the looks exchanged between him and Shiloh. She wasn't sure of their history, but imagined their separation must have taken a toll on them.

"No, none had a problem with it." He then paused a moment and a frown settled on his features. "However, there was someone named Rita."

Jules lifted a brow. "Rita?"

"Yes, Rita Crews. She was a member of my band for a time. A damned good guitarist. She and I had a no-strings affair for a few months earlier this year. But she began getting possessive—she even had a couple of altercations with fans who she thought were giving me too much attention. I ended up letting her go."

"You fired her?"

"My manager fired her, but she knew I was behind it."

"When was this?"

"Around four months ago. I haven't seen her since. She tried calling a few times, but I wouldn't take her calls."

Jules nodded. "You said she was a good musician. Has she hooked up with another band?"

"Not sure. I would think so, but I don't know. It will be fairly easy for me to find out."

"Please do."

"Surely, you don't think Rita had something to do with Saturday night," Caden protested.

Jules stood to disconnect her tape recorder. "I still can't say whether it was intentional or accidental. But given there aren't any bars in the area, unless the driver parked while intoxicated—or attended your party, Shiloh, then—"

"My party?" Shiloh asked with expressive eyes.

"Yes. I hope no one left the party drunk, but it's possible. Did you notice anyone drinking excessively?"

"No, not at all."

Jules nodded. "It would be helpful if I could get a list of the invitees."

"Not everyone who came received an invitation," she said, smiling over at Caden. Returning her gaze to Jules, she added, "But I will give you the list I have. And there are video cameras inside the shop, and they were turned on that night."

"Perfect. Are there any cameras in the courtyards?"

"Yes, but none facing the streets."

"I'd like to view what you have if I may."

"By all means. You can stop by anytime to pick them up," Shiloh said.

"Would tomorrow be okay?"

"Absolutely. Tomorrow is just fine."

Jules released a deep breath. "I wish I could have checked for tire prints on the road to see if there were skid marks. That would tell me whether the person had lost control of the vehicle. It's too late for that now. But I do have a friend with the Charlottesville police department. I'd like to see whether any vehicles were caught on camera speeding through that intersection during the time frame we're looking at. The video camera from the traffic light should shed some light on that. There are a few other things I want to check out, as well."

"So, do you have any initial thoughts right now?" Jace asked.

"It's too soon to say just yet. I still have a lot of unanswered questions and I need to do more investigating."

Jules glanced over at Caden. "In the meantime, I wouldn't take anything for granted. In other words, watch your back."

* * *

Caden couldn't help noticing that Shiloh was quiet on the drive home from Shana's place. He wondered whether bringing up the situation with Rita had anything to do with it.

He walked her to her door and wondered if he would be invited in. He hoped so, because they needed to talk. He was aware that the idea of his involvement with other women during their breakup was something that had bothered her. But, as much as he regretted it, it had happened, and they needed to be able to move on. Together. Just as he'd told her a number of times, and like he'd told Jules tonight, he'd truly loved only one woman.

She had told him earlier that day about her lunch with Dr. Aiken and how she'd been honest with him about Caden. She said he was very gracious and had wished both of them the best, and he said he was glad she was happy.

Caden intended to make sure she stayed that way.

"Jules asked a lot of questions tonight," he finally said, breaking the silence as they stepped off the elevator.

"Yes, that's probably the only way she's going to find out the truth." They stopped in front of her door, and she dug into her purse for the key.

"We're still on for this weekend?" he inquired, needing to make sure, since he couldn't read her thoughts or her mood.

She lifted her gaze to his. "Yes. Why wouldn't we be?"

He shrugged. "You've gotten all quiet on me."

She didn't say anything for a moment and then drew a quivering breath. "Because before tonight there was never any reason for me to assume what happened last weekend was anything but an accident. But now…"

Deciding he didn't want to discuss anything in the hallway, he took the key from her hand and opened the door. Closing the door behind them, Caden leaned against it and watched as she put her purse on the table and kicked off her shoes before dropping down onto the sofa.

Locking the door, he moved toward the sofa and sat beside her. Reaching out, he lifted her into his arms and placed her on his lap, tucking her head beneath his chin. He loved the way she felt in his arms. He loved her scent. He loved every single thing about her.

"I don't want you to worry about anything, Shiloh. Personally, I still believe it was an accident."

She drew back and tipped her head to look at him. "But what if it wasn't, Caden? What if that woman who used to be in your band is getting back at you? You said she'd had several run-ins with fans over you. That lets me know she had a mean, jealous streak. And a jealous woman will do just about anything."

He shook his head, wishing he'd never had to mention Rita in the first place. "First of all, we shouldn't jump to any conclusions. For all we know, Rita could have been performing in L.A. or somewhere else on Saturday night. I'll call around and see what she's up to. In the meantime, I don't want you worrying about anything."

He paused a moment and said, "When you got quiet

on the ride home, I thought my mentioning Rita had upset you."

Shiloh drew in a deep breath. "No, I'm over that, Caden. No matter who you might have been with in the past, you're with me now, and that's all that matters. I'm yours, and you're mine. I love you."

Caden felt as if he couldn't breathe, because when he stared down into her eyes, he could plainly see all the love she'd spoken of. He didn't think he could love her any more than he did at that exact moment. It took him a moment to gather his composure to say, "And I love you, sweetheart."

Their gazes locked and held as he continued to feel their love and hope she felt it, as well. She had once been his playmate, then his best friend, his lover and now the woman who had his heart.

He reached down and raked his hands through her hair, loving the texture of the luxuriant softness. Then he moved his hands to caress the back of her neck. She was tense, and he could feel it. Making her relive Saturday night at Shana's had done a job on her. And like he'd told her, he didn't want her to worry about anything.

He held her gaze, looking into a pair of dark, beautiful eyes, while his hands continued to trace the contours of her neck. Years ago, when they'd been forbidden to speak to each other, they had begun communicating with their eyes whenever they would pass in the hallways at school, or when he'd been standing off somewhere with his group and she'd stood with hers. And they were silently communicating now, purposely building heat between them.

He leaned down and took her mouth, kissing her softly yet hungrily, not understanding how he could do both. When he heard her moan, he deepened the kiss, increasing the tongue play in a way that conveyed just how much he desired her. He almost trembled with the depth of that need.

His stomach tightened, and his erection throbbed at the feel of her breasts pressing against his chest. He could feel the hardened nipples through her blouse, and it made his penis thicken even more. She was kissing him back, ravaging his mouth as much as he was ravaging hers. Flaming his passion, stroke after sensuous stroke of her tongue. He heard raw, undiluted desire in her moans, and they continued to set his own desire ablaze.

She pulled back, breaking off the kiss, and he saw more than burning passion in her eyes. He saw fire, hot and blazing, and it was burning him all over, urging him to strip off his clothes right then and there. And when she leaned in and traced the lines of his beard and mustache with the tip of her tongue, he pulled her back into his arms and hungrily kissed her again.

This time, he was the one who broke off the kiss. Lifting her off his lap, he stood and eased her to her feet. "I want you, Shiloh. Now. Here."

Spurred by a frantic need to make love to her, he began tearing off his clothes. She followed his lead and stripped off hers. The sight of her naked flesh pushed his desire to the limits. Reaching out, he pulled her to him and began raining kisses over her face, her neck, chin and throat, and then laying claim to her breasts. Sliding a nipple between his lips, he held it hostage while licking the torrid bud with his tongue, then sucking on it hard.

"Caden!"

His name on her lips had him lifting her into his arms and stretching her out on the sofa. He began licking her all over as her intoxicating scent and taste stirred his primitive maleness and his heart rate increased with anticipation. By the time he reached her womanly core, she had tilted her hips upward to receive his mouth. His greedy tongue slid inside of her, and immediately he was bombarded with sensations that rammed through every part of his body. It was always that way whenever he tasted her here, and he used his tongue and nibbling teeth to pleasure her, stunned by the force of his greed for her.

He cupped her hips, locked his mouth on her and went wild over her taste. She groaned and pushed against his lips, while he plowed her with kisses that were long and deep.

"No more. Please. I can't take any more."

He was just getting started. Caden lifted his mouth and eased off the sofa to grab his pants to retrieve a condom packet from the pocket. While she watched him, he rolled the condom over his hard erection.

"I like seeing you do that."

He glanced over at her. "Why?"

She smiled. "I like seeing what I'm going to get."

His gaze raked over her naked body, spread out on the sofa. He had licked and massaged every inch of her. "I like seeing what I'm going to get, as well."

He moved back to the sofa and eased his body over

hers, fitting perfectly in the vee of her thighs and liking the feel of his erection pressing against her legs. He leaned in and kissed her once more, this time beginning with a slow, languorous connection, taking his time to enjoy her and letting her enjoy him. He could feel a tingling sensation starting at the base of his shaft and spreading all over him when he deepened the kiss. Caden needed to get inside her, and his erection went unerringly to her center, right to her core. He lifted his head and gazed down at her.

Shiloh's breath caught at the intensity she saw in Caden's eyes and, reaching up, she wrapped her arms around his neck. She loved him. She wanted him. He was her world as he'd always been.

With gazes locked, she felt him slide into her, stretching her wide, burrowing deep; she could feel every inch of him. Her inner muscles felt him, too, and instinctively tightened around him and began milking his erection and loving the feel of the hot contractions taking over her womb.

And then he began moving in and out of her. His thrusts were firm and strong, stroking her to the point of mindlessness in the most primitive way. No matter how many times they made love, the sensations he could arouse in her were always overwhelming, overpowering. Pushing her to the brink fulfilled his every need.

She felt his body tense and a rush of mind-splintering pleasure took over her entire being. She felt her legs tighten around him, her arms grasped his neck and her hips lifted off the sofa. He pounded into her and she met each thrust with a power of her own. Their lovemaking was so potent it was impossible to tell where he ended and she began. Shiloh began to feel her climax build in every part of her body. She became convulsed with pleasure as he continued to grind into her in rapid succession, firing her loins and leading her to wanton pleasure. Her heels dug into the center of his back, making him thrust even harder, and she knew he would take all of her. He was so deeply embedded inside of her that she actually felt a sexual ache.

When he cried out her name just seconds before exploding, that same blast ripped through her. She was engulfed in sensation after sensation that led her straight into rhapsody. He leaned down and captured her lips, taking control of her mouth as shudders continued to rack their bodies.

They remained entwined, becoming boneless, unable to move. Somehow he managed to shift his body off hers and pull her closer into his arms, holding her as if he never wanted to let her go. She felt the kiss he pressed against the side of her neck. The brush of his beard against her skin sent even more sensations through her. Sighing in contentment, her body instinctively curled into his.

At that moment, she didn't want to think about anything except the man who was holding her so protectively in his arms.

A few hours later, Caden eased out of Shiloh's bed. What had started in her living room on the sofa had continued in her bedroom, and he expected her to sleep until morning.

He glanced down at her before grabbing his phone off

her nightstand and going into the living room. Sitting down on her sofa, he immediately placed a call to Grover Reddick, his manager. It was late, but Grover would still be up. He wondered when the man took time to sleep.

"Hello."

"Grover, this is Caden."

"What's wrong? Tired of playing CEO?"

"I wish it were that easy. I'm calling for information."

"About what?"

"It's who," Caden said, trying to keep his voice down so as not to wake Shiloh.

"Well, *who,* then?"

"Rita."

"Rita Crews?"

"Yes."

"Why would you want information on Rita?"

Caden told his manager what had happened last Saturday night and how Rita's name had come up during the investigation.

"Shit, man, Rita can act crazy at times, but she's not *that* crazy…. When I released her from the band she did say some crazy stuff, but I just put it down to the heat of the moment."

Caden lifted a brow. "What kind of crazy stuff?"

"Crap like you would be sorry for letting her go. She was going to make you pay. She was the only woman for you. That kind of crazy stuff. The reason I didn't tell you is because I didn't take her seriously. I figured she was merely blowing off steam. Surely you don't think she'd pull a stunt like that, do you?"

"Hell, I hope not. I told Rita the score before we got involved. I wasn't serious. She knew that."

"Well, I guess she saw things differently. She's a damned good bass player, but we all know there can't be any cause for friction with the fans. Concert tickets aren't cheap, and your fans are the ones putting food on our tables."

Caden nodded. "I agree with you. Look, I'm sure Rita's with some other group now, and I need to know who. And I need a copy of their schedule."

"No problem. I'll get that information for you."

"Thanks, Grover. And while I have you on the phone, there's another favor I need to ask."

Thirty-Five

Dalton drove through the gates of Sutton Hills, thinking he knew the reason that Jace had summoned him today. Okay, he'd been missing in action at work today, but everyone deserved a mental health day every now and then. So, he'd taken one.

He had left the office early yesterday to pull himself together, and after that date last night, there was no way he could have gone in today. The woman had been a looker, but he'd been with her only a few minutes before he'd regretted asking her out. She had spent the entire time talking about her ex. He had been so glad when the date had ended. And when she had invited him to her place, he had refused. He had gone home and had spent the rest of the evening with a bottle of vodka while listening to B. B. King sing the blues. He couldn't recall the last time he'd gotten boozed up, and then he had awakened that morning with a doozy of a hangover. Now, several cups of coffee and a good-ass nap later, he felt a lot better.

Dalton had been smart enough to call in and give Jace a heads-up about not coming in; otherwise, Big Brother would have shown up on his doorstep to find out why he wasn't at work.

Around three, Jace called saying there was a family meeting at Sutton Hills at six. He couldn't help but wonder what the fuck it was for, but he hadn't been in the mood to ask. Maybe Jace and Wonder Woman had called off the wedding. Probably not possible with her being knocked up and all. Jace would do the honorable thing, whether or not he loved Shana. It must be something else.

He parked his car and decided not to rack his brain about it since he would find out soon enough.

"I heard Dalton's car outside," Caden said to Jace, pouring a glass of Scotch, something he felt he'd need when they dealt with Dalton. First, they would tell him about the incident Saturday night, since he had every right to know. They would also be telling Dalton about their mother, wanting him to hear it from them.

Grover had called back a few hours ago to say that Rita was now performing with Phrase 3. The group's last concert had been three weeks ago, and they wouldn't go back on the road for another couple of weeks.

Just because Rita hadn't performed anywhere last weekend didn't mean she'd been in Charlottesville. All the same, he had passed the information on to Shana, who would in turn tell Jules. According to Shana, her sister had the means to check further into Rita's whereabouts last weekend.

Caden glanced over at Jace, who seemed relaxed and in control. There was no doubt that Shana was good for Jace. His brother was happy, and he was happy for him.

"Ready for your trip?" Jace asked.

"Yes," Caden said, smiling. "We leave first thing in the morning. I'm sorry I won't be here for Brandy's funeral service. I'm glad Dalton agreed to go with you. Do you think Shelton Fields will attend?"

"I spoke with him earlier today, and he said he plans to go. Also, I wanted to tell you that Shana's waiting to hear from Bruce about what he finds on Brandy's computer. Bruce suspects information was wiped from a remote location and he's checking into that, among other things."

"What happens if his suspicions are realized?"

"Then we call in Marcel at the FBI to do an investigation. He would need to determine whether Brandy was involved—along with Freeman and Arrington—in divulging trade secrets. You saw the video that Security gave Dalton. Brandy was clearly searching his office for something, but the question is, what?"

Caden shook his head and was about to say he had no answer for that question when Dalton walked in, pulling off his aviator sunglasses. His bloodshot eyes told Caden everything. "No wonder you stayed out today."

"Whatever," Dalton said, glancing around. "Where's Hannah?"

"She's left already."

Dalton raised a brow. "Left?"

"Yes," Jace said, sitting on the sofa. "She does have a home to go to, you know."

Dalton shrugged as he plopped down on one of the chairs. He tended to forget about the small cottage Hannah owned that sat on the grounds of Sutton Hills. Their grandfather had left it to her in his will. In fact, their grandfather had left Hannah pretty well-off and, as far as Dalton was concerned, she deserved everything she got. She had worked with the Granger family for close to fifty years and she was like family herself. "I'm so used to her being here that I often forget about her own place." He sniffed the air. "Did she cook anything before she left?"

Caden rolled his eyes. "You're pathetic, and you look pathetic. Should I even ask why you have bloodshot eyes?"

"None of your damned business." He then glanced over at Jace. "So, what's this meeting all about?"

"A couple of things," Jace said, studying his brother.

"Such as?"

Caden came and sat down on a chair opposite Dalton. "The first matter involves me."

"What about you? And please don't tell me you've knocked the wine lady up already."

"Shiloh isn't pregnant," Caden said, frowning.

"Thank God for that. So what's going on with you?"

"It involves that accident on Saturday night."

Dalton leaned back against his seat and stretched his legs out in front of him. "What about it?" he asked nonchalantly.

"There's another theory being floated around about what happened."

Dalton frowned confusedly. "So, tell me about the other theory."

Caden paused a moment and then said, "It may not have been an accident—it might have been intentional."

Dalton went still, and then he slowly sat up straight in his chair. Shock covered his face. "Intentional? Are you saying there's a chance someone tried to kill you?"

Caden let out a deep breath and then said, "Yes, that's exactly what I'm saying."

Dalton stared at Caden for the longest time as the shocking news ran through his mind, infiltrated his brain waves and registered in his thoughts. "Why would you think it was intentional?" he asked, not wanting to believe what he was hearing.

"I didn't come up with this myself and, quite honestly, I'm still not sure that it was intentional. We're having the matter investigated, since there have been some new developments," Caden explained.

"What kind of developments?" Dalton wanted to know.

"Mainly to do with Rita Crews—she used to be the bass player in my band. We were lovers for a brief time, but she got carried away, became possessive and began antagonizing the fans and causing too much trouble with other band members. When things got worse, I knew I had to replace her. Just last night, I found out from my manager that she had made threats about me. Then, to cap it off, today he told me that her current band has been on hiatus for the past while—including last weekend. Apparently, one of the band members said she'd told him she would use her time off to settle a score with someone."

"And you think that someone was you?"

"I don't know, Dalton. That's why we've hired a private investigator who'll check on Rita's whereabouts last weekend."

Dalton shook his head as he stared at his two older brothers. "You should have told this Rita girl up front what the deal was. Then you wouldn't have this problem."

Caden rolled his eyes. "She *knew* what the deal was. I didn't lead her on."

"You must have done something if she's now out to get you. Man, Caden, you don't know how to handle business with your bed partner." Dalton paused, then added, "Compared to you two, I am a genius when it comes to the ladies."

Ignoring his last comment, Caden said, "Rita's involvement is merely speculation. She might have been talking about something else altogether and there's a fifty-fifty chance she wasn't anywhere near Charlottesville last weekend."

"Well, for your sake, I hope that's the case. When will this private investigator know something?"

"Hopefully in a few days."

Dalton drew in a deep breath. He sincerely hoped the speculation involving Rita Crews was merely speculation. Nothing could be worse than jealous women— there was no reasoning with them. At the first sign any woman was possessive or obsessive, he would drop her like a hot potato.

"You said you wanted to discuss a couple of things, so what's the other one?" he asked Jace.

Dalton didn't miss Jace's hesitation and he noticed that Caden seemed uneasy about something, as well. "What's the other thing, Jace?" he repeated, wondering what on earth it could be.

"It's about Mom."

Dalton felt a nasty twinge of concern as he exhaled and said, "Mom? What about Mom?"

Dalton saw the quick glance between Jace and Caden, the twinge becoming an uneasy feeling twisting in his stomach. "I'm going to ask just one more time," he said, getting to his feet. "What *about* Mom?"

It was Jace who answered. "We found out that she was involved in an extramarital affair."

Dalton didn't say anything. He just stared at Jace, a complete absence of shock on his face.

Jace concluded there could be only one reason for that.

"You knew," Jace said in an accusing tone as anger rattled his senses. "You knew Mom was being unfaithful to Dad."

"Yes, damn it, I knew, but what was I supposed to do? Tell Dad?"

"I don't see why you couldn't have," Caden said with an edge of steel in his voice. "Jace and I have been pulling our hair out trying to think of the best way to break this news to you, and you knew already."

Dalton frowned. "The reason I didn't tell Dad or anyone was because Mom made me promise not to tell."

"And of course, you did anything she asked you to do. You were always her favorite, and now I know why. You knew all her secrets."

"Damn it, Caden, I did not know all her secrets. I was only a little kid at the time. I only found out she was having an affair by accident."

Dalton sat back down and didn't say anything for a minute, and then he began talking. His tone was low and deadly serious. "It was the year before she died, so I must have been around ten or eleven. I was lying low after school. I'd been acting out in class that day and they told me my teacher would be calling my parents to let them know. I figured I could hide out somewhere until their anger wore off." He didn't say anything for a minute, and then he said softly, "That's when I saw Mom...with a man who wasn't Dad. They were kissing and about to take their clothes off. She saw me, but the man never did. Later that night, she came to my room and made me promise not to tell anyone."

And of course, he promised, Jace thought. Dalton had adored their mother, and he'd done anything she had asked of him.

A deep frown covered Caden's face. "Where were they?" he asked in a curt tone.

Dalton glanced over at his brother. "The boathouse."

"The boathouse?" Jace exclaimed in a loud, angry voice. "Mom had the nerve to bring her lover to Sutton Hills?"

"And to think Michael Greene was behaving all holier-than-thou at the party last Saturday night. Had I known he had disrespected our family, especially our dad, I would have beaten the crap out of him right then and there."

Confusion spread over Dalton's face. "What the hell are you talking about?"

"Michael Greene," Jace said. "He used to work for Granger years ago."

"Yeah, I remember him. He's Deidra Greene's dad. Deidra gave me my first blow job when I was fourteen."

Dalton's statement left both of his brothers speechless. "Deidra was a lot older than you," Caden said, recovering himself. "At least four years older."

Dalton shrugged. "Is that supposed to mean something?"

"Apparently not," Jace said, staring at his brother. "But the fact still remains that Michael Greene had the damned nerve to engage in an affair with our mother, and he used the boathouse at Sutton Hills as if it were a damned hotel."

"Hey, wait a minute," Dalton interrupted. "I don't know where you got your information, but the man Mom was with that day at the boathouse was not Deidra's dad. It was *not* Michael Greene."

Thirty-Six

Jace shifted his body and eased up to sit on the side of the bed. He couldn't sleep. All he could think about was the conversation he'd had with his brothers earlier that evening.

"Jace?"

He glanced over his shoulder and saw Shana look over at him as she wiped the sleep from her eyes. "Sorry, sweetheart. I didn't mean to wake you."

Pushing hair out of her face, she said, "I'm fine. I was so tired last night I don't remember you coming to bed. How did things go with Dalton? How did he handle finding out about your mom's affair?"

"He already knew."

"What?"

"Yes," Jace said, lying back on the bed. Pulling Shana into his arms, he tucked her head beneath his chin. "He'd been hiding out in the boathouse when he got into trouble at school and saw Mom there with her lover."

"At the boathouse? At Sutton Hills?"

"Yeah. I guess she felt safe in doing that because nobody but her went down there on a routine basis. She used to claim that was her private place and that the lake would relax her mind."

"What did she do when she realized Dalton was there? Did he walk in on them?"

"He didn't actually walk in on them—he was hiding in a closet. But Mom saw him sneak out. He says he didn't see anything other than two people kissing and undressing. But that was enough for him to get an idea of what they were about to do. Dalton wasn't a dummy where sex was concerned, even when he was eleven."

Jace paused a moment and then added, "Mom confronted him about what he'd seen that night and made him promise not to tell anyone. It was wrong for her to do that, but she knew she could get away with it because Dalton thought the world of her. He worshipped the ground she walked on. Dalton believed Mom was perfect, and I suspect it was hard on him to discover she wasn't."

Jace drew in a deep breath then said, "And he kept her secret all this time, telling no one what he saw that day. At one point, I suspected he thought Dad did kill Mom, and I can understand why he would. He knew what Mom had been doing and figured Dad had a motive."

"Do you believe he still thinks your dad is guilty?"

Jace shook his head. "No. I think, after a while, he put the pieces together and acknowledged Dad's innocence like the rest of us. It's just not in our dad's nature to hurt anyone."

"But an angry person will do just about anything if pushed hard enough," Shana said.

"True. But I've always admired my father's control, especially under pressure. If anything, he would have asked Mom for a divorce. But he would never have killed her."

Shana nodded. "Your mom was murdered at the boathouse, right?"

"Yes."

"Then the person who killed her knew her routine or knew she went there often enough. If I were your father, I would have someone check out the Greenes' alibi again to verify they really were on a cruise when your mom was killed."

"But here's the shocker, Shana. The man Dalton saw with Mom that day wasn't Michael Greene."

Shana pulled from Jace's arms to look up at him. "You're sure?"

"He's positive. If that's the case then she must have been seeing two men and, evidently, she was sleeping with both."

"Who was the man Dalton saw?"

"He said he didn't know him but that he would recognize him if he ever saw him again. He saw the man that afternoon, but the man didn't see him. More than likely, Mom never told him that Dalton had been there."

Shana didn't say anything for a minute. "What if this other lover found out about her affair with Michael Greene and killed her in a jealous rage or something?"

"I guess that is a possibility. The one thing I do know is that my dad didn't commit murder," Jace said with unwavering certainty.

"All quiet on the Granger front at my end," Striker Jennings reported to his boss, Roland Summers.

"Good. I've heard from the other members of the security detail, as well. It seems as if Shep's sons have made things easy for us tonight.

"Everything is set for Caden's trip this weekend?" Roland asked. Once Striker had discovered that Caden Granger would be taking a trip out of town for the weekend, Roland thought it would be best for someone else to shadow Caden. If Caden were to see Striker in Vegas and recognize him as the man who had saved his life, his cover would be blown. Until Carson said otherwise, Sheppard Granger's sons would be protected, and Roland would do everything in his power to ensure Sheppard's desire that professionalism and discretion be maintained at all costs.

Roland ended his call with Striker and leaned back in his chair. He recalled the first time he'd met Carson Boyett. He'd been a cop intentionally set up to take a fall. As a result, he had been sentenced to fifteen years.

He had served three years when his wife, Becca, hired Carson to fight to have his case reopened. She did so, risking her own life in the process. In retaliation, Becca was killed, and Carson had come close to losing her own life. But somehow Carson had persevered and had managed to expose the team of bad cops on the take. All five had been charged with his wife's murder, along with a number of others.

It was through Carson that Roland had first met Luther Thomas, another man who had been wrongly convicted. Through her he'd also met Sheppard Granger. It had been Sheppard and Luther—now the Reverend Luther Thomas—who'd approached him to set up a security detail for Shep's sons. Striker Jennings was one of those men. Some of the guys working for Roland were, like him, innocent of the crimes they'd been accused of. Some, like Striker, had committed crimes but had served their time and had now taken their rightful place back in society. They were all good men, men he'd been lucky enough to bring into his organization. Hardworking men and dedicated to a fault.

Roland was about to get himself another cup of coffee when his phone rang. "Roland Summers."

"This is Stonewall."

Stonewall Courson was the person who'd been assigned to keep an eye on Shep's youngest son, Dalton. "Yes, Stonewall, what's happening?"

"I guess the natives are restless. Dalton Granger decided to go out for the evening."

Roland checked his watch. "It's after midnight on a Thursday night. There aren't too many places still open at this hour."

"He's headed down the interstate in that sports car of his. At least he's keeping to the speed limit. Maybe he just wants to ride around or something. I do that myself when I have a lot on my mind. I just wanted you to know it's not going to be an early night for me like I thought it would be."

Roland chuckled. "Sorry about that, and thanks for checking back in. Just stay with him."

"Don't worry, I will. If he hangs out all night, so will I."

Thirty-Seven

"You're still not telling me where we're going?" Shiloh asked, smiling over at Caden. She was sitting across from him in the private jet he had rented to take them from Charlottesville to the surprise location. Caden was doing a good job of keeping his lips sealed. As she continued to hold his gaze, she couldn't help but think what a gorgeous pair of lips they were. She definitely liked the neatly trimmed beard he had begun sporting a few months ago. Caden had always been a good-looking man, but as far as she was concerned, the beard made him look even more handsome, and the way it lined his mouth made his lips that much more desirable, more kissable and so darned delicious.

"Shiloh?"

"Yes?"

"I asked if you were comfortable."

She nodded. "Yes, now that the plane has leveled off."

He chuckled. "I'd forgotten that flying isn't your favorite pastime. But I hope you believe me when I say I'll make it worth your while."

"I hope so, since I didn't bring a stitch of clothing with me other than what I have on." And that was the truth. She had followed his instructions to the letter. No undergarments, toiletries or change of clothes. According to him, they would purchase anything she needed when they got to their destination.

Caden was sitting in the seat facing her with his long legs stretched out in front of him. He was wearing a pair of jeans and a long-sleeved white button-down shirt. Although she had no idea where they were going, she didn't have any doubt in her mind what they would do when they got there. His eyes had been roving over her body from the minute they'd boarded the plane. And sitting across from him was giving her the full Caden Granger effect. He had a way of looking at her that could turn her insides to mush, creating a deep throb between her legs and making her breasts ache.

She could pretend they didn't want each other, sit here and suffer through the entire trip. Or she could take matters into her own hands, and her fingers itched to do just that. She'd never been a bold person when it came to sex. In fact, Caden had taught her everything she knew. She had saved herself for him, and at twenty-two, she had experienced her first sexual encounter. He had made it worth waiting for.

"What are you thinking?"

His question interrupted her thoughts. "Sure you want to know?"

"Yes. Tell me."

Could I? Should I? Why not? "I was sitting here thinking about how sexy I think you look and how your eyes are deliberately trying to turn me on."

"Are they?"

"I think so."

She watched as a smile touched the corners of his lips, making the throb between her legs intensify. "Is it working? Am I turning you on, Shiloh?"

She didn't mind being honest. "Yes."

"What are you going to do about it?"

Now, that was a thought-provoking question. "Not sure I can do anything."

"Sweetheart, you're the only woman who can."

His words not only stirred her insides but also filled her with the degree of confidence she needed to unbuckle her seat belt. She glanced around. "The pilot is—"

"Flying this plane. And I didn't think we needed a flight attendant. It's just the two of us in here."

She glanced around again. It was a mini-jet, not as large as the one owned by her uncle Rodney. Because he had business interests all over the world, her uncle's jet was spacious and had been designed for his comfort with sleeping pods and a full-service kitchen. While this jet was nice, it lacked the amenities her uncle's plane had.

But she would make do.

Easing out of her seat, she knew he was watching her. Waiting. Sometimes she thought he knew her better than she knew herself. "Since you won't tell me where we're going, I guess I'll just have to entertain myself until I get there."

"Help yourself."

"I intend to."

He lifted an eyebrow, and she smiled. Maybe he didn't know her all that well after all. At least, this no-holds-barred side of her. He was the only man she'd ever slept with. Even during those four years they had been separated, the thought of sharing her body with another man was something she hadn't had the courage to move on and do. When she thought she had been ready, Caden had stepped back into her life. And he'd let her know in more ways than one that he was there to stay.

She stretched her body, lifting her hands over her head, knowing his gaze watched her every move. She then went to him and leaned toward him, placing a hand on each of his thighs. "I like you, Caden Granger."

"Do you?"

"Yes. Although I don't know if you're taking me north, south, east or west."

"I'm taking you with me, and that's what's important," he countered.

She smiled, knowing he was right. Right now, the only thing that mattered was that they were together. She unbuckled his seat belt and settled onto his lap like a Cheshire cat ready to be petted. And when he wrapped his arms around her, she curled into him, feeling content for now.

"You smell good," he whispered close to her ear.

"So do you." And he did. It was part cologne and part man. The combination was arousing. Incredibly so.

She could feel his erection pressing against her backside, and it was throbbing mercilessly against her. Letting her know what it wanted and what it needed. In turn, his throbbing was causing the area between her legs to throb.

She shifted her body to slip off his lap. She slid down in front of him on her knees with her head between his thighs. She looked up at him and intentionally licked her lips. She saw the flare of heat in his gaze. There was no need for him to ask what she was doing down there because he knew. And if he didn't, then he would soon enough.

"Stand up, Caden," she said in a voice so filled with want and need that she could hear it shaking.

He must have heard it, too, and stood while looking down at her with those oh-so-sexy eyes of his. She reached up and slowly pulled down the zipper of his jeans. In the time it took him to pull in a deep breath, she had freed his penis and held the engorged erection in her hands. She was thinking what she always thought whenever she saw this part of him. Not only was this a very useful tool that could bring her a lot of pleasure, but it was also a beautiful piece of art. The shape, size and texture totally captivated her. Very impressive.

She could see blood rushing through the engorged veins and couldn't imagine any other man being this well-endowed, this magnificently crafted and designed. What good was eye candy if your mouth couldn't enjoy the delicious taste of it every once in a while? And she intended to enjoy this. She intended to enjoy him. And without wasting any time, she leaned in and guided the shaft toward her mouth.

Opening wide, she slid his erection between her lips,

and the minute it was in her mouth, she began doing all the erotic things he had taught her to do, coming up with her own ideas, as well.

Caden sucked in a sharp breath. Seeing Shiloh on her knees with the full length of him in her mouth was an erotic image being branded on his brain. She'd given him blow jobs before, but there was something different about this one. Her tongue was working overtime. His hands gripped the arms of the seat when erotic sensations rushed through him, making him weak in the knees.

He moaned her name, and she looked up at him while he was still fully embedded in her mouth, almost reaching her throat. And when she began bobbing her head up and down, he growled in pleasure.

Reaching down, he stroked the tip of his finger down the center of her throat in a sensuous motion over and over again and watched her eyes darken with need. That need was affecting him, driving him to want more than her mouth. He needed to be deep within the essence of her.

She continued to gobble him up in a way that had him clutching the sides of her head while throwing his head back and moaning deep in his throat. Lord, she was blowing him away. Literally.

He couldn't take any more. Her mouth was too much. More than he'd expected but everything he'd wanted. Every lick of her tongue was driving him deeper into one hell of a sensuous abyss. When he felt himself about to come, he quickly pulled back, and she released him with an involuntary sigh.

Hungry for her to the point of being delirious, he pulled her from her knees, and his hands went straight under her skirt to tug down the lacy panties covering her femininity. And then turning her around to brace her hands on the arms of the seat, he lifted her skirt to expose her bottom. Spreading her thighs apart, his shaft homed in on her from the back.

His erection was throbbing to the point of madness when he tilted her backside and entered her. Holding tight to her hips, he began thrusting in and out of her, while her wet, hot inner muscles clenched him. The feel of those muscles contracting and constricting was driving him into mindless ecstasy.

He kept pounding into her over and over again while she cried out his name, told him to keep going and not to stop. If he could, he knew he would remain inside of her forever. Then it seemed the plane shook, and at first he thought it was turbulence but realized it was his body coming apart in one hell of a climax.

Caden threw his head back and shouted her name when he felt her come. His nerve endings seemed ready to explode as he kept up the rhythm and continued thrusting. Nothing was better than making love to the woman he loved, adored and cherished.

He had just pulled out of her and was gathering her into his arms when the pilot announced over the intercom to fasten their seat belts for landing. He watched her slide back into her panties and straighten her skirt while he zipped his jeans.

Reaching out, he pulled her into his arms and kissed her, hoping she felt all the love he felt in their kiss. Then, sweeping her off her feet, he carried her to her seat and buckled her in before taking his own seat and snapping the seat belt in place.

When he glanced over at her, he realized he'd made love to her without any protection. "I didn't use a condom," he said, disgusted with himself. Dalton had mocked him often enough but he was right—it was something he should never forget.

"That's okay. I'm on the pill, so it's okay if you want to stop using a condom."

Oh, yes, he thought, smiling. *I want.* He loved the feel of being skin to skin with her.

She glanced out the window, and then she looked back over at him and smiled. "You're taking me to Vegas."

"Yes. I want us to replace bad memories of Vegas with good ones."

She nodded, smiling. "I can't wait."

Thirty-Eight

"Oh, Ben, tonight was simply wonderful. I can't remember having so much fun. And all those songs brought back so many great memories. Thank you for bringing me to New York."

Ben smiled at Mona as they caught the hotel's elevator. "You don't have to thank me, Mona. I'm enjoying myself as well and I should be thanking you for agreeing to this trip."

They had arrived in New York yesterday. The plane ride from Charlottesville to NYC had been smooth, but catching a cab from LaGuardia to their hotel in Times Square amid rush-hour traffic had been challenging and at times downright scary. Being her eyes, he had told Mona about all the bridges they'd crossed over and the tall buildings they'd passed.

After checking into their connecting rooms, they freshened up before enjoying dinner at a restaurant within walking distance from the hotel. The next morning, they shared breakfast together before taking a tour of the city on a double-decker bus. Seeing all the excitement and happiness on her face touched him profoundly, and he wished he could keep her in such a cheerful mood forever.

"I'm glad you enjoyed yourself tonight," he said, tucking her hand in the crook of his arm and stepping off the elevator onto the floor where their rooms were located. "I didn't know you could sing."

Tonight they had taken in the play *Motown: The Musical.* He could still hear the songs, some of which had been his favorites, playing in his ear…probably because Mona was still humming them. And what he'd just told her was true. She had a beautiful singing voice, something he'd discovered when part of the musical included a sing-along with the audience.

"I can't sing. You're imagining things," she said, chuckling.

"I know what I heard. Your voice is as beautiful as you are." When she got quiet on him, he glanced over and saw the blush in her cheeks. "You're even more beautiful when you blush," he whispered, after leaning over.

Turning down the corridor that led to their rooms, he said, "We'll sleep in tomorrow and do room service for breakfast since we don't have to meet Phil and Nina until lunch." Phil Rodriquez had worked with Ben on the police force in Boston. They had retired around the same time, Ben moving to Charlottesville and Phil returning to his hometown of Queens. Phil and his wife, Nina, would meet them for lunch, and then tomorrow night the four of them would attend a Broadway show.

They stopped in front of Mona's room, which was

connected to his. "Sure you don't need me to come in while you get settled?"

"I'm sure," she said, smiling. "You did such a great job when we first got here."

He had. Upon check-in, he had walked her around her hotel room, telling her where everything was located. Then he had stood back and watched as she felt her way around the room without his assistance, getting familiar with the room on her own. He admired how she refused to let her disability keep her from living a fulfilling life. During the months he'd known her she had always been so positive.

"I'm looking forward to meeting your friends tomorrow, Ben," Mona said.

"And they are looking forward to meeting you, too. I told them all about you."

She tilted her head and grinned up at him. "And just what did you tell them, Mr. Bradford?"

"That I've fallen hopelessly in love with you."

He watched her amusement fade somewhat. "Oh, Ben."

This wasn't the first time he'd told her he loved her; however, he knew just like all those other times, she wasn't ready to accept his feelings. That was fine. He was a patient man and wouldn't push. That was why he'd reserved separate hotel rooms. When she was ready to take their relationship to the next level, she would let him know it. In the meantime, he would continue to be patient. He had all the time in the world.

He leaned down and placed a gentle kiss on her lips. He then reached behind her, and using the key card, he opened her hotel-room door. "Get inside before I throw you over my shoulder and haul you to my room."

The amusement returned to her face. "You wouldn't dare."

He chuckled. "Don't tempt me, woman. Now get in that room."

When she stepped over the threshold, he took a step closer and kissed her again. This one was slow, lingering and filled with all the passion he always felt around her.

Ben broke off the kiss and whispered, "Dream about me, sweetheart."

She smiled up at him. "I will."

He closed her hotel-room door. Sighing deeply, he walked next door to his room while whistling an old Motown tune.

Twelve times, Mona thought, lying in bed hours later. Tonight had made the twelfth time Ben had told her he loved her since the day they'd first met. However, she had yet to share her feelings for him. Fear had made her keep quiet.

Yes, she was afraid. She was terrified that once she told him she loved him, it wouldn't be long before he got tired of being her seeing-eye companion. The thought of having a blind wife was what had driven her husband off. Deep down, she knew that wasn't totally true, since her ex had been looking for a way to dump her anyway. The auto accident had made it easy for him to get out of the marriage with her and get into one with the young secretary he'd been having an affair with.

But right now she didn't want to think of her ex. She wanted to think of the wonderful guy in the next room who had made her feel better than Fred had made her feel in all the years they were married. Ben always gave her compliments, even on those days she hadn't looked her absolute best. He told her he loved her and that she was pretty, smart and intelligent.

Ben treated her like a queen, saying he treated her the same way he expected his daughters to be treated. With respect. And he'd told her he loved her. Twelve times. What kind of man did such a thing?

Benjamin Bradford.

She shifted in bed. It was way past midnight, and she was still trying to go to sleep. Tonight had been wonderful. The stage show had gone by in a blur, and she could still hear the sounds of Motown in her head. It had been a special night.

Getting out of bed, she slowly felt her way around the room and made her way to the window. She wasn't sure why she wanted to stand there when she couldn't see a thing—not the bright lights or the tall buildings New York was famous for. Ben had told her what he could see when he looked out her hotel-room window.

She turned away from the window when she suddenly sucked in a sharp breath. Something passed before her eyes, and it hadn't been just a flash of light like before. Just now, she'd seen color, shapes and objects—she was sure of it. She strained her eyes but couldn't see anything else. It was all just a dark blur.

Then, when she'd given up, assuming she had imagined the whole thing, it happened again. This time it lasted longer, coming in clearer than before. The bed-spread was green, the carpeting brown, and a silver ice bucket sat on a table. Then the image was gone again. But she *had* seen it!

Instantly hope filled her. Dr. Oglethorpe had told her when she had reported seeing flashes of light months ago that that was either a good sign her sight was re-turning…or a bad sign it was about to leave her perma-nently. She had hoped and prayed for the former, but the tests the doctor had performed hadn't been conclusive.

Mona couldn't wait to get back to Charlottesville and make an appointment to see Dr. Oglethorpe again. She wouldn't get her hopes up, but what she'd just seen moments ago was real. She wouldn't mention it to any-one, not even to Ben. She didn't want to get his hopes up, either.

Mona heard a sound and realized it had come from the room next door. Ben's room. He was still up? Couldn't he sleep? She slowly moved away from the window to sit on the side of the bed. Ben wanted her the way a man wanted a woman. She was very aware of that. Even without her sight, she felt the vibes. But he wouldn't rush her. He would be patient and let it be her decision when they became intimate. Now maybe it was time to show the man who'd told her that he loved her twelve times another way.

Maybe it was time to show him that she loved him, too.

Ben was searching around the hotel room for the television remote when he heard the light knock on the connecting door. He quickly moved toward it, wondering whether Mona needed him for anything. It was past midnight, and he figured she would be asleep by now.

He quickly opened the door. "Mona? You okay?" She was braced in the doorway, and he tried not to notice she was wearing a bathrobe belted around her waist, revealing the top part of her nightie.

She smiled at him. "I'm fine. I wasn't asleep. I heard you moving around and wondered if you were okay."

"I'm fine. I couldn't find the television remote. Sorry if I disturbed you."

"You didn't. Like I said, I wasn't asleep anyway."

He couldn't help staring at her skin and how gorgeous she looked, even without makeup. If he'd thought it once, he'd thought it a number of times that she was a beautiful woman. And why did she have to smell so good?

"Did you find it?"

Her question lassoed his thoughts back in. "Find what?"

"The remote."

"Oh. No. Not yet."

"I would help you look but…"

He smiled at her joke. "Don't worry. It's around here someplace. I probably accidentally knocked it under the bed or something." He studied her and realized she was trying to make small talk. Did she want him to invite her into his room? The thought that she did stirred hope inside of him, and he figured there was only one way to find out.

"Do you want to come into my room and keep me company while I look for it?"

"You sure it's okay?"

His laugh was easy. "It's okay with me. Is it okay with you, Mona?"

She laughed, too, at the absurdness of her question. "Yes, it's okay with me."

"Then that's all that matters." He stepped aside. "Come on in."

When she stepped into his room, he closed the door behind him. When he turned back around, she was standing in the middle of the room. In the bright light he saw that her robe matched her gown. Yellow. He'd once told her yellow was his favorite color and wondered if it was a coincidence that she was wearing it.

"My room is similar to yours," he said. "There's a chair at three o'clock if you want to sit down." Early on in their relationship, she had explained that it was helpful to advise her of directions by going clockwise.

She turned to him, and almost unerringly, she met his gaze. "And where is the bed?"

Desire he'd tried controlling all night shot through him. "Ten o'clock."

She nodded and moved to the bed to sit on the edge. Just seeing her sitting on his bed sent all kinds of intense emotions spiraling through him. He cleared his throat. "I guess I need to look for the remote," he said, stepping away from the door to check around the television. Moving toward the desk area, he looked over his shoulder and saw that Mona had shifted from the sitting position on the bed to lie on her side to face him. He lifted his brow. "You're okay?"

She smiled at him. "I'm fine, but I've decided to be honest with you about something."

"What?"

"You've told me a dozen times that you love me, and I've thought about that."

"Have you?"

"Yes. And each time I dwell on it, I'm in awe that you feel that way."

"I told you, I fell in love with you the moment I saw you, the first time we talked. You took my breath away."

"I couldn't see you clearly, but your scent aroused me. That has never happened to me before. Now with my sight gone, I rely a lot on my sense of smell, and you smelled good that day. You smell good every day."

Ben chuckled. "Thanks."

"You're welcome."

Ben didn't say anything for a minute as he looked over at her, stretched out on his bed. God, he wanted her. And he needed to know something. "Why are you here, Mona? Why did you come to me? What do you want to be honest about?"

He watched as she slowly got up off the bed and, feeling her way around it, she moved toward him. When she reached him, she stopped and said, "I'm here because I felt it was time for you to know something."

"What?"

"That I love you. I love you so very much. I thought I would never say those words to another man, but you proved me wrong. You also proved that not all men are made the same. There are some who are nice guys. And you are my hero, Ben. You are my everything."

Ben hadn't expected that. Any of it. And that made her words that much sweeter. Meaningful. Heartfelt. He reached out and tugged her into his arms, needing to hold her close to his heart. This woman who'd brought joy to his world after so many lonely years. Back then he'd had his girls and, at the time, that was all he'd needed. His girls and Sharon's memory.

Mona felt good in his arms like she always did, and he was very much aware of how closely her body was pressed to his. When she pulled back and glanced up at him, he dipped his head and captured her mouth, snatching whatever she was about to say right from her lips.

He loved her taste. It was tantalizingly sweet and sent warm blood rushing through his veins. He felt his entire body firing up with a primitive need that he'd managed to control over the years. But with Mona, that control was wavering.

She broke off the kiss and drew in a deep breath, and he did likewise while watching her lick her bottom lip with the tip of her tongue. His stomach tightened, and his body was on fire with full awareness.

Wrapping his arms tightly around her, he began backing her up slowly toward the bed. Once there, he kissed her again.

Mona was beginning to feel things she hadn't felt for a long time, if ever. Ben had a way of turning a kiss into something so sensual that her body shivered at the onslaught. She felt hot and tingly all over.

He released her mouth and, reaching out, tipped up her chin with warm fingers. "I want you, Mona."

His words, spoken in a deep, husky voice, sent even more shivers through her. "And I want you, too, Ben."

Her body tingled with awareness when she felt him undressing her. After he'd removed her robe and gown, she felt his callused hands stroke over her skin. The heat of his touch flowed through her, and when he leaned in and whispered how beautiful he thought she looked, sensuous shivers rippled up her spine.

She reached out, wanting to undress him, as well. He was wearing a T-shirt, and she lifted it over his head, tossing it away. Her hand went to his chest, and she moaned when she ran her fingers through the curly hair there. It was soft to the touch. And then she let her fingers run down the planes of his stomach and heard his quick intake of breath. She marveled at the fact that she was responsible for the sound.

Her hand lowered, and when she realized he was wearing pj bottoms, she tugged downward to push them past his hips and thighs. He assisted by stepping out of them. Knowing he was now as naked as she was sent a sensual sensation rioting through her. It had been a long time since she'd been intimate with a man, and this was the first time since becoming blind. She would have to feel her way through this, and that was what she intended to do.

Her hand lowered still, and she boldly cupped him, finding him so aroused that her breath caught. His breathing changed. She liked that. She also liked how he felt in her hands. He was hard and hot, and the heat actually stirred her hunger. The same hunger she had kept a lid on for years.

"Let's get into bed, sweetheart," he whispered against her ear.

She nodded and released him. She lay on the bed and he followed, tugging her into his arms to lie beside her. She knew him. He intended to take things slowly, treat her as if she were a china doll, but she didn't want that. She wanted him to handle her the way a man handled a woman he wanted intensely. She needed that and wanted to have it that way.

She sat up and ran her hands all over him, needing to continue to touch the skin she couldn't see. He felt soft in some places and hard in others. He was hairy, and her fingers traced a path from the hair on his chest past his stomach muscles and all the way to his groin area. And then she took him into her hands again, loving the feel of him and the way his erection was hardening, stronger and stronger beneath her fingertips.

"Mona, baby, you're killing me."

She heard the words ground out through clenched teeth and wished she could see the expression on his face. She held on to hope that one day she would.

"I need you now, sweetheart."

And she needed him. She heard and felt him shift in the bed, adjusting the pillows at her head. He shifted her onto her back and the heat from his body covered her own.

And when he leaned in and captured her mouth in

his, she could only moan at all the sensations rapidly mounting inside of her. Sensations so far gone and out of control she could only lie there and savor them.

While he continued to kiss her, his knee nudged her legs apart, and he broke off the kiss long enough to say, "When the girls went off to college, I decided they would be the only two children I'd ever want. I had a vasectomy many years ago."

She nodded and whispered, "I always wanted a baby but Fred never did."

"I know."

Yes, he knew, because she'd told him the score with her ex. "And if we were younger, Mona, I would give you the baby you wanted."

His words set emotions off within her, because he'd offered to do something her own husband had refused to do. Just knowing he meant the words touched her deeply.

"Now you can share my grandbabies with me."

Those words only added to the emotions she was feeling. He was talking as if he wanted her to not only be a part of his present but also a part of his future. "Grandbabies? You think your girls will give you more than one?"

He chuckled softly. "I figure I'll get at least two or three from Shana. The jury's still out on Jules. I can't wait to meet the man who will topple her off that high horse she's on."

And then she felt his fingers making their way to her breasts, cupping each in his hand. Continuing the search, his hand found her stomach and then the area between her legs. "You're beautiful," he whispered, sliding a finger inside her.

His featherlight caresses sent more sensations escalating through her, and she closed her eyes to feel and savor his touch. As he kissed again she felt him gliding inside of her, not stopping until he was buried deep.

"You okay?" he asked with concern in his voice when their bodies were locked together.

"Yes, I'm fine." And at that moment his features appeared before her eyes, an incredibly handsome face. The surprise of seeing it made her suck in a shocking breath before everything turned black again.

"What's wrong, baby? Did I hurt you?" he asked in a concerned tone.

A part of her wanted to share what she had glimpsed, and then a part of her held back. If she never regained her sight, at least for that one brief second she had been blessed with a glimpse of the man who had her heart.

"No, I'm fine, and you're beautiful," she whispered, fighting back tears. "And I love you, Benjamin Bradford," she said, reaching up and cupping his face in her hands.

She felt him smile against her hands. "And I love you, Mona Underwood."

And then he began moving, slow at first. Gentle. Sensual forces that were rapidly taking control of her seized him, and he began moving in a rhythm that had her moaning while he leaned in and planted a row of kisses around her collarbone. His thrusts became hard, going deep, then deeper, and driving her over the edge.

Wanting more, her body arched, her hips rose, and he came down with hard strokes each and every time.

And then she felt her body explode at the same time his did. He tightened his hold on her hips, and she dug her fingertips into his shoulders as she was pushed into waters that drowned her senses while every cell in her body erupted in deep, undiluted pleasure.

"Ben!"

"I'm here, baby. I will always be here."

A promise she believed in, and at that moment, she knew how it felt to be loved both physically and mentally. He was destroying all the pain she'd ever endured in her life. Ben was replacing the pain with joy and hope.

And when she began to shake violently from the force of her orgasm, he held her, caught up in his own throes of ecstasy. And they scaled the walls of pleasure together.

Thirty-Nine

"Still keeping secrets, I see," Shiloh said as she stepped out of the bedroom of the suite they were sharing at the beautiful Venetian Hotel on the Strip. She was dressed for an evening that she was clueless about other than it would begin with dinner at Caesars Palace.

After getting settled at the hotel, he had taken her on a shopping spree, buying her everything, particularly the gown he had chosen for her to wear tonight. Green had always been his favorite color, and the moment they had walked into the exclusive shop and he'd seen the teal-green silk gown on a mannequin, he'd had the sales clerk bring one out in Shiloh's size. And from the way he was looking at her, it was obvious he liked seeing her in it. She slowly twirled around, giving him a full view of the backless floor-length gown.

"Yes, I'm still keeping secrets," he said, walking toward her while brazenly raking his gaze all over her. "But it's all good, and I think at the end of our trip, you will agree with me."

When he came to stand in front of her, he smiled and said, "Baby, you look good. No, better than good—you look simply gorgeous."

She appreciated his compliment but rolled her eyes, knowing he was exaggerating. "You're saying that only because your favorite color is green."

He chuckled. "It was Granddad's favorite color, too. I miss the old man."

Shiloh reached up and caressed his cheek. "There's no doubt in my mind that Richard Granger is proud of his grandsons for keeping the promise they made to him. The three of you are bringing the company around."

"There's a lot of work to do. And we still need to find out why Brandy was snooping around in Dalton's office. Her memorial service was yesterday. Jace, Shana, Dalton and other employees attended. It's still hard to believe she would commit suicide."

Shiloh nodded. "Have you heard anything from Jules Bradford regarding Rita Crews's whereabouts last Saturday night?"

"No, but I don't want to think about Rita or anyone or anything else. This weekend belongs to us, and I intend to make it special with a few surprises."

"What kind of surprises?"

He reached out and tweaked her nose. "If I told you, then it wouldn't be a surprise now, would it?"

She playfully frowned up at him. "I guess not. And you look good in your tux, by the way. I assume since we're all dressed up that after dinner we're going to some fancy place."

"I guess you can assume that." He smiled when her frown deepened. "You look so pretty when you smile— remember that," he said, taking her hand and leading her toward the door.

"I'll try," she said, deliberately giving him her best smile.

Shana hung up the phone and paused a moment before turning to Jace, who was coming into her kitchen. He'd been outside washing her car. "That was Bruce," she said.

He glanced over at her. "And?"

"He said Brandy's hard drive had been wiped clean from a remote location. Now the question is, by whom?"

Jace drew in a deep breath as he sat down at the table. "I felt like a hypocrite at Brandy's memorial services yesterday when Barbara Holden from our HR department stood up and said what a model employee Brandy was. Now, less than a day later, we find out she might have been involved in heaven knows what."

"Which makes me wonder if she really committed suicide," Shana added. "What if someone…the person behind what she was doing or was looking for…decided she was a liability instead of an asset?"

"Then she would probably be eliminated without much thought," Jace said, running his fingers over his chin. "And the D.C. police haven't changed their minds about it being anything other than a suicide," he added.

"That assumption might change if the FBI gets involved. I need to let Marcel know. He and his men will decide how they want to proceed in their handling of this."

Jace stood up from the kitchen table. "And here I thought everything was over with the arrests of Arrington and Vidal. When do you plan to call Marcel?"

"First thing Monday morning. The sooner he is apprised of the situation, the better." She paused a moment and then said, "Jules called while you were outside washing the car."

Jace could tell by the look on Shana's face he would not like what she was going to say.

"And?"

"And Jules checked the major airlines."

"Go on."

"She found out that Rita Crews did purchase a ticket from Dallas to Charlottesville the same weekend of Caden's accident."

"Damn."

"I know the feeling."

"I need to let Caden know," Jace said.

"Jules hired someone to keep an eye on Rita. She's back in Dallas, so Caden isn't in any immediate danger for now."

"I'm glad I don't have to call him, then. He's planned a special weekend for Shiloh, and I wouldn't want to ruin it by calling to tell him about Rita Crews."

Shana nodded, understanding completely. "Thanks to Jules placing surveillance on her, you won't have to."

"You're a beautiful sight for sore eyes."

Shiloh turned and smiled at the older gentleman

standing in front of her. "Grover, this is a nice surprise. It's good seeing you again." Caden had introduced him years ago as the manager of his group, and she knew Caden thought the world of him. Grover had always been nice to her, even during those times when she hadn't been Caden's favorite person.

"Same here, Shiloh, and you look ravishing tonight."

And she felt ravishing. Caden hadn't been able to keep his eyes off her during most of dinner and kept complimenting her on how she looked. "Thanks. Caden was here a few minutes ago. We had dinner together, and then he had to go to the gentlemen's room and hasn't returned yet. That was almost ten minutes ago." She glanced around. "You haven't seen him, have you?"

A wide grin covered Grover's face. "Yes, I ran into him, and he gave me orders to take you to him."

She lifted a brow. "He did? Why? Where is he?"

"All he told me to tell you was that it was part of this weekend's secret surprise."

A smile touched Shiloh's lips. "He's been so secretive. I didn't know we were coming to Vegas until we landed. It was quite a surprise."

"Well, if you'll come with me, I'll take you to him," he said, offering his arm to her.

"Okay," she said.

They walked through the beautiful Caesars Palace, past the area where all the slot machines were located before taking the escalator to another section of the Colosseum—a smaller concert room referred to as the Arena.

Grover opened large double doors to a room that

could probably seat a thousand people. When she glanced questioningly up at Grover, he said, "You're attending a concert."

She lifted a brow. "I am?"

"Yes. Caden will join you in a minute."

"We're kind of early, aren't we?" she said, looking around. "There's not another soul in here." Because it was empty, the beautiful room seemed kind of eerie.

Grover chuckled. "No. In fact, you're right on time. Take a seat up front and enjoy the concert."

And then he left, closing the door behind him, and she frowned when she heard a distinctive click. Had he just locked her in this room? Why? She had to be mistaken. She was about to try the door when a female voice came across the speaker and said, "Please take your seat. The show is about to begin."

"What in the world?" Shiloh muttered when the houselights dimmed. How could the show start with no one in attendance but her? She was about to pull her cell phone out of her purse and call Caden when the room got dark and the stage lit up. That was when she walked up the aisle and took a seat in the fourth row from the front.

Within moments, the huge curtain came up, and she caught her breath when she saw that Caden's band members were onstage. Then that same female announcer who'd told her to take her seat earlier said, "Let's give a round of applause for the man who has become one of the greatest saxophone players of all time, Caden Granger."

Shiloh's breath caught when Caden walked onstage

amid the bright lights. He looked so good in his tux, and when he turned toward the audience, namely her, the huge smile that curved his lips made him look even more handsome.

And then he spoke. "I'm here tonight in the Arena of Caesars Palace to do a once-in-a-lifetime performance. I have only one number to perform, a number I wrote years ago after being inspired by a certain beautiful woman. Thus, this tune is aptly titled 'Shiloh, My Love.'"

And then he lifted the sax to his mouth, and the moment he belted out the first note, tears ran down Shiloh's cheeks. He was playing the song he had named after her, undoing all the painful memories of their past and replacing them with these—memories of a Vegas she would remember forever.

Usually, during a Caden Granger concert, he would close his eyes while performing to block out the view of the audience and concentrate solely on his music. But not tonight. Tonight, he was performing with both eyes open and he was staring at her. He not only wanted her to listen to what he was playing, but he wanted her to look past the sax and into his soul, as well.

And she was, and she did. The music was as beautiful and moving as it could possibly be. She could feel deep emotions in what he was playing—the love, the commitment, the promise—all in heartrending clarity. Caden was a gifted saxophonist, and tonight he was playing from his heart and soul just for her. And only for her.

The music continued, and so did her tears—she

couldn't stop. The man onstage, immaculately dressed in an expensive black tux, was her world. He always had been and always would be.

And then the music ended, and she got to her feet to give him a one-woman standing ovation, clapping as loudly as she could. He smiled before taking a bow. She watched as he set his sax aside to leave the stage and walk toward her, his steps as sexy as he looked himself. He came to a stop in front of her, and her breath caught when he took her hand in his and lowered down on bended knee.

Looking back up at her, he asked, "Shiloh, will you marry me? Not next month. Not next year. But now, this weekend, in Vegas. Let's do what we should have done four years ago—what we had planned to do. More than anything, I want you as my wife. We'll have a reception later at home, but I want to marry you now. Will you marry me and return to Charlottesville as my wife?"

Shiloh stared down at him in shock as she swiped at her tears. Her heart soared at the thought that Caden wanted to marry her. Now. This weekend in Vegas. His proposal wasn't just a surprise; it was a gift. The precious gift of a second chance for both of them.

She smiled down at him. "Yes. I'll marry you, here in Vegas like we always planned to do."

There was clapping, whistles and catcalls. She glanced around to see Caden's band members, along with Grover, smiling, then lifting their instruments up in salute. Smiling, Caden stood, pulled her into his arms and kissed her.

Less than two hours later, they were married. Part

of the Arena was transformed into a wedding chapel, and with Grover and his band as witnesses, they became man and wife.

"I'm waiting for you to get out of that gown."

She glanced down at the ring Caden had slid on her finger hours ago. It was a stunner, absolutely gorgeous. She then looked across their room to where Caden sat in a chair, his legs stretched out in front of him. His tie was undone, his jacket tossed aside and his shirtsleeves rolled up. Her husband was ready for business.

Her husband. She liked the sound of that.

With his hands casually resting on his knees, he was looking at her in a way that let her know just what he wanted. "I thought you liked this gown on me," she said, smiling over at him, feeling his heat from across the room.

"I do. You look damned good in it. But I know you're going to look just as good out of it…so take it off."

He wanted her to strip, and he had a good seat to watch her do it. She decided to tease him a bit. "You sure you want me to take it off? You're absolutely certain?"

Without smiling, with a look on his face that was as serious as he could get, he said, "You either take it off or I'll take it off for you. But be warned—I don't know what shape the gown will be in when I finish, because I intend to tear it off of you."

Shiloh looked down at her gown, knowing he meant every word. She definitely didn't want that. This was her wedding dress, the one he had purchased for her, and she had already planned to keep it and cherish it forever. "In that case, I will take it off myself."

And she did, making it pure torture for him to watch as she slowly exposed her body to him inch by inch. Caden wasn't sure how many times he shifted in his seat when his erection became almost unbearable. Its insistent pressing against his zipper was pure torment.

Her breasts were full, inviting, and the juncture of her thighs made his mouth water. She shimmied out of the gown and took the time to lay it across the arm of the love seat. When she was left in nothing but her thong and high heels, he felt his pulse rate increase. His wife was perfectly made from the top of her head to the soles of her feet.

He watched as she slid her thong down a pair of gorgeous thighs. She tossed it to him and he caught it, bringing the flimsy piece of black lace to his nose, inhaling her scent. His manhood throbbed even more.

And when she stood totally naked in front of him, he stood and began stripping off his own clothes. He crossed the room and picked her up, and instead of carrying her over to the bed, he carried her over to the desk in the room.

"Can't make it to the bedroom," he said, pushing everything out of the way and sitting her on the edge of the desk, spreading her legs in the process.

"I understand. Let me help you," she said, reaching out and taking hold of his erection and guiding it to her womanly core.

He was glad she understood, and she definitely had things under control. The moment he entered her, he thrust hard and went deep. Grabbing hold of her hips, he began thrusting inside of her again and again. The urgency, the need and greed that drove him, could not be defined or explained. It just was, and he doubted he would ever tire of making love to his wife.

The feel of her inner muscles tightening around him almost sent him over the edge, and he kept pounding inside of her, needing her in a way he had never wanted a woman. Knowing she would always and forever be his sent his heart rate increasing and his pulse pounding.

Several times, he virtually lifted her from the desk in his overwhelming need to go deeper, and when she screamed out his name at the top of her orgasm, he followed her, drowning in a pleasure so exquisite he knew he could die from it. He felt his own body explode, and Caden knew what it felt like to want a woman to the point of craziness.

The spasms that tore through his body were magnetic, forceful and had him totally out of control. Never had a climax been so intense and electrifying. He leaned in and captured her mouth, needing to kiss her, taste her and brand her forever.

Breaking off the kiss, he gazed down at her and whispered, "I love you." And he meant it with his entire heart.

"And I love you, Caden."

A smile touched his lips, and with their bodies still locked, he lifted her hips off the table, and she automatically wrapped her arms around his neck. They would continue this in the bedroom.

Forty

Upon returning to Charlottesville on Sunday night, Caden and Shiloh went straight to Shana's house. After arriving at the airport, they received a text from Jace asking to meet them right away.

When Jace opened the door, all it took was to look into Caden's and Shiloh's smiling faces to know Caden's mission had been accomplished this weekend. "Congratulations, you two. Come in."

"Thanks," Caden said, giving his brother a bear hug. "This weekend Shiloh and I completed what we'd started four years ago, and we're very happy," he said, pulling Shiloh to his side and placing a kiss on her temple.

Caden glanced behind Jace to see Dalton was already there. Caden smiled and said to him, "You're still in a bad mood?"

Dalton shrugged. "Maybe. Maybe not. But I can still congratulate the two of you," he said, also giving his brother a bear hug and giving Shiloh a hug, as well.

"It would have been nice had you told me what you planned to do this weekend. I had to hear it from Jace an hour ago."

"Only because no one could talk to you this week, Dalton. That woman you hired the P.I. to find must have done some kind of number on you."

"I don't want to talk about it," he said in a quiet voice, letting his brothers know that it was still a sore subject with him.

Shana came from the kitchen and congratulated the newlywed couple before saying, "Jules is on her way over here with information she wants to share with us."

"Jules? Who is Jules?" Dalton asked.

"My sister. She's been checking into a few things regarding Caden's accident."

"Did she find out whether Rita was in Charlottesville that weekend?" Caden asked, sitting down on the sofa with Shiloh by his side.

"Yes. She discovered a ticket had been purchased in Rita's name that weekend for a trip from Dallas to here."

Caden slowly shook his head. "I just don't believe it. Jealousy is one thing—killing someone is another."

"Yes, but Rita Crews did make those threatening comments about you to your manager. And why would she come to Charlottesville? Do you know whether she has relatives or friends here?" Jace asked.

Caden released a disgusted sigh. "I don't know, but I don't think so."

"Well, we'll know soon, because a P.I. Jules knows in Dallas is talking to Rita."

"Talking to her?" Dalton asked angrily. "Why hasn't the woman been arrested?"

"Because, Dalton," Jace said, answering instead for Shana and trying not to let Dalton annoy him, "we have no evidence of anything. Caden didn't call the police that night, so there's no open investigation of anyone trying to do him harm. Just because Rita purchased a ticket here that weekend doesn't mean anything. That's the reason Shana's sister arranged for this P.I. friend in Dallas to talk to her."

Dalton rolled his eyes. "Does anyone really think this Rita woman is going to confess to anything? I say bring the police in, tell them what we have and let them take over."

"Again, Dalton, we have no evidence. If Rita is guilty of anything, then we'll find out," Jace said, determined to not let Dalton try his patience…or anyone else's, for that matter. His brother needed to take a chill pill.

"So, Shiloh, tell us—how did Caden pop the question?" Shana asked, changing the subject and defusing the tense moment between Jace and Dalton.

Jace gave Shana a silent thank-you and used that time to pull Dalton aside to say in a low tone, "Hey, man, will you ease up a little?"

Dalton shrugged. "I don't like the idea of someone out to get my brother—for any reason."

"And you think I do?"

"Of course not, but it seems all of you are putting a lot of stock in what Shana's sister thinks. What is she? A cop or something?"

Jace was about to answer when the doorbell sounded.

"That's probably Jules now." He left Dalton to head for the door.

Dalton sighed and turned his attention to the conversation already in progress. Shiloh was telling him how Caden had arranged a concert just for her at Caesars Palace when he heard a feminine voice approaching—a voice he recognized immediately. This was the same voice he hadn't been able to get out of his mind for weeks.

He whirled around, and his gaze met the eyes of the one woman he'd hoped never to see again. "What the hell are you doing here?"

Jules was equally shocked, and it took her a minute to regain her composure to fire the same question back at Dalton. "What the hell are *you* doing here?"

The entire room fell silent as the two seemed to dismiss their surroundings and face off. Jace stepped in the middle of the fray and calmly said, "I take it that the two of you already know each other."

"Yes!"

"No!"

Jace shook his head. Jules had said yes, and Dalton had said no. "You either do or you don't, and I suspect you do. We're here to listen to Jules's report on Rita Crews, but I think before we can do that, the two of you have personal business that should be settled in private." It was apparent he had already figured things out.

"No, we don't, and no, it shouldn't," Dalton said angrily. "I'm out of here. You and Caden can fill me in later." He headed for the door, swearing under his breath, and slammed it shut behind him.

* * *

Jules just stood there, trying to get a handle on the fact that the man she'd come to think of as *Dick* was really Dalton Granger, Jace's brother. She drew in a deep breath and saw everyone looking at her. "I didn't know who he was," she said in disgust. "He told me his name was Dick."

"Dick?" Caden asked, trying to keep amusement out of his voice.

Jules shrugged. "He said it was a nickname for Richard."

"Which is partly true," Jace said. "Since his name is Dalton Richard Granger. The Richard came from our grandfather."

"Look, Jace is right about you and Dalton needing to straighten a few things out, but I prefer hearing what you have to say about Rita first," Caden said. He'd seen Dalton's anger directed at Jules, and although he didn't know the full story, he did have a clue based on the little he knew. And if what he suspected was true, it would take more than one talk between the two of them before the matter was resolved.

"All right," Jules said, coming to stand in the middle of the room. "I agree that Dalton and I have a private matter to resolve, but I'm here to discuss what I found out about Rita."

"Okay," Caden said, his hand tightening on Shiloh's. "What did you find out?"

Jules took the seat Jace offered. "Rita admitted to coming here to confront you, but after she arrived she talked herself out of it. She has proof she never left the hotel she checked into. She claims she didn't even rent a car. She took cabs to and from the airport. She claims the hotel staff will verify her story that she was holed up in her room for those two days."

"But why did she come at all?"

"She thought she could talk to you about the situation. She wanted to apologize. She wanted to give you her word it wouldn't happen again. She also wanted to ask that you rehire her. It seems she's having problems adjusting to the group she's in now."

Caden shook his head. "Rita knows me. She knows I don't put up with bullshit and that there's no way I would hire her back. I don't know why she would even think that I would."

"Evidently, your manager, Grover Reddick, gave her the impression that maybe you would and suggested she come talk to you."

Caden frowned. "That's odd. I talked to Grover. In fact, I called him to find out what group Rita was now playing with, and I told him about the situation Saturday night and what was suspected with Rita. That's when he told me about her threats."

"And he didn't mention anything about telling her to come here and that he knew she had been here that weekend?"

"No," Caden answered.

"That *is* odd," Jules agreed. "When was the last time you talked to Grover Reddick?"

"In Vegas this weekend. He helped me pull off everything with my surprise proposal to Shiloh. He was instrumental in arranging everything—the wedding, the venue and contacting the band members so they would be there for my private concert."

Jules nodded and glanced down at Shiloh's hand. "Congratulations." She then stood. "I guess now I need to check out Grover Reddick."

Caden waved off her words. "Don't waste your time. Grover is my manager and has no reason to want to hurt me." Caden chuckled. "If anything, he needs to keep me alive and well if he wants me to return to the touring circuit in January. He wasn't crazy about the idea of my putting my music career on hold to fulfill the promise I made to my grandfather, but he did understand."

"So you trust him?" Jules asked.

"Absolutely. We've been business partners for years."

Jules nodded. "Probably the same way Jace trusted Vidal Duncan."

Jules's reminder of what Vidal had been capable of doing came as a blow, one from which Caden quickly recovered. "Grover has no reason to want to hurt me, and especially no reason to want me dead, Jules."

"Let me find out whether that's true." She shoved her hands into the pockets of her jeans. "I will check out Rita Crews's alibi and will also check out Grover Reddick's whereabouts that weekend, as well. If you happen to talk to him, don't mention anything."

Caden frowned. "I won't." He then glanced at the people in the room who were staring at him. "She's not going to come up with anything on Grover. You'll see."

The next morning, Ben glanced across the break-fast table at his daughter. Jules had called that morn-

ing and asked if he was cooking breakfast. He hadn't
planned on it, but since she'd asked, he figured there
was a reason she wanted to come over…and he had an
idea what that reason might be. Yet she'd been here for
an hour now, and she hadn't asked a single thing about
his weekend in New York with Mona. In fact, Jules had
been unusually quiet over breakfast.

"I thought you would have grilled me to death by
now," he said, glancing over at his daughter while taking a sip of coffee.

Jules glanced up and looked at her father questioningly. "About what?"

"My weekend in New York with Mona."

She blinked. "Oh. Right. How did that go?"

Ben smiled. "It went fine. We had a great time."

"I'm glad."

Jules went back to moving her food around her plate.
Ben figured she had something on her mind since she
wasn't eating her favorite breakfast. She had stirred
her grits around so much they were looking downright
soupy.

"You want to tell me what's wrong, Jules?"

She glanced back up at her father. "Why do you think
there is something wrong?"

Ben chuckled. She must be kidding. "Because I'm
your father, and I know my girls. I know when something is bothering them, and anytime you aren't trying
to get into my business, that means something is wrong
with you. So what gives? And remember you can tell
me anything."

Jules smiled. That was one of the reasons she loved

her father so much. He could read her and Shana like a book. Her sister hadn't called her last night after the debacle at her place. Jace had probably convinced Shana to leave her alone to work out her own issues. If that was true, then she appreciated her future brother-in-law for doing that for her.

"Jules?"

She sighed. "A month or so ago, I met this guy while working undercover one night. He was nice-looking, smooth and kind of pushy. He asked for my contact information, and I told him if he wanted to get to know me he'd have to find me."

"And?"

"He did find me. Last week, he showed up at my office. He must have hired a P.I. to hunt me down."

Ben chuckled. "Well, you did tell him to find you."

"Yes, but I really didn't think he would. At first, I was flattered. But then he turned me off. It's obvious he's used to getting any woman he wants."

"But, of course, you were going to make sure you were the exception."

"Yes. We didn't exchange real names."

"Why?"

"Because I didn't know him and wasn't sure I wanted him to know me. Anyway, I came up with a plan to put him in his place and did something that pissed him off."

Ben nodded. "And you probably did so thinking you'd never see him again."

"Right. But I ran into him again. Last night, in fact."

"Where?" Ben asked, taking another sip of his coffee.

"At Shana's."

"Shana's?" Ben asked, lifting an eyebrow.

"Yes." Jules released a deep breath. "I found out last night that the man I had pissed off is Jace's brother Dalton. And, needless to say, seeing each other last night didn't go well."

"I can imagine."

Jules shook her head. "No, Dad, you can't begin to imagine."

"That bad?"

"Yes, and his brother is marrying my sister. He and Jace are as different as black and white."

"So are you and Shana. The two of you are sisters and not clones—you are as different as chalk and cheese. But I think you and the young man should bury your animosity. If for no other reason than for Shana and Jace. We're having a wedding in two weeks, and it should be a joyful occasion for everyone."

"I know, but I don't want to think about burying anything with Dalton Granger. Forgive me for saying this, Dad, but he's such an ass."

"Ass or not, he's still Jace's brother, and somehow the two of you need to try and get along."

"Maybe," she said, not convinced something like that could ever happen. "I've agreed to check out a few things regarding an investigation into what happened to Jace's brother Caden two weekends ago. I'll be too busy to get sidetracked by anything…especially by Dalton."

"Putting it off might not be the best thing, Jules."

She took a sip of her coffee. "We'll see, Dad."

* * *

The next morning, when Caden opened his office door, Dalton was standing there waiting on him. "You're early, aren't you?" Caden asked, hanging up his jacket.

"I want to talk to you about Shana's sister."

"What about Jules, Dalton?"

"I don't like her."

Caden smiled as he took a seat at his desk. "I think your dislike of her was pretty obvious last night. And your not liking her only means I don't have to worry about you hitting on her every chance you get. No big deal."

"Damn it, Caden, it *is* a big deal."

Caden frowned. "What is the big deal, Dalton? Maybe she's one of the few women who didn't fall for all your bullshit. She's one of the rare few who doesn't think your piss is made of liquid gold."

"That isn't funny!"

"Trust me, you don't see me laughing. To learn that a man I consider a friend is a suspect in trying to bump me off isn't anything to laugh about, either. It's a problem I'll have to deal with—if it's true, though I honestly believe that it's not. Still, excuse me for saying it, but I have enough on my plate dealing with my own problems. I don't need to take on any of yours."

"I'm not asking you to take on my problems."

"Good, because I won't. This weekend, I married the woman I love. I'm happy and I wish everyone else could be just as happy as we are. But I want to give you something to think about."

Dalton glared at him. "What?"

"Jace and Shana are getting married in two weeks, and the woman you claim you don't like is Shana's sister. And knowing Shana like we both do, she's not going to take any of your bullshit when it comes to her sister, and I don't blame her."

Dalton's glare deepened. "So you're blaming me?"

"Let's just say I know you, Dalton. You're used to having your pick of women. You met Jules, and she didn't make things easy for you. I say good for her."

Dalton didn't say anything. He stared at Caden for a few minutes, and then he stormed out of the office.

"You okay, Sheppard? Ambrose called and said you needed to talk to me."

Shep nodded when Carson entered the conference room and closed the door behind her. Without saying anything, he crossed the room, pulled her into his arms and seized her mouth in a long, slow and lingering kiss.

When he broke it off moments later, he drew in a deep breath. "I needed that."

Carson licked her lips, loving his taste. "What is it, Sheppard? What's wrong?"

He led her over to the table where they could sit down. "Jace called Saturday morning and finally told me what had happened with Caden. Of course, I didn't let him know I already knew about it."

"And?"

"He hired Shana's sister, who owns a P.I. firm, to look into it, and there's a strong possibility that Caden's former female band member might be involved. She and Caden were involved in an affair earlier this year, and when he discovered she had a jealous streak, he broke things off. She made threats."

"So it had nothing to do with you?"

"That could be the case, but I still want my sons watched. Someone sent me that email, and until I find out who and why, I still don't want to take any chances."

"I understand and I will let Roland know to maintain the status quo until I let him know otherwise."

"Just keep me posted of any new developments."

She smiled. "I will, and there is something I need to report."

"What?"

"To ensure that Caden didn't get suspicious of anything, Striker switched places with Quasar at the last minute. And Quasar followed Caden to Vegas this weekend."

"Vegas? Why?"

"It seems your middle son eloped and got married on Saturday."

Shep's eyes widened in surprise. "Caden?"

"Yes. So act surprised when he calls and tells you himself."

"Who did he marry?"

"Shiloh Timmons."

Shep chuckled. "Well, I'll be damned."

He couldn't help but recall Caden's attitude the time his sons had come to visit a few months back and Shiloh's name had come up. "Those two were always close as kids. I figured when they got older something more would develop, but after I'd heard that Samuel Timmons forbade Shiloh to have anything to do with my family after I went to jail, I just assumed that the two of them had severed their connection."

Carson lifted a brow. "Then how did Samuel Timmons end up becoming an investor in your company?"

"When Dad needed money to keep the company afloat, he approached Samuel. Evidently, Timmons was willing to put aside his dislike of us to invest in the company. For him, it was all about money."

Carson nodded. "Why did Samuel Timmons dislike your family so much after you were sent off to jail? Before that, the two of you were close, right?"

"Not all that close. But our families did do things together from time to time, either as couples or with our children. Sylvia was a lot closer to them than I was. At one time, she and Sandra Timmons were thick as honey. I figured since they thought I had killed Sylvia, they wanted to end any relationship they had with my family."

Carson shrugged. "For some reason, I think there's more to it than that."

"Who knows? Samuel would roll over in his grave if he knew Caden and Shiloh were married."

"So you're happy for Caden?"

Shep smiled. "Yes, I'm very happy for Caden."

Forty-One

"So, what do you think, Marcel?" Jace asked.

The three Granger brothers were seated in the conference room with FBI agent Marcel Eaton. They had all just watched the surveillance video showing Brandy going through Dalton's office.

"Well," Marcel said, leaning back in his chair. "She was definitely looking for something. Did any of you notice the expression on her face?" he asked.

Both Jace and Caden replied that no, they hadn't noticed anything unusual. Dalton shrugged and said, "I'll probably burn in hell for saying it, but the only thing I noticed was the way she bent over to pry open the drawers to my desk."

Marcel, Jace and Caden just stared at Dalton as if they couldn't believe what he'd just said. He stared back at them. "Just keeping it honest."

"Spare us your honesty," Jace said and then transferred his attention away from Dalton to Marcel. "Anyway, Marcel, what do you think?"

"She was definitely looking stressed," Marcel said. "Her features were intense, almost to the extreme. It was as if she'd been given an order she had to comply with. By the way, what is the significance of that particular painting on the wall—the one with the fireworks? She definitely seemed interested in it or what she thought might be *behind* it."

"I noticed that, as well," Caden said.

"Who had that office before it became Dalton's?" Marcel wanted to know.

"It had been empty for years, and I don't know who had it last. But it will be easy to find out," Jace replied.

"Find out whether any redecorating had been done or whether any of the furnishings have been changed out, or new pictures added and any old ones taken down or replaced. There's something about that picture, or the spot where the picture hung, that held Brandy's attention, and I want to know why."

"Okay. I'll check that out," Jace said, jotting down notes on a writing pad.

"I'm going to officially talk—on the record—to the D.C. authorities and let them know there's a chance we'll be reopening Brandy's case. They might have ruled it a suicide, but now I'm beginning to wonder."

"You actually think she was murdered?" Dalton asked, sitting up in his chair.

"I'm not sure yet. It could have been a murder set up to look like a suicide. There's also the possibility that Brandy got herself too deep into something, then guilt set in, and she saw suicide as the only way out."

"What's the story behind her being in D.C. that weekend?" Caden asked.

"According to the report I received from the D.C. police, the apartment where she was found is leased to Nellie Borland. She and Brandy had been friends since childhood. Borland got a job in D.C. after college. She works as a computer programmer and travels a lot. Nellie told the authorities she got a call from Brandy at the beginning of that week claiming she had a lot on her mind and needed to get away for a few days.

"Borland told Brandy she would be out of town on a ski trip but that she could come stay at her place while she was away. Borland left for her trip before Brandy arrived, but talked to her on the phone the day Brandy arrived to make sure Brandy knew where she had left the key to the apartment. That was the last she heard from her."

"Brandy's mother doesn't believe her daughter committed suicide. I'm sure she would be glad to hear the case is being reopened," Jace said, rubbing his hand down his face.

"Yes, but what she might get is information that her daughter was involved in something illegal," Marcel said, standing. "I'll let you know what I come up with. In the meantime, if I can get the background information on Dalton's office, I'd appreciate it."

Jace nodded. "We'll take care of it."

Shiloh looked up, hearing the knock on her door. She had a feeling whom her early-morning visitor might be and she wasn't exactly looking forward to this meeting. "Come in."

The door opened, and Sedrick walked in. "I tried calling this weekend and couldn't reach you. Everything okay?"

She smiled. "Yes. I went away for the weekend."

"By yourself?" he asked, sliding into the chair across from her desk.

"No, I went away with Caden." She watched as Sedrick's features tightened.

"I can't believe you're still messing around with him."

For someone who'd always known how she felt about Caden, she found his comment odd. "Yes, I'm still messing around with him. In fact, we took our *messing around* to another level and eloped this weekend," she said, placing her hands on her desk in full view so he could see her wedding ring.

Sedrick was out of his chair in a flash. "What the hell? What did you do?"

She frowned at his reaction to her news. She hadn't expected him to be ecstatic, but she hadn't expected him to act like their father, either. "What I did was marry the person I love. Maybe that's something you should consider doing instead of stringing Cassie along."

Sedrick's face hardened. "We're discussing you and Caden Granger, not Cassie and me."

"There's nothing to discuss regarding Caden and me. We're married."

Sedrick rubbed his hands down his face in frustration. "Do you care what marrying him will do to Mom?"

"Honestly, no. What she and Dad schemed to do, keeping Caden and me apart while I was in the hospital fighting for my life, is unforgivable. And if Mom couldn't stand Caden so much, then why did she go to him and tell him the truth?"

"Damn it, she thought he already knew."

"Well, he didn't. So, in a way, I should thank her for doing something I couldn't. It doesn't matter anymore, because this weekend we did what we wanted to do four years ago, and that was to become man and wife, regardless of who may or may not like it."

Sedrick stared at her for a long moment. "I think you've made a mistake."

She got up out of her seat, fed up with his shitty attitude. She leaned over her desk. "When it comes to Caden, I don't care what you think, Sedrick. I don't even know what you're thinking anymore. Earlier this month, all you cared about was my happiness, but now you're singing a different tune. My happiness doesn't mean a thing to you."

"That's not true!"

"Isn't it? What do you have against the Grangers?"

"Do I need to remind you that Caden's father killed their mother?"

"He did not!"

"Oh, and I suppose a jury found him guilty just for the hell of it," Sedrick stormed.

"Caden and his brothers believe in their father's innocence and plan to prove it."

"I hope for your sake they don't."

Shiloh was taken aback by his words. "What do you mean?"

Sedrick shoved his hands into the pockets of his jeans. "Nothing. Forget what I said. You and Mom are the only family I have, and I was hoping that the two of you would reconcile your differences. Now your marriage to Granger will make that nearly impossible."

Without saying anything else, he turned and walked out of her office.

"Just checking to see how you've been," Shana said to her sister, adjusting the cell phone against her ear. This was the first chance they'd had to talk since Jules's confrontation with Dalton on Sunday.

"I'm fine—just busy with my investigation on Grover Reddick," Jules said, pushing away from her computer.

"How's that going?"

"It's going. I should have my report finished within the week. How are the wedding plans coming along?"

"So far so good. I can't wait."

"I guess not. Best to get it done before the baby bump appears."

Shana chuckled. "I really don't care."

"You've changed. There was a time when you would have cared. What happened?"

"Jace Granger happened. He's simply wonderful."

"He's definitely nothing like his younger brother," Jules muttered.

Shana didn't say anything for a moment. "I'm sorry

you and Dalton didn't meet under the best of circumstances."

"So am I, but I promise to try to get along with him for your sake, Shana. I will be civil to him—at least I promise to do my best."

"And that's all I can ask for."

Forty-Two

A week later, Jules asked to meet with Caden regarding her final report on Grover Reddick. He invited her to Shiloh's place, where they both now lived. Jules entered the apartment and came up short when she saw that, besides Caden and Shiloh, Dalton, Jace and Shana were also present.

Dalton took one look at her and turned to the window to stare out, ignoring her. She was fine with that and figured the sooner she told Caden what she'd discovered, the sooner she could get out of there.

"So what did you find out?" Caden asked. He was seated on the sofa beside Shiloh. Jace and Shana were sitting diagonally across from them on a love seat. Dalton was still standing at the window, but Jules had a feeling he was listening attentively.

"First of all, I want to thank Shiloh for providing me with a list of the invitees to the party as well as the video taken inside the shop that night. I've gone over everything and found nothing suspicious."

Dalton glanced at her and she tried not to come unglued from his heated stare. "Just so you know, my investigative firm works with a team of other firms that are all part of a security network. Their work is concise and on point. With that said, Rita's alibi checked out. The hotel confirmed she arrived at the hotel by cab and that she didn't leave until she caught a cab back to the airport that Sunday morning." Jules paused a minute and then said, "I'm going to tell you something that will no doubt be shocking to you, but I believe Grover Reddick is the man who tried to run you over that night."

Shiloh gasped, but Caden remained unmoved, his features unreadable. "And you base your assumptions on what?" he asked in a disbelieving tone, letting her and everyone else know he didn't believe this allegation for one second.

"I was able to locate an airline ticket from L.A. to Charlottesville in Grover Reddick's name. I also obtained records on the car he rented at the airport. Furthermore, I was able to get photos from our police department. The photos show all the cars that went through the intersection—less than a block from here—around the time of your accident. A definite match was made between the car we suspected was involved and the one Grover rented."

Jules saw Caden's jaw twitch, and he finally asked in disbelief, "Why? Why would he do such a thing?"

Instead of answering immediately, Jules pulled out a document in the folder she was holding. She placed it on the coffee table in front of Caden. "Were you aware that Grover has a million-dollar insurance policy on you?"

Caden rubbed his hands down his face. "No. Yes. Hell, I don't remember. I think I recall signing papers for him to do so. It was close to eight years ago when that policy was taken out. Such a thing isn't unheard-of in the music industry. In fact, it's usually standard practice. He managed the group and probably has policies on all key members."

Jules simply nodded and placed another document in front of him. "Were you aware that Grover has a gambling problem and that he's strapped for money? He has outstanding gambling debts, and—"

"Enough!" Caden said, standing and shoving his hands into the pockets of his jeans. "He could have asked me for the money. Why would he go to these lengths? It doesn't make any sense."

"A gambling addiction never does make any sense. It seems he is addicted pretty badly and has been for years. He's also been embezzling some of the band's profits to pay for his habit."

It was obvious from the look on Caden's face that he hadn't suspected a thing about the embezzlement of the band's profits. Jace came to stand beside his brother. "So, with all this information, can an arrest be made, Jules?"

She shook her head. "No. Since a police report of the incident was never filed, it would be Caden's account of what happened that night against Reddick's. We can probably get him on the embezzlement charges, though. It's something a good accountant can trace. That's the best that can be done."

"The best that can be done, my ass. That's bullshit,"

Dalton said, leaving his place by the window to come stand beside the sofa. "A man tried to kill my brother, and you want us to believe nothing can be done?"

Jules lifted her chin. "That's right. Nothing can be done…unless…"

Caden raised a brow. "Unless what?"

"Unless Grover confesses."

"Don't hold your breath for that to happen," Dalton sneered.

"Wait!" Caden said, holding up his hand to stop Dalton from getting started. "I have an idea—something that might get the confession."

Jules's eyebrows rose. "Okay, let's hear it."

Two days later

"Mr. Reddick, Caden Granger is here to see you."

Grover glanced up from the papers on his desk and frowned. "Caden? Okay, send him in," he said, wondering why Caden was in L.A. Was he here to tell him he was ready to go back on the touring circuit the first of the year? Maybe ready to start working on a final tour schedule? He could have called or emailed to do either of those things.

Caden walked in and glanced around Grover's office. There had been many memories made in this room. Good memories. He glanced over at Grover standing behind the desk. Today, the man looked older than his forty-four years.

"Caden, my man, this is unexpected. What are you doing in L.A.? Did you bring Shiloh with you?" Grover asked, coming from behind his desk and offering Caden his hand.

"I had some business to take care of here," Caden said, taking his hand and wishing he didn't have to. "And no, I didn't bring Shiloh with me."

"I'm so happy for both of you. I was so glad to have been there to witness the ceremony. The whole thing was classy and beautiful."

"I thought so, too." Caden paused, then said, "I want to talk to you about something serious that came up while the private investigator I hired was checking out Rita's alibi."

"Oh, and what is that?"

"That you were in Charlottesville that same weekend." He saw surprise flare in Grover's eyes and surmised Grover never expected to be caught out. "Why didn't you tell me? We could have gotten together. Shared a drink."

Grover waved off Caden's words as they both sat down. "I wasn't in the city that long. Just flew in to check out this new group of singers. Three ladies who can really sing and—"

"You were there for a few days?"

"Yes, but I was busy."

"Why didn't you mention it to me when we talked that night on the phone?"

"I didn't think it was important."

Caden nodded. "Any reason you tried to run me down that night in front of Shiloh's place? Did you think *that* was important?"

Grover sat straight up. "What are you talking about, Caden? Why would I run you over?"

"To collect on that insurance policy you took out on me in order to settle your gambling debts. Why, Grover? Why did you do it, man? I thought we were friends."

"I don't know what the hell you're talking about."

Caden nodded slowly. "I came here today hoping you would level with me, but I see you won't, so I intend to take what I have to the police. Maybe you'll be more cooperative with them." Caden stood.

"The police? Wait, Caden! Hold up and let's talk about this." When Caden did not reply he realized the jig was up. "Okay, I fucked up. But you weren't saying when, or if, you would be back with the band, and I had pressing bills to pay. You seemed to enjoy playing Mr. Corporate America, but I needed money."

"I could have loaned you the money."

"You would have asked too many questions."

"So killing me instead was the best option?"

"I didn't want to kill you. Damn it, Caden, I told you I needed the money, and those bastards were breathing down my neck, making threats. I screwed up and that guy jumped out of nowhere. I figured—"

"What? Figured I should live?"

"Yeah, and I immediately regretted what I did. I sort of went crazy with the pressure and the threats." Changing tack, he added, "You're happily married, and I helped you pull that off. Let's leave the police out of this. I'll resign and find other work. You know me. I'm not a bad person."

Caden wondered whether Grover was even listening

to himself. How could someone admit to having tried to kill him, and then say he wasn't a bad person and should get off scot-free? "I trusted you with my career, my business, my life, Grover."

"Fuck you and your life. Poor little rich kid who wants to play musician whenever he feels like it. I've done everything to make you a success. I needed the damned money, and you owed it to me," he shouted. "You owed me," he repeated. "My life was being threatened. They wanted their money and—"

"So, your solution was to kill me, cash in the insurance policy and get on with your life."

"Yes!" Grover screamed. "I would have killed you to get it! I tried. I fucking tried. It would have solved all my problems. Damn you!"

Caden stared at the man he'd had so much faith in, so much confidence in—the man who had been his manager for years. Rather than saying anything else, he turned and headed for the door.

"Wait, Caden! If you go to the police, I'll deny everything. People know me in L.A. I'm a model citizen. They won't arrest me. All you have is circumstantial evidence."

When Caden got to the door, he reached into the top pocket of his jacket. "No, I have more than circumstantial evidence." He held up a mini-recorder. "I have your confession."

"It won't hold up."

"If this won't hold up," he said, showing him the recorder, "then this will." He opened the door, and three policemen walked in. "They heard your confession, as well."

One of the officers spoke up. "Mr. Reddick, you're under arrest for the attempted murder of Caden Granger. You have the right to remain silent…."

Caden kept walking, refusing to look back. He went straight to the elevator and rode down as a cold chill ran through his body.

As he stepped off the elevator Shiloh was waiting for him. He pulled her into his arms, needing to hold her. And then he kissed her, needing her taste to consume him and make him feel whole again.

He broke off the kiss and took her hand in his. "Come on, baby. Let's get out of here and go home."

Forty-Three

Sedrick Timmons looked around the warehouse, waiting to meet the person who had summoned him. He turned up the collar of his coat. The air had turned cold. Shit, he didn't want to be here and wanted no part of this.

"Glad you could make it."

Sedrick turned around. He hadn't heard anyone approach. "What do you want? Why did you ask me to come here?"

"It's about your sister."

Sedrick frowned. "What about her?"

"I heard she married Caden Granger."

Sedrick frowned. "And what if she did?"

"Nothing, as long as she convinces her husband not to reopen his father's case. And *you* are going to make sure that happens."

"And if I don't?"

There was a harsh chuckle. "Oh, but you will. I know about your part in Richard Granger's death. He would have survived that heart attack if you hadn't administered the drug in the hospital that tightened his muscles so much that there was no way he could survive."

Sedrick rubbed his hand down his face. "What do you want?"

"I told you. As far as everyone knows, Sheppard Granger is guilty. For the benefit of all of us, it had better stay that way."

* * * * *

Look for Dalton's story next in
THE GRANGERS *series,*
available soon from Harlequin MIRA.

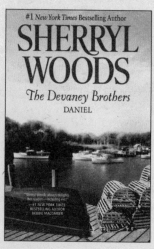

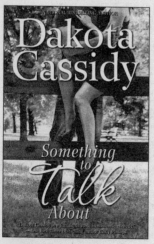

REQUEST YOUR FREE BOOKS!

2 FREE NOVELS
FROM THE ROMANCE COLLECTION
PLUS 2 FREE GIFTS!

YES! Please send me 2 FREE novels from the Romance Collection and my 2 FREE gifts (gifts are worth about $10). After receiving them, if I don't wish to receive any more books, I can return the shipping statement marked "cancel." If I don't cancel, I will receive 4 brand-new novels every month and be billed just $6.24 per book in the U.S. or $6.74 per book in Canada. That's a savings of at least 22% off the cover price. It's quite a bargain! Shipping and handling is just 50¢ per book in the U.S. and 75¢ per book in Canada.* I understand that accepting the 2 free books and gifts places me under no obligation to buy anything. I can always return a shipment and cancel at any time. Even if I never buy another book, the two free books and gifts are mine to keep forever.

194/394 MDN F4XY

Name   (PLEASE PRINT)

Address   Apt. #

City   State/Prov.   Zip/Postal Code

Signature (if under 18, a parent or guardian must sign)

Mail to the Harlequin® Reader Service:
IN U.S.A.: P.O. Box 1867, Buffalo, NY 14240-1867
IN CANADA: P.O. Box 609, Fort Erie, Ontario L2A 5X3

Want to try two free books from another line?
Call 1-800-873-8635 or visit www.ReaderService.com.

* Terms and prices subject to change without notice. Prices do not include applicable taxes. Sales tax applicable in N.Y. Canadian residents will be charged applicable taxes. Offer not valid in Quebec. This offer is limited to one order per household. Not valid for current subscribers to the Romance Collection or the Romance/Suspense Collection. All orders subject to credit approval. Credit or debit balances in a customer's account(s) may be offset by any other outstanding balance owed by or to the customer. Please allow 4 to 6 weeks for delivery. Offer available while quantities last.

Your Privacy—The Harlequin® Reader Service is committed to protecting your privacy. Our Privacy Policy is available online at www.ReaderService.com or upon request from the Harlequin Reader Service.

We make a portion of our mailing list available to reputable third parties that offer products we believe may interest you. If you prefer that we not exchange your name with third parties, or if you wish to clarify or modify your communication preferences, please visit us at www.ReaderService.com/consumerchoice or write to us at Harlequin Reader Service Preference Service, P.O. Box 9062, Buffalo, NY 14269. Include your complete name and address.

ROM13R

#1 *New York Times* Bestselling Author

DEBBIE MACOMBER

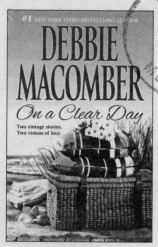

**Two vintage stories.
Two visions of love.**

A Man's Future…

Rand Prescott believes his chances
for happiness are limited because
he's going blind. When he meets
Karen McAlister, he begins to
imagine a different future—one
filled with love. Karen already
knows she wants to be with him for
the rest of her life, but Rand refuses
to bind her to a man who can't see.
Brokenhearted, she's prepared to
walk away. Can he really let her go?

A Woman's Resolve…

Joy Nielsen's latest patient, businessman Sloan Whittaker, is confined
to a wheelchair after a serious accident—and he's lost the will to walk.
Joy is determined to make sure he recovers, and once he does, she's
prepared to move on to her next patient, no matter how strongly she
feels about Sloan. There's only one problem. She doesn't think she can
get over him.…

Available now, wherever books are sold.

Be sure to connect with us at:

Harlequin.com/Newsletters

Facebook.com/HarlequinBooks

Twitter.com/HarlequinBooks

HARLEQUIN® MIRA®
www.Harlequin.com

MDM1624